Oliver H. Growden

Matthew Redmayne

A New Zealand Romance

Oliver H. Growden

Matthew Redmayne
A New Zealand Romance

ISBN/EAN: 9783744771788

Printed in Europe, USA, Canada, Australia, Japan

Cover: Foto ©Andreas Hilbeck / pixelio.de

More available books at **www.hansebooks.com**

MATTHEW REDMAYNE

A New Zealand Romance

BY

OLIVER H. GROWDEN

GEORGE ROBERTSON AND COMPANY

LONDON   SYDNEY
MELBOURNE   ADELAIDE

1892

CONTENTS.

MATTHEW REDMAYNE.

PART I.

A WIFE'S CONFESSION.

" My Dear Husband,

"When you read this your wife of a day will be dead. I cannot convey to you how earnestly I wish you to credit what I am about to say. I could not rest in my grave if I thought the disgrace which has covered me in my lifetime should rest upon my memory when I am gone. Think of me as speaking from the dead; and remember that however improbable some of the things I relate may seem, I am not likely to write anything but the truth now, and least of all would I think of doing so to you.

"It is part of my diary—the only part bearing upon those facts of which I know you must so intensely desire to learn the truth. As it was written then, so it remains now.

"Since the day when I was dragged from before you in the cabin of your yacht, I have never known a happy hour. It was a heavy burden that was laid upon my shoulders then; and never for a moment has it been lifted from them. *You* believed me guilty—and oh! my dear, dear Matthew, it was in *that* that the bitterness of it lay. Everything has been against me;—every one has believed me to be a guilty, wicked woman, and I dared not open my lips to defend myself. The trial came on; evidence was piled up against me; there was not a man or woman in the land that did not condemn me. I saw it in the faces of the gaping crowd that came every day to stare at me; in the stern looks of the judge, the jury—everywhere. I wonder I did not go mad. I have sometimes wished they had found me guilty, for then I should have escaped the slow torture I have endured since.

"And yet I was innocent.

"I might have cleared myself, but I could not bring myself to do it. It was not that I was careless of life; on the contrary, I had the one thing that should have made life happy. I knew then, as well I know now, what I was giving up; but there was only one thing that weighed with me—and that was your love, my dear Matthew, for I may call you so now. I made the choice; and had I my life to live over again, I could not but choose to do the same again. Believe me, I had a reason for what I did; and, much as you must have suffered, before you have read to the end of this Confession you will admit it was no light reason.

"The struggle to contain myself in silence has been a hard one for me. I have often heard about you. The world is a small place after all, and it has come to my ears in many chance ways how you have lived since that fatal epoch in our lives. I have heard how you have shut yourself out from society; how you have gone from country to country an aimless and hopeless wanderer; how you have been pressed again and again by those who had every right to advise you, to get a divorce from one who was but your wife in name, to whom you had attached yourself by a hasty boyish pledge, and who had, apparently, proved herself so base and unworthy of you. I know, too, that you have remained true in spite of all. Think then, if you deem me worthy of the bestowal of a thought, how I must have suffered in my obscurity when I saw from what I had shut myself out, and whether I would have condemned you and myself to all this without a weighty reason. That reason, dear Matthew, it is now my purpose to show you.

"And when you have read this Confession, and pass judgment upon my poor afflicted sister, who has been the unwitting cause of it all, do not forget the calamity that had befallen her. She was not responsible for her terrible act. Had she been sane she would have been incapable of even conceiving the thought. She had had much wrong, and had been basely deceived. She was an instrument in the hands of a just Fate. My heart is fit to break when I think of her and all the terrible misfortunes that overwhelmed her through one rash act. My poor Catherine!

"May you be happier henceforward than you have been while I lived to blight your prospects. May you learn to forgive her who entered into your life only to ruin it, but who would gladly have given her existence to make you happy had Providence ordered our lives more kindly than it did. Would that I could convey to you by some other means than pen and paper what I feel towards you at this moment of writing. Though misfortune has come down upon me like a thick darkness, my life has known one green spot in its dreary wilderness—through all my love for you has remained as strong as on the day when you first won the admission from me. I may confess it now; for when this reaches your hand the grave will have hidden all the faults and follies of

"Your loving wife,
"ESTHER.

"*October* 9, 1888."

THE DIARY.

I.

JAN. 15, 1885.—How strange it seems to me to be seated in this room writing in my diary to-night. I can scarcely realize that I am the new governess, and that I am at The Peak. The advertisement was: "Wanted, young lady of education and refinement as governess. Knowledge of languages required in addition to ability to instruct in ordinary curriculum. Terms, £40 per annum. Apply, The Peak."

Well, I was a young lady of education and refinement. I knew French and Spanish passably, was well acquainted with Latin, had a slight smattering of German (very slight, I may say), besides English, which of course didn't count. I flattered myself I knew how to instruct in the " ordinary curriculum "—which I supposed meant the three R's—and above all, I wanted that £40 badly. I applied for the place, got it, and here I am, tired to death with travelling for the last two days, and with my daily portion of diary-writing, which I have religiously pledged myself to do, still staring me in the face.

To-day was one of those unseasonable days occasionally met with even in mid-summer. Thick clouds of mist were drifting over the hills as we set out from Wellington this afternoon, and in about half an hour it began to pour down in torrents. The driving sheets of rain made the scenery a mere indistinguishable blurr, and I lay back in the carriage in despair of finding anything from without to interest me. I was full of a feeling of timid nervousness. I had not yet seen Mrs. Shaw, the lady by whom I had been engaged, for I had applied for the situation in writing, and I wondered what she would be like. I took out the letter she had written in reply to mine, and read it over again. It was kindly enough worded, assured me of having a very comfortable place, that the two little girls it would be my duty to instruct would be found *exceedingly* docile and teachable, and all that ; but it was written in a thick heavy hand. The t's had no upstrokes, and had great black bars dashed across them ; the tails of the g's and y's were as stiff and unbending as pump-handles, and the ends of the words ran away into mere ragged lines. Altogether a grim, forbidding kind of hand ; a hand that brought up a vision of a woman with a little too much will of her own, a set, severe face, and tightly-closed lips. I did not like the picture I had conjured up, put the letter back in the reticule, and looking out of the carriage window again, found I was in sight of The Peak.

From the valley road along which we were slowly crawling —I could call it nothing else—I caught sight, through the gray cloud of rain, of a large rambling building perched apparently on the top of the highest hill. The coachman pointed to it with his whip, and said that was "It." From the valley it was impossible to form any idea of what the place was like, for I could only make out the dim outlines of a number of high-shouldered gables pushing up above the trees ; a great straggling place it seemed, all the bigger and more unwieldy from the mists that hung about it. Then it was shut out again, and we began to ascend a hillside, so steep that the horses had to go in an abrupt zig-zag to lessen the strain. The trees, heavy with the rain, overhung the banks at the roadside and brushed against the coach windows as we passed. Then, without in the least knowing how we got there, I found myself jolting along a rough narrow mountain path, with The Peak in the midst of its wide grounds lying below. Behind the house, the mountains rose giddily upward till their tops were hidden in dense clouds of mist, that closed, and opened, and changed, and hung down the steep hillsides like masses of tangled drapery. A cold icy wind had arisen and was sweeping keenly along the heights ; a wide, bleak prospect opened out ; on every side stretched rugged brown hills studded with the blackened stumps of charred tree stems, with random patches of native bush showing here and there through rifts in the mist, and having an indescribably wet and draggled look about them. I wondered what could have possessed any one to build such a house as the one before me, and then hide it away in a wild, barren, out-of-the-way spot like this.

A few more turns in the road, and we stopped before a
pair of tall iron gates, which the driver opened. Then we
wheeled up a broad pebbly yellow-sanded sweep of carriage
drive, and halted before the hall door, and stepping out, I
found myself fairly arrived at The Peak at last.

It is not the most comfortable feeling to entertain at the
beginning of such an engagement as mine, and I may be
wrong, but I have an unpleasantly strong idea that Mrs.
Shaw and I will not be the best friends in the world. She
received me herself in the drawing-room on my arrival to-
day, and I was surprised at the closeness of her resemblance
to the picture I had formed in my mind. She was tall,
gaunt and bony, with eyes severe, and dress of formal cut.
Her eyebrows were bushy—too bushy for a woman; and
her forehead, though she was by no means an elderly
woman, was full of wrinkles. Her nose was pointed; her
ears stood out sharply from her head; and in the very first
moment of my introduction I was conscious of a certain
grim, disagreeable air of sanctimony about her.

She rose from her chair as I was announced, and stood
with one arm crossed in front of her, and the other by her
side, steadily looking at me. She took in every point
before she spoke. Then she said, " You are Miss Gower,
I presume. I am glad to see you. I trust we shall get on
very well together." *I* trusted we should get on very well
together, added what I thought the occasion required, and
presented my credentials.

" You will be tired after your journey," she said, when
she had made me thoroughly uncomfortable by the critical
way in which she seemed to read over the letters. " The
servant will show you your room." She rang the bell, and
a servant girl appeared, who piloted me up a flight or two
of stairs and along a dreary stretch of passage to the
quarters assigned me, where I have remained ever since,
Mrs. Shaw being considerate enough to indulge me with tea
in my own room.

And now I am just about tired out. The bed looks inviting, and I think I have done enough for one day.

II.

JAN. 16.—First day over, and I am not sorry for it. I want an hour or two's leisure to decide whether I like the place or not. I think it will do. Mrs. Shaw, whose chief characteristic seems a pretty strong will and a pretty quick temper, is not so bad as I thought she would be. I concluded last night that she was not a lady—by a good deal, and she left the impression upon me to-day that she has not always been used to her present style of living, and is afraid of the fact being known. It appears she is a widow. Mr. Shaw died at sea, about thirteen months ago. Besides the two young girls I am engaged to teach, she has one son, the offspring of a previous marriage. He is at the University, she told me to day, and she expects him down almost immediately. His name is Edgar Stadding, and he is spoken of (by his mother) as a rising man in the scholastic world.

My two pupils seem only ordinary specimens of child life. Mediocre in every way —nothing remarkably good, bad, or clever about them, and consequently a very fair field to work upon.

The Peak is much more comfortable than one would think from its surroundings. It is an isolated, bleak place certainly, but it has its advantages —among them a magnificent view. The grounds are of great extent, and are well laid out that is, from my point of view. The paths are full of odd twists and turns, and reveal all sorts of unexpected attractions at unexpected places. The shrubbery is cut into a variety of strange artificial shapes, which is the one point in the gardening I do not like. The whole place, both grounds and house, is sadly neglected. The house itself is a very substantial affair, having been built in times when the Maoris were troublesome, and when the possibility of a raid on their part was among the things which might reasonably be calculated upon. There is even now some legend extant about a solemn league and covenant having been made between the earliest representative of the Shaw family and a certain Epuni, who, in those days, was chief of a tribe of savages called the Ngatiawa, and a mighty man in the land.

Jan. 18.—Great preparations were being made for the arrival of Edgar Stadding all day yesterday, and the place is even yet in a state of mild uproar. Things had been left to the last moment, too, and the object of all this fuss arrived in the midst of the confusion. He came very unexpectedly, and without sending any word. I had the rather doubtful honour of seeing him last night before any one else in the house, and there was something in his behaviour that puzzled me then, and which I am at a loss to understand now.

It was a beautiful night. The moon had just risen, and the dew was glittering in the silvery light. I had wandered from the house, and found my way to the low stone fence that borders the garden. I stood there enjoying the fresh beauty of the night, looking along the road that stretched away in the moonlight like a long gray ribbon till it was lost in distant windings among the hills.

There was a spire of tufted grass growing out from between the stones of the wall, and nodding in the breeze. It was such as Goethe's Marguerite might have said her charm over—"He loves me, he loves me not"—and I plucked it, and choosing two words, repeated them as she did, picking a blossom at each word. I came to the end, and held the stripped blade in my hand.

I was to be unfortunate!

I laughed and threw the blade away, and turned to go into the house again, but paused. Slowly there grew out of the silence a faint rattle that gradually took the sound of carriage wheels, and two dots of flame, like twin stars, floated out into the dimness far along the road. As it came nearer I saw that the lights belonged to a dog-cart, which had two men in it. It stopped suddenly when directly opposite me, and one of the men, giving a hasty exclamation, sprang out, and the next thing I was conscious of was that a young man was approaching me with lifted hat and outstretched hand. I was more than surprised. I had never seen him in my life before, but he seemed, in some unaccountable way, to regard me as quite an old friend. He was tall and over-dressed—even in the moonlight I caught the flash of jewellery on cuff and shirt-front—and the fingers of the hand he held out had several rings on them.

"Ha," he said, as if he were greeting some familiar acquaintance, "who the unmentionable would expect to see you hanging over a fence at this hour? How the deuce did you get here, of all places? You've stolen a march on me, you puss; begad you have. Good heavens!" he said, stopping short in comic despair within a pace of me. "Is it not—can I have made a mistake?"

He certainly had, and I went so far as to say so. "Puss," indeed! the impudence of the fellow.

"Indeed, I—I beg your pardon. I thought I had the pleasure of meeting——"

The man in the cart laughed, and the other, murmuring some apology which I could not distinguish, scrambled back to his place in what I thought a very ungraceful and undignified way, and drove on again. As I walked towards the house, wondering how such a strange mistake could have arisen, I heard a peal of laughter from along the road, and looking back, saw the dog-cart take the turning that led up to the house, and it at once crossed my mind that it was Edgar Stadding who had taken this informal way of returning home, and that it must have been he who had spoken to me. And I should like to know who on earth could he suppose me to be, that he

should have the unheard-of impudence to call me
" puss !"

Jan. 19.—I saw him again to-day. He introduced
himself the other night in a way that prejudiced me pretty
strongly against him, and my dislike—for it amounts to
that; I always go by first impressions—was increased this
afternoon, though he seemed to put himself to some pains
to make himself agreeable. As I was walking by myself
in the garden after the day's lessons were over, I saw him
lolling on one of the old-fashioned garden seats that are
scattered here and there over the grounds. He had a
number of letters beside him on the seat, and seemed to be
reading one very attentively; he kissed it once or twice
too, if I am not mistaken. From " puss," I suppose. I
wonder who the creature can be? How that word does
annoy me, to be sure! Presently he caught sight of me,
and, thrusting the letter into his pocket, came hurrying
along the path after me.

" Oh, Miss Gower," he said, as he overtook me, " I have
just been over to the post-office for our daily batch of
letters, and here is one for you."

I took the letter, thanked him, and was passing on when
he said—

" I hope you have forgiven me for my stupidity of the
other night, Miss Gower. It was the dim light did it;
and you really are so much like—the party I took you
for."

I felt anything but flattered by the resemblance !

" There is nothing to forgive, Mr. Stadding," I said,
tartly. " I had forgotten all about it."

It was a case of antipathy at first sight. Without there
being any one thing in his manner or appearance that one
could single out as *the* objectionable feature, there was
something about him that roused my dislike at once. If
he thought to use the letter as an excuse for opening
a conversation, as I supposed he did, he had chosen the
worst possible means for his purpose, for it was in my

sister's hand, and I was anxious to get away to my own room and read it. But he stood right in my way, flicking the flowers with his riding switch, and apparently determined not to go till we were better acquainted.

"You are very kind to say that, Miss Gower," he said; "you have no idea how I have been tormenting myself about my awkwardness. I am afraid you will find The Peak very dull," he went on, after pausing to see if I would speak, "especially after being accustomed to living in town."

"I don't think I shall find it at all dull. I prefer country to town."

"Do you? Well, I don't. Awful bore, I think it. Tells on a fellah, you know—least, it does on me. Gives me the miserables, and I make for the town the first chance I get. Course, being a university man—student, you know, and all that" (he looked out of the corners of his eyes with elaborate slyness as he said it, but I carefully avoided his glance)—"er—town offers me many advantages."

I said, "Indeed," endeavouring to reduce myself to a lump of inanity in the hope that he would drop the conversation, but he went on as cheerfully as ever.

"Oh, yes, six months in the country would make me into an unmitigated clod-hopper" (a great deal less than that would do it, I commented mentally). "*Allow* me," and he picked up the letter, which had slipped from my fingers.

"Do you know, Miss Gower, I can do a little at the second-sight business," he said, desperately trying to keep up the conversation, as he held out the letter, and gazed impudently into my eyes. Everything he did was more or less impudent, it seemed to me.

"Yes?" frigidly.

"Yes. Shall I give you a sample of what I can do? For one thing, now, I can prophesy good news for you in this letter. Shall I go on?"

"By all means, Mr. Stadding, tell me all you know; only I am afraid you are not recommending yourself as a letter-carrier for the future."

"Oh, I say," he said, with a stupidly depreeating air, "that's—that's very severe. But, now—you couldn't cross my palm with silver, could you, in true gipsy style? No change? Oh, very well. Your letter, then," and he gazed abstractedly into space, and let the words drop slowly, one by one, from his lips, "is from one near and dear to you—whom you haven't seen for some time—a female, a mother—no, not a mother, nor an aunt—let us say a sister; let us further say her name has nine letters, and that the first is C. Am I right as regards the writer so far, supposing it is from her?" and he assumed what he meant for an engaging smile.

"Quite right, so far," I said, somewhat surprised.

"Good breeding requires that I must not allow myself to pry too closely. She is an actress, tall, dark, has—well, in fact, has a temper of her own, and—yes, meditates very shortly paying you a visit."

"Why, Mr. Stadding, you must surely be acquainted with my sister to know all this!"

"Performance is over, Miss Gower" (another smile), "it merely remains to pass round the hat."

"But, tell me, do you really—you must know my sister Catherine."

"To those who have the gift of second sight, ordinary conditions don't apply. We know 'em all, any one you like, without the preliminary of introduction. I have that marvellous gift, and it enables me to know that the Grand What's-his-name of Thibet is a humbug, and that the Czar Alexander looks under the bed every night before he goes to sleep."

"Oh, but," I said, impatiently, " without any nonsense, do you know my sister Catherine?"

"I know Catherine's sister   —"

He was interrupted by a shriek of laughter, and little

May Shaw, one of my two pupils, came running along the path, her hat hanging round her neck by the strings, her hair flying out behind her.

"Oh, Eddy, hide me quick! She wants me to go to bed, and I won't go-o-o," shrieked the child, trying to hide behind him.

"Confound the child! go away; don't bother me with your nonsense now," he said, irritably, pushing her away.

"Oh no, of course not," and the child fell back a pace and pouted, "'cause you want to talk with Miss Gower," she added, with the charming frankness of her years.

"May Shaw!" I said, severely.

"You impudent young monkey!" said Mr. Stadding, at the same time looking at me and smiling as if there was a perfect understanding between us.

"Miss May," said a sharp voice, "come along and let's have no more nonsense," and the nurse, a cross, vinegar-faced woman, appeared round a sudden bend in the trees and seized the child by the wrist. She looked sourly from me to Mr. Stadding, and back again, and was turning away without speaking, when Mr. Stadding said ill-temperedly—

"I wish you could manage to keep those youngsters a little more under control, Mrs. Hetherwick."

Now, Mrs. Hetherwick, I have reason to know, occupies a peculiar position in the family. She is generally spoken of as "the nurse." That is her official capacity. She came into the house with her mistress, and from their long acquaintance has drifted from the position of servant into that of confidante. She is allowed considerable authority, and, from what I have seen of her, seems to exercise it in the most disagreeable way, and is heartily detested by the other servants. She has the reputation, too, of being the most consummate of gossips, and has unusual facilities in the way of learning local scandal, being related to the land-lady of the Truss o' Straw, a hotel at the Hutt, a place not far from here, where such news naturally collects.

She turned upon Mr. Stadding at once, with crest erect.

"Indeed, Mr. Stadding, I think I know my place better than some others I could name, if it comes to that," she snapped. "I am sorry if the little thing *interrupted* you. There are times, I know, when children are in the way." She looked spitefully at me as she spoke, and I began to wake up to the fact that I was being placed in a very unpleasant position.

"Hoity-toity, marry come up," said Mr. Stadding, mocking her. "Do we know who we are speaking to, Mrs. Hetherwick?"

"Yes, we do, Mr. Stadding, and it would be better if some others in the house were just as careful who they talked to. I know my own place, at least—and know how to keep it, that's what's more."

"If I had my way, that last is just what you wouldn't do, madam."

"Oh, I dessay! And I think I know some who would be just as sure of their place if you had your way, sir—which the Lord forbid you ever should!" she said, shaking her head at him fiercely.

"You take my advice, Mrs. Hetherwick, and don't go too far. I didn't ask you for any impudence, you know, and when you speak to me you'll be good enough to remember the difference in our positions. If you are allowed liberties elsewhere, you'll lay aside your Jack-in-office airs with me. I've no more words to waste on you. Miss Gower, may I see you into the house?"

I had felt *de trop* during this passage, and did not wish to appear to identify myself with either party. I was irritated at the conduct of Edgar Stadding, whose thoughtlessness had placed me in a very false position. It was impossible not to understand the point of Mrs. Hetherwick's reference to myself, and I dreaded how she might use her influence with Mrs. Shaw if her enmity were once aroused.

"Thank you," I said coldly, "I shall stay out here a little longer."

He lifted his hat, without speaking, and passed on after Mrs. Hetherwick, who was striding up the walk to the house, dragging little May with her, who was continually looking back and tripping up, and being jerked on again till a turn hid them from sight.

The evenings are raw and cold up among these bleak hills, so, giving them a few minutes to reach the house, I turned to go in also. As I passed up the stairs to my room I heard the voice of Mrs. Hetherwick saying, "Take my word for it, she's too good-looking by half. I know 'em of old." I heard no more, but my modesty could not make me doubt as to who it was that was under discussion, and I have serious misgivings as to how this will end.

Edgar Stadding was a true prophet. The letter *was* from Catherine. It was very short, and contained little more than the intimation that the company with which she was travelling would shortly be in Wellington, and that she hoped to be able to get time to visit me soon after I received her note.

As I finished reading the letter I remembered what Edgar Stadding had said in the garden. Could he really be acquainted with her, and did he by some means know that she intended coming here?

A thought strikes me: We were always considered very much alike. Can this be the explanation of the strange mistake he made the other night? I sincerely hope it is not!

III.

JAN. 22.—I have seen Catherine to-day for the first time for five years! She is very little changed, and I feel quite sure now that it must have been she that Edgar

Stadling mistook me for on the night of his return; and the knowledge is very far from being pleasing to me. I not only dislike him personally—and I frankly admit that I do, as I have said before—but his tone, when he spoke to me, both on the first occasion and since, was to my thinking a deal too familiar and—well, disagreeable, to say the least. From what I have seen of him during the last day or two, I believe him to be a selfish and unprincipled man.

Catherine is staying at the Truss o' Straw, at the Hutt, where she established herself this morning. She sent a note telling me she had arrived, and as soon as my work for the day was over I went down to see her. I inquired for "Miss Ada de Bonville," which was the name—a foolish one, I thought—on the note she had sent, and was shown up to her room, where we committed all kinds of extravagances in the first joy of meeting after so long a separation as ours has been. At least, I know I did; and when my first lucid interval occurred, I found myself, with tumbled hair and dress, sitting on the sofa opposite Catherine, and both of us in a generally confused state of half laughter, half tears.

When I say she is little changed, I mean as to her appearance; in other respects there is a change, though what it is I scarcely know, except that I have an uneasy sense that it's there, and that I wish it was not. But beyond this it is the same dear self-willed impulsive Catherine of old.

We sat and talked as girls will talk after they have been long parted, but what it was all about I haven't the faintest idea now. The long summer evening closed in upon us all too soon, and as I wished to be back at The Peak before dusk, I rose to go. I was standing in front of the glass arranging my head-gear with Catherine beside me, when I was struck anew by the resemblance between our faces, and at once recalled my first interview with Edgar Stadling, and the mistake he had made.

"Catherine," I said, suddenly, "do you know any one named Edgar Stadding?"

She started, and then laughed guiltily, and began to colour up.

"We are in the way of knowing a good many people in our profession," she said, evasively. "It's different to a governess's, you know—considerably."

"Well?"

"Well, what?" with a short laugh.

"Do you know Edgar Stadding?" I repeated, determined to have a direct answer to my question.

"Well, as I say, one knows so many—but why do you ask?"

"Because I'm pretty sure he knows you, and knew you were coming here too."

"Oh, that's very likely," she answered, carelessly, "and so did five thousand others, for the matter of that. It was in the papers about our coming long enough, goodness knows. Besides, more people know Tom Fool—you know the rest."

"Yes, but he knew more about you than he got from any paper. The papers didn't say you were my sister, or give your right name, did they; or say that you were tall and dark, and had a temper of your own?"—(Or speak of you as "puss," I was going to add, but checked myself in time.)

"Did he say that?" she said, her eyes sparkling. "You know him—you've spoken to him, then?" and she glanced up at me quickly.

"Or rather, he has to me—and I'd thank him not to in future."

"And why, indeed! Isn't he good enough for your ladyship?"

"I don't say anything as to his goodness or badness, though I have my doubts about the former. But I don't like him—for one thing."

"Indeed! And what is the other thing, may I ask?"

wavering between jest and earnest, with a growing inclination to the latter.

"Simply because he doesn't know how to speak when he does do so—as far as I have seen as yet, at any rate."

"That sounds very like a 'bull,' doesn't it?   Did he say anything very shocking?"

"It's not what he has said to me altogether, but to others, and his manner in general.   But that has nothing to do with my question as to whether you know him or not—though I scarcely need ask you now."

"What a persistent little fool it is!   Why, of course I do—that is, we have a slight acquaintance—platonic, you know.   The fact is, he is an artist, and appreciates good acting——"

"*And* actresses," I said, with a curtsey.

"I accept the amendment.   *And* actresses, as you remark," with a return of the curtsey.

"He may be an artist, but he's certainly not a gentleman, nor the kind of person I would choose for—for—well, a friend——"

"Oh, nonsense.   Don't be so absurd.   What do you know about him to form an opinion on, and what's your opinion worth when you have formed it, I'd like to know? I'll be bound you haven't spoken to him half a dozen times altogether."

"No, indeed I haven't, and don't intend to, that's more. I found twice quite enough for my taste."

"Twice!   There you are, now!   The very idea of running away with an opinion of a man's character after seeing him twice!   I wonder you were introduced to him at all."

"It would be a good while before we'd become acquainted if he waited for that, I'm afraid.   We weren't introduced; he doesn't wait for such old-fashioned formalities as that. He introduced himself, and that, too, in a way that was a good deal more peculiar than agreeable."

"He has a free and easy way with him, I know."

"Yes—very much so. The first time he saw me I've a shrewd idea he took me for some one else." I looked hard at her, but she met my eyes with a look of childlike innocence.

"I shouldn't wonder if he did. I doubt if he would have the courage to speak to such a little dragon of propriety, if he knew. You always were a little prude, you know that yourself. But who could he take you for?"

"Can't you guess!"

"Not the faintest idea," she said, shaking her head.

"Shall I tell you?"

"Please."

"Ada de Bonville."

"Ada de Bonville! Me! Never!" she exclaimed, with well-simulated surprise.

"Come, come," I said, mischievously, "you're not on the stage now. It's well acted, but only acted after all. You know it was you he must have mistaken me for if he mistook me for any one."

"Go along with you, you impudent minx! How should I know? He might have taken you for one of the old maids of Lee. As likely as not—you look the part. But tell me—what did he say?"

"No more than you might expect any other young man to say who found himself in a very ridiculous position. Mumbled something I suppose he intended for an apology, got back into his dog-cart, and drove off again—and all with the worst grace imaginable."

"Mumbled! He didn't mumble. But surely that wasn't *all* he said. What were his words what did he say?"

"Bless my heart, I don't set so much store by his words as to be able to repeat them verbatim a week after hearing them. Something about an unexpected pleasure, and how on earth did I get there. Which I think it was like his impudence to say." (I still suppressed the "puss.")

"And was that all he said?" she asked, with a certain air of relief, as if she had been afraid he had said a good deal more.

"As far as I remember that was all he said."

"Ha! ha! ha!" she laughed, "the very idea of his taking you for me! That *is* good. Well, we are alike, certainly—in looks, anyway. I suppose you were highly indignant at the innocent mistake he made?"

"Indignant? Why should I be, at his saying to me what it would be appropriate to say to any one else in a like position?"

"Oh, but you were always such a straight-laced little prude of a thing. You know you were."

"A prude," I said, irritably. "I think you told me that before this evening. I'm not quite sure what you call a prude. If it's prudish not to like any one who doesn't know how to behave himself, then I'm a prude, and mean to remain one."

"I'd better count ten before I add anything to that, don't you think, Ettie? Don't let us quarrel over it."

"Quarrel! I don't want to quarrel. But what do you say such ridiculous things for? And all for the sake of a——"

"Let us change the subject, Ettie," she said, stopping me by putting her hand over my mouth. "When shall I see you again?"

"I'm afraid I shan't be able to call here often. Come up and see me at The Peak. I've got a room to myself."

"Thank *you*," she said, with another curtsey. "I've no wish to see your puritanical old Mother Hubbard up there. Besides, what would she think of the governess who defiled her house by bringing an unregenerate, painted actress into it; and that actress her sister, too?"

"Why, what can you know about Mrs. Shaw?" I asked, in surprise.

"Oh, I know plenty about her. I know her a good deal better than you think," and she nodded her head wisely.

"From Edgar Stadding," I commented mentally, and then aloud—"Have you ever spoken to her?"

"Not I, but I know what kind of woman she is, all the same. I have means of hearing. What? The time? Oh, well, if you must go. Will you have a ticket for the theatre? 'Deeds Done in Darkness.' Come and see your sister filling the *rôle* of the 'Deserted Wife' as played by her for two hundred and fifty nights before enthusiastic audiences in all the leading cities of the colonies, an impersonation universally admitted to be unique in its boldness of conception and minute conscientiousness of detail—ahem! Can't I reel off the patter? I got that from one of the notices written by a newspaper fledgling I charmed in the stalls one night. Won't you come? I'd like you to see it. I'm sure you'd like it. We begin in Wellington in a night or so. My leave is up to-morrow."

"Thanks. I'd like to go; but then you know——"

"Oh, yes; Mrs. Shaw, propriety, and all the rest of it. I'd go in spite of the old cat, if I had to climb out of the window. What's it got to do with her, I'd like to know."

"But being an irreclaimable prude I couldn't do that, you see."

"*You* climb out of window! I don't believe you could persuade yourself to leave a house afire if you had to save your life at the risk of your ankles being seen. What is it Miss Mowcher says about that? Well, what must be, must be, I suppose. I should like you to see it, though, at the same time. I rather pride myself on my 'Deserted Wife.' You wouldn't believe what a hold it has taken of me. I quite terrified myself the other night when I woke up in the middle of a dream, and found myself going through the scene on the floor of my room."

"I should like to see you too, Kate; but if I can't see you in the part of a Deserted Wife, perhaps I'll see you have a still longer run in that of an Old Maid in the Comedy of Life, so cheer up."

"No, that indeed you won't—not while leap year's in

the calender and I've got a tongue in my head. Good-
night, old chap. I can see you are taxing yourself to work
up a joke on something about a ' drop-scene ' and a ' curtain lecture,' but I don't care to hear it. Here, take this
ticket in case the spirit should move you to try the window-
climbing business. Ta, ta !"

IV.

JAN. 24.—Mrs. Shaw has treated me very coldly since
the evening when Edgar Stadding spoke to me in the
garden, and I am glad that that gentleman has of late been
away pretty frequently at one place and another, and that
when he does meet me he makes no attempt to engage in
conversation. I think he understands me pretty well now.
Mrs. Hetherwick ignores me altogether—of which I should
be glad did I not doubt she is only waiting a favourable
opportunity to injure me in the eyes of her employer.

Mrs. Shaw surprised me yesterday. I have mentioned
that I was struck with a certain grim suggestion of sancti-
moniousness about her at our first interview, and that
impression has been made a good deal stronger lately.
She is the very last person in the world I should expect to
see patronizing a theatre or, indeed, any other amusement ;
yet last night she not only went to the theatre herself, but
took her retainers with her—me along with the rest. I
wonder what she would think if she knew my reason for
being interested in the play ? Early in the morning she
received a visit from a certain Dr. Carmichael—a tiresome,
good-natured old man, who officiously superintended my
work with my pupils during the forenoon, and seemed to
think his gray hairs justified him in playfully pinching my
cheek and pulling my ears, which he *would* persist in doing
—and I think it must have been on his persuasion that she

allowed herself to be led so far out of her ordinary humdrum groove. I had taken the ticket Catherine had offered me, but without any hope of using it, for I was anxious to avoid doing anything that I thought might displease Mrs. Shaw—and I was pretty sure my going to the theatre would displease her—but I felt very much disappointed, for I was really curious to see how Kate could act. Mrs. Shaw is one of those persons who have gained us the reputation, as a nation, of taking our pleasures sadly. She called the two servants and myself into the drawing-room yesterday, where she was sitting in company with Dr. Carmichael, with Mrs. Hetherwick knitting and glowering in the background. She surprised them even more than she did me by saying she had gone to the expense of buying tickets for the theatre. She was opposed to the habit of theatre-going. It was, generally speaking, a Thriftless, Worldly, even Immoral practice; but on this occasion the piece seemed different from those usually given, and was advertised as being of a strictly moral tendency, and specially adapted to appeal to the young, and it was for the purpose of assisting a good charitable object. She approved of that—she emphatically approved of that. She was a charitable woman herself, and always wished to help a good object with her humble mite. But still, those who did not wish need not go, and she would write an appropriate text on their tickets, which they might keep instead. Both the servants assumed an air of infinitely preferring the text, but being compelled by a disagreeable duty to go to the theatre.

"And which will Miss Gower have, the text or the play?" said the doctor, with a sly smile, sidling up to me. "I am going to the play, myself. Gratify an old man by saying you will go to. Miss Gower smiles. I answer for her, Mrs. Shaw; Miss Gower will go to the play, and you can give her the text afterwards."

Mrs. Shaw, who was no doubt vexed at the others declining the text, received my decision with a very bad grace,

and silently offered me a ticket. I did not wish to place
myself even under the trifling obligation of accepting it,
and in consequence I allowed myself to commit a piece of
very bad generalship.

"Thank you," I said, "I have a ticket."

"Oh, indeed," she said, icily. "I was not aware of that."

Something like a muttered, "Well—upon—my word,"
from Mrs. Hetherwick's corner, as if the speaker had
almost lost the power of speech from amazement, showed
me the mistake I had made.

"Very good. You see, Miss Gower's charitable feelings
have anticipated yours, Mrs. Shaw," said the doctor, who
seemed to understand the situation.

"Quite so. It is a very commendable feature in a young
person's character," said Mrs. Shaw, with a frigid stare.
"I can quite understand the ticket was bought with no
other purpose than that of charity."

Her temper was still ruffled when we set out for Wellington, and was made worse by the sudden appearance of Edgar
Stadling, who had been away during the first part of
the day, and who now declared his intention of accompanying us to town. I, too, could have wished he had not
put himself in evidence, for though I was not looking at
her, I knew Mrs. Shaw at once set herself to keep a vigilant
watch upon me; and when we entered the theatre, I took
care to take the seat farthest away from Mr. Stadling.

I had very seldom been in a theatre before—never, of
course, under like circumstances—and I sat with a feeling
of nervous distraction upon me, waiting for the rising of
the curtain, and the appearance of Catherine upon the
stage. The house was not half full as yet; and a confused
buzz of conversation arose from the continual throng of
new-comers making their way in. As I was wondering, in
my simplicity, how Catherine would ever be able to go
through her part before so many people, and thinking how
impossible it would be for a nervous creature such as I to
say even half a dozen words in the presence of such a

battery of eyes, I was startled by a face I caught sight of on the opposite side of the circle. It was that of a tall, dark man, who had just been obsequiously ushered to his seat, and was standing waiting, with a certain statuesque pose, for two ladies, who were making their way towards him. He was a spare, powerful-looking man, with a closely-cut black beard, and one shoulder a very little higher than the other.

"Who is that man?" I said, laying my hand on the arm of Doctor Carmichael, who sat next to me.

"Who? Where? How your hand trembles! What is the matter?"

I knew my hand shook, for I was excited, though I did not know why.

"That tall dark man opposite us, who is showing the lady into her seat. There, he has just sat down, and is reading his programme."

The doctor, who is rather short-sighted, put up his glasses.

"That," he said, focussing his glass, "is Llewellyn, the owner of Scythe-bearer, the disputed winner of the Auckland Cup, that we have heard so much of ever since the race. This is the first time I have had the chance of a good look at his face, and what an evil-looking one it is, isn't it? He could play the part of Mephistopheles without change of dress, and no one would notice the incongruity. Here, just look at him through this," and the doctor offered me his lorgnette. Llewellyn raised his head as I brought the glass to bear upon him, and I had a good view of his face. As the doctor said, it was indeed an evil-looking one. But its chief characteristic, and that which fixed the attention to the exclusion of all else, was the expression of the eyes—deep-sunk, black, and piercing, with a depth of hidden passion and fire in them.

"Miss Gower, you shuddered, I'll take my oath you shuddered! How would you like a man like that for a husband, eh? You wouldn't care to cross his purpose, would you?"

"No, that indeed I shouldn't," I said. "I hope our paths in life may never meet." And then the curtain went up.

I could wish that my record of the evening ended here, for, as a matter of fact, I blush even in the privacy of my own room, when I think how I disgraced myself; and I am really ashamed to think I could let a mere piece of make-believe sensationalism have such an effect upon me.

It was the last scene of the third act, the central tableau of the piece, and was, to my thinking, horribly realistic. It represented a glade in a forest at midnight, so dimly lighted that one could scarcely distinguish the actors. Two men had met, and were talking angrily. Presently they closed furiously in a death struggle. In the midst of the combat, the stage moon burst out from a bank of canvas clouds, and revealed one man in the act of plunging a knife into the other. The wounded man sank upon the ground; the murderer, alarmed at what he had done, made off—and all was done in such dead silence that it made one quite nervous. Then, from among the bushes, Catherine, in the character of the Deserted Wife, rushed towards the fallen man, who was no other than her faithless husband. He struggled to his knees as she came near, and dumbly held out his hands to her, and clutched her dress. She snatched up the knife from where it had fallen upon the ground, seized one of his wrists, and brandished the dagger over his head. Her action was so terribly life-like I could not bear to see more, and I covered my face with my hands. I heard her clear voice ringing through the building, "Let me finish the work!" There was quietness for a moment, and then a burst of applause, that died away on my ears as if I had been plunged under water, and then—well, and then I must admit I was guilty of the weakness of fainting.

When I recovered, some one was holding my head up, and some one else was chafing my hands. There was a crowd of people round me—a pyramid of curious eyes piled almost to the ceiling, it seemed to me in my confusion, and the first face I distinguished, as the mist cleared away from my eyes, was that of the man Llewellyn looking down at me over the shoulder of Edgar Stadding. Then, I saw Mrs. Shaw, who seemed, by her looks, to have been disappointed in detecting the moral tendency of the play, standing grim and silent beside me, with my shawl dangling from her hand. Then, I found myself outside, and revived as if by magic with the breath of the keen cool night air. The carriage drove up. Doctor Carmichael, who had monopolized me as completely as if I had been a piece of his property, gently lifted me in, and we were soon trundling homeward again. Had it not been for the doctor, I think we should have been absolutely the dreariest party of pleasure-seekers that ever rode on wheels. I remained dumb under a sense of my own humiliation and disgrace, and the humiliation and disgrace I had brought upon my rigid mistress by making her, upon the one occasion on which she had relaxed, the centre of a scene in a theatre. She had insisted on having a light in the carriage—owing to her uncertainty as to what further weakness I might betray, I suppose, and she sat next me, bolt upright, angular, mute. Once I thought I heard her mutter, "Moral tendency, indeed!" but that was all. Doctor Carmichael was saying, "I was disappointed, too, in the piece—I must admit that I was disappointed in the piece. There is too much of the garments rolled in blood about it to my thinking."

"Dev—er—jolly good play, I think," said Edgar Stadding, "as plays go nowadays. I hate your milk-and-water crossbreds between a Sunday-school picnic and a Methody prayer-meeting. Give me something hot and strong before your tea-and-cake-in-the-garden business."

Mrs. Shaw glared, but said nothing.

"I don't know," said the doctor. "I've got a theory on the point. I believe, and have always believed, that an actor's character is affected by his profession. He unconsciously takes upon himself the features of the part he represents."

"Oh, that's all stuff," answered Mr. Stadding, in his delightfully frank way. "You mean to say that a man is more likely to become a murderer because he pats a man on the sconce with a brown-paper club—why, what rot."

Mrs. Shaw glared harder than ever, but still said nothing.

"What seems ' rot ' to you, sir, as you elegantly term it," said the doctor, gripping the head of his stick very tightly, and getting red in the face, "may seem sound common sense to other people with perhaps equal powers of judgment. I mean to say that a conscientious actor, who sinks his own individuality, and for the time being assumes that of a murderer—though there is no necessity for flying to that extreme, mind you—forces himself into the same frame of mind, and acts as a murderer would act—he is, I say, simply putting himself through a course of criminal education. And that's the long and short of it."

"And that's your theory, is it? If you saw murderer and murdered over their oysters and beer after the play, you'd see what nonsense it is."

"Upon my word, sir, you have a peculiar way of putting your argument," said the doctor, growing redder in the face, and taking a fresh grip of his stick. "I repeat, and I speak from a pretty wide professional experience of human nature, that, given the provocation, a man, who, by repeatedly acting the part, has lost the salutary horror of crime, which is the best safeguard against it, will be prone, much more prone, to—to—to——"

"Commit murder, for instance," suggested Edgar Stadding, with a grin.

"Well, if you will persist in going to that extreme, sir,—even to commit murder than if he had not had such an insidious training."

"Oh, query, query, query," said the other.

"Oh, it's easy to cry ' query, query, query ' ; but that's no argument. And let me add, that the chances would be increased tenfold if he were under the influence of drink, or was delirious, or ——"

"Or mad."

"Or mad, especially if mad. I'm glad you follow me."

"I follow you! Not at all. The way you were running on naturally suggested 'mad' to me."

"Upon—my—word!" gasped the doctor, with long intervals between his words, his face of an apoplectic hue. "You're impudent, sir. You're talking of what you know nothing about."

"One of us is, I'll take my oath," admitted the amiable Edgar.

"I quite agree with what you say, doctor," said Mrs. Shaw, opening her lips for the first time. "And I beg of you never to ask me to go to such a place again. I consider myself imposed upon, and my charity abused. Moral tendency, indeed!"

"We didn't stay long enough to see that," put in Mr. Stadding, with another grin; "the moral tendency didn't come out till the last act."

"I am very glad you do agree with me, Mrs. Shaw," said Doctor Carmichael. "I am sorry if you have not enjoyed your evening; but theatre-going is apt to lose its charm for people of our years, I know."

"Considering this is the first and last time I have ever been in such a place—and considering I was only induced to go under the mistaken idea that I was doing good—I fail to see why you should use the word '*theatre-going*' in connection with me, doctor," said Mrs. Shaw, ill-temperedly, and speaking very rapidly. I don't think she liked the doctor's last phrase.

"I beg your pardon; I did not mean to offend," he answered. "And what is your opinion of my theory, Miss Gower?" he said, turning to me.

"I have never given the subject any consideration, doctor."

"And therefore hold the same views as Doctor Carmichael," put in Stadding, apparently thinking he had said a very good thing.

"Perhaps, sir, you will allow Miss Gower to give her own opinion! When you are as old as I am you too will probably see fit to draw the same conclusions as I do."

"Hm, most things would be excusable under those circumstances!" with spiteful significance.

The doctor drew in his breath hard; but before he could answer the carriage drew up at the gates of The Peak, and he stepped out in wrathful silence.

*   *   *   *   *   *

Jan. 28.—Edgar Stadding went away to-day on a visit to some friends in the country; and I am glad of it.

Feb. 10.—A good long while since my last entry, and a good deal has happened in the interval. It has come at last. I am the most unfortunate girl that ever lived. I have dreaded it ever since I overheard Mrs. Hetherwick's flattering remark concerning myself after her quarrel with Edgar Stadding in the garden that day—of which quarrel I suppose I may regard myself as in a measure the innocent cause. But it has come from a most unexpected quarter, and has arisen from a source whence, unless I am much mistaken, more trouble may be looked for.

I have left The Peak. Have been ignominiously dismissed, in fact, and am writing this at the Truss o' Straw, where I have temporarily taken up my quarters in the room in which I saw Catherine.

Ever since I had the misfortune to rouse the dislike of that vindictive old creature, Mrs. Hetherwick, the tide in my affairs has steadily set against me, until the climax has been reached in my summary discharge.

And what is the reason?

A charming, romantic, Gretna Green elopement, if you please, between that detestable Edgar Stadding and Catherine, who is now Mrs. Stadding! She must be mad! I would not trust my happiness in such hands for any earthly consideration. I do hope there may not be the seeds of future unhappiness for her in thus recklessly throwing herself upon the mercy of that man ; for I am convinced of nothing more surely than that ho is utterly unworthy of being trusted. I may be wrong ; I hope for her sake I am. But I am afraid she is blinded to his faults, and that her awaking will be a bitter one. The future will show—the future will show !

V.

FEB. 10.—Knowing Catherine's disposition as I did, there was one thing that surprised me even more than the elopement itself, and that was that she should have written to me about it ; for, though ordinarily as frank and open as a child, she had a horror of letter-writing. From the date—more than a week back—it had evidently been delayed. If it had only come to my hand a day or two earlier, I should not have allowed Mrs. Shaw the opportunity of turning me away—an opportunity of which she availed herself in the most venomous way. This is what Catherine had to say for herself :—

"*Auckland, February 2nd, 1885.*

" MY DEAR OLD ETTIE,—

"Whatever will you think of me ! You remember what you said when you saw me at the Truss o' Straw about my having a long run in the Comedy of Life in the part of an old maid? Well, neither you nor anybody else will ever see me in that character. Ettie, *I am Mrs. Edgar Stadding !* What do you think of that ? And I haven't had to wait for leap year either. I know you are not over fond of Edgar, but I hope you will try to like him better now he is your brother-in-law." (Indeed, I shall do nothing of the sort. Brother-in-law, indeed !) "Really, he is very kind, and all that one could look for in a husband. If he has been wild, it was because he had nothing to steady him—never had a wife to be cared for, or to care for him.   I do not think you will find it in your heart to blame me, though I know what a dear, strict, old-fashioned thing you are in these things.   I had no one to confide in but you, and I was afraid to ask your advice, for I knew from what you said that night at the Truss o' Straw how you would take it.   You will like Edgar ever so much when you come to know him better, and he speaks in the very kindest way of you, and seems to have formed quite a high opinion of you.   We are staying at the Bay View in Auckland, and all we want to make us perfectly happy would be to have you with us."   (No doubt!)   "To show how considerate he is, he wishes our marriage kept perfectly secret till he sees his way to reconcile his mother to the match, because he does not know how it might affect your position at The Peak if it were to become known now. This, I assure you, is his only reason.   Indeed, he has told me as much himself, and says he knows his mother is of such a hasty temper she might do or say something in her excitement which might make your position uncomfortable. I know I must have ruined his prospects by allowing him to throw himself away upon such a useless creature as I am. So you see how unselfish he is, and how full of consideration for others.   We must keep everything secret for the present, and I know I may depend upon you *not to breathe a word to any one.*   I have no more to say, so good-bye.

" Your loving sister,
" KATE STADDING.

"P.S.—It will be useless to write, for we leave Auckland in a day or so.   I will write again soon."

The letter came upon me with the unexpectedness of a thunderbolt.   I could scarcely believe my eyes when I read it.   I had neither seen nor heard anything that would have led me to suspect anything of the kind on the part of either Stadding or Kate.   The former, from what I saw of him, seemed to be living idly and contentedly enough at The Peak.   He was away the greater part of every day either shooting or fishing—that is, he would set out with gun or rod, but I can scarcely recall a single occasion on which he returned with anything in the shape of spoil. What little time he spent at home he passed either lolling about the grounds, the embodiment of indolence and *ennui*, or annoying Mrs. Hetherwick, who appeared to entertain an absolute hatred for him at last, and showed it in the most unmistakable way in her behaviour. Several times latterly he had sought to break the monotony by drawing me into conversation, but I made it a point to treat him with the frigidity of an iceberg; so he gave up the attempt, but always remained scrupulously polite and conciliatory. Of his mother, who is fond of him to idolatry, he took scarcely any notice—whole days passing without their even seeing one another, for of late she had been kept indoors by an attack of rheumatism.

Catherine I did not see as often as I wished, owing to her obstinate determination not to call at the house—a determination I can very well understand now. On the few occasions when I did see her she never even mentioned Edgar Stadding's name, and I began to flatter myself that what I had said had caused her to break off her acquaintanceship with him. She had always been frank and unreserved to a fault, and she was the last person in the world I should have thought capable of keeping such a secret to herself; and yet here was her letter, showing her to have been the strictest observer of the lovers' creed.

In spite of Edgar Stadding's precautions to keep it secret, the knowledge of his escapade had evidently reached Mrs. Shaw's ears, the information, I can well understand, being furnished by Mrs. Hetherwick, who would have heard sufficient from her relative, the landlady of the Truss o' Straw, to form her own conclusions.

Mrs. Shaw is a woman of decision. Being unable to revenge herself upon the real culprit, she did the next best thing and turned upon the culprit's sister, and poured the vials of her wrath on my devoted head.

Though she allowed her feelings to carry her the length of turning me away at a moment's notice—and that, too, with the bitterest words on her lips—I cannot help feeling an odd kind of pity for her. Yesterday was her birthday, and in consequence my two pupils had a holiday, and a number of guests had been invited. I saw them wandering about the grounds in twos and threes all the afternoon as I sat reading in my room. They seemed to be thrown pretty much upon their own resources for amusement, and a spirit of depression hung over them. All the arrangements were left in the hands of Mrs. Hetherwick—Mrs. Shaw, who appeared worried and generally out of spirits, not showing herself more than the requirements of politeness rendered absolutely necessary. As the place seemed all in confusion, and there were more things to be done than hands to do them, I had thought of offering my services; but the amiable Mrs. H., whose face was flushed and whose temper was heated by the flurry of preparation, treated my advances with such sour incivility that I deemed it wisest to efface myself, and remained effaced for the rest of the day accordingly. I knew what the cause was quite well. Edgar Stadding, who had promised to return from his visit to a friend in the country for the occasion, had not done so, and in consequence the whole affair was very much like the play of "Hamlet" with the Prince of Denmark left out.

During the evening I had left my room to enjoy the fresh air in the garden, and was returning when Dr. Carmichael, who was one of the guests, met me in the passage.

"What! Miss Gower?" he said, drawing my arm through his. "The very person I've been looking for. Where have you hidden yourself all day, you rogue? I haven't so much as caught the whisk of your petticoat?"

"Improving my mind by reading in my room, doctor."

"Been improving its mind, has it?" he said, pinching my ear. "I can't help pinching your ear, Miss Gower—

such a pretty little ear. What advantages the gray-heads have over the young ones, haven't they?" .

"Yes, I find they have," I said, putting my hand to my ear.

"Does it tingle? It'll tingle worse than that some day."

"Then I hope it won't be soon, nor from the same cause," I said, with some trepidation.

"'My face is my fortune, sir, she said,'" chirped the doctor. "Make your mind easy, Miss Gower, it's bound to be soon; only it will be some young humbug's plausible tongue instead of an old man's fingers. I wonder where your fate is to-night, Miss Gower. I wonder——Listen!" A beam of yellow light streamed through a half opened doorway along the passage, and a peal of merry laughter floated to our ears. "Perhaps he is there," he said, pointing to the room ahead. "I have a laudable desire to assist fate to-night; let us go and see."

I drew back. "No, no. I am not—Mrs. Shaw would not——"

"Tut, tut. Come along; don't say 'no' to me. Mrs. Shaw," he said, as that lady appeared coming slowly along the passage; "here's a young girl who not only wishes to shut herself up in her room, which is an unnatural thing for a young girl to do, but would throw the blame of her imprisonment on you."

We were standing under the chandelier. The light fell full upon Mrs. Shaw's face as she approached, and I was struck by its paleness, its look of irritation and illness. She stopped for a moment as the doctor spoke, and looked closely at me, her lips pressed tightly together. There was a look in her eyes such as I had never seen before. If we had been alone, and if there had been anything to cause ill-feeling between us, I should have thought she was almost about to strike me. Then she passed on again, saying, "Pray do not let me stand in the way of your enjoying yourself *to-night*, Miss Gower." It was very ungraciously said, and her manner and appearance were so strange that I stood looking after her as she walked away.

The doctor was saying, with an air of having spoken several times before, " Really, Miss Gower, I shall be forced to make it tingle again if you don't pay more attention to your seniors."

" I beg your pardon ; I was not listening. You were saying——?"

" That I am anxious to join the other young people. Come along."

Further protest was useless, and I allowed the doctor to lead me into the brilliantly-lighted room where the company were collected.

" Mr. Forth," he said, to a stylishly-dressed young gentleman with a *pince-nez*, who was passing, " allow me to introduce you to Miss Gower."

Mr. Forth held his head back for a moment to bring his glasses to bear on me, bowed, and was charmed to make my acquaintance.

" He belongs to our own day, *he* does," said Dr. Carmichael, as my new acquaintance passed on, being taken possession of by two young ladies in pink. " He's a special correspondent for half a dozen provincial newspapers at Home, and passes his time in gleaning and retailing what he calls ' good stories.' He has quite made up his mind that there is nothing serious in life, and is voted the very best of company—you'll find him everywhere. He has fiefie stories for the ladies—see how those two creatures in pink are giggling now—who rap his knuckles with their fans, and say he's a wicked fellow, and that they won't listen to him ; stories he tells over the mahogany at my Lord Tom Noddy's, and stories that only bear ventilation in the genial atmosphere of his club. A club—do you know what a club is ? "

" Everlasting *ennui*, with cigars, wine, and a little more wine, isn't it ? "

" Don't know but what it is," said the doctor, with an

air of deliberation. "Not bad that—for a young lady of your years. Well, our Special was born for the club. He is possessed with a talking devil; his tongue is a living justification of What's-his-name's theory—it's swung in a vacuum, and having no force of gravity to check it, it goes on for ever—observe?"

"Who is that he is speaking to now?"

"Doctor Johnson," said the doctor, promptly.

"Doctor Johnson?"

"*Alias* the Rev. Simon Quinzy, but a true and faithful copy of the Lexicographer even to the stains on his waistcoat. You'll hear the oracle deliver himself of something in six syllables later on. Come, and I'll introduce you."

"However, they are married," a young-old lady was saying to the Reverend Simon as we came near. "These things are different to when I was a girl. Marriages are much harder now."

"Yes, begad they are," said the Special, *sotto voce*, dividing a wicked leer between his two companions impartially, by giving one the beginning and the other the end of it, "much harder—especially after the ceremony;" and the young lady in pink who clung to his left arm put her fan before her face and giggled modestly.

"Nephew of Colonel Grimsby, wasn't he?" said Dr. Johnson to the well-preserved lady, who nodded her head mysteriously.

"Ah, yes, old Grimsby," broke in the Special again, peering about through his glasses; "know a good story about him. He was a doctor before he entered the army, but do what he would he couldn't work up a connection. y'know. 'No,' said his friends, 'and till you marry and have a stake in the place you never will.' 'Well,' said the colonel, when he told me the story, 'being a constitutionally bashful man, and of small means besides, what was I to do?' A buzz of conversation and laughter drowned the Special's voice, and when I heard him again he was saying, "'She blushed, he popped, and begad they were married in

a fortni't.'" The young ladies in pink giggled in concert,
and the one on his right said—

"Really, Mr. Forth, how *vulgar* you do grow!"

"She is a native of Switzerland, you say?" went on
Dr. Johnson to the old lady. "There is no objection on
the score of nationality—a good race, a fine race."

"I don't know so much about that, sir," remarked the
irrepressible Special, who was in the very best of good
spirits. "The Swiss I've known are mighty poor specimens
of the genus forked radish."

"Sir," said Doctor Johnson, who seemed irritated at the
constant interruptions, and fronting the Special with ex-
panded chest—"there are those who elevate every chance
acquaintance into a national representative, and condemn a
whole race because they dislike an individual."

"There he goes; he's off," said Dr. Carmichael to me
behind his hand. Then to Dr. Johnson, "That's very good,
sir; that's an epigram."

"No, it's the truth," said the perpetrator of the alleged
epigram, "and an epigram is the falsest thing outside
the columns of a newspaper," with a severe look at the
Special.

"Phew," exclaimed the latter, "that's the unkindest
cut of all; that's one for my knob—eh, Miss Tracey?"

"Really, Mr. Forth, you are so *vulgar*—I don't understand *slang*," minced the elder of the two young ladies
in pink. "But what about the surprise you promised
us?"

"Ah, yes, b'the way; we're forgetting. Time's up;
this wa-ay, ladies and ge'men," he said, with the affectation
of the air of a showman. And led by the volatile Special
the company made their way into an adjoining room.
Here a number of chairs were arranged in a semi-circle
near one end of the apartment, and we all seated ourselves.
Everything was evidently understood by the others, but I
was completely in the dark as to what it all meant. There
was a babel of talk and merriment going on all round.

The Special was sitting directly behind me, and was in the midst of a "good story." "Of course," he was saying, "I knew what the meeting was, and I knew newspaper men weren't wanted there, and the colonel was the first to notice me. 'What name?' says he, in his jerky way. 'Forth,' says I. 'You are aware of the nacher of this gathering,' says he; 'may I ask if you also are a landed proprietor?' 'Oh, certainly,' says I. 'Forth of Fourth Estate, begad.' The others laughed, and the colonel blushed pretty loudly—you know his way of colouring up at everything—and sat down."

Some of those around the Special laughed, and one of the Misses Tracey said "Yes?" in a perplexed way, as if there were more to come, and she had failed to see the point.

"Well?" said the Special.

"What was the joke?" asked the lady, in bewilderment.

"Forth—Fourth Estate, don't you see?" explained the Special, sheepishly.

"O-h—yes," said Miss Tracey, vaguely, leaving the Special boring his glass into his eye, in silent chagrin at having his story spoilt.

Presently a curtain that had been stretched across the room in front of us was drawn aside. Some one carefully got up in the character of a typical Irishman, with a sprig of shamrock in his button-hole, and a blackthorn under his arm, entered by a side door, and then I knew that it was a charade that was about to be performed.

"Miss Gower," said a voice in a harsh whisper, and looking round, I saw Mrs. Hetherwick standing at the entrance to the room. "You are wanted if you please, miss."

I was surprised at her tone and the expression of her face. She looked almost pleased—which was a bad omen.

"Mrs. Shaw would like to see you in her room if you are not otherwise engaged," she went on, with a disagreeable suggestion of irony in her manner, and I followed her to Mrs. Shaw's room.   She entered after me, and sat down in the corner farthest away from the light.

Mrs. Shaw was sitting with her elbow on the table and her head resting on her hand.   There was a letter and envelope lying beside her, where they appeared to have been tossed.   She pushed a small pile of coins towards me and said: "There is your salary, Miss Gower.   I have paid you in full for two months in lieu of a month's notice—to which you are entitled, I believe," she added grudgingly.

A sleek tortoise-shell cat, which had been sleeping on the hearth-rug, got up, stretched herself, walked away, and sprang into Mrs. Hetherwick's bony lap, where it lay, filling the room with its purr in the dead pause.   Mrs. Hetherwick sat with her eyes frozen open and glittering in the shadow like the cat's, and fixed in a steady glare on my face.   She sniffed contemptuously as Mrs. Shaw spoke, which, being translated, meant she scouted the idea of my being entitled to anything.

"I do not understand you, Mrs. Shaw," I said, in bewilderment.

"I said that that is the amount of your salary, with a month's pay in addition in lieu of a month's notice.   You will please consider your engagement with me at an end," repeated Mrs. Shaw, speaking with painful distinctness.

"May I ask why you have taken this step, Mrs. Shaw?" I ventured, scarcely believing my ears, and wondering what could have happened.   "Have I not given satisfaction?"

"As far as your instruction to Annie and May are concerned, I've no particular fault to find.   It's not on account of inefficiency."

Another sniff from the corner. Translation of same: "Granting her too much even at that!"

"I should like to know, then, what is the ground of complaint.   I am not aware of having offended in any way."

A sniff that was almost a gasp from the corner this time. Mrs. Shaw, whose face was shaded by her hand, looked steadily at me before speaking.

"I must confess you surprise me, Miss. Gower. You are not aware of *anything* that would urge me to take this step?"

"Ha, indeed!" came a hoarse whisper from the corner.

I scarcely know what indistinct suspicion flashed upon my mind and made me hesitate as I said—

"No, Mrs. Shaw, I do not. I flattered myself I had afforded no room for dissatisfaction. From the fact of my being dismissed in this way I should suppose that something serious——"

"It *is* something serious, Miss Gower. You associate, I believe, with a person named Bonville—Ada de Bonville, as she calls herself?"

Do what I would I could not prevent my colour rising as she spoke. I thought of Edgar Stadding's absence, and something like a suspicion of what had taken place—and which I must, I think, have imbibed from the air—began to take shape in my mind, and held me speechless and overwhelmed with confusion. A sniff, eloquent with suggestion, from the corner, increased my embarrassment. Mrs. Shaw, whom it had plainly cost an effort to restrain herself, rose from her chair and approached me with her hand clenched and half raised as if she were about to strike me. I knew how passionate she could be when excited, and I drew back. Mrs. Hetherwick started up so quickly that the suddenly-awakened cat flew out at the door with an angry spit.

"Emily, Emily," she cried, sinking all appearance of the servant in the confidante, "don't forget yourself! Don't demean yourself by touching the nasty, scheming thing."

Mrs. Shaw stopped within a pace of me, and pushed her face close up to mine. Her lips were white and twitching with passion.

"Oh," she said, "if I had only known your character at the beginning as I know it now, my lady—the unprincipled *hussy* that you are!"

"Mrs. Shaw!" I cried, in amazement, "what does this mean? To whom are you speaking?"

"You *brazen*-faced thing! Do you attempt to carry it off with me that way?"—("Don't demean yourself, Emily; don't demean yourself," interjected Mrs. Hetherwick).—"This is what you and that painted Jezebel from the theatre have hatched out between you! You may well blush to steal into an honest woman's house and—and—and—— You rile pair, to trap such as he is into a marriage with such as *you* and your set are. You planned it from the first—you know you did——"

"Didn't-I-see-them-together-in-the-garden-and-wasn't-she-the-go-between-for-that-creature-at-my-sister's?" clattered on the Hetherwick, breathlessly, and so rapidly that her sentences ran together into one long word. "I-knew-from-the-beginning-what-it-would-be-but-what-was-the-use-of-my-saying-anything! Don't dem——"

"You *hold* your tongue," with a passionate stamp.—("Oh, indeed!" from the amazed Hetherwick.) "Now, madam, I'll bandy no more words with you, for fear I should forget myself. There's your money—take it and go! Pack up your traps and leave this house to-morrow morning, bag and baggage, and never darken my doors again. D'ye hear?" And Mrs. Shaw stamped on the floor again, the natural vulgarity of her character displaying itself in every word and gesture.

It is one of my failings to be for ever unequal to an emergency. I was unequal to this one. When I should have spoken hotly in my own defence, the only words that came to my lips were, "Very well, Mrs. Shaw;" and though I felt the spirit of resistance strong within me, words refused to come, and I turned and walked from the room.

As I passed along the passage I met the company trooping out of the room where I had left them ; and though I was too agitated and nervous to consciously heed what they said or did, yet in a dull mechanical way I saw every flirt of fan or hand, and noted every word that passed. The Special was among the foremost, and was explaining to some one beside him, " *Pat* and *riot—Patriot*. Don't you see ?"

" Oh, how *clever* you are ! How *ever* did you come to think of it ?" said a voice, a female one, in accents of tender admiration, as they turned into another passage, and passed beyond ear-shot.

When I entered my room Catherine's letter was lying on the table. That explained everything, though there was little that required explanation.

I had not possessed a very extensive wardrobe when I arrived at The Peak, and had added little to it afterwards, so my preparations for departure were soon made. I arose early in the morning, and not wishing to risk a meeting with either Mrs. Shaw or the Hetherwick, I made an undignified exit before any one was out of bed, and came down here to the Truss o' Straw, bringing all my worldly possessions with me in a portmanteau and a brown-paper parcel.

<hr>

VI.

Fernridge, March 29. There is a tinge of dazzling lustre on the hills, and the dawn is abroad in all the freshness of an autumn morning. I have risen early to make up my lee way with my diary, and there is not a soul stirring in the house. Through my open window comes the breath that has been wandering all night over the breasts of the mountains and fields, and between sweet-scented hedges. I can just catch the sheen of the daisies on the upland. Beyond is the white line of breakers on the beach, their thunder hushed to a loud rustle.

This is the first entry I have made headed " Fernridge," though it must be something like six or seven weeks since I came here. I am beginning to think I am not the most unfortunate girl that ever lived after all. I am rather ashamed of having written it, in fact ; but whatever I have written I have written, and shall let it stay.

Looking back at the time I spent at The Peak—if it were not for the dates I should not be able to say whether it were weeks or months : time has flown so quickly and pleasantly since then—and leaving out of consideration, of course, the circumstances under which I left, there is nothing beyond the groundless spite of Mrs. Hetherwick that I can recall as particularly unpleasant in itself ; but life there was ground down to such a monotonous, routine kind of existence, that when I left, it was with a feeling akin to escaping from a prison. Life at The Peak and life at Fernridge are two very different things ; and Mrs. Shaw and Miss Winterson are two very different people. I feel grateful to Dr. Carmichael for having been the means of bringing me here.

And as I mean this to be a complete register of all that happens to me—I have the same confidence as A.S.P. in *A Day's Ride* that I am anticipating a future biography —I had better make a note of how that came about.

It was my second day at the Truss o' Straw, and I was becoming unpleasantly conscious that Mrs. Beazely, the landlady, was keeping a close watch upon me, with a view, I suppose, of forwarding a few more items to The Peak, for, from what Mrs. Hetherwick had said, it was plain enough Mrs. B. had already acted the part of spy upon Catherine. She was continually meeting me at the most unexpected times and places, always with an elaborate appearance of accident, always with apologies for her intrusion. Fortunately for me she had a dry, irrepressible cough. That cough was in the atmosphere all day long. I heard smothered explosions in the passage, under the window, outside my door ; boards creaked with her stealthy approach, and visions of a dirty drab petticoat were for ever meeting my eyes at odd corners. I grew sick to death of the creature's razor face—she has the features of Mrs. Hetherwick, with the addition of a pair of blank, expressionless, gray eyes, and a pointed nose with an everlasting and vivid blush on it, suggestive of a liberal indulgence in her own wares.

I had been so suddenly thrown upon my own resources that I had not the slightest idea as to what it would be best to do, beyond a vague intention of looking somewhere for another situation; but one thing I had made up my mind upon, and that was to leave the Truss o' Straw and its spying mistress at once.

I had done what little packing up there was to do, and was on the point of paying my bill preparatory to setting out for I scarcely knew where, in search of I scarcely knew what, when Mrs. Beazely put her head round the door in her stealthy fashion and said a gentleman wished to see me.

" Excuse me, my good woman," said a familiar voice in the passage, and the landlady drew back, and Dr. Carmichael came into the room.

" My dear Miss Gower," he said, coming forward with extended hand, " how *do* you do ? "

" Thank you, doctor," I said, smiling—for I was really glad to see him—" I am very well."

" H'm," he said, sitting down and wiping his forehead. Then, in his direct way, and with a quizzical look in his eyes, " So you've done it now, it seems ? "

I was not sure how much he knew, and answered cautiously

" Yes, unfortunately I have been unlucky enough to offend Mrs. Shaw."

" It's that old cat Hetherwick I'll take my oath it is," said the doctor. " I know the old beldame of old. There's no mischief going but what she has a finger in the pie."

" You may say the whole hand in this case, doctor," I said.

" Yes, I'm convinced of it." He paused and looked at the floor in silence for a moment or two. "And now, what do you suppose you're going to do? You've not been foolish enough to wear your heart on your sleeve for that red-nosed hussy I found outside your door to peck at— you've not let her worm anything out of you?"

"Nothing," I said, laughing at his odd way of putting it. "I've done my best to keep her at a distance—which I find a pretty hard thing to do."

"The old catamaran—she's left the print of her nose on the lock of the door as it is. But about what we are to do with you. You know, my dear, I've been in the world long enough to understand your position," he said, leaning forward in his chair, and speaking in a confidential tone. "You're young and you've got a pretty face of your own -- and, by gad, before you're half my age you'll wish you had to run the Bank of England sooner than have *that* responsibility. Now, what are you thinking of doing with yourself?"

" I'm afraid, doctor, I'm not fitted for much else than the kind of place I've just left."

"Not fitted," he said to himself, shaking his head. "The modern girl, the modern girl, the Lord deliver us from the modern girl. Well," he went on after a pause, "I know an old lady, one with no Hetherwick about her to set you by the ears, either. She's more or less of an invalid, and needs some one in the shape of a companion some one to read to her, and so on the poor old lady's eyes are not what they used to be; she has a preference for Dr. Watts' hymns and the Psalms in metre on Sundays, and is a nice old-fashioned body I think you will take to immensely."

" No children ?" I asked : and I scarcely know whether I was pleased or disappointed a little of each, I think, and for different reasons--when he said--

"No children *nor* followers," which latter he threw in as an afterthought. "She has a sister, a confirmed invalid, who lives with her, that's all. Come, shall I say it's a bargain? She commissioned me to find a suitable young person who could always be near her, who was of good principles and dressed plainly. She stipulated for nothing else except that a cripple would be preferred."

"A cripple?"

"A cripple. You will understand that after you've known her a week. She has a number of quaint old bodies she calls her pensioners, who live on her bounty. And if you were only far gone in consumption, or had a wooden leg, you'd make her life happy, for she'd feel then that she was helping some one who needed it."

"You said something about a sister —" I began.

I am sure Dr. Carmichael would have been quite justified in showing some impatience at the half-hearted way in which I met this kind offer, but he said, just as good-temperedly as ever—

"My dear girl, you needn't concern yourself about the sister. Miss Maria Ann, I am sorry to say, is paralytic; she mostly keeps her own room, has her own attendant, and will in no way interfere with you. Now," he said, "you are not an ordinary chit of a girl. If you were I should not take the interest in you that I do. The people are good people, and you should get on well with them. As a woman of common sense, you know you have yourself to provide for and your own way to make in the world, and you'll find the world a very rough world, where the weakest go to the wall. As for marriage——" He shrugged his shoulders, hopeless of saying what he thought on *that* point, and stopped and looked at me for my answer.

"Doctor," I said, "you have been very kind, and I should be very ungrateful if I didn't accept — —"

"Then it's a bargain," he said in a tone that ended the matter, and putting up his hand to stop anything in the way of thanks, "and you can pack up your traps for Island Bay as soon as you like? I'll write your letter of introduction," and he sat down at the table at once. The letter was a very short one, but by the time it was finished the doctor had changed his mood. He got up from his chair, took a turn or two thoughtfully up and down the room, and then coming back again said perplexedly—

"Esther, what is all this pudder at The Peak? Mrs. Shaw tells me that Edgar has made a fool of himself with an actress, and that you are mixed up in it. But what between temper and tears—and they are the first tears I have ever seen on Mrs. Shaw's face—and the screechings of the Hetherwick, I haven't an idea what it's all about; but I am afraid she's very much cut up over it. Do you know what it is?

What was I to say? After the kindness he had shown me I couldn't treat his question as I should have liked to do, and avoided it. In any case I should not have cared to tell him what had really happened, and now I was of course bound to strict secrecy by Kate's letter. Though there was a smack of eccentricity in everything that he said and did, I had every confidence in the doctor's prudence; and had the time for it not gone by, his advice would have been the first I should have sought; but it was too late for anything of the kind now.

I gave the only answer that presented itself, and I know it was suspiciously like a white lie.

"I never liked Edgar Stadding from the beginning," I said, "and never even spoke to him if I could help it, and I think much less of him now. As for having anything to do with his last escapade, I had not the slightest idea what he was going to do. And if I had, it would have been the last thing in the world I should have thought of to advise any one to trust their happiness in *his* hands," I added, with a touch of bitterness I could not keep back.

"H'm," said the doctor, thoughtfully, prodding the carpet with his stick. "You speak pretty strongly; but I thought as much—I thought as much. You have no idea who the girl—but of course you haven't. Some scheming chit off the boards, I suppose, who wanted to catch a husband," he went on, looking at me in an absent-minded way, as if I was a long distance off, and apparently not noticing the hot flush his last words had called to my face. "I'm sorry for Mrs. Shaw. She has no one in the world but the two bits of girls and Edgar—and all her hopes were built on him. She thought there was a career before him, and expected a great deal from him—a great deal too much in my opinion, from what I know of him. And now all that's over, for God knows where this will end with such a man as he. Yes, I'm very sorry for Mrs. Shaw. I don't think you understood her, or her you. You didn't agree; you were like acid and alkali."

"Very like acid on the one side," I admitted, tartly. "*I* am sorry for——"

"For the girl," he said, as I stopped confusedly; "and so am I. Her future—Heaven knows what her future will be with such a man! I know him well." He stopped and shook his head despondently, and looked at his watch. "Well, well, I must go. You won't forget to put yourself in evidence at Island Bay as soon as you can?"

My own fears on Catherine's behalf were revived by what the doctor had said, and I longed to question him further, but before I could find words—which, in my position was not an easy thing to do—he had shaken hands and gone.

I arrived at Fernridge next day, and took a decided liking to the place and its mistress at once. It has an odd, old-fashioned air for so young a country. You would almost think it had been brought bodily from some out-of-the-way nook in the Old Country and set up here, like a tabernacle in the wilderness. I suppose this is owing to the fact of its being built on the lines of an old water-colour picture that hangs up in the best room, with the inscription, "Our Old Home," under it. Miss Winterson has a very sentimental regard for this picture, and had her present residence built to resemble it, so as to remind her of the old place where she passed her girlhood. "I did

the house myself, my dear," she said, when she saw me
looking at it, " and Miss Maria Ann " (she always speaks
of her sister by her full name) "did the scenery. Here
was mother's room, where she died I am afraid to think
how many years ago; this was mine, and this Miss Maria
Ann's by the chimney here. What a long, long time ago
it does seem, to be sure ! Do you think the house and the
picture alike ?" I certainly did. I had noticed it at once,
and pleased the old lady intensely by telling her so.

The house is a great deal larger than is necessary for
two old ladies and their one or two servants, and is full of
jutting gables that thrust themselves out on the paths, and
so obtrude themselves on you and prevent your seeing the
whole line of frontage at once, that in walking around the
house, and seeing it a bit at a time, you would think it
much larger than it really is. Nearly every room has
French casements ; and creeping plants quite cover the
front and sides of the house—and that so closely that
abrupt openings are cut in the foliage around each door
and window. At the back is the fruit garden ; at the
sides and in front, except for a delicate oblong box-hedged
little patch of flowers opposite each window, are about two
acres of smooth, green, velvety turf, without a single shrub
or anything to break the beautiful close-cut surface ; and
over this lawn the gardener, a very ancient retainer,
ambles for two or three hours every day behind a clattering lawn-mower, with a loudly-checked handkerchief
fluttering round his head to protect him from the heat,
and his shoulders stooped so low down, and his elbows
stuck so far out behind, that he looks like some giant
grasshopper. On three sides the grounds are bordered by
high lines of thick-leaved evergreen trees, which almost
completely shut out the view. In front there is a low
holly hedge, with a gate painted green to correspond ; and
looking over this hedge—as you can do from any of the
front windows—you see a stretch of daisy-spangled plain,
which dies away at the distance of about half a mile into

a broad border of yellow beach, on which the waves foam
and beat all day long, sometimes in a hoarse muffled roar,
sometimes with a scarcely audible rustle. As I look out
at them now they stretch in a long line of milky white
between the two craggy grass-crowned bluffs that stand at
either end of the beach. Running in a kind of zig-zag,
midway across the plain is a narrow road, bordered with
furze, which seems almost to blaze in the sunlight, with its
garish yellow bloom. The road is so seldom used that,
except for a strip along the crown, the grass has covered
its sides very nearly throughout its whole length. Altogether it is a delightful place to be in, and I don't think I
was ever more completely satisfied in my life. I could live
and die here with perfect satisfaction.

I have already said that the Misses Winterson and Mrs.
Shaw are very different people, and so they are. One
would scarcely suppose they belonged to the same race.
The two Misses Winterson are natives of England, and
why they should ever have left it, and come out here, is a
mystery, for they have not an atom of the material which
either colonists or emigrants are made of. They seem to
have come out quite alone and unprotected too,—indeed,
from what one can gather from their conversation, one
would scarcely suppose there had ever been a male in their
family at all. Only once have I heard an accidental
reference to a certain legendary brother. Miss Dorothy
Ann (it is only now and then I see Miss Maria Ann)
always speaks of their life in England in a wistful,
regretful sort of way; she was plainly sorry to leave it,
but never yet has she expressed a wish to go back again.

There are only two servants, John, the gardener—
he apparently has no surname, or else has given it up
as obsolete and unnecessary—and a girl named Martha
MacDougal who attends upon Miss Maria Ann. I do
not see much of her, and what I have seen I do not like.
As is often the case with people who attend on the sick,
her temper which I should not suppose had ever been very

good, has been spoiled beyond redemption, and is made
even worse by the constant criticism she is subjected to on
the part of John. whose " wut " is more remarkable for its
breadth than its point.

VII.

ONE would scarcely credit what a call there is upon the
Miss Wintersons' charity. They have comparatively quite
a number of old men and women on their list. But
many though they are, there are no impostors among
them, for long experience has made Miss Dorothy Ann as
sharp as the sharpest beadle in Bumbledom in deciding
on the claims of would-be pensioners. They include two
widows of soldiers who were killed in the Maori war, who
do not receive sufficient recognition from a grateful country
to enable them to live independent of charity, and other
families whose breadwinners have in some way been taken
from them. If she did not care for the poor old bodies,
Miss Dorothy Ann says, just as Dr. Johnson might have
said, they would have to go to the Benevolent Institution,
which is quite true, and that she says she could not bear
to think of.

April 3.— I have already made several friends among
the people here, and gained an admirer yesterday in the
person of the most remarkable boy it has ever been my
fortune to meet. He has the quaint name of Pure-in-
Heart Love-God Bundle, and is the strangest mixture of
childishness and precocious intelligence one can imagine.
It is hard to say which quality is the most marked. It is,
I suppose, the outcome of the lonely, isolated kind of life
he has been compelled to lead, for he is a helpless cripple,
and has been so from his birth. He comes out strong in
conversation, his brain having developed beyond his years,

while his body has shrivelled under his disease. He is the most lovable little fellow I have ever known.

I made his acquaintance through visiting his mother in company with Miss Dorothy Ann yesterday evening. The widow Bundle's house stands in the corner of a piece of ground a quarter of an acre in extent, and is remarkable as being the oldest building in the place. It is built of the trunks of fern-trees, which have numberless little green sprouts growing out from the chinks and crannies on the outer side of the walls. It has a tottering, old-fashioned chimney, built in the slap-dash style of the early days, and so full of wrinkles and cracks that it gives every promise of descending upon the roof before long in an avalanche of bricks and mortar.

Mrs. Bundle, with her daughter, was in the midst of her meal of meals—tea—when we entered. As far as neatness and cleanliness go, both the old lady and her belongings were beyond reproach, but she seemed to consider it necessary to say in an apologetic way, as people in her position *will* persist in doing, as she dusted a couple of chairs with her apron, that she had been up to her eyes in work just before we came, and was all in a muddle. The room was so dimly lighted, that, though it was still early in the evening, it was only when Mrs. Bundle threw a remark into the dimness at one end of the room that I became aware there was any one else present besides herself and her daughter.

"Pure-in-Heart," she said, in that tone of make-believe gaiety in which mothers speak to sick children, "here's two ladies come to see you. You remember Miss Winterson, don't you? His memory for some things is a'most gone, ma'am; he seems to have forgotten a many things sin' he's bin away," she said in an explanatory aside to Miss Winterson, who had made her way to the child's side and was speaking kindly to him.

"Oh, but he remembers me; don't you, Pure-in-Heart?" said Miss Dorothy Ann. "And here's another friend I've brought you. This is Miss Gower—you can think of 'Gower,' can't you?"

"Yes, ma'am," said the little fellow in the faintest of voices, smiling up at me as I stooped down and kissed his mite of a face. Sarah Bundle threw some sticks on the fire, and the flames shot up and lighted the room. A moment before I had had a vision of a little shrunken body and weazened face turned up to mine in the dusk, but now I found I was holding the hand of the smallest child of his age I had ever met. He must have been thirteen or fourteen years old; and though his limbs were those of a mere child, his face had the worn, troubled look of one who had almost lived out his allotted span. He was hopelessly deformed, and so weak that he made no attempt to move from his chair, where he was half sitting, half lying. He had that look of patient intelligence beyond his age so often seen in invalid children, and which always strikes upon one with such a sense of pity and foreboding. There was an ancient-looking, well-thumbed volume lying on the table near him, and seeing me glance at it, he drew it towards him.

"Would you like to see what I've got here, miss?" he said, clasping it in his arms and smiling, and holding the leaves ajar to inflame my curiosity with a glance inside, and then clapping them together again tantalizingly.

"You must know that I don't let every one look into this," he went on in a tone to make me duly value my privilege. "This is like the wishing-cap of What's-his-name to me, and you'd never guess what it is never. Though I can't move, I can travel most anywhere I like. I may have nobody but mother and Sarah in the room, and yet have half the world around me. I can sit here in this weary old chair of mine, and yet be in a palace. I can lie quite still and close my eyes and sail away, away, over the ocean, and be in India or China or what not—and all through the magic of this musty old book. Now, guess," commanded the oracle.

It was quite exciting. Mrs. Bundle and Sarah looked on and smiled, and grew so interested that they let their tea grow cold. Miss Dorothy Ann was a victim to the pangs of a morbid curiosity, though I suspect the inscrutable conundrum was not as new to her as she made out.

"A history?" I ventured.

"No," with a self-satisfied shake of the head, and a hug at the book.

"A book of travel?"

"No," with another shake and another hug. "You're quite cold yet. Not near it."

"Arabian Nights?" suggested Miss Dorothy Ann, recklessly.

"No—O," said little Pure-in-Heart, with such open derision that Miss Dorothy Ann quite collapsed. "Not within—oh, you can't guess at all," he said, in despair of making anything of Miss Dorothy Ann.

"A picture book?" I said.

"No-o," said Pure-in-Heart, hesitatingly, and pursing up his lips as he seemed to find himself becoming closely pressed; "but you're pretty hot—you're getting nearer now."

"A portrait album?"

"Well, you're right and you're wrong," announced Pure-in-Heart, oracularly, now almost at bay; "for there are pictures of faces in it too. But I expect you're as near as you'll get. That's as near as most people get with me," he said, with the consciousness of being a master in his art. "You'd never guess, if you tried for ever so long. There," he concluded, with a grand burst of revelation, "it's a Book of Stamps!" and he dazzled us by throwing it open before us.

"Here's China, India, Canada, France, Italy — oh, most every place in the world, he rattled on, excitedly, "and here's one—I gave it a whole page to itself—one from Cyprus. You've never seen anything like this before, have you, Miss Gower?" he asked, with an abrupt pause, and speaking a voice divided between pride in his ex-

traordinary treasure, and apprehension lest somebody else
might be able to boast a rival display.

"Never," I said. "Why, you're a regular little Post-
master-General.'

"Yes, ain't I?" he acquiesced. "I don't suppose," with
sudden thoughtfulness, "there's anybody anywhere got a
collection like me. You see, it takes up a good deal of
one's time to do it thoroughly. But people are very good
to me, and bring me all the stamps they can lay hands on,
because they know there's nothing I care for as I do them.
And then you know I can take out my book and sit down
quiet of a night in front of the fire without bothering
any one—and I know I've been a great burden," he added,
opening his eyes widely, "it's a wonder, indeed, I was ever
reared——"

"Bless his kind little heart," interjected Mrs. Bundle, in
a stage whisper, to Miss Dorothy Ann, "the patient little
sufferer that he was!"

"And how carefully you must have taken them off,
Pure-in-Heart," I said, for I could not see a defaced stamp
in the whole collection.

"Oh, that," said Pure-in-Heart, "is because I never *peel*
them off the envelope, you know. I used to at first; but
the best way is to cut the stamp out and leave the piece of
the envelope sticking on underneath it. See, all mine are
done that way, and I never tear one of them. And then
I tell myself stories about 'em for hours in my way of it,"
he went on in a low voice, looking in a dreamy way into
the fire, "stories I make out of my own head, you know.
I open the book and come across India, p'raps, a stamp
that's had Hindoo hands on it, and been carried through
towns and towns of India, and regularly got the flavour of
India worked into it, as it were, and come miles and miles
over the ocean among thousands and thousands of people.
And I think how first of all some bird, very likely an
eagle, dropped a seed, and it grew and grew, and the rain
fell on it and watered it, and the sun shone on it and

scorched it, but still it grew up into a bush. Great slimy monsters in some river may have swam under it and snapped at it with their great teeth, or poor little dead children that their mothers had thrown into the Ganges may have come floating by it, or some tired pilgrim going to some shrine may have lain down in its shade and slept while the birds sang to him out of it. And clothes were made out of it and worn, and sold to some paper-mill; and yet it was meant some day to fall into the hands of a sick little cripple miles and miles away, and very likely not born then, in the shape of a square little bit of paper with the Queen's head on it."

Mrs. Bundle and Sarah listened and looked on in silence, quite oblivious of there being such an institution as tea in existence. Miss Dorothy Ann sat with her eyes bent upon the little fellow with a look of sympathetic interest. I had to suppress my very strong doubts as to the correctness of his natural history, but it was impossible not to feel interested.

"Yes, it's a wonderful thing is a stamp," said Pure-in-Heart, stroking the open page of the book reflectively, "and they've all of 'em got a history of their own if one only knew how to read it. Some come on black-edged envelopes I remember one coming lo-o-ng ago when poor father was killed—and then I can fancy people crying over them; some tell of fortunes made and lost, and good luck and bad luck, and all sorts of secrets, and all that goes on in the hurly-burly world that I can never join in." There was a tone of regret in his voice as he paused for a moment, but he went on again as cheerfully as ever. "But what I can't help thinking of, Miss Gower, is, how impossible it is to keep a particular stamp from coming into my hands if it's meant to come. *I* don't think there's any such thing as chance, y'know—and who knows but what the same Power that sets all these going just to please a poor weak little invalid, mayn't somehow make some use of what *he* does in *his* turn."

"The very idea," said Mrs. Bundle, in her tearful tremor

again; "but that's how he always rattles on.   He would be quite contented, he says, to be just as he is all his life if only in some way he could be made of use—as if his innocent bits of stamps could be of use——"

"Well, mother," mildly protested little Pure-in-Heart, "who knows but what they may be. *I* don't know how, *nobody* knows how; but still it *may* be, mightn't it, Miss Gower?"

"Quite right, Pure-in-Heart," put in Miss Dorothy Ann. "You know what Milton says in that book I gave you, where the leaf is turned down. 'They also serve'—you know the rest."

"'They also serve who—who only'——"

"'Who only stand'—yes, go on," said Miss Dorothy Ann, nodding encouragingly.

"'And wait'—'They also serve who only stand and wait.' I've got it," cried the delighted Pure-in-Heart, with a triumphant flourish. "I'll go and look it up," and with a dexterity that spoke more plainly than anything else could have done of the length of time he had been condemned to that means of moving himself from place to place, he wheeled his chair into the next room.

"What a remarkable boy, Mrs. Bundle," I said, turning to his mother.

"Yes," said Mrs. Bundle, looking at me with very red eyes—she had been crying quietly into her handkerchief—"everybody says so that sees him. And it's that that makes me fear for him more than anything else. I wish, d'y'know, in my own heart, he was more like other children. It's his book knowledge and his style of talkin', and his odd old-fashioned ways and what not, that makes me think oftentimes I shall lose him—he's more like a man of fifty in his talk than a boy of fourteen. And I've noticed it all the more sin' he's come back from havin' bin away from home; his memory's a' most clean gone, and he talks more out of his own head than he used. He'd repeat by the whole hour together, if you only encouraged him, what he'd picked up from books—rhymes and bits of things—but now he scarce remembers one of the people he used to know, though he won't own it, and makes believe he does. And he does go on so about heaven, and goodness only knows what all, when there's no one about—oh dear."

"Never mind, Mrs. Bundle; you mustn't think of it in that way. His talents are given to him to make up for his affliction," said Miss Dorothy Ann.

"Besides," put in Sarah, with an effort at consolation, "he hasn't got so *much* talent."

"I hope it may be nothing more, ma'am, I'm sure," said Mrs. Bundle, doubtfully; "but it makes a body's heart ache to hear him run on so. It's like as if it were true as my poor Bundle used to say—his lips have been touched with a cinder from the altar. It was my poor Bundle as give him his name, you remember, ma'am," she added, with an apologetic quaver in her voice, and a sidelong look at me— 'Pure-in-Heart Love-God Bundle.'"

"And a very good name, too," said Miss Dorothy Ann, promptly.

"It's good enough, as far as that goes, and with a good meaning to it, I'm sure; but one doesn't know," and Mrs. Bundle paused doubtfully, as if she thought there was a good deal in a name. "It's the old-fashioned ones as I like myself. Here's S'r' Ann, now; I named her myself—Sairey being my mother's name, and my mother's mother's, Ann having been my own"—she referred to the fact of her once having a name as something vague that had ended with her youth. "Just plain Sairey, and she's as good a girl as ever was, and I haven't a fault to find against her——"

"I'm quite sure of that," interjected Miss Dorothy Ann.

"Thank you, ma'am. She's goin' away to service is Sairey this coming week—a Mrs. Llewellyn's, over at Monkses's Bridge."

"Llewellyn!" I thought at once, and the recollection of

the Mephistopheles I had seen at the theatre that night at once recurred to my mind.

There was a scir-r-r of wheels, and little Pure-in-Heart shot back into the room again on his chair.

"I hope you'll have a very comfortable place, Sarah," said Miss Dorothy Ann. "It will be strange at the beginning, as it's the first time you've been away from home, but you'll soon get over that."

Sarah said, " Yes, ma'am," and little Pure-in-Heart, who seemed to have changed his mood, chimed in with, " And don't you forget to send me all the stamps you get, mind."

" I won't forget, Pure-in-Heart. I'll send you every one I get—every one," said Sarah.

" Honour bright, mind," said Pure-in-Heart, holding up his finger.

"Yes, on a bright," said Sarah, thinking she had the mystical formula all right.

"You've got something in your hand, child. What is it?" broke in Mrs. Bundle.

" It's— it's only something for Miss Gower, if she'll have it," said the little fellow, blushing a rosy red and steering his chair round beside mine. " It's a real genuine ostrich feather that came all the way from Africa, and is worth ever so much. It's no good to me, Miss Gower, being a boy, and if you'd like it——"

I knew it would please him, and I said I should like it of all things.

"And you'll wear it?" he said, peering up at me, and drawing the feather slowly between his fingers.

" You shall put it in yourself, Pure-in-Heart," I said, getting my hat, "and I'll wear it just to remember you by."

Pure-in-Heart's face was radiant as I put my hat in his hands; and he looked it over and flourished the feather about it with an air that would have done credit to a milliner, as he hesitated where to put the ornament to best advantage.

"I think it would show best there," he said, sticking it in at the side with a look of mature criticism, holding the hat at arm's length, and turning his head from side to side to observe the effect.

"Quite right," said Miss Winterson. "You've made an excellent choice, Pure-in-Heart. We'll make a milliner of you."

"Now, let me see how it looks when you put it on," he said, and I put the hat on and walked across the room, Pure-in-Heart watching with his head still held critically on one side.

"Splendid," he exclaimed, delightedly, clapping his hands, while his pinched little face took quite a new expression in his enjoyment, and turning to his sister, he said

"You'll know Miss Gower anywhere now, won't you, Sarah; you could tell her ever so far off, couldn't you?"

"Yes," said Sarah, looking at the feather with an expression that had a dash of good-natured envy in it, as we made preparations to set off homewards. "I shall always think of Miss Gower when I see the feather."

I can't help thinking what a strange, lovable little fellow he is, and of the odd idea he consoles himself with in his helplessness—that his innocent fad of collecting stamps may some day be of use. My woman's vanity suggests—if he had said *the feather*, now, for that does improve the hat wonderfully, and I shall always wear it in memory of him. There is a flavour of *kismet*, too, in his idea of Providence concealing a purpose behind everything we do. I wonder if it's true. If it is, what possible purpose could be hidden behind the commonplace experiences I have just recorded. for instance?

As I lift my eyes from my writing and look through the window everything has changed. A storm is threatening. The trees are being tossed in the first breath of the blast. There is a dark foreboding of what is coming in the atmosphere—as if the powers of the air were drawing a deep breath before they clash and grapple in careering chariots of storm-cloud, the blinding sabre-flash of lightning, and the burst and rattle of thunder. The distant waves have a hoarser roar as they break in angry discoloured masses on the beach. Black banks of cloud hang threateningly over them. And fluttering up above the horizon like the wing of a bird, a chance streak of sunlight falling for a moment in a white gleam over it, I can see the sail of a yacht. The brass-edged clouds on the horizon glow dully like the mouth of a furnace, and presently, from their midst, the first keen streak of lightning writhes out. The thunder bursts forth with a deafening bellow, and roars and echoes among the cloud caverns and hollows overhead; and as if the spell were broken, the rain rushes down and fills up all the space between earth and heaven with a furious swirl of gray vapour.

The atmosphere clears again somewhat, and I look out with a painful interest to the spot where the yacht was when the storm burst upon it. She is past the island in the bay now, and pretty close in shore, and rises and falls on the brown breaking water; the tall masts sway about in what seems to me a dangerously unsteady way; the sails are now bellying out in the breeze, now taken aback and fluttering against the mast. Suddenly part of the canvas is drawn in, and part comes down with a run, and the vessel rides steadily at anchor under bare poles. Now —though rather indistinctly, for the rain is coming on again in a heavy, monotonous downpour—I can see a boat put out from the yacht and make for the shore. Now it is hidden from sight again. The gray rain-mist closes in steadily, steadily, and blots out everything—the yacht, the sea, the sky, the scenery—everything is swallowed up and lost in thick wrappings of gray vapour.

*　　　*　　　*　　　*　　　*　　　*

There is a bustling and confusion and a running to and fro in the passages below, and an opening and shutting of

doors. Somebody has arrived. I wonder can it be any
one from the yacht ?   I feel the most——

VIII.

April 4, 1885.—I was called away yesterday by Miss
Dorothy Ann before I could finish the entry in my diary,
and on descending to the lower regions I found her talking
in the drawing-room with a tall, dark, weather-beaten
young man, who had made his appearance at the house as
suddenly as if he had been dropped from the clouds. There
was something unmistakably suggestive of the sea about
him. I had noticed a long, clinging overcoat hanging in
the passage as I came down. It was dripping with wet,
and gave off a powerful odour of salt water ; and I at once
jumped to the conclusion that the young gentleman had
come ashore from the yacht, and that it must have been
his arrival that had caused all the bustle in the house.

Miss Dorothy Ann, who makes it a point to treat me in
all matters as an equal, introduced me to him, and hoped
we should be good friends—which I am sure we shall. I
have always had a strong partiality for those who go down
to the sea in ships ; and the chief charm in the personality
of Mr. Matthew Redmayne—to me at any rate—is a
certain breezy, sailor-like unconventionality he has with
him. He is not a handsome man. Long exposure to wind
and sea has given him a complexion bordering on copper
colour, and there is not an inch in his six feet of stature
that owes its attractiveness to cosmetic or tailor. He was
dressed to-day in a baggy suit of blue serge, which, I
suppose, it is only in the fitness of things that a sailor
should wear. He has a square, rugged, masculine breadth
of forehead, which has a habit of wrinkling when the brain
behind it begins to think : the whole face, indeed, is a
good, manly, confidence-inspiring one, and—yes, and one

I felt an instant liking for. There is an atmosphere of
security and protection about him, which will be a glorious
inheritance some day for the fortunate woman he selects
for his wife. And yet, at the same time, I am sure there
would be a trace of another feeling too—a spice of fear of
at any time bringing down his displeasure upon herself. At
least, that is how I should feel, I know. (It's my own
diary, why shouldn't I say it?)

I may as well put down all I know about him at once,
for I suppose it is the first and last time his name will
appear in my diary. He comes of a family whose fortunes
were broken at Home, and who have more than retrieved
them in the colonies. They are the proprietors of large
plantations in Fiji, and have a number of vessels constantly
engaged in going and coming between here and there, the
trade being done mostly in sandal-wood, and cocoa-nuts, or
copra, or vegetable oil, or something of that kind. At any
rate, it has enabled them to make an immense amount of
money; and they have the reputation of possessing a
marked capacity for keeping it when made . . . Though
I have nothing definite to go upon, I have a shrewd idea
that Mr. Redmayne and his people do not get on very well
together. He has travelled a good deal, and mostly in company with a certain Dick Drugget, whose name, together
with that of the *Meg Merrilies*, his yacht, is constantly
cropping up in his conversation. . . . The said Dick
Drugget came up to the house yesterday with Redmayne,
but forcibly made his exit when he heard that there was
not only a young woman in the house, but that she would
presently be invited down to meet him. The thought of
the encounter filled him with alarm, and he made off to
the yacht, where he has remained in seclusion ever since.
The one desire of my life now, woman-like, is to make the
acquaintance of this Dick Drugget.

Redmayne had just returned from the front door, whence
he had been throwing fruitless requests to come back, after
the retreating figure of the shy Drugget, and was still in a

simmer of laughter at his friend's behaviour when I went into the room.

I had not closed the door on entering, and a partially-suppressed cough told me that some one was concealed behind it. Miss Dorothy Ann laughed, and the familiar figure of Dr. Carmichael came forth from his temporary eclipse.

"I've just come along with Redmayne, Miss Gower, to give you a look up before leaving. I'm going Home to-day."

"I am very sorry," I said. "Must you go?"

"I must indeed, or I shouldn't be here. I have been left a pot of money by a certain old relative of mine, who had made his nest so high up among the branches of the family tree that I was not even aware of his existence; and if it had not been for his lawyers publishing an 'if-this-should-meet-the-eye' advertisement I might never have heard of my good luck."

"But you will come back again," said Miss Dorothy Ann, with the true spirit of a colonist. "You'll never be able to stay away from the colonies after all these years."

"Say rather from old friends, Miss Winterson," replied the doctor, with the same air as I am sure Dr. Johnson must have used towards Mrs. Thrale. "That's just what they said when I came out here in the first place—Lord, Lord, how many years ago was it? No, I don't think I shall, but I shall be away for three or four years anyway."

"And then?" I said.

"And then I shall be back among you again. I wonder how I shall find you all—I wonder what changes will have taken place."

"None I hope, unless for the better," said Miss Dorothy Ann. "To what good fortune do we owe you and Matthew coming together?"

"Well, I intended paying you this visit and intercepting

the coach here as well, and as Mat was bound hitherward
as well we came together. We've cut it rather fine, too,
what with backing, and filling, and reefing, and tacking,
and one thing and another; and thanks to Redmayne, I
run a very fair chance of missing my boat."

"Redmayne is not responsible for the ten thousand
changes in sea and air and heaven," said Mr. Redmayne,
laughing. "All things considered, the *Meg* made a splendid
run."

"I watched you beating up, from my window," I said,
"until the storm came on and hid you."

"Did you?" exclaimed Mr. Redmayne, with gratified
pride. "Didn't she behave beautifully?"

"I don't suppose my opinion on the point is worth
much "—(" Quite so," put in the doctor, parenthetically)—
"but I certainly think she did. It must be delightful to
be the owner of a yacht."

"It is, I assure you——" began Mr. Redmayne, enthu-
siastically.

"It's almost as good to be the next best thing," said the
doctor.

"And that is?" queried Miss Dorothy Ann.

"That's a conundrum," answered the doctor, with a
look of unfathomable slyness at Mr. Redmayne, who
laughed self-consciously, as if what the doctor had said
derived its point from something that had previously passed
between them.

"Pray consider the *Meg Merrilies* as your own property
whenever she is in the harbour," he said, looking from
me to Miss Dorothy Ann, "with my services into the
bargain."

"Not old enough to be trusted, Mat," said the doctor;
"besides the bad effect of sea air at this time of the
year."

"Why, Dr. Carmichael," exclaimed Miss Dorothy Ann,
laughing, "where's your consistency? It was yourself told
me that the one thing I wanted was a breath of sea air."

"Then why not take that breath on the decks of the *Meg?*" asked Redmayne, eagerly.

"*I* advise you to take sea air," said the doctor, interrupting his friend again without the least compunction. "Take a camp-stool and sit on the beach an hour before breakfast, and you'll get all the sea air you need, I warrant."

"Nonsense," said Mr. Redmayne. "There's nothing like a genuine sea breeze for health, Miss Winterson, and that breeze can only be properly got on shipboard. Look at me for instance."

"Look at him, indeed," said the doctor, who seemed to take a malicious pleasure in opposing his friend's proposal, "a living testimony to what the sea can do towards turning man into mummy. A complexion between a brick and a Red Indian, and a hand like a nutmeg-grater from hauling tarry ropes. Ha, ha, ha!"

"Miss Gower would enjoy it, too," went on Redmayne, ignoring the doctor, who really was very irritating.

"Miss Gower would do nothing of the kind—she'd be sea-sick."

"No, I'm sure I shouldn't," I said. "I was never sea-sick in my life."

"For the best of reasons—you've never been to sea."

"Oh, but I have; I've made the voyage from Australia, besides having been over the Straits two or three times."

"Miss Winterson, you must settle the question. Say you'll go. The doctor only opposes for the sake of opposing," and the yachtsman appealed to Miss Dorothy Ann.

"If it rests with me, I don't know what to say," said Miss Winterson, doubtfully. "I never feel safe in these bits of boats—not meaning your yacht, Matthew, of course."

The doctor looked into my face with the most irritating enjoyment of my disappointment—for I really was disappointed: a trip on a yacht at this time of the year is so enjoyable.

"Quite right, Miss Winterson. The idea of two ladies trusting themselves, with only a flimsy plank or two between them and the deep blue sea, to the mercy of a slip of a yachtsman not more than—by the way, how old *are* you, Redmayne?" said the doctor, with unblushing impudence.

"That's certainly not a fair question," said Miss Dorothy Ann. "Don't answer him, Matthew."

Mr. Redmayne has an excellent temper.

"I don't intend to," he said. "If he doesn't know, no one should, for our acquaintance was of the earliest, I believe. But about this trip——"

"God bless my soul, how many 'Noes' does the boy think go to a refusal? Miss Winterson has said 'No' once—be content with that."

"Take no notice of him, Matthew. I have every confidence in you. I'll leave it to Esther—what do you say, my dear?"

Miss Dorothy Ann looked at me, Mr. Redmayne looked at me (a little anxiously, I thought), the doctor looked at me, his head on one side, and with an unspeakably knowing look on his face, as if he knew what the answer would be before it came.

"I should—that is, I think the sea air would really do you good, Miss Winterson, and I think I should be in favour of going," I said, demurely.

The doctor, who seemed to have a faculty for making himself disagreeable, said "Hem!" passed his handkerchief over his lips, and looked up at the ceiling; and then, without moving his head, let his eyes travel from Mr. Redmayne over to me and back again, and then said "Hem!" again. I am quite sure the reason I gave was the only one in my mind, and yet I never felt so thoroughly hypocritical in my life as when the doctor said "Hem!" in that uncomfortably pointed way.

"That's settled then," said Miss Dorothy Ann, somewhat doubtfully. "You have Miss Gower to thank, if you think there's much to be thankful for in cumbering your boat with two useless women, Matthew."

I suppose Mr. Redmayne is not good at making conventional speeches, for he seemed unaccountably confused as he said—

"I am very much obliged to you, Miss Gower. It—it—will do Miss Winterson a great deal of good, I'm sure." And as he looked at me I noticed for the first time what a deep hazel his eyes were.

"Disinterested young people! Of course it will—eh, Miss Winterson?" said the doctor.

"I hope so, I'm sure. It's very good of Matthew to make the offer."

"Yes, indeed. You are overflowing with goodness to-night, Redmayne," the doctor began, ironically.

"Listen, doctor," said Miss Dorothy Ann, suddenly, holding up her hand, and we heard the rattle of coach wheels in the distance. "That is your coach coming at last."

The doctor took his farewell of us with a studious avoidance of anything approaching sentiment, which was quite in keeping with his character, and then, as we all stood at the door, he paused with his overcoat thrown over his arm and his portmanteau grasped in his hand, and looked at me.

"Well," he said, "the next best thing to being the owner of a yacht? Have you solved it?"

"I am not good at that kind of thing, doctor; I am afraid I must give it up."

The driver of the coach drew up his team with a flourish opposite the gate. The doctor took a step in that direction, paused, and then said, "Ask Redmayne; he knows," and with a last round of handshaking was off. At the furthest turning, a hat—presumably the doctor's, and apparently elevated on the end of a stick—was flourished for a moment above the hedge that hid both the coach and the owner of the hat from view, and the volatile doctor was gone.

IX.

APRIL 8, 1885.—I had really formed a strong liking
for Dr. Carmichael—all the stronger, I think, because of
certain harmless oddities he had, and which were only skin
deep. Yet, to be honest with myself, I cannot say I feel
that sense of loss which should follow the departure of a
friend. A month or so ago I should, I am sure—and why
not now? It is strange, for I have always had the reputation of forming strong attachments for the few friends I
have been lucky enough to gain. Change of scene, I
suppose.

Mr. Redmayne is still at Island Bay, passing his nights
on the yacht, and the greater part of every day here, the
yacht meanwhile floating in the Bay, as idle as a painted
ship upon a pointed ocean. He *says* she is undergoing
some kind of repairs, which Dick Drugget is attending to.
But I don't believe it. For Miss Dorothy Ann and I have
paid several visits to the boat, and beyond the repainting
of the name there is not a sign of anything having been
done to her. I should be pleased if it were only an excuse—
and I believe it is! It is strange that he should select
such a dead-and-alive place as Island Bay to make a long
stay in. I should have thought it the very last place to
furnish any attraction for a young man who has travelled
so widely and seen so much of the world as he has.

He has announced his intention of remaining until we
are ready to make our promised trip, which is being put off
day after day by Miss Dorothy Ann, till I am afraid the
winter weather will set in and prevent it altogether.
Which will be simply maddening.

April 9.—I have lately made several visits to the
Bundles' on Miss Dorothy Ann's behalf. The road is a
long and lonely one, and I have been each time under the
escort of Mr. Redmayne. He is an old friend of the family,
and very popular at the cottage, little Pure-in-Heart hail-

ing him in what was for him quite a boisterous fashion, and demanding stamps. The little fellow was pleased beyond expression to see the feather he had given me still in my hat, and regaled Mr. Redmayne with a full and particular account of how it had come into my possession, and the conditions under which I had bound myself to wear it . . . Sarah I did not see. She left home to go to her situation yesterday.

It began to rain soon after we left the cottage to-day. We plodded along in silence for a time, holding ourselves all askant to avoid the full rush of the shower, and then Mr. Redmayne said—

"Will you not take my arm, Miss Gower? We should get along much better."

It was the first time he had ever offered the friendly conventionality, and he did it in a very hesitating and embarrassed manner. I thanked him, and accepted the offer, just as absurdly embarrassed on my part. Then we plodded on again, but we certainly did not get along any faster. Mr. Redmayne grew stoically indifferent to the rain—seemed rather to enjoy it, in fact—and in spite of what he had said a moment before, was very careful to walk slowly, so as not to hurry me. I am under the impression we must have walked *very* slowly, and tired as I was, wet as I was, uncomfortable as I was, I was sorry— actually sorry—when Fernridge came in sight. I have always flattered myself on the possession of a certain amount of common sense, yet I found myself childishly wishing we had only just set out and had all the walk before us again . . . When we were about five minutes' walk from home, Mr. Redmayne woke up from a long silence, and with a sudden attempt at conversation asked—

"Do you enjoy life here, Miss Gower?"

"Yes, very much indeed," I said, and added (with malice aforethought), "but I wonder that you, who have passed so much time in travelling and have seen so many places, and must be so fond of change, are not tired of such a dull place."

He is not good at paying compliments, and the one he now paid—or rather perpetrated—came with sledge-hammer force, and laboured under the additional disadvantage of being uttered in a rainstorm.

"It—it all depends on the company one falls into, you know," he said, "and in that respect I have never found any place so much to my liking as this one."

Before I could collect myself sufficiently to answer he added—"Are you good at guessing, Miss Gower?"

I said naively that that all depended on what it was I had to guess about.

"Oh, it is a very simple thing. It is whether you cannot guess why I should have stayed here so long—though it has seemed anything but long to me?"

It was naturally difficult to tell for certain in the rain, but I thought he sighed as he spoke.

"Why," I answered, with the artless surprise we feminine hypocrites always assume in such circumstances, "you have already said it was because you liked the company you had fallen into."

He is as bad at the exchange of anything in the form of badinage as he is in other small graces, and he replied disconcertedly, but with an earnestness that was almost ludicrous—

"There—there is something beyond that, Miss Gower."

"Then I can only suppose it is because you are good enough to wait till Miss Winterson can avail herself of your kindness in placing your yacht at her disposal."

I think he gave it up then as hopeless. Ah! if he had only known how difficult it was to keep up appearances!

"Is that the *only* reason you can think of, Es Miss Gower?"

"That is the only reason I can think of, Mr. Redmayne," I said, all in a flutter at his merely pronouncing the first syllable of my name.

We had arrived at Fernridge by now, and he opened the gate with a ridiculously depressed air.

"I hope the wetting will not injure you, Miss Gower," he said, standing aside as if he had no intention of entering.

"Thank you, I do not think there is any fear; but are you not coming in?"

"No," he said, with the spirit of depression still heavy upon him; "I will go on board the boat at once and change my things. Good-bye."

I am not usually of a malicious disposition, and yet I certainly did derive a positive feeling of pleasure from the knowledge that I had made him miserable.

April 16, 1885.—The auspicious season upon which Miss Dorothy Ann has set her heart will not dawn for a day or two yet, and the yacht—still undergoing the same vague process of repair—has been lying in the bay all the time. Redmayne has been as constant in his visits to the house as if it were a shrine, and he were a pilgrim. He seems to realize that what he was about to say during that walk in the rain a week ago was premature—(Answer, my heart! Was it?)—and he evidently has formed a pretty correct idea of the state of mind I am in on the subject, and carefully refrains from saying or doing anything likely to embarrass me. He has, in fact, acted just as he should act. But at the same time he makes the most eager endeavours to take the fullest advantage of anything I say or do that has the least appearance of an inclination to break through the barrier of reserve I have set up; and I have a humiliating suspicion that in spite of all my wise and maidenly resolves, that inclination does make itself evident occasionally.

I am afraid that of late I have allowed my attention to be so much taken up with other things that I have been growing forgetful of old friends. Poor little Pure-in-Heart, whose health is causing his mother a good deal of anxiety, has been worse than usual for the last day or two. I saw him to-day for the first time since I heard of his illness, and short as the time has been, he is much changed. He is, nevertheless, just as interested as ever in collecting stamps, and gleefully showed me a fresh batch he had received from his sister.

"Good-bye, Miss Gower," he said to-day as I was leaving the cottage. "It don't look like as if what I'm doing is going to be of very much use in the world now, does it?"

"Never mind, Pure-in-Heart," I said, with vague encouragement, "we none of us know what our actions may lead to; and even if it does nothing else, your collection has interested you and given you something to occupy your mind."

"And then there's the feather, isn't there?" he said. "That's ornament if it isn't use."

"To be sure," I said, "there's the feather, and that's both ornament and use too. It's made a shabby hat as good as ever it was."

"Ah, it isn't the hat that people like about you, Miss Gower; it's what's under it."

Mr. Redmayne was there. I did not think he had noticed the very obvious flattery, but on the way home he took occasion to remark what a shrewd little fellow Pure-in-Heart was, and that there was more truth in what he said at times than one might suppose.

There was a volume of meaning in his words as he spoke, but much more in the look that accompanied them. I promptly assumed the mask of simplicity and innocence which is the refuge of my sex, and said I thought so too.

I wonder how many times I have read Kate's letter lately. It seems to read very differently to me now from what it did at first. Foolish Kate! I should like to hear from her, and yet, since that last letter, never a word. Or perhaps she has addressed her letters to The Peak, and they have been detained there. I have not thought of that before. It is possible. But then she was always the most inconstant of correspondents; I don't suppose she has ever written a line.

April 19.—If there were a feminine form of "Hurrah,"
I would use it now! At last Miss Dorothy Ann has made
up her mind! She will embark upon the long-talked-of
trip to-morrow! True, it is only for two days, but that is
better than nothing. The momentous decision was given
in my presence a few minutes ago, just as the little French
clock on the mantlepiece indicated twenty-five minutes
past three. She had been consulting a certain infallible
almanac which is sent to her every year, as she has done
regularly for the last week or so, when she took off her
spectacles and folded them up with the deliberation of one
who had formed a great resolve, and said in a steady,
collected tone of voice—

"Esther, my dear, if it is not too sudden for you, I
think we may say we will go to-morrow. I shall tell Mr.
Redmayne when I see him this evening."

And now it is a case of "hurre, hurre, hop, hop, hop,"
to get ready, though for my own part it has been hanging
over my head so long that I have very few preparations to
make.

* * * * * *

April 20.—I don't think I have ever passed a more enjoyable day than I have to-day. Mr. Redmayne and Dick
Drugget had made arrangements and seen to the stowing of
most of our things over-night, so that this morning there
was little else to do but make ourselves comfortable on
board till the time of sailing. Beyond remarking as to the
comfort of what "Mr. Gilbert" said in the storm about
being as near Heaven on the sea as on the land, Miss
Dorothy Ann showed no sign of disquietude after arriving
on the yacht. She says she has every confidence in
Matthew—and the almanac, which she ranks only second
to the Prophets in point of reliability, and which is quite
positive in its assurance of a week's fine weather.

Ever since his behaviour the first time he came to the
house I had intended to make friends with Dick Drugget;
but, though he doesn't seem to mind Miss Dorothy Ann.

he withdraws himself into an impenetrable shell if I happen
to so much as address a word to him. Yet one cannot help
being pleased at a certain quiet way he has of trying to
make things as agreeable as possible for those about him;
—which I have noticed he sometimes accomplishes only at
considerable inconvenience to himself.

It is delightful to sit up there on the deck, with the
sunlight spangling the water around one and the fresh
sea-breeze blowing over one, and watch the great hills go
floating by. As I have said already, it must be one of the
greatest pleasures in life to be the owner of a yacht—which
reminds me of what the doctor said about the "next best
thing." I wonder what he could mean, or if he meant anything at all, and why should I have to go to Redmayne for
the answer? And that again reminds me that the latter
did not give us a great deal of his company to-day, sinking
the host in the sailor, and leaving us to read or talk, or do
pretty much what we liked, while he attended to the navi-
gation of the vessel. I was greatly disappointed in him,
for the weather has been so calm that neither Miss Dorothy
Ann nor I have experienced the least inconvenience in
remaining on deck, so that there could have been no
necessity for such a careful display of seamanship. I have,
of course, endeavoured all day to keep up an air of enjoying the partial neglect rather than otherwise. Two or
three times he came towards me as if intending to say
something, and then turned away again without speaking.
If he only knew how irritating that is, he wouldn't do it.
On the few occasions when he did enter into conversation
he seemed oddly preoccupied and absent in his manner.
In fact, all his abilities to entertain and amuse seem to
have been left on shore. Strange—very. I wonder why?
He is generally anything but dull company. I hope there
will be a change to-morrow.

X.

April 21, 1885.—There *has* been a change! I can hardly write the words, my hand trembles so. He has declared that he loves me, and has loved me from the first day he saw me!

I had made up a prudent little bundle of maxims of my own, as to what it would be "proper" to do and say ; and was quite clear that the difference in position between a mere governess and a wealthy merchant's son was so great that any attachment between us could have no other than an unhappy ending—for me at least. And I have acted as any other woman, placed as I was, would have acted—that precise little code of mine has been as completely blown to the winds as if it had never existed—and that at the first word he uttered.

The day passed much the same as yesterday, Matthew—he is my Matthew now!—behaving in much the same unsatisfactory way as before. A brisk little breeze sprang up and sent us gaily over the water ; but towards evening it died away, the sails hung loosely from the yard-arms, and we came to a dead standstill—if that is the right word. The sun had become entangled among the gilded masses of cloud that hung about the horizon, and his beams pierced through the gaps in their golden lining in long fan-shaped rays, passed over our heads, and fell afar off upon the green breasts of the hills beyond us. It was lovely—lovely as Eden, but like Eve in Eden I was discontented—all through Matthew, I suppose.

"It is a beautiful evening, is it not, Miss Gower?" broke in upon me so suddenly that I started in surprise. I looked around, and saw Matthew standing beside me. Miss Dorothy Ann, who had been on deck a little while before, had gone below.

"It is," I said. "If I could only paint, and could put that blazing yellow mass of cloud on canvas!"

"What would you call it if you did?" he asked, biting

nervously at his moustache, his eyes fixed on the changing tints of the sunset, and his thoughts fixed, I was sure, on something much nearer home.

"The Gates of Heaven," I said. "I don't think even they could be more beautiful than that."

"I am glad you have found something to enjoy, Miss Gower, for I have an uncomfortable idea that, not to put too fine a point upon it, I have proved a failure as an entertainer."

In my own mind I quite agreed with him, and *therefore* answered—

"Not at all, Mr. Redmayne; for my part, I've enjoyed myself beyond anything I expected. Besides, you have the ship to attend to," I added—rather inconsequently.

"Yes," he said, nervously; and then, "Do you remember that time we walked home from the Bundles' in the rain, Miss Gower?"

"From Bundles' in the rain?" I repeated, with a weak, hypocritical attempt at having almost forgotten it. "Oh, yes. It was *very* wet that day, wasn't it?" I said, sweetly.

He did not answer, and the inevitable awkward pause followed. I had what is called an intuition that something momentous was threatening, and in a headlong attempt to defer that momentous something I broke in upon the silence with the first words that came to mind. They were what the doctor had said to me when leaving for Home, and I began at once—

"I have a question to ask you, Mr. Redmayne."

"Indeed. What is it? I shall be happy to answer if I am able."

"It's Doctor Carmichael's conundrum: 'What's the next best thing to being the owner of a yacht?' He referred me to you for an answer."

"The answer," he said, dropping his unnatural air of seriousness and his eyes dancing with laughter as they met mine—"is, that the next best thing to being the owner of a yacht is to be"—(a pause)—"his wife!"

Instead of deferring that momentous something I had brought it measurably nearer! Awkward does not describe what I felt, and I took refuge in the most imbecile reply that ever occurred to mortal mind—even when that mind is a woman's. I said "Oh," and waited, mute and helpless, for what would happen next. It was not long in coming.

"Miss Gower," he said, earnestly, "if I have seemed absent-minded and neglectful of you and Miss Winterson, there is no one who should know the reason better than you."

"Better than I!" hypocritical (*i. e.* feminine) to the last.

"We did not understand one another on the occasion I spoke of just now. I am afraid it was ill-timed on my part. I should not have spoken so soon. But I wish to say now what I tried to say then. And that is—you cannot misunderstand me, Miss Gower. Believe me, my heart is in this. I have been afraid to speak; but—but—but I must, Miss Gower"—and he took both my hands in his, and his eyes met mine entreatingly—" you *must* have seen, you *must* know that I love you. Say you love me a little in return."

I did not answer—I could not.

"Esther—Esther," he pleaded. "Answer me. You you are not offended? Say at least that you are not indifferent to me."

*   *   *   *   *   *

——No. I cannot write it even here. Has any one ever loved and been loved before, and had that love declared to them, and felt as I feel now? I can hardly believe it. It seems as if the delicious experience were mine, and began and ended with me.

Our voyage is at an end to-day. Those are the lights of Island Bay. Only two days since I saw them, but the world has turned round twice between then and now. Then I was a girl; now I feel that I am a woman, and have entered upon a woman's inheritance.

April 22.—I should be happy. And yet—always an "if" or a "but" or a "yet"—while I am every way justified in believing my happiness founded upon a solid Reality, I allow myself to be tormented by nothing more than a Dream. It was about Catherine. There are dreams and dreams. This is the evening of the nineteenth century, and nobody confesses to thinking there's anything in dreams, and I don't myself—of course. But at the same time there are dreams that will not down at the first smug shibboleth one brings to bear upon them in the almighty name of latter-day enlightenment; and this one of mine has a distressing reality about it, and has haunted me persistently all day. I saw a vision of Catherine's head and shoulders—nothing more. It appeared at the end of the room and came on towards me—came towards me till it was within an inch or two of my face, and I closed my eyes and shrank back from it as I would from the face of a corpse. When I looked again it was once more at the end of the room, and came forward in the same dead, resistless way as soon as my eyes rested on it, till I closed them and shrank away as before. And so on, time after time, till I was quite worn out with the effort and terrified with the thought that soon I should not even have the strength to shrink back or close my eyes, and the horrible thing would touch my face and cling to me. The dead face was white, and the eyes looked out from a cascade of loose black hair that streamed down around it. But what frightened me most was the thought which the vision somehow conveyed to my mind. It did not speak, or move its dead blue lips, but as it came nearer and nearer the thought was repeated and repeated and repeated with inconceivable rapidity, till my brain throbbed again, as though soundless voices were pouring it into my ear in a hideous voluble chorus; and the thought was—"I'm mad—I'm *mad*—I'm MAD!"

I wish I had not dreamed that dream. I cannot away with it.

PART II.

A WIFE'S CONFESSION (*continued*).

XI.

May 4, 1886.—In this out-of-the-world corner a year soon slips away, and if it were not for the calendar I could scarcely believe that it was more than twelve months since I first arrived here. Twelve months, and not a word nor a line from Catherine all that time. Though it was a year ago the memory of that dream clings to me still, and fills me with a foreboding and distrust of the future.

Matthew, who has been here and away again several times during the interval, is about to be taken in as junior partner in the firm of Redmayne, Redmayne, and Co., and is in a state of comic horror as he sees the toils of business threatening him more and more closely every day. Yesterday, after a stay in port of barely two hours, he was peremptorily summoned away by a letter from his father, and is now engaged, miles up the coast, at a place with an unpronounceable Maori name, in the carrying out of some commission for the firm—a commission, he darkly hinted, foisted upon him simply for the purpose of "trying" him, and seeing what business capacity he has. Whatever it may be, it is likely to delay him for a considerable time.

I received a letter from him to-day. It is delightful to read, but what *am* I to say in answer? He has resumed in the most determined way, through the hard, matter-of-fact medium of the post, what he began by word of mouth just before he was called away.

"Dearest Ettie," says the letter, "now that I am

becoming mixed up in the infernal (excuse the term : it expresses my meaning exactly)—the infernal mechanism of the Firm, I am not sure of my movements for a single day. Even now, you see, my father has employed me on this commission for him, which is likely to keep me employed for days yet—worse luck. He and I have not been on the best terms lately, because he objects as a man of business, and as a man of business who wants his son to be a man of business after him, to my free and easy way of roaming about the world. He holds that I must have what he calls a settled purpose in life ; and with the idea of supplying that settled purpose he holds over my head this menace of making me a partner in the firm. Of course he's right in what he says, and Dick Drugget, and the *Meg,* and all the rest of it must go. But, my darling, there is one thing that must *not* go. Between now and the time of my entering business life I have strong reasons for wishing that our marriage may take place. I spoke to you about this before I was called away, but perhaps I may be able to think more clearly · if I may say so—and speak more clearly by letter. Once fairly entangled in the meshes of the firm, and Heaven alone knows what complications may arise. Anyhow, I don't mean to risk it. Do not, my dear Ettie, say that this is too sudden. Where is the use of our putting it off ? We can never know one another better than we do now ; and I am sure I can never love you better than I do now. You are your own mistress, and have only your own heart and the happiness of us both to consult. I do not wish to hurry you, my love ; but for the sake of yourself and me, try and come to a decision."

And now I am given over to the demon of Irresolution. This *is* altogether too sudden. I did not expect anything of the kind for ever so long. If he were only here I could show him how unreasonable he is ; but you must hear all a letter has to say. You can't interrupt it or argue with it. What is it best to say, now—what is it best to say ?

May 7.—Another bit from another letter. He is still a
prisoner, and cannot get away :—" My dear Etty, have you
quite used up your little bundle of arguments ? There are
three blisters on the letter. You cried when you wrote
it " (which I did). " I have kissed them three times three
each. All you have said, my darling, would be true
enough if the circumstances were different, and if it were
a different man from myself and a different dear little
woman from *yourself*. Are we to begin to doubt one
another already ? You surely do not distrust my love for
you. Esther, dear Esther, I stake all my happiness, my
prospects, my future—everything, on your love. I am not
speaking without a reason for it. Believe me, it is *not*
mere caprice. I can more than guess what course events
will take when once I become mixed up in business affairs ;
and before that time comes, and while I am my own master,
I must make sure of my happiness by making sure of You.
Dear Esther, can you not— will you not—trust me ? Why
should there be delay ? Are you not, my dearest, mistress
of your own actions (*for the present, that is* [1]), and am not
I my own master ?"

What can I say in answer to such a letter ? Of course I
trust him. What he says is all very well from his stand-
point ; but then he is a man, and looks at it from a man's
point of view. I look at it from a woman's point of view,
which is a very different thing. There is a suspicion of
mystery and secrecy about it, and mystery and secrecy I
detest. Besides, I do not wish to begin my married life
under such compromising circumstances. " Am I not my
own mistress ?" Yes, I am, indeed—too much my own
mistress. I wonder, does his reference to the consequences
of his becoming a member of his father's firm mean that
his people have other plans for him—plans which would be
destroyed by his marrying one who is only a governess ? If
I thought that—— Well, if I thought that, I should love
him still—love him well enough and weakly enough to let

[1] The very idea ! For the present, indeed !—E. G.

him spoil his prospects by marrying me. Humiliating to own it, even to myself, in my own diary, but still the truth. And now for the answer.

May 24.—Extract number three. He gets more and more positive each time ! " My dearest Etty, I am not going to budge one hair's-breadth. When I see you next—in a day, or two days, at farthest—I shall come with the License in my pocket. I have said it. So now, my darling, let us have no more doubts, no more hesitatings ; but be a good girl and surrender the point, and you shall have all your own way afterwards (perhaps). Do not, my love, disturb yourself trying to solve the large problem of secret marriages. I admit everything you say on the matter, and think all the better of you for it—for it could only come from a good and pure mind. I would not be so unreasonable as to ask you to do anything to which you were conscientiously opposed. But I do not wish our marriage to have, nor will it have, any secrecy whatever about it. Miss Winterson shall be admitted fully and freely into our confidence, since you wish it but on the morning of the day only."

What a headstrong, resolute, self-willed man it is ! What can I do? What is there to do but give way? I feel what feeble opposition I could offer swept away and scattered to the winds.

Kismet ! It is fate. I bow to it.

My last shred of argument is destroyed by the concession he has made at the end of the letter, for I asserted myself so far as to say I positively *would not* consent to the marriage without consulting Miss Winterson, who had proved herself so kind a friend to me. It would have been unworthy of myself, and ungrateful to her. I am a girl with a Conscience. I have my limits. And I am not going to have any romantic nonsense in the matter of my marriage that I am determined on. One elopement in a family is quite enough, *I* think.

XII.

May 26, 1886.—Matthew has been as good as his word, and has returned to-day—marriage licence and all! I had been expecting him and looked—ah, how eagerly!—from my window with the very first streak of dawn this morning, and I cannot describe the rush of feeling that took my heart by storm when I saw the sunlight falling on the white sails of the yacht in the harbour once more. Some one—I thought I could recognize him, though he was diminished to a mere pigmy by the distance—was moving about on the deck—moving about impatiently, I told myself, anxious for the time to arrive when he might come ashore to see Somebody else.

Matthew, of course, was well aware of the hours kept at Fernridge, and would be sure not to put in his appearance much before ten. Up till that hour my time was my own. In fine weather I usually spend it in wandering about on the cliffs, where I could enjoy the fresh sea-breeze. *This* morning was a fine morning, and accordingly, at my usual hour, I set out for the cliffs.

In passing over the smooth-shaven lawn in front of the house, I came in full view of the yacht, and before I was half way across I noticed the Pigmy on board all at once cease pacing up and down and go temporarily out of sight. Then a boat put out from the vessel's side and came scudding over the water to the shore; and a minute or two after I had reached my regular promenade I saw Matthew hurrying towards me. (How impulsive some people are in greeting any one after even a temporary absence. Matthew is one of these, and is very impulsive—very.) Then we walked, he and I—I with my arm in his—up and down the narrow beaten track above the cliffs, and he showed me the mysterious document, the License, which he had brought with him from Wellington, as he had said he would—though I had not believed he was half in earnest when he said it.

"Now, Etty," and he frightened me by opening out the License in a dangerously business-like way, "this will allow us to marry in just a fortnight's time from now, and seeing we've known each other for such a long time——"

"We've known each other for just a little more than twelve months," I objected, and till that moment I had not myself realized how short the time had really been.

" —— and we've both made up our minds——"

"Only twelve months, Matthew; think how short— " I began again.

"Miss Gower, we went over all that ground in our letters, and I got the best of the argument. You talk as lightly of twelve months as if you had come in for your inheritance of eternal life. Listen to your own words: 'Adjective, adjective Matthew, I consent' (you scratched that out and re-wrote it three times, fickle-minded Miss, before you made up your mind); 'but on condition that Miss Winterson *is not kept in ignorance*' (you have carefully underlined that). Now, I have consented that Miss Winterson should not be kept in ignorance; and if you breathe another word I shall think you no longer love me."

"Oh, Matthew."

"Another thing. See this." And he produced an unopened letter from his pocket and waved it before me. "I received that last evening, and I have taken a solemn oath that whatever it may contain it shall not be opened till I am the happiest man in New Zealand. The last message I got took me away from you for weeks. 'Once caught, twice shy.' If I don't open it, I can't know what's in it— logic that, isn't it?"

"But, Matthew—how foolish! You don't know what may depend upon it. Some one may be dying for all you know."

"Can't help it," he said, putting his hand—one hand; the other was occupied—in his pocket, and shaking his head resignedly. "Some one may be dying; some one may be dead. I expect it's something of the kind. They wouldn't write for nothing, I dare say. The fortunes of the house of Redmayne may be hanging on it, but there that letter remains until you allow me to break the seal. So now you know the responsibility that rests on your shoulders."

"Nonsense; it isn't fair. Read it at once, sir!"

"No, Miss Gower; never a line," he said, obstinately. He took it out again, and looking at it, and addressing himself to it, said reflectively—"Isn't it hard on a man? Here's a message that's come scores of miles to his hand; it may mean life or death or ruin or ten thousand things, but open it he must not—read it he must not—and all because of the obstinacy of a woman, and that woman his affianced wife."

"Matthew, I—I *have* promised, and that should be enough. If anything should happen you'll never forgive yourself ——"

"You'll never forgive *yourself*, you mean; it lies with you."

"Oh, but it doesn't lie with me. I won't take any such responsibility. It is sent to you, and you should read it at once."

"Esther, my dear girl," he said, with mock solemnity, "a time will come (soon, I hope) when you will know me better. I've made up my mind " (and he began to check off on his fingers in the most obstinately positive way the number of things on which he had made up his mind) "that you're the best and dearest girl in all the world to me. I don't intend to change it. We've both—*both*, mind—made up our minds to marry one another. *I*, at any rate, don't intend to change on *that* point. I've made up my mind that until you've fulfilled your promise— nothing more than your promise, remember—and I can claim you as my wife before the world. that letter remains unopened."

"Matthew," I said, determined to make him see my side of the question, "it is foolish ——"

“ Foolish to love you, darling ?”

“ To act like this. Who knows what that letter may contain ?”

I spoke almost angrily, but he answered with his immovable good humour—

“ You said that before, my dear ; I am surprised at you hesitating so long when it lies with you to set both our minds at rest. Seriously, Esther, you have promised to be my wife ; why not soon as well as late ? As for the letter —what if I open it ? Ten chances to one it will call me away again, and so open the way for ten thousand things to come between us. No, Esther. To-day, who knows, we may be standing at the very turning-point of both our lives—our future happiness or misery may depend on your decision. Why not decide ? I promise you I shall read the letter when we reach the church door, but not one instant sooner. Come, say Yes.”

He was pressing me hard, but I was not going to give in yet.

“ Matthew, how—how——”

“ Pig-headed, say.”

“ How headstrong you are.”

“ Only masculine resolution, my love, I assure you : nothing more than simple masculine resolution. May I take it for granted that your ladyship says yes ?”

Her ladyship was very slow in giving her decision. To have a personal appeal made to one by the man one loves is a very different thing from receiving the same appeal, even though it may be in the same words, through the cold medium of ink and paper. And, notwithstanding the preparation which our letters to one another had afforded, it came upon me with an embarrassing sense of suddenness. It is a strange thing to me to love as I do, and to inspire such love in return. Ever since mother died I have had no one in the world to love or to be loved by but Catherine, and her calling has kept us so much apart that my life has for the most part been a lonely and friendless one.

I leaned my head upon his shoulder and wept quietly. His sympathetic nature understood mine; his strong hand sought my weak one and pressed it, and five or six times we walked up and down the narrow beaten path in silence, my head still resting on his shoulder, and his arm thrown protectingly around me.

When we parted, he to return to the yacht, I to return to the house, he said—

"Then you promise ?"

"I promise."

A cloud passed from before the sun just then, and the yellow flood of light came rippling down the pathway to our feet.

"A good omen !" he said. "Your future shall be my future—and it shall be a happy one for both of us. Good-bye !"

And that future begins in a fortnight !

June 6.—I am becoming quite frightened at Matthew's obstinacy concerning the letter ; and to-day, to make matters worse, a telegram came. Every day since the arrival of the letter I have urged him to open it. But no ! He only waves it at me and laughs, and puts it in his pocket again. It has become quite discoloured and all worn at the edges from being constantly carried about. I am astonished that he can so control his curiosity. I wonder what it can contain ? It has become a veritable nightmare to me. I have dreamt about it for three nights in succession—a dream that always frightens me, and always wakes me up with tears on my face, but which, try as I will, I can never recall clearly to memory afterwards. It is foolish to allow such a trivial thing to influence one, but somehow it fills me with a vague foreboding and dread for the future. And the arrival of the telegram to-day has naturally made me more nervous than ever. It doesn't affect Matthew one iota. He looked at it and laughed when it was put into his hand to-day, and said—"*Your*

sting is drawn for three days yet, anyhow! Meanwhile
——" and without another word he clapped it and the
letter together into his pocket-book, and put them in his
pocket. He smiled in the most irritating, self-satisfied
way when he saw I was about to speak. "We'll take it
as read, my love," he said, waving his hand easily. "I
know what you are burning to say, but there's time enough
yet; we're both young, and we'll live to see the end of it,
never fear."

June 7.—Worse and worse. Another telegram came
to-day. He smiled grimly, but seemed not the least in the
world inclined to open it. "In it goes with the others!"
was all he said, and in it went beside the others accordingly.

"Matthew," I remonstrated, "you are a very, very
foolish fellow. You don't know what may be the consequence of what you're doing."

"Let 'em telegraph," he observed easily, "it's only a
matter of copra or cocoa-nuts, I expect, when all comes
to all; and copra and cocoa-nuts can wait, and I can't."

If another comes to-morrow I don't know what I shall
do. Copra and cocoa-nuts, indeed!

June 8.—*It has come!* This is terrible! I was terrified
when he showed it me. All I could say was—"Oh,
Matthew?"

"Oh, Esther!" he said mockingly, and spread out all four
—three telegrams and a letter—as if they were something
to be proud of.

"In it goes with the others!" he said again, grimly,
and in it went. "Copra and cocoa-nuts, my love, I'll
stake my existence it's only copra and cocoa-nuts. You
don't know the governor as well as I do. He's often taken
that way."

"Matthew, you—you must be *mad!*"

"Mad because I prefer you to copra and cocoa-nuts, my
love? I want to show you before our marriage how little
anything weighs with me against my regard for you, dearest.
I mightn't have the chance afterwards," he said, lightly.

I believe his own resolution is shaken, though he won't own it, and that he only persists from sheer obstinacy. Masculine resolution, only masculine resolution again, I suppose.

To-morrow is the day ! What will be the outcome of all this ? Rather what may *not* be the outcome of it for both of us ? I do trust it may not be the forerunner of some dreadful disaster. I shall not sleep an hour to-night. God grant this may end well, but—I am afraid, I am afraid.

June 9, morning. —One difficulty over. The day has begun well—but will it end well ? The first thing this morning I told Miss Winterson everything. She was amazed, and though she tried—the dear old soul !—to hide it out of consideration for me, who, I am sure, do not deserve it, I know she must have felt hurt, but whether at my conduct itself or my not taking her into my confidence earlier, I am at a loss to decide. But she is a dear, kind old lady, and has risen to the occasion with the best grace in the world. She left me only half an hour ago, after coming to me in my own room and treating me so kindly that I feel quite guilty and shamefaced when I remember how deceitfully I have behaved towards her.

What with the nervousness natural to my position, and the dread of what those telegrams may reveal, I am almost distracted. I have very little of the feeling of a bride. This will never, never do.

This is the last entry *Esther Gower* will ever make ! I do not know—he will not satisfy me on the point whether he has received another telegram or not. I do hope he hasn't. His last words as he left me were, " You shall know all at the church door."

Perhaps it is only copra after all.

Oh, wretched ! wretched ! wretched ! What a day this has been ! Oh, Matthew, this fatal obstinacy ! He has gone. What may not have happened before we meet again.

He kissed me and left me as we came out of the church. He read the letter and the last telegram only; he had received one—one urgent one—this morning, and would not open it until after we had been married.

[THE LETTER.]

"*Levuka, Fiji, May* 2.

" DEAR MATTHEW,

"Please return to us as soon as you can do so conveniently. I am uneasy about father's health. It is nothing serious as yet—he even persists in pursuing his business as usual—but there is no certainty as to what it may develop into, and the doctor either will not or cannot give us any satisfactory assurance. As to the transaction with the Messrs. Burnett about the copra, which he hinted to you last mail he would employ you on, I believe he has abandoned it. In any case you will be of more use here if anything should happen to father, especially now that our uncle is in England. There is no occasion for anxiety, but please do not delay your return unnecessarily.

"Your affectionate sister,

" ELLEN."

[THE TELEGRAM.]

"Urgent.　　　　　　　　　　　"*Levuka, June* 9.

"Have telegraphed again and again. Why do you not reply? Come at once; father is dying.—ELLEN."

Oh that that were all. A letter lay on the table when I returned—how we returned, whether we rode or walked, I scarcely know. It is from Kate. God help her and me!

It is unsigned, and barely readable. She has apparently been interrupted in writing it. Oh, my God, what can have happened? What can have happened?

"*Happy Valley Road, June* 7.

" DEAR ESTHER,

"Come to me at once. I have been deceived and deserted. He has treated me worse" (here the writing was illegible) "and has shut me up here as a *mad woman*. I do so need your help. *Take no one into your confidence, but come at once.* The house at the bottom of the hill, below the three pine trees. Bring some money to——"

Postscript.—You have now read, dear Matthew, all that I have entered in my diary. My confession would not be complete without the statement I am now about to make. Had it been possible for us to meet, and for me to have made by word of mouth the explanation I am now putting on record, there are some things in it I might have kept back. But when you have read this it will not matter how unreservedly I open my heart or how complete the confession I make. I have not altered a single word or line, and to much of it your own memory will bear witness. In what follows, however extraordinary it may seem, I only ask that you will believe it as implicitly as that portion of what you have just read, and which you know from personal experience to be true.—Esther.

XIII.

My mind had misgiven me from the moment I heard of the reckless match Catherine had made. While I had been at The Peak I had seen quite enough of Edgar Stadding to convince me he was a selfish and unprincipled man; but it had never once crossed my mind that he could be the heartless villain this letter showed him to be. . . . It may have been foolish, but I had attached so much weight to Catherine's request, in the letter she had written from Auckland just after her marriage, asking me to be faithful and not reveal her secret, that I had scarcely mentioned her name to either Matthew or Miss Dorothy Ann. They knew I had a sister travelling somewhere about the country, and that was all. Now that this misfortune had come upon her I was glad I had kept to my resolve so well, though it left me without a friend to whom I could turn for advice.

It was one of those emergencies that bring out all the weaknesses of my character. Catherine's letter was urgent —more than urgent—and I should have set out at once to her assistance; but the trial and suspense of the morning had left me wretchedly weak and ill. I was incapable of the effort. I did not even leave my room. Miss Dorothy Ann came to my door once, tried it, and called my name softly. I did not wish to be disturbed, and had not answered; and she—thinking, I suppose, that I was asleep —had gone away again.

I passed a sleepless night, thinking what I could do to help poor Catherine, and wondering what the end of it all would be. . . . When I arose in the morning my resolution was taken—indeed, there was but one thing to do: I would go to Catherine at once. Happy Valley Road, the place mentioned in the letter, was only a few miles from Island Bay, and I hoped to be able to get there and back before evening. . . . I knew the place well: a dismal stretch of roadway winding through a dark, precipitous gorge, with a few wretched tumble-down buildings scattered along its length —so few, and so few of them fit for human beings to live in, that I could have no difficulty in finding the one in which Catherine was shut up.

So much had happened on the previous day, and I was still so upset and confused, that I was simply incapable of grasping the situation intelligently and considering what it would be best for me to do. Beyond the vague intention of visiting the place and seeing Catherine, I had as yet formed no plans for her assistance. It did not even occur to me whether I should encounter any difficulty in gaining an interview with her when I had succeeded in finding out where she was imprisoned.

Martha brought me my breakfast into my own room. I knew I should have need of all my strength before the day was out, and, though I was but little inclined, I ate a hearty meal. . . . It was still early in the morning, but I knew Miss Dorothy Ann was up, for I had heard her moving

about in her room. I wished to see her before I set out,
but how I was to account to her for my absence for the
remainder of the day I did not know. It was impossible
to tell her the truth ; it was impossible to meet her with a
subterfuge. In the difficulty, I came to the worst possible
decision : I resolved not to see her at all if I could avoid it,
but to leave a note on my table telling her not to be
alarmed, and that I should return before evening. I wrote
the note—it was very short, and yet the words were very
hard to choose—and then stole quietly out of my room and
down the passage, hoping to pass Miss Dorothy Ann's
apartment without being discovered; but as I came opposite
the door it opened, and Miss Dorothy Ann stepped out.
She started when she first looked at my face, and said in
her kindly tone—

" You are up early, my dear. Are you not well you
look pale ?"

"Quite well, Miss Winterson, thank you," I said,
guiltily. " I I am going for a long walk : I think it will do
me good." (It was not so impossible to meet her with a
subterfuge after all.)

" That's right, Esther ; you are wise not to think too
much, nor too seriously, about what has happened. I trust
things are not so bad as they appear with Mr. Redmayne,
and that Matthew will soon be back among us again. Fiji
is not the North Pole, you know."

" I hope he will, I'm sure. But—but I can't help
thinking that, however innocently, it was still through me
he was prevented from visiting his father in his illness."

" Ah ! my dear," said Miss Dorothy Ann, smiling, and
taking both my hands in hers, " I have known Matthew
longer than you have ; and—as yet, perhaps—I understand
his disposition better than you do. He is a thoroughly
good fellow, or he would not have taken the notice he has
of an old woman like me ; but he is only human, like other
men ; and has a temper of his own, and a will of his own,
and I've seen him when he's had occasion to use both. The

first, perhaps, *you* may never see; but the second you
certainly will—as you have already, in the matter of the
telegrams—and when you have had a longer experience of
him as his wife—— There now, don't cry, my dear, or I'll
never forgive myself; I didn't mean to hurt your feelings.
You must try and not give way like this, my dear."

"It is not that, Miss Winterson; that is not all that is
troubling me; nor—nor was that all that happened yesterday——" I was ashamed of my tears, and felt it necessary
to say something in apology, and had gone thus far before
I checked myself.

"Not all, Esther! What else was there—what else do
you mean?"

"I received a letter—a letter with bad news from a
friend," I said, turning my head away, for my tears began
to come afresh.

"Poor child, poor child," she said, kindly. "And can I
not help you? Do not tell me, if you do not wish to; but
can I not share your trouble with you? I have suffered,
too, in my time, Esther. I can sympathize with you, dear,
believe me."

"You are very, very kind, Miss Winterson, and if I were
free to speak you would be the first——" and then, between
the tears in my eyes and the lump in my throat, I could go
no farther. She saw that the interview was becoming painful to me, and had the kindness not to prolong it.

"We all have our troubles, Esther; try and keep up a
good heart under yours, and be sure you have always a
friend in me, whatever happens," she said, and left me.

The thought crossed my mind, now that I had spoken to
Miss Dorothy Ann, whether it would be wiser to leave the
note where I had placed it, or destroy it. I took a pace
towards my room with the latter intention, hesitated,
decided it would perhaps be best to let it remain after all,
and turning, left the house.

The path to Happy Valley Road lay for a few miles along
the beach, and was so rough, and so strewn with great

boulders, that had it not been broad daylight, it would, to me, a woman, have been almost impassable. There was a lurid crimson blaze in the sky as I set out, a foreboding of storm in the atmosphere. The tussocks, which grew here and there in patches on the steep hill-sides, and down close to the beach, were so long, that they interlaced across the pathway; and they were so saturated and heavy with dew, that before I had gone far on my journey my boots and the bottom of my dress were as wet as if I had been out in a heavy shower of rain.

After a little more than an hour's hard walking, or rather scrambling, I left the beach, and turning to the right, dragged wearily through a waste of dry sand until I entered the Happy Valley Road. The sun had become hidden behind tangled masses of black, rain-charged, spongy clouds; the broad light of mid-day was dwindling to little more than a murky twilight, and the steep wall-like hills on either side of the road made it still darker. A moaning wind was rising. The storm, which had been threatening when I set out, was about to break; and I hurried on, hoping to reach my journey's end before it burst upon me in its full fury.

I had often been in the neighbourhood before, but I could not call to mind ever having noticed the three pine trees Catherine had mentioned in her letter, and I kept a sharp look-out for them as I walked along. Presently I saw them. A sudden break in the changing masses of vapour overhead allowed the sunbeams to struggle through, and they fell for a moment in a blaze of light upon a dome of white cloud that had formed low down near the horizon; and against this background of white, I saw the silhouettes of three trees, close together, standing out sharp, black, and solid, startlingly like the picture of the Three Crosses outside the walls of Jerusalem on the morning after the Crucifixion. It was only for a moment. Then the sunlight died out, the white cloud was swallowed up and lost in the swelling sea of black vapour around it, and the dull

twilight shadow stole over the landscape again. "The
house at the bottom of the hill, below the three pine trees,"
the letter had said. These, then, were the trees; and
below them must be the house where Catherine had been
shut up by Stadding. Now it was too late, doubts and
difficulties that had never before occurred to me began to suggest themselves. If Catherine had been imprisoned under
the circumstances the letter stated, Stadding must have
consigned her to private keeping, and not to an asylum ;
and if to private keeping, would he not have taken every
precaution against any one but those in his confidence
gaining access to her ? I was only a woman, alone,
unprotected, unassisted—what should I do if admittance
were denied me ? My heart well nigh failed me when I
thought how desperately Catherine stood in need of
assistance, and how little it was in my power to render
her; and fearing the worst, and resolutely steeling myself
to meet it, I went forward. The wind that had been
rising died completely away, and a silence, still, dead,
oppressive as a nightmare, reigned. I walked on till I
reached the summit of a rise in the road just beneath the
hill where I had seen the trees, paused for a moment, and
then—weak and woman-like—closed my eyes. I closed
them involuntarily. I closed them because I knew that
when I opened them I should see Catherine's prison-house,
perhaps only a few yards from me.

XIV.

. . . It was a big, dilapidated, two-storied building —
like a disused farm-house. It stood at the bottom of the
slope in a little lap among the hills, and faced a narrow
stretch of winding roadway. From where I was, only one
side of the house was presented to view, and all the
windows on that side were boarded up. The roof, which
was of iron, was brown with rust, and here and there there

were great gaps in it. There were several chimneys, all crumbled and weather-worn into mere tottering piles of brick, save one, from which a heavy stream of smoke, suggestive of damp wood, was rising. In one corner of the roof was a sky-light; and by some mental process which I cannot describe, I at once became aware—became aware beyond any possibility of doubt or question—that the room beneath it was the room in which Catherine was imprisoned. I lingered for a minute or two with some insane hope of seeing a signal waved to me from it; and then, descending the hill, approached the house by the rough cart track which led to it from the coast.

It is a humiliating and dishonourable confession to make —but then I was only a mere girl, nervous, imaginative, and timid, and the sight of that grim, forbidding, deserted-looking place terrified me: I was sorely tempted--tempted almost beyond my feeble power to resist—to turn my back and make the best of my way home again. Prudence whispered that it would be the very height of improbability to suppose that Stadding would allow a second opportunity to occur of rendering assistance to Catherine if the first were not taken full advantage of. I was ignorant, un-sophisticated; I did not know what the extent of his power over Catherine might be, or what villainous resources might not be ready to his hand. Would it not be wiser, after all, to set aside Catherine's desire that I should not confide in any one, and go back and try to procure such assistance as would ensure success even if the opposition I was now beginning to dread were offered?

I know now that this is what I should have done. I do not exaggerate one jot when I say I would give my right hand at this moment to rectify the tremendous con-sequences that have resulted from following a contrary course. I did not know, as I stood hesitating that day on Happy Valley Road, with the first heavy drops of the storm beginning to plash around me, and the first rumble of the thunder sounding behind the hills, that the fate of my whole future life hung trembling in the balance, and that by deciding the question I was then putting to myself I should finally and for ever fix my destiny for weal or woe. But so it was. I know it now.

I told myself it was cowardly to turn back. I conjured up a picture of Catherine, deserted by her treacherous husband, and suffering I knew not what hardships in her imprisonment, waiting and wondering what would be the result of her letter—her desperate, despairing letter, written I was afraid to think under what circumstances—and whether I would move hand or foot in her aid. Days had now gone by since the letter had been written;—what might not have happened since then?

No; having gone so far I could not draw back. I turned resolutely towards the house, and walked along the cart-track—walked along it rapidly, for fear I should again be overtaken by my pitiable indecision—till I halted in front of the house. There was an ill-conditioned tabby cat squatting on the doorstep. Beyond this there was not a sign of any living thing about the place. The upper windows, like those at the side, were boarded up. Of the two lower ones, that to the right was hidden by its shutters, and had plainly remained so for a considerable time, for a portion of the spouting above it had fallen out of repair, and the course of the water escaping from it was indicated by a green slimy track which traversed the shutter and wall of the house down to the ground. The blind of the window to the left was drawn down. . . . Had it not been for the column of smoke arising from the chimney I should have thought the house was deserted.

I walked up the path to the door—the cat rising and arching its back and bristling its fur as I approached and knocked. My heart seemed suddenly to trip up and alter its beat, and its pulsations grew heavy, slow, and choking. I waited one—two—three full minutes. No answer came. The cat, which I noticed now had an ugly red lump where its right eye should have been, began to claw at my dress, and then, with a suddenness that made me start and cry out, it sprang on to my shoulder and rubbed its head against my face. I tried to shake it off, but it clung so tightly that its great claws pierced my flesh, and I had perforce to let it remain. If I had allowed myself to pause another moment, the little courage I had would have failed me, and in spite of my resolution I should have given way to the temptation that was again besetting me, and beaten an ignominious retreat.

I knocked again. It was an effort of will, an effort to which I urged my weaker self as a slave-driver might drive a slave. . . . There was a sound of footsteps walking softly along the passage, and the door was opened by a feeble, little, old woman, very much bent with age, with an evil-looking, erysipelas stricken face, and a tattered shawl drawn round her shoulders. She fixed her eyes on a point in space apparently two or three feet in front of me, and stepped back as if to make room for me to enter.

"Ah, my dearie," she said, with unaccountable familiarity, and in the wheedling tone one might use to a child in arms; "have you come back already? I didn't look for you so soon——"

She was interrupted by the cat, which hurled herself from my shoulder to that of the old woman with a shock that fairly made her stagger.

I had expected to have my entrance disputed, but here was the most unlooked-for readiness to grant admittance—a readiness so surprising that it roused my suspicions.

"You must be mistaken," I began. "I do not think   "

"Good Lord, ma'am, I beg your pardon," said the little old woman, suddenly dropping her ingratiating tone, and coming very close up to me, with the spectral-looking cat poised on her shoulder, and peering up in my face. "I'm that short-sighted." She passed her hand—which I noticed shook very much—over her eyes as if brushing away something that impeded her vision. "I could only make out it was some one in petticoats, and I thought it was my

Gertie come back. Gertie—that's my daughter. And what may you want with me, ma'am?"

"I came to see a person who, I understand, is— is staying here," I said, thinking it best to state my purpose at once, and feeling, too, that at the vital moment when perhaps the whole success of my object depended upon my self-assertion and confidence I had stated that purpose in the feeblest and least impressive manner.

The old woman's face slowly took upon itself a look of low cunning and impassiveness. She shook the cat from her shoulder, folded her arms very tightly under her shawl, and holding her head on one side, looked up at me with a faded air of coquettishness.

"I'm an old woman, and I'm a little dull of hearing," she said, leaning forward with an air of careful attention, and presenting one side of her face to me, so that I might speak directly into her ear. "I didn't catch what you said."

. . . "Ho! and what's his name?" she asked, when I repeated the object of my visit.

"It's a lady, and her name is Catherine—Stadding," I answered sharply, hesitating in spite of myself over the hated name.

"*Stadding*—Catherine *Stadding! Catherine* maybe, but *Stadding* devil a bit," she said slowly, and with a maddening sneer. "There's no such person here—no, nor yet any-wheres else either, for that matter, if I knows my man," she added, with a thick laugh. "You've come to the wrong shop, my fine lady."

"I've made no mistake," I said, "I know she's here. I have a letter from her. I demand admittance to her. How dare you keep her shut up here! How dare you prevent me seeing my own sister?"

"Oh—ho," cried the old woman in a shrill quaver, throwing her head back, and placing her arms akimbo, "we're sisters, are we? Oh, the dear creature! How proud we must be of her! And how proud her mother'd be, if she could see her darling now! *To* be sure!"

"Stand out of my way, woman, and let me go to her at once," I said, and with an appearance of resolution I was very far from feeling, I made as if I would step past her into the house.

"Ah-h; would you—would you—would you?" she cried menacingly, catching my wrist in her bony grip. "Don't you rouse the devil in me, or I'll spoil your beauty for you, my pet—I'll spoil your beauty for you."

"Catherine, Catherine," I called, "where are you?"

There was a confused sound of footsteps somewhere overhead, followed by a shock, as if some one had thrown herself against a door, and a shower of blows rained upon the panels.

"Here, here, here!" I heard in a hoarse voice. "Is it you, Ettie? Is it you? Here, here, here. Come and help me. Come and help me!"

"Back, you little she-devil you," screamed the old woman. "Back, I tell you, or I'll tear the eyes out of your head."

The blows, which had ceased for a moment, descended upon the door again with redoubled violence.

"Ettie, Ettie, Ettie!" called the voice—I should never have taken it for Catherine's—it was so harsh, so hoarse, so unfeminine. "Don't go away and leave me. Don't let her drive you away. It's my last chance. There's only the old wretch herself to deal with. Come and help me. Come and help me. I'm locked in!"

"Hear her," said the old woman. "'Only the old wretch to deal with'—'only the old wretch.' You'll pay for this, my lady, later on," she shouted, in the direction of the noise. "I'll pay you out for this by and by. I'll make short work —"

"Give her drink," said the voice from up-stairs. "It's drink she wants."

"Let go my hand," I said. "If it's money you want, I'll give you what I have; only let me see my sister."

The change in the old woman's manner was ludicrous in its abruptness.

"Na, na," she said, "if you're really her sister, I'm not the woman to keep you apart, though, maybe, you'll not be so pleased as you fancy when you do see her. It's few pleasures an old woman like me can get, and if you happen to have the price of a pint about you—why——" and she twitched her fingers expressively, without finishing her sentence.

I had often read of murders being committed for the sake of the few shillings one might carry; and, as I took out my purse, I was careful to let the old woman see how empty it was. What other money I had—it was very little, and I had only brought it with me because of Catherine's request—I carried loose in my pocket.

The noise above our heads began again, and as her hand closed over her bribe, the horrible old woman shook her fist at the invisible disturber of the peace, and uttered a volley of ready blasphemy that made me shudder.

"Come on," she said, leading the way up a rickety flight of stairs, and fumbling in her pocket for the key, "and make her stop this infernal clatter, or she'll break the door down before she's done, and there'll be the devil to pay when Gertie comes back. Comin', you mad jade, d'ye hear —comin'. Will that satisfy you? Comin', *comin'*, comin', I say!" raising her voice to a petulant shriek.

After reaching the head of the stairs she led the way for a few paces along a landing, thrust the key into the lock of a door, and waited till I had caught up to her.

"You don't happen to have so much as the price of another pint about you, young woman, do you?" she said, framing her request as if she expected No, and looking most unmistakably as if she expected Yes. "It's risky work this. I had strict orders not to let anybody into the house. It's lucky for you you only had an old woman like me to deal with, and not Gertie. *Have* you got so much as the price of a——"

"Not now," I said, impatient to see Catherine, and doubtful of the policy of exhausting at once my only means of influencing the old woman. "I'll give it to you after I have seen my sister; not before."

"Are you there, Ettie?" came the voice from the other side of the wall. "Give her what she wants, and let her go. Come to me—come to me, for Heaven's sake."

"*That's* a dear," said the vile creature, with a smirk, pocketing the coin I gave her, with a deftness that almost amounted to sleight of hand. "Now she shall see her sister and welcome."

She opened the door to allow me to pass through, and as soon as I was on the other side, clapped it to again and locked it.

"You're caught now, my fine lady," she chuckled. "You got in for your own pleasure, but whose will it be when you come out, my pretty bird—whose will it be when you come out, eh?"

The room was quite dark, and I realized the danger I was in at once.

"How dare you?" I cried. "Open that door and let me out, instantly!"

"Are you there, Ettie?" asked the voice. It came from an inner room—apparently next to the one I was in. I had not from the first recognized it as Catherine's, and a horrible doubt suggested itself to me that it might not be Catherine at all, and that I had been enticed into a trap.

"Who are you?" I cried in terror. "Is that you, Kate?"

"Yes, yes," came the answer. "Don't you know my voice? Why don't you come to me, Ettie? What is keeping you?" and she rattled the handle of the door impatiently.

Before I could answer, a slide in the panel of the door by which I had entered was slipped back, and the face of the old woman appeared at it.

"Here, take this, you little fool. I was only joking with you," she said, tossing a key through the opening, "though there's better than you had to make this their

quarters against their will. There, that's the key of the
door in front of ye."

"And why is this door not unlocked? What right have
you to treat me like this——" I began, my fears thoroughly
aroused by the conduct and evident character of the old
woman.

"Safe bind, safe find, dear. Make much of her while
you've got the chance. She's all your own for half an
hour——"

The door of the adjoining room was shaken again
petulantly, and the voice called to me—

"Ettie, Ettie, how can you leave me like this? There
is nothing to be frightened at. Lock yourself up in here
if you are afraid. Do—do come to—me——"

The last words were almost lost in sobs, but I was so
alarmed and suspicious of the old woman, who was standing
leering and smirking wickedly at me through the opening,
that I still lingered.

"Ettie, Ettie," sobbed the voice. Was it—could it be
Catherine's, or was there some deception about to be
practised on me?

"D'ye hear?" said the old woman, pointing a shaking
finger towards the room. "She's callin' ye, pretty."

"Kate," I said, in an agony of doubt, "is it really you
that's speaking? It is not your voice I hear."

There was a sound as if something were being dragged
heavily along against the wall; then a long, quivering sigh
—a sigh laden with an expression of anguish beyond words
—and then the voice said again, slowly and wearily, as if
it had not the strength to say more—

"Yes, yes; it is I."

I recognized it now. It was Catherine's; and I unlocked the door and was in the room in a moment.

XV.

"CATHERINE!"

Yes, it was Catherine. She was standing in the farthest corner of the room, her face buried in her hands, her long rich brown hair, of which she used in the old days to be so proud, falling in a cascade almost to her waist. As I paused and looked at her, her shoulders heaved with a suppressed sob.

"Kate, dear Kate," I said, going up to her, and putting my arm around her. "How long have you been here? Did you think I was never coming, poor girl?"

She did not answer, but let her head sink upon my shoulder, and continued her silent fit of weeping. One hand stole out towards mine and grasped it; the other she held closely pressed before her eyes. I could feel her tremble from head to foot—her emotion was so great—and waited till she should recover herself before speaking to her again.

The room was lit by a sky-light—it was, in fact, the room I had decided upon as I stood looking at the house from under the three pine trees. Had it been a cell in a prison it could not have been more comfortless. It was as dirty as if it had not been entered for years; there was no fireplace; and save for a table and a couple of chairs, not an article of furniture in the room. The opposite end from where we were standing was divided off by a thread-bare red curtain, which, being partly drawn aside, allowed the faded coverlet of a bed to be seen.

"I am glad you've come to me at last, Ettie," said Catherine, trying to compose herself, but with an angry sob catching her breath between every few words. "I was afraid you had not got my letter. I did so long to see a face I loved again. You don't know what I've suffered —since we saw one another last—he's never been near me since he—shut me up in this horrible den."

"Poor girl; how long have you been here? Could you

not have let me know sooner?" I said, and led her to one of the chairs, and sat down beside her.

"I scarcely know how long it has been," she said, clasping and unclasping her hands in her lap. "I have lost all count of time since he brought me here. Oh, Ettie, if you knew all, you would pity me—you would pity me. And yet he was kind at first. He said he loved me——"

"But you are his wife, Kate, and he dare not continue to treat you like this now—now his conduct is known," I cried.

She moaned and hid her face upon my shoulder, and then, after hesitating a moment, mutely put her left hand on my lap.

There was no ring on it !

I could not speak for a moment, and when I did the only words that came to my lips were—

"Oh, Kate, poor Kate ; is it as bad as that ?" And because I knew that, sensitive as she must be to her position, she might misinterpret the most accidental expression of feeling that might escape me, I clasped her the closer to me.

"I thought I had told you in the letter," she said, sobbing so bitterly that her words were scarcely intelligible. "He—he kept up the deception till near the end—we quarrelled one night—and he tore the ring off my finger——"

"Do not tell me, dear, if it distresses you," I said, for her sobs had choked her utterance. "Let us think how we are to get you away from this place."

"No, let me tell you all, now I've begun." She pushed me from her and began pacing up and down the room. "He tore the ring from my finger, and put his foot on it, and laughed in my face. 'You my wife,' he sneered. 'I thought you had been long enough on the boards to know a sham marriage from a real one. We've kept up the game long enough,' he said, 'and now let's end it, for I'm sick of it.' He was drunk, and when he is drunk he is brutal. I would not believe him, but he took a wicked pleasure in repeating it and throwing my shame in my face. I went on my knees to him that night, Esther—I did—I was nearly mad. He was raising a glass of wine in his hand; he paused and listened, and I besought him, if what he said was indeed true, that he would make the only reparation he could make me. And, oh, I did—I did plead with him so," she said, with an eloquent, piteous gesture of her hands. "What did he do? Oh, Esther, you don't know what a devil a man may become. He listened to all I had to say, and then deliberately, maliciously, with a smile on his lips, dashed the wine in my face. 'Does that satisfy you? Get up,' he said, 'and be —— to you. The time for all that kind of thing is over with me now. You knew what the game was as well as I did, for all your pious show, you jade, you. I only drop you where I picked you up. Go back to the profesh. again, for by gad, if you can act as well on the boards as you do off them, why there's a career before you.' I don't recollect what happened next, but I was ill—ill with the fever for weeks."

She burst into a passion of weeping again, but motioned me off when I rose to go to her. A deluge of rain was falling, and the wind had risen and was blowing in fitful gusts that struck the house with the solid impact of sea waves, making the rickety old building rock again, and rousing a deafening clamour among the loose sheets of iron on the roof. The lowering clouds overhead had been throwing deeper and deeper shadows into the room. Suddenly the gloom was rent, like the veil in the Temple, by the livid glare of lightning, and then descended again, denser and blacker than ever by contrast. The rattle of the thunder died away in space; the wind re-asserted its sullen buffeting of the house; and the rain pattered upon the roof, sweeping in flashes of white spray across the sky-light above our heads.

But momentary as that gleam of light had been, it had

lasted long enough to reveal that which made me shrink and cower in my corner of the room.

The flash of lightning had taken Catherine in an unguarded moment; her face had been turned towards me, and I had caught the full play of expression that animated or rather distorted it. . . . When I had received her letter, while I had been talking with the old woman at the door, when I had first entered the room where I now was, it had never for an instant occurred to me that Catherine's alleged madness was other than a wicked invention of Stadding's. Now I knew it was true, and that my sister was a madwoman!

It was not the deceptive and unnatural effect of the blaze of light that had beat about her; it was not the misinterpretation of a chance expression of the moment, nor the result of predisposing doubts or suspicions; for, as I have said, I had neither. It was vivid, instinctive, infallible conviction. I do not know whether I should be ashamed to confess it as selfish and timid, or whether the feeling was natural and excusable in one of my disposition, and situated as I was—my love and pity for her—and I did love her and pity her—became supplanted by a still keener feeling—a feeling of apprehension for my own safety. I did not know but what she might, at any moment, spring upon me and do me some violence.

The semi-darkness had fallen again so quickly that I did not think she had noticed my start of recognition, and as well as my distraction would let me I concentrated all my powers of self-control in one effort to conceal the fact of my terrible discovery.

. . . On entering the room I had locked the door, and the key was still in the lock. Catherine removed it, and then commenced pacing up and down the floor again.

. . . I was glad she had not noticed the ring which I had so lately become entitled to wear, for I feared it would excite her; and while her back was turned to me I quietly slipped it from my finger and put it in my pocket.

"I haven't told you half, nor nearly half," she went on. "I feel if I told you all he has done I should go mad—as he says I am already. But *you* don't believe it—you don't think I'm really mad?" she said, breaking off suddenly, and wheeling round towards me.

"No, dear; of course not," I said, with a pitiable attempt to assume a matter-of-course air. "Why should I?"

"And suppose I was ever to get out of here—of course it is only nonsense," she said with a simper—but keeping her eyes furtively on my face the while ; "but if I was, do you think people would take me for a madwoman or not?"

Her question pained me inexpressibly.

"Why, Kate dear," I said, "of course you'll be able to get away from here—I shall see to that myself." (Did I really mean what I said? Heaven forgive me! I do not know whether I did or not. Some vague idea of rendering her assistance I know I had.) "What have you done that you should be made a prisoner of——"

"What have *I* done?" she said, fiercely. "What have *I* done? It is not what I have done that has made a prisoner of me—of me, his wife, for morally I am his wife, though I should loathe and scorn myself——"

Another vivid streak of lightning shot into the room, played for a moment over her in a gleam of livid fire as she stood checked in the attitude of passionate hate, and was gone again—swift, momentary, silent. There was a pause, and then the shriek of the wind and the furious rush of the rain overhead were drowned in the hoarse roll and echo and re-echo of the thunder.

. . . "What does that tell you, Ettie?" she said, taking a torn scrap of paper from the bosom of her dress and holding it up before me. It was so creased and wrinkled that what it contained was barely readable, and it was with difficulty that I made out the words : —

". . . . I declare . . . . no other . . . . I can think of . else . night. My whole heart and affec . . . . . bound . . . . . the two words, Amelia Ll——" (the last word was unfinished).

"'I can think of no one else day or night. My whole heart and affections are bound up in the two words, Amelia Ll——'" Catherine repeated, folding up the piece of paper and putting it in her dress again. "I saw him write it. It was one night when I was lying ill with the fever – one night after he had thrown the wine in my face—and he came to me and said he was sorry for what he had done.

"'Shake hands, Kate,' he said, 'and let bygones be bygones.'

"I could have forgiven him and tried to forget, if I could only have believed him. But I knew he had come to me with a lie on his lips and in his heart.

"'Let bygones be bygones if you will, Edgar,' I said, 'no one can have less desire to remember the past than I have. There's only the future left to me, and only the future left for you to undo the wrong you've done me. Before you touch my hand in friendship again, you must give me back what you took from it.'

"'You mean the ring,' he said.

"'I mean the ring,' I answered.

"'I know I said more than I should, and did more than I should, the other night. I don't remember what it was exactly,' he said slowly, as if he were choosing the words that would deceive me most readily. 'I wasn't in my right mind or I wouldn't have done it; but whatever it was, I beg your pardon, and I'll make what amends I can in the future. I can't say more than that. And now,' he went on, as if he had done all that could be expected of him, 'now I've got a letter to write. Are we good enough friends for me to stay and write it here, or not?'

". . . "I scarcely know why—except that I had learned only too well to suspect him most when most friendly, and that I had suspected him all the time he had been talking to me—but as he sat and wrote I got up softly and looked over his shoulder, and this," pointing to her bosom, " was the letter. When he came to the name of the woman he was writing to, I became so excited that I forgot myself and leaned forward to look more closely, and he heard me. He half turned his head, and started as if he had seen a ghost.

"'Confound you,' he cried, putting his hand over the letter. 'This is too much. I'll teach you to play the spy upon me.'

"I knew now why he had taken the ring off my finger and thrown the wine in my face. . . . I said nothing, but went to the door, locked it, and took out the key. Our room was in the second storey, and I went to the window and threw the key into the street. I heard it ring on the pavement below. He watched me all the time with an air of being completely at ease.

"'Hul-lo, hul-lo,' he drawled, ' what's the little game— what's the little game?'

"'Now,' I said, ' who is that letter for?'

"'I'll read it to you when I've finished, my love,' he said, 'now that you have been kind enough to prevent anything in the way of interruption by locking the door, just to see how a woman enjoys playing second fiddle in this kind of game.'

"'Don't drive me too far,' I cried, and I took up the lamp and held it above my head. ' I give you three minutes to tell me who that letter is to, or I'll pitch the lamp among the bed-curtains and fire the house. We're locked in, and we'll burn together.' And I meant it, and he knew I meant it. I hated the woman and I hated him, as I hate them now. . . . He's a coward, and he turned pale ; but he tried to put a bold face on it, and half rose from his chair.

"'Move a step if you dare!' I cried, and I swung the lamp as if about to dash it among the curtains.

"'God's sake, you mad woman, mind what you're at with that lamp. Give me a moment to think —'

"'No,' I said, 'not another instant. Once for all, am I to know who that letter is to?'

"'Curse you! Do your worst!' he said, and holding up his arms so as to shield his face, he made a blind rush at me. I stepped back a pace, and then hurled the lighted lamp among the curtains. They burst into flames in a moment, and seizing the opportunity I secured the letter from the table—and I've got it yet. They never found it on me through all.'

"'Help, help, fire!' he shouted, pulling down the curtains and trampling on them. 'You madwoman, would you murder me?'

"But the flames spread over the room, and I laughed at him, and fanned them into a stronger blaze. The thick smoke rolled round him like a cloud, and dazed and choked him, and he staggered towards the window and threw it open, I thought with the intention of jumping out; but the height was too great, and he turned to the door again and kicked through one of the panels in his desperate efforts to break it open. Then there was a sound of shouting outside, in the street and in the passage, and the door was burst in.

. . . "I can only remember three things after that. I awoke for the first time, and I was lying in bed in a dark room with some one sitting beside me who forbade me to speak. I awoke for the second time, and the country was flying past a railway carriage window, and Stadding was seated near me. I awoke for the third time, and found myself here. All the interval between the awakenings seems like one long nightmare, that always in some way or other resolves itself into that scene you remember in the theatre at Wellington——"

The torrent of words stopped suddenly. Catherine had acted rather than narrated her story, often raising her voice to a shrill scream, so that I might hear her above the incessant clamour of the storm without, and grew so excited —especially towards the end—that I became alarmed. She paused now, and pressing her hands to her temples, staggered, and would have fallen had I not sprung up and caught her in my arms.

"Oh, my head, my head!" she said, as I supported her to a seat. She sat down and rested her head on my shoulder —sat so long, so silent, and so motionless that I stole a look at her face to see whether she might not have become insensible. Though the wind was blowing and the rain falling as violently as ever, the atmosphere had cleared so that one could see plainly in the room, and I was shocked to find her watching me stealthily between her fingers, her shoulders quivering with suppressed laughter, and an expression of insane, elfin enjoyment on her face.

"Catherine!"

She did not move, but her eyes fell, her laughter ceased, the expression died out of her face.

"Esther," she said, presently, raising her head, "I've not told you yet why I sent for you." Her eyes met mine, and their expression frightened me. "Ever since I was brought here, I have only had one desire—to escape; and I have desired to escape only, for one thing—to revenge myself upon Edgar Stadding. Never a day or a night, that I have not watched my opportunity; but it has never come. It was the scheming of days and weeks to get that letter away, alone. I did not send for you because I wanted your sympathy. Had that been all, I would have died sooner than let you know. You remember the night you came to me at the Truss o' Straw?" she said, abruptly.

"Yes."

"And your telling me that Edgar Stadding mistook you for me, the night he returned home?"

"Yes."

We had both risen, and Catherine stood with her hands held firmly on my shoulders, as if she expected me to resist, and was prepared to overcome me by sheer force of strength, if I did.

"Since I have been here, I have found out—no matter how—that he is about to marry the woman he was writing to that night, Esther," she said, sinking her voice to a deep, tremulous whisper. "If I die for it, he shall never do it.

He shall never marry her while I live—never, never! He thinks he has put me out of his life, but he will find he has not; he will find he has to reckon with me yet. There is only one thing between him and me now, and only one thing between me and freedom. Do you know what that is?"

I trembled, and felt her hands close more tightly upon my shoulders.

"No."

"Yourself!"

"Catherine!"

"As Catherine Stadding, I know, for I have tried, I can never go out from this place. As Esther Gower I must, and shall. That is why I sent for you. Now do you understand?"

"No."

"Edgar Stadding mistook you for me," she said, rapidly and excitedly. "Are the eyes of that old beldame sharper than his? Had you come yesterday, when her daughter was here or to-morrow, it might have been different."

"Kate, dear Kate, if there is anything I can do to help you, you know I will do it—it was for that I came. Only tell me what it is. If it is in my power I will do it."

"It *is* in your power," she said, slowly. "But you will not do it."

"I will indeed, Kate. Tell me what it is. Only tell me what it is. I will do it, believe me, if I am able," I said eagerly.

"It is very simple, Esther; we often do it on the stage. We'll double our parts."

"I don't understand you, Kate."

"We'll change clothes, then. I will leave in your place; you will stay behind in mine."

She spoke slowly and calmly, but her hands clutched my shoulders with the grasp of a strong man. We stood for over a minute gazing silently into one another's eyes. The wind beat against the house; the rain splashed on overhead.

"Do you consent?" she said.

Think of the position I was in. We were alone in the room. She a madwoman, and I in her power. She was stronger than I, and I knew that if I resisted she would use that strength with the desperation of madness. If I consented —— I shuddered when I considered what that might mean.

"Do you consent?" she said.

"No, no, I cannot; you do not know what you ask."

"You do not know what you refuse," she cried, furiously; and with a single exertion of her strength she forced me to my knees, and stood threateningly over me. "You do not know how I have set my heart on it; you do not know what I am ready to do to gain it. Once for all, do you consent, or must I tear the clothes from your back?"

"Catherine, Catherine, have mercy. Let me go. I came to do what I could to help you—I did indeed. Let me go. I have friends. I will speak to them. They will help you —will help us both."

"Your friends! Who are your friends? Once outside of here, you and your friends would forget me—would be ashamed to own me if you did remember me."

"No, Kate, they would not; indeed they would not. Only try me; only let me go. We will help you; we will see you righted and set free from this horrible place. We will do more for you than ever you could do by yourself, even if you succeed in escaping. You have your rights— you have your remedy at law, and we will secure them for you, and give you a greater revenge against Stadding than you could win without our help. What can you do alone against him? He has been too strong for you once, and he will be too strong for you again."

"My remedy at law, my remedy at law," she said, bitterly, still standing over me and still holding me down. "You would give me law, not justice; you would blazon my shame all over the land, and have every finger pointing at me and every tongue wagging at me. You would give

me a revenge I cannot gain by myself?   No, you wouldn't.
What can I do alone against him?   I'll show you that.
I'll show you and every one whether the law could give
me a revenge I am not able to take for myself.   Only
let us meet face to face.   I tell you, Esther, unless he
makes the one reparation he can make, I'll kill him—I
will, I tell you, or he will kill me——"

"Oh, hush, hush, Catherine——!"

"Hush!   I will not hush.   I tell you I will.   He has
robbed me of happiness, he has robbed me of honour, he has
robbed me of freedom, he has robbed me of reason—for I'm
mad, Esther, mad, though I try to hide it—mad, mad.
Robbed me!   Oh, my God, what has he not—what has he
not robbed me of?   And you talk of what you will do and
what your friends will do, and tell me I should go to law.
Keep your law to yourself.   Keep your friends to yourself.
I have none.   None would own me for a friend.   Do you
think I care a jot for my own sake whether I am shut up
here or whether I am free?   Not I.   Why should I?
What is life to me now?   What has he left me to live
for?   Nothing.   Nothing but revenge; and for that I will
sacrifice myself, I will sacrifice you, I would sacrifice anything.   I have bided my time—I have watched; and now
the time has come, do you think you will persuade me from
it?   Come, I would not do you an injury.   But do not
make me forget you are my sister—do not madden me by
refusing.   Do you consent?"

"Hey, hey, hey, in there," cried a voice from outside,
and the door was rattled loudly.   "How much longer are
you going to be?   Time's up half an hour ago.   D'ye hear
me?   D'ye hear me, I say?"

"Say a word if you dare?" muttered Catherine, in my
ear.   "Take care; I am desperate."

I tried to struggle to my feet, but she held me like a vice.

"Let me go, Catherine," I pleaded.   "Let me go.   I
will come again.   I will get help——"

"No, I tell you—no, no, no!" she said, in a fierce whisper.

"Hey there, d'ye hear? Come, clear out o' this. You bin there long enough."

"Hel ——"

"A-a-h; would you?" Before I could utter the cry that rose to my lips, Catherine's hand glided with the swiftness of lightning from my shoulder to my throat, and closed round it in a merciless grip. Tighter and tighter I felt her grasp become. I tried to speak again, but could not. A blood-red cloud formed before my eyes. I could not breathe. I was conscious of Catherine in the midst of the silent struggle controlling her voice to speak calmly, and giving some answer to the woman outside, and then I became insensible.

When I awoke I felt sick and faint. I was lying on the bed in the portion of the room I have spoken of as being partitioned off by the red curtain. I was stripped of my outer garments. Those which Catherine had been wearing, but which she had now taken off, lay in a heap beside me. Catherine herself, with the curtain, partly drawn back, grasped in her hand, her body half bent, stood looking down at me, as if she had been checked in the act of taking a step towards the door. She was dressed in the clothes she had taken from me. She shook her clenched hand at me.

"Utter a sound if you dare!" she said, and she strode to my side threateningly.

I sank back with a shudder. She looked keenly at me again, as if to satisfy herself of my helplessness, and then walked to the door. I watched her half stupidly. I did not realize fully where I was, or what had happened. A ray from the skylight fell on little Pure-in-Heart's feather in her hat as she paused to put the key in the lock, and in another moment she had passed out. I rose and tried to make my way to the door, but before I had gone three paces my legs gave way under me, and I sank down. I tried to cry out, but my voice scarce rose above a whisper.

"Well, I hope you're satisfied," I heard a thick,

uncertain voice say. "Thank your stars you've come out with a whole skin on your bones, my lady. Not so fast, not so fast. Na, na. Lock it, lock it, lock it—let me see you lock it, and pass me the key through the hole here, before I undo this door to ye. I want no more of her mad rushes. I can't stand 'em—I'm an old woman, and I can't stand 'em."

It was the old woman talking to Catherine.

There was a sound of a door being opened and closed, a sound of retreating footsteps, a sound of another door being opened and closed somewhere below—and then silence.

The old woman had not detected the deception. Catherine had escaped, and I was left alone in the house.

This was on the tenth of June.

*　　　　*　　　　*　　　　*　　　　*　　　　*

The discovery of the fraud, the return of the old woman's daughter, my fruitless appeals to be set at liberty—all that happened during the time I remained shut up in the lonely house on the Happy Valley Road, I pass over. They have nothing to do with this statement.

I come to the third day, the twelfth of June.

It was evening, and I had been lying down from sheer exhaustion. I had scarcely slept an hour from the moment I had first entered the house, and had fallen into a wakeful, disturbed slumber. I was awakened by a confused sound of voices, among which I recognized the harsh, masculine tone of Gertie, the old woman's daughter; the shrill, broken treble of the old woman herself; and—was I mad or dreaming? I sat bolt upright, with my eyes fixed on the door. There was a scurrying of footsteps in the passage. The old woman was swearing dreadfully, her daughter was threatening. The door was thrown open; some one was hustled into the room. It was Catherine!

It was Catherine; but how changed. Her face was pale, thin, and drawn; her eyes wild and sunken, her dress disordered. She staggered helplessly to a seat and sat down, and rested her head upon her hands without even casting a glance around her.

"Catherine, Catherine, you have come back," I cried, going up to her, and placing my hand upon her shoulder. "Where have you been these three days?"

She raised her eyes to my face, gazed at me vacantly for a moment, shook her head, and let it fall upon her hands again. I thought she had not recognized me, but presently she rose from her seat, and after pacing up and down the room, turned to me and said with a thick laugh—

"I have been somewhere and to some purpose. You'll hear the country ringing with it when you go back among your friends, Ettie."

"What do you mean?" I said. "What has happened?"

"I have met Stadding."

"Catherine!"

"He is dead!"

"God forgive you, Kate!" I cried, recoiling in horror. "You have not killed him?"

"Have I not?" she said slowly with a horrible significance, and speaking more to herself than to me. "Have I not?" Her eyes sought the floor at her feet as though, it seemed to me, they rested upon something that had fallen there prone, face-downward, lifeless.

"Hush, hush, Kate. You do not know what you are saying. You could not have done it."

"Why not," she cried, her face distorted with the fierceness of her passion. "Why should I spare him? Did he spare me? What did I say I would do if we met? Well, we have met, and my revenge is completed."

She came close up to me. I forgot she was not responsible for what she had done. I forgot the wrongs she had suffered. My mind took in only the one fact of her crime. I shrank back from her touch.

"Oh, heaven," I cried; "you have done this—you, my sister——"

I do not know what sudden light may have broken in upon her poor disordered brain. Perhaps it was a momentary gleam of sanity. A look of unspeakable pathos, a look of confused intelligence, as of one suddenly awakened from a dream, came into her eyes. They filled with tears, and she threw herself at my feet and clasped me round the knees.

"Keep my secret, Ettie," she said in a hoarse whisper, and so indistinctly that she seemed scarcely able to articulate. "Do not betray me."

Her hands unclasped and dropped limply by her side, and before I could stoop to assist her, she fell to the floor insensible.

I loosened the things about her neck, and called loudly for help. The door was thrown open, and Gertie rushed into the room.

"Fainted," she said, bending over Catherine's senseless form. "Help me put her on the bed. There, now, leave her to me. She'll be right in ten minutes. Off with them rags as don't belong to you, and take back your own. I've had enough of this game. You're the first and the last that gets in here on this lay, I can tell you; and you can think yourself lucky to get out of this hell upon earth as well as you have."

. . . In ten minutes I had resumed my own clothes again, and without being permitted to remain long enough to see whether Catherine showed any signs of returning consciousness, I was hurried from the house, and found myself once more on the Happy Valley Road.

I felt in my pocket for my wedding ring, which I had taken from my finger during my interview with Catherine. The pocket was torn and the ring was not there.

PART III.

IN WHICH THE AUTHOR TAKES UP THE STORY.

XVI.

[It will be noticed that Esther's confession chronicles the events occurring up to the 12th of June, 1886. The confession did not reach Mr. Redmayne, to whom it is addressed, till April 24th, 1889. What happened between those dates it is the purpose of the following to record.]

THE following extract is taken from the *Evening Post* of the 12th June, 1886 :—" Though fortunately the late severe gale which swept over the country has not resulted in loss of life, we have several narrow escapes to record. On the evening previous to the day on which the storm burst upon us, Mr. Matthew Redmayne (the son of Mr. J. W. Redmayne, the well-known merchant of Fiji), who had been staying for a time at Island Bay, put to sea in his yacht—the *Meg Merrilies*. He had scarcely had time to get well started upon his voyage, when the vessel was over-taken by the storm, which increased to such a degree of violence that the *Meg Merrilies* was soon being driven helplessly before it in the direction of the coast whence she had set out not many hours before, and she was headed straight for Island Bay. When the fury of the elements was at its height, and only a few minutes before the yacht entered the bay, her foretopmast was snapped short off, and the top hamper becoming entangled in such a way that the vessel bade fair to become unmanageable, Mr. Redmayne made his way aloft to cut away the wreckage. In the midst of his efforts he lost his footing, and had it not been for the exercise of the greatest agility he would in all probability either have fallen overboard and been inevitably lost, or been crushed by falling upon the deck. As it was he managed to save himself; but in doing so he injured his right leg so severely that when at last he reached the deck he was quite unable to stand. It was fortunate that the *Meg Merrilies* a few minutes afterwards made the lee of the island, and so escaped the fury of the gale. The vessel came to anchor under this friendly shelter, and Mr. Redmayne was brought ashore at the first opportunity, and at once taken to the residence of Miss Winterson, where he promptly received the most efficient medical aid. We are glad to report that though the leg was severely strained and contused, Mr. Redmayne will be well enough to resume his voyage as soon as the necessary repairs to the yacht are effected."

XVII.

"Now, Matthew, what *is* the use? Try and compose yourself; do try and compose yourself a little," and Miss Dorothy Ann, whose eyes were very red and swollen, and who looked very far from being composed herself, paused and put her handkerchief to her eyes. "This constant worry, worry, worry, will only make bad worse. Goodness *knows*, this has been a trying time for us all; but I do trust it may turn out all right in the end——"

Redmayne started so impatiently that the bandaged leg stretched out in front of him gave him a twinge that made him bite his lips to keep from calling out.

"Compose myself," he said, bitterly. "Look at me lying here and playing the sick man with my wife gone heaven knows where, and my father on his death-bed—— She said nothing, you say, as to who could have written the letter, or why she was going away?" he broke off to put the question he had put a score of times before, and which had been answered a score of times before in just the same way as it was answered now.

"None, Mat, my poor fellow, none," said Miss Dorothy Ann, looking over her handkerchief. "She set out the morning after you sailed. She looked pale and distracted, and said she was going for a long walk, because she thought it would do her good—and, poor girl, she looked as if she needed something to keep her up," and the red eyes went down behind the handkerchief again.

"That is, she looked more distressed than could be accounted for by what happened on the day before—do you mean?"

"I am afraid, Matthew, that is just what I do mean."

"But what could have happened more than we know of? You know of nothing in her past life that could——"

"I know nothing, Matthew. All she said was that your sudden departure was not all that had happened to trouble her, and she seemed to blame herself, too, for being the cause of your delay."

"But you told her she was not in the remotest way——"

"Of course I did." Miss Dorothy Ann hastened to say. "I told her she was not in any way responsible for what had happened, and that she was foolish to let such a consideration trouble her for a moment. But it was her manner, more than her words, that drew my attention." Miss Dorothy Ann paused and thought for a moment. "I am still of opinion something had happened to distress her that we know nothing of—and judging by her manner, something serious. Besides that, there's her note. Quite inexplicable it seems to me after our meeting, and what we said to one another."

"Yes, there's the note; much light it throws on the subject"; and Redmayne drew the note from his pocket, and read it again disconsolately. "Dear Miss Winterson," it ran, "do not be alarmed if you do not see me during the day. I was anxious to see you before leaving, but I did not like to disturb you. I shall be back, I trust, by evening. I received a letter yesterday, and it contained an appointment to meet a friend, whom I have not seen or heard of for many months, and I could not forgive myself if I neglected it. Yours faithfully—ESTHER."

"You are sure she has never spoken to you of any friend who would be likely to write such a letter as this?" asked Redmayne, folding up the letter slowly, and thrusting it into his pocket.

Miss Dorothy Ann had already put this question to herself, and placed her mind upon the rack to suggest an answer, all to no purpose; and even now she paused again and considered before answering.

"Quite sure I know of no one," she said, hopelessly, "unless, perhaps, her sister. I remember she has mentioned she has a sister."

"I know; she has mentioned her to me once or twice," said Redmayne, knitting his brows; "but one wouldn't be likely to receive a letter, such as she mentions, from a sister, I should say. Do you—do you really think she received a letter at all?" he asked, suddenly.

"Why, of course I do," said Miss Dorothy Ann, surprised at the question. "Why?"

Redmayne took out the note, and read it again thoughtfully before answering, and then said—

"The morning you spoke to her, did she seem so excited as to lead you to suppose her mind was—was affected in any way?"

"She was agitated—agitated, it seemed to me, in a rather unaccountable way. But that was just her disposition; she is so nervous and sensitive. I think the trial of the week before—telegram coming after telegram, and the suspense—had unnerved her—."

"My cursed obstinacy!" he cried, passionately, crunching up the note in his clenched hand. "I might have known it; but I give you my word, Miss Winterson, I thought my father was playing me, like a trout, to see what I was made of before he took me into the firm—I did; upon my word I did. He did it before, and I thought he was doing it again. She did not appear," he began, and then paused, and went on again—"like one who would—would kill herself."

"No, no, Matthew! Don't entertain that thought," said Miss Dorothy Ann, clasping his arm, and speaking very emphatically. "She would not do that under any circumstances, I am very sure. It was not that; whatever it may have been it was not that, thank God. I know my poor girl better than to think that."

"Some accident—Good God, Miss Winterson, who knows but she may have fallen from those cliffs into the sea. Fallen? She was out in that storm; the wind would have blown her before it like a wisp of straw—And I cannot so much as put my foot to the ground. It maddens me."

"Don't let us fly to the worst conclusion, Matthew. Something, of course, must have happened; but I hope it is nothing serious—I trust it is not so bad as you fear. It may turn out better than we think."

"That letter—that letter. I wish to heaven I could find out where it came from, or what it contained—or if she received a letter at all. A friend—what friend could it be that could call her away in such a manner and without a word of explanation to any one? She could have had no secrets she could wish to keep from you, Miss Winterson?"

"No unworthy secret, Matthew, I am very sure," answered Miss Dorothy Ann, gravely, with as near an approach to reproof as circumstances would permit; "but secrets we all have, and, poor girl, she had hers, no doubt."

"It is strange she mentioned nothing to you. I cannot understand it. There is some mystery beneath it all— some mystery I fear we are not likely to have cleared up. Oh, Esther, my wife," he cried, with an uncontrollable outburst of feeling, and raising his hand to his brow, "I would give my right hand to know where you are to-night, or for the power to set my foot to the ground to seek you out. Three days! Shall I ever see you again? Oh, if it had not been for my insane folly in not opening those telegrams before I did—What could have possessed me——"

"Nay, now you are as unreasonable as she was in blaming herself for keeping you from going to your father. If you had opened and read them ever so often, she would have been called away by that letter just the same."

"How do you know she ever got the letter she says she did?" he said, returning persistently to the one thought that seemed to weigh most heavily upon his mind. "How do we know what effect that suspense and that sudden parting may have had upon her? *I* do not know—my rough man's nature did not feel it; but how do I know how it may have affected her. Before heaven, Miss Winterson, I fear I stand guilty of unhinging her mind by my madman's freak—I do—and if I never see her again I shall never forgive myself——"

"Oh, hush, hush, Matthew—you are letting it prey upon your mind too deeply. You are no more to blame than I. How can any of us tell what the future may bring forth?" Miss Dorothy Ann knew she was saying what was conventional and commonplace, but what else was there to say? And after all it showed that she did sympathize with him.

"Ay, and who can tell what the last three days may have brought forth," and Redmayne's head sank upon his breast dejectedly.

There was a knock at the door, and Dick Drugget entered. Redmayne looked up at his face anxiously as he came towards him.

"No news?" he said: but he knew there was none before he asked.

"No news," said Dick Drugget, sadly. "Every nook and cranny for miles round has been searched, but there is not a trace of her anywhere—not a trace anywhere."

"Oh, my God," sighed Redmayne, "this is terrible. I would have given ten years of my life to have been with you."

"Don't give way, Mat, old man," said Dick Drugget, sympathetically, his inveterate awkwardness asserting itself even in his sympathy. "We did all we could. You couldn't have done more if you had been there yourself——"

"Yes, yes, Dick; I'm sure of that—I'm sure of that. But she is not found—she is not found."

.   .   .   .   .   "I called down at the yacht this afternoon, too," said Dick Drugget, after a long pause. "They've finished the repairs, and she's all ready for sailing."

"I can't help it, Dick; I can't go—not now, not tonight. I'll wait till morning now. Something may turn up. Was ever a man placed as I am?" he exclaimed, a deep flush rising to his face. "I am almost distracted between the two."

"As well sail as not," said the other, with awkward persistence. "You will do no good by waiting; the search will go on just the same whether you go or stay, and if anything turns up you can easily be let know."

"I think Mr. Drugget is right, Matthew," said Miss Dorothy Ann. "You cannot join in the search if you remain; and you would only fret yourself to death lying there. Trust me to let you know if anything happens."

There was another pause, and Dick Drugget looked from the distressed face of the one to the distressed face of the other, as if he had something more to say, but was doubtful whether it was the right time to say it.

"They say there was a body found out at Lowry Bay ——" he began.

Redmayne and Miss Dorothy Ann looked up swiftly. "A body? Of a woman?" demanded the latter.

"No, no, no, no," cried Dick Drugget, putting out his hands, and speaking very rapidly, so as to prevent his hearers dwelling even for a moment upon the wrong conclusion he saw they had jumped to at once, "of a man, of a man, of a man."

"Murdered?" It was Miss Dorothy who asked, but with little more than an affectation of interest. As for Redmayne, he had sunk back again, and was lost in thought.

"From the marks—yes."

"Is it known who he is?"

"Stadding was the name," said Dick Drugget, leaning forward with a kind of nautical roll, and resting his elbows on his knees, and clasping his hands. "Edgar Stadding, from a place called The Peak, I think."

"Stadding?" said Miss Dorothy Ann, starting with vague alarm. "Are you sure of the name?"

"Yes; Stadding was the name, I'm sure. He was found with his head beaten in, and quite dead," said Dick, with slow circumstantiality.

"Have they arrested the man who did it?" Miss Dorothy Ann's interest was something more than affectation now.

"It's doubtful whether it was a man at all or not," said Dick, wisely, as if he had an opinion of his own on the subject. "No; there's no one been arrested that I know of. There are 'extras' out about it. The body was found this morning. You'll know the name, perhaps?" he said, looking up in Miss Dorothy Ann's face.

Redmayne had not spoken as yet. He had been sitting with his head leaning upon his hand, apparently paying no attention to what was being said. Suddenly, a thought seemed to occur to him.

"Stadding, Stadding, Stadding?" he said, questioning himself vaguely, and turning slowly towards the others. "Was not that the name of Mrs. Shaw's son—Mrs. Shaw, where Esther was staying before coming here? I am sure I've heard his name from her."

"Hush!" said Miss Dorothy Ann, starting up from her chair, and laying her finger on her lip. "I saw some one pass the window in the dusk. Please God, it is Esther herself. Listen!"

Dick Drugget got up abruptly, and sidled towards the door, ready to execute a prompt retreat if occasion should arise. Redmayne sat bolt upright in the attitude of one whose whole attention is concentrated in the one act of listening. Miss Dorothy Ann stood motionless, her eyes looking downward, her head partly turned towards the door, as if she was half afraid of what was about to be revealed.

The lock was turned, the door swung back slowly and hesitatingly, and in the dusk the figure of a woman entered the room. She advanced a pace, and then stopped and hesitated, as if bewildered. Her face was pale and haggard, and her dress torn and travel-stained.

"Esther!" cried Miss Dorothy Ann.

A deep, fervent "Thank God!" burst from Redmayne.

Miss Dorothy Ann saw that she was about to fall, and hurried to her side and helped her into a chair.

"She has fainted," cried Redmayne. "She is ill!"

"Esther, my love, look up. Here is Matthew!" said Miss Dorothy Ann.

The mention of the name was like magic. The closed eyes opened and the pale face flushed. She looked past Miss Dorothy Ann to where Redmayne was lying upon the sofa, and started joyfully to her feet with his name upon her lips; and Miss Dorothy Ann, saying something about getting sal-volatile, went out of the room, though she knew there was no other restorative needed. Dick Drugget had executed the meditated retreat as soon as the door had opened, and was by this time half way towards the yacht.

"Matthew," cried Esther, throwing her arms round his neck and kneeling down beside him, her haggardness and paleness swept away by the lovely wave of colour that mantled in her face. "What has happened? What has brought you back? Are you hurt?"

"Nothing has happened; head winds have brought me back, and the hurt is nothing," answered Redmayne between the kisses he pressed upon her lips. "But now —What has happened? What has brought you back, and are you sure you're not ill? You looked ill just now. Tell me all about it."

"Never mind, now that you have me back, Mat dear," she said, her new-found strength seeming to leave her again, and the paleness and weariness coming back into her face at the question.

"Poor girl," he said, stroking her hair and gazing fondly into her eyes. "You are tired. You will tell us all about it after you have rested."

"Tell me what has happened to you first," she said. "I did not hope to see you back so soon. Have you heard from home since?"

"They think I am on my way to them now. I sent a telegram saying I was coming, and of course they do not know we have had to put back. But now you've come back to us, I shall start at once."

"But are you strong enough?"

"I was strong enough to come ashore, my dear, so I suppose I am strong enough to go on board again. But how ill you look again, darling; and you have not told me where you have been these three days."

"I am not ill, Matthew, only tired. I am better since I have seen you," she said, sinking her head restfully on his shoulder. . . . . . "Matthew, dear," after a pause.

"Yes, my love."

"Will you take me with you when you go on board the yacht again? Please do. You are hurt; you will need a nurse. I do so want to go."

"Why, certainly, my dear. Not half an hour ago I would have given all I had in the world to have taken you with me in the first place. I shall never leave you alone again—never."

She seized upon his words eagerly. "Promise that you never will, Matthew," she said, shuddering a little, and pressing closer to him.

"I promise, my love," he said, and sealed his promise in lover fashion. "Ah, when I think how near I have come to losing you —— No! I shall never leave you again," he repeated.

"Oh! Matthew, how I wish you never had. How I wish you had taken me with you instead of leaving me here," she said, with a sob.

"Never mind it now, Ettie. It's all over, and you are safe back again, and no harm done after all," he said, easily. "Don't let it bother your pretty little head. I was wrong to leave you; but then, you see, none of my people knew of my marriage, and under the circumstances I thought it best to go alone."

"I know," she said, "I know; perhaps I shouldn't ask to go now; but you won't mind; you'll take me, won't you? I'll put up with anything if you'll only let me go."

"Of course you shall go, Ettie. What! The wife of a day, and must she plead so hard to be taken with her husband? And after I had so nearly lost you for ever!"

"It's too late now, Matthew, but if you had only taken me at first," she said again, with a sigh, "everything would have been prevented."

"I wish I had now, dear," he said, putting his own construction on her words, and little dreaming what they really meant. "It has been an anxious time for us all, but thank God you are safe back again—and now let us forget all about it. It might have been worse. But what made you set off in such an unceremonious way, without a word to anybody? Was it the letter? Miss Winterson has told me all about that. But above all, where have you been, and what has happened to you these three days?"

"It was the letter, Matthew. It was from a—a friend who was in great trouble, asking me to go to her assistance."

"And like the dear little impulsive soul that you are, you went?" he said, bending forward to look into her eyes.

"Yes."

"But who was she, and where does she live, and what kept you three days?—She is not one of Miss Winterson's friends in Newtown?"

"No."

"Where then?"

"Matthew, forgive me, but I cannot tell you. She bound me to secrecy both in her letter and—and afterwards." Her head was nestling so closely on his shoulder that he could not see her face.

"But you can tell me where you were during the three days you were away?"

"To tell you that would be to tell you all, Matthew. I cannot say. Can you not trust me?"

"Trust you—yes, my love. But when you set out you expected to be back by nightfall. It is strange that you should be kept three days. We all thought something had befallen you."

"Well, Matthew dear, something did befall me. You do not think I would have caused all the anxiety I have if I could have helped it," said Esther, reproachfully, but never lifting her head from his shoulder. "I would have let you know if I could, but I could not. I regret—oh, more than I can tell you—all the distress you have felt through me; but it was not in my power to let you know the truth. You believe me, dear?"

"Yes, Ettie, of course. And now, one more question— Is your friend still in need of help, and can I help her? Or, rather, since it is your sovereign will that I must act in the dark, can I help you in helping her?"

She pressed his hand and looked up at him gratefully, as she said with unconscious simplicity—

"And you will not try to find out my secret?" and then added quickly, as he flushed at the question, "No; forgive me, I should not have said that."

"That was a true woman's question," he said, and laughed lightly. "Had you been a man I doubt if I ever should have forgiven you."

"But I am not only a woman, but a wife; and some day, perhaps soon, Matthew, I may ask you to redeem your promise."

"When you get absolved from your dark oath of secrecy, eh?" he said.

"Yes."

"And till then what has happened during these three days must be a sealed book?"

"Please," she said, with a sigh of relief and a grateful upward glance that amply rewarded him for his forbearance.

"Very well then, my dear; my curiosity is dead from this moment. You are sure you are strong enough to stand a sea voyage," he said, looking doubtfully down at her face.

"Say rather I am too weak to be left behind. That would be the greater trial of the two, Matthew."

"But I believe you are ill, though you won't admit it. And we start in an hour; I must not lose another moment. I have delayed too long—much too long—already."

"I am ready now, Matthew."

"By the way," he said, glancing at her hands, "do you always wear gloves in the house? You have kept them on ever since you came in. I hope there's nothing on a certain third finger you are anxious to hide. Let me take them off."

It was said in jest, but pale as her face had been before, it went a shade paler, and then flushed crimson, as she snatched her hand away with an affectation of playfulness, and went out of the room on the pretence of looking for Miss Dorothy Ann.

XVIII.

. . . . One would have thought that Esther's return would have put an end to all the distress and anxiety Miss Dorothy Ann might have felt on her behalf; but it had not. It may have been that something had passed

between her and Esther during the time they were together,
while preparations were being made to convey Redmayne
to the beach—for he would not delay his departure an
instant now, in spite of the pain the slightest movement
cost him, and in spite of the night having closed darkly in
—or it may have been that her keen woman's insight was
not so easily satisfied as Redmayne's unsuspecting nature.
At any rate, after Redmayne and Esther and Dick
Drugget—who had returned under cover of darkness—had
taken leave of her, and she stood watching them as they
moved away towards the sea-shore with their lanterns
glinting here and there in the darkness, the look of
trouble that had been on her face for the last three days
was still there.

The lights dwindled away in the distance till they looked
like so many pale stars, and then came to a standstill, and
Miss Dorothy Ann knew that Redmayne was being put on
board the boat that was waiting to take him off to the
Meg Merrilies, lying waiting in the harbour. Then the
stars separated; one returned towards Fernridge; the other
two floated away in the darkness, and then went out as
suddenly as if they had been extinguished.

"Poor Esther! Poor Matthew!" she said, shaking her
head with a vague pity.

John, the gardener, who had assisted in conveying
Redmayne to the boat, approached the garden gate with
his swinging lantern, and, as he passed through and paused
for a moment, a horseman dashed up and said something
to him breathlessly. There was a quick interchange of
question and reply, and then the horseman dashed off again
at the same furious rate, and the clatter of his horse's hoofs
died away in the direction of the beach. John remained
standing for some moments at the gate with his lamp held
high in the air, and his head craned forward peering into
the darkness.

Miss Dorothy Ann left her stand at the door and walked
down the path towards him.

" Who was that, John ? " she asked, anxiously.

" Ane o' the pollice, mem," said John, still holding up his lamp, and still peering forward.

" What did he want ? "

" I'm thinkin' it's the young leddy, mem," throwing the answer pettishly over his shoulder, as if annoyed at the interruption.

" The young lady ? — Do you mean Esther — Mrs. Redmayne ? "

" He named naebody, mem ; but I kent weel eneuch wha he meent by the description."

" What did he want with her—did he say ? "

John lowered his lantern and turned towards his mistress with the barely suppressed impatience of a spoilt servant.

" He named naebody, mem ; an' he didna say what he wanted wi' the young leddy excep' speerin' whaur she had gane."

" What did you tell him ? " asked Miss Dorothy Ann, looking away towards the beach, where a couple of lights were glancing about. " Hark, what was that ? somebody shouted something ; what was it ? "

" They're cryin' on the *Meg*, if I'm no mista'en," putting up his lantern and craning his head forward again. " I'll awa' doon an' see what's wrang."

" Stay a moment, John. Answer my question first, and then you may go. What did you tell him when he asked where Esther had gone ? "

" What did I tell him ? " repeated John, slowly, who did not relish being checked in this way, and who was, more-over, somewhat scandalized at such a question being put to him. " What did I tell him ? " he said again. " What wad ye hae me tell him ? What wad I be likely tae tell him but the truth ? I tel't him she had gane aboord the *Meg Merrilies* wi' her guidman."

" Listen, there's that shout again ! What was that ? "

" Aye, they're cryin' on the *Meg*, I tell ye, mem.

A-a-ay," he said, with a long-drawn note of surprise, "they're daein' mair nor cryin' on her; they're chasin' her, mem. Dae ye see that licht comin' roun' the pint, yonner, mem?"

"Oh, dear me—what can this mean, John?" and Miss Dorothy Ann was all in a tremble with apprehension. "What can they want with Esther? What can have happened?"

"'That I cudna' say, mem," said John, indifferently; "unless—maybe—but na, that cudna' weel be.".

"What could not be? What do you mean?" demanded Miss Dorothy Ann, quickly.

"I wis thinkin', mem—but na, that cudna' be."

"You were thinking what? What could not be? Tell me what you mean," cried Miss Dorothy Ann, distractedly.

"Aweel, mem, I wis jist thinkin' o' the body they fund the day oot at Lowry Bay—but, as I said afore, that cudna' weel be. But I can sune settle a' doots by gaun doon till the beach——"

"Do, John; go at once, and come back and tell me what happens."

*   *   *   *   *   *   *

The two lanterns in the boat were placed so that they shed very little light on the occupants, but it was sufficient to let Redmayne catch the expression of sadness on Esther's face as she looked away shorewards.

"It is always sad to leave a good friend, Ettie," he said, in answer to the look, "but I trust you will find almost as good where you are going. You will like my sister Ellen."

"Yes," answered Esther, her eyes following the track of old John's lantern ashore, as it traced the way back to Fernridge, "Miss Winterson has been a good friend, and it is sad to leave her; but sadder for her than for me, for she will be all alone in the old house now, while I will always have you."

"Always, Ettie," he said, "always;" and his arm stole protectingly around her.

Both were silent for a while, their eyes following the course of the spark of fire on shore. Dick Drugget was the oarsman, and only the regular clank of the oars in the rowlocks, and the swish of the water around the prow of the boat broke the stillness. The blades of the oars glittered like polished steel as they flashed up noiselessly out of the black-looking water, and caught the light of the lanterns.upon them.

"You remember Mrs. Shaw, Esther?" said Redmayne, suddenly. "Did you know her son Edgar Stadding was dead—found murdered out at Lowry Bay."

He felt her shudder convulsively, but she turned her head away, and he did not see the look that shot across her face, or hear the half-uttered "Then it is all true!" that escaped her lips. There was a cold biting air rising and stealing over the water, and he thought it was that that had made her shudder.

"You are cold, dear," he said; "draw this cloak round you."

She was a long time arranging the cloak to her satisfaction, and though she tried hard to control her voice, it trembled as she forced herself to say·

"I—I did hear something about it; but I did not I had hoped it was not true.

"Too true, I'm sorry to say. You would know him, of course. I have heard you speak of him."

"Yes, I knew him, but was never on very friendly terms with him. I am shocked that he should have met such an end."

"Had he offended you very deeply? You never told me why you disliked him?"

"He had offended me and deeply. But is it not known who—who——?"

"Who it was that killed him? No, not as yet."

"Nor any one suspected?"

"I believe not.   There is no clue as to who did it, Dick, is there?"

"Scarcely anything," said Dick, "but what there is makes me think it was a woman."

"A woman?—why a woman?" demanded Esther, quickly, turning towards him.

"Yes, why a woman, Dick," said Redmayne, rather surprised that Dick should have acted so much out of character as to express an unsolicited opinion.

"Because they say there was a ring found beside the body."

"A ring?" said Esther, faintly, shrinking into the shade of the cloak to hide the deathly white that stole over her face.

"A ring," said Redmayne, still more surprised that Dick should support his opinion after he had expressed it. "There can't be much evidence in that, Dick, I should think—it may have been the man's own ring."

"No; this was a woman's ring, and more than that, a wedding ring."

"It's a hard matter to distinguish one wedding ring from another," observed Redmayne, feeling that, in the light of recent experience, this was a subject he might be considered to have some knowledge of. "It is lucky for us I had the forethought to have our initials engraved inside ours, since wedding rings are lost in this haphazard fashion—eh, Ettie? Why, Ettie, dear girl, what's the matter?—Light here, Dick—good heavens, she's fainted!"

"No, no, Matthew; I've not," cried Esther, recovering herself with an effort. "I'm better now—I am tired and had almost fallen asleep—that was all. Where is the yacht?" she asked, looking about her in the darkness and shuddering again. "Let us get on board as soon as we can, Matthew—let us get on board as soon as we can."

A few minutes after, Dick Drugget shipped his oars, and the boat glided round to the further side of the yacht. Esther remained in the boat with her husband, watching

the preparations that were made for his removal, and did
not leave it till she had see him safely hoisted up on to the
deck. Then she too ascended, and helped him to his cabin ;
but had no sooner seen him comfortably settled there than
she expressed a wish to have a last look at dear old Island
Bay, and went on deck again. Redmayne did not go to
the trouble of formulating the thought very clearly to
himself, but as he lay back on his couch it struck him that
feminine human nature was somewhat inconsistent : when
Esther was in the boat she was so exhausted that her
keenest desire was to get on board the yacht ; once on
board the yacht her first act was to wander on deck again.
Ah, well.

.   .   .   .   .   It was a relief to Esther to find
herself alone in the dark. While she had been with
Redmayne, with the tell-tale light shining upon her face,
she had been afraid to dwell for a moment on the thoughts
that crowded upon her, for she was not one of those who
can think and yet not have her thoughts reflected upon her
face. She did not know how long she had stood in the
friendly darkness lost in deep and bitter reverie, but she
was startled and roused from it with the bewilderment of
one aroused from sleep. It was probably the effect of the
conversation in the boat that she should have grown
unduly suspicious of things about her. Two lights were
moving about in the direction of Island Bay, and on the
instant she felt unaccountably suspicious of them. She
felt that they meant something, and that that something
concerned her. The yacht was now under weigh, and the
distance between it and the shore greatly increased ; but
the breeze was blowing from the land, and Esther was
convinced she was not mistaken when she thought she
heard the vessel hailed from the shore. Dick Drugget was
standing with a rope half-coiled in his hand, and he started
too, apparently at the same sound, but seemed doubtful
whether his ears had not deceived him. He hesitated a
moment, glanced shoreward, and then went on with his

work. Presently the same sound came over the water again —only fainter; but Esther was on the alert now, and she was quite sure some one from shore was hailing the yacht. Dick Drugget had heard the hail also, and he dropped the rope and went aft. As he did so he passed close by where Esther was standing. Acting on the impulse of the moment, she placed her hand on his arm. He had been gazing as intently at the lights ashore as if they had mesmerized him, and he started at her touch.

"I beg your pardon, Mr. Drugget; did I startle you?" she said.

"I—I did not know you were on deck, miss," he said. He was confused, and let the word slip from him unawares; and then, in still greater confusion, began an incoherent something in the way of an apology.

She had her gaze turned towards the lights on the land, and did not seem to be paying the least attention to what he was saying, and broke in eagerly upon him—

"You will not stop the vessel?"

"I thought I heard a hail from ashore, ma'am." ("Ma'am," with careful distinctness.)

"It can be nothing. Some stupid joke."

"Still, a hail's a hail," he said, unanswerably.

"Yes, but who can it be? There's no one in Island Bay who can want anything of us."

"Not that I know of, there isn't," he said, with heavy impassiveness; "but something or other— -"

"And Mr. Redmayne is so anxious not to be delayed," she interrupted, anxiously.

"Yes, I know that," said Dick, doubtfully, for he still felt strongly that a hail *was* a hail. "I could ask him what he thinks."

"No, no! I had rather you didn't. I—I do not wish him to be disturbed. I am sure he would not wish any attention to be paid to every chance noise we may hear. I am sure this can only be some silly trick of some one who wishes to delay us."

"Very well, mi—that is, ma'am; if you think so, of course there's nothing more." And Dick, still unconvinced, was turning away again when he became aware of another light suddenly revealing itself to windward, and which was rapidly bearing down in their direction. The idea that they were being pursued at once occurred to Esther, and acting once more on the impulse of the moment, she stepped up beside Dick Drugget again, and said—

"Could we not put out our lights, Mr. Drugget?"

She was standing just within the radius of light thrown by the binnacle lamp. She raised her left hand as she spoke, and the light streamed full upon it as Dick turned his puzzled face towards her. . . . . There are circumstances that suggest the same train of thought to two minds, like sparks struck from the same flint. Both Esther's hands were gloved, but Dick's eyes happened to fall upon the left hand only; and though he was not naturally suspicious, and had not up till that moment even given serious thought to the murder that had been discovered that day, in some spontaneous, unaccountable way a chain of evidence pieced itself together in his mind, and drove home its conclusion with the force of an inspiration— The ring found beside the body—her acquaintance with Stadling—her three days' mysterious absence—her agitation in the boat when the murder was mentioned—her evident dread of pursuit—above all, that gloved left hand, that ring found beside the body.

Their eyes met. The process that had flashed through Dick's mind was reflected in Esther's. She drew back, and stepped out of the ring of light instantly, and without a word hurried into the cabin. As the door closed behind her she heard for the third time a hoarse hail borne across the water.

Redmayne had been dozing, but he started up as she entered. He gave one rapid glance at her face.

"Esther," he cried, "you are frightened; what has happened? What is the matter?"

"Nothing, Matthew," she said, in a faltering voice, "and —and I am not frightened."

Pale, worn, and haggard as her face had been before, it bore another expression now, after the mute, unmistakable accusation she had just encountered on deck. It was a look that at once appealed to him as something more than could be accounted for by mere bodily weariness, and he began to wonder whether after all he had made the wisest choice in bringing her with him. And then the events of the mysterious three days occurred to him, and with something that was almost a shudder he drew her close to him.

"Yes," he murmured half aloud, "it is—it must be for the best."

"What must be for the best, Matthew?" she asked.

"To have brought you with me, dear. It would break my heart if we were ever parted again."

"Nothing shall ever part us now, Matthew," she said, in desperate contradiction to the nameless fear that was rising within her heart.

"Hark!" he interrupted. "What is that? Somebody has come alongside us."

They both listened.

"Well, well," said Redmayne, relaxing from his listening attitude with easy confidence. "Dick's on deck. It'll be all right."

There was a murmur of voices, lasting for two or three minutes; a sound as of the footsteps of several people approaching the cabin; a pause, and then some one knocked.

"Come in," said Redmayne, wondering what could have happened, and Dick Drugget entered and clapped the door sharply to, and stood with his back against it.

"What's the matter, Dick? What are we stopping for?"

Dick never had a very ready supply of words at his command at any time, but at this moment he seemed more than usually at a loss. He remained leaning mute and helpless against the door, looked from Redmayne to Esther and back again, and then let his gaze drop nervously.

"Who is it that has come aboard, Dick?"

Dick raised his eyes, as if he were about to speak, but they rested on the white, scared face of Esther, and fell again. There was a restless movement outside the door. Dick straightened his legs out stiffly, planted his feet flatter and more firmly on the floor, and leaned against the door still more heavily, as if he expected resistance from outside, and was prepared to overcome it. Redmayne heard the noise and said impatiently—

"What is it, Dick? Why don't you speak? What has happened? Who is it that has come aboard?"

"It—it is something of the greatest importance to you, Mat," said Dick, in desperation at last, and speaking in short gasps; "but perhaps Mrs. Redmayne——"

"Nonsense, man; never mind Mrs. Redmayne. Let us hear what it is, and be done with it."

Dick shifted his feet again, and looked appealingly at Esther; but she avoided his glance and wound her arms more closely about her husband's neck.

"What do you say, dear?" said Redmayne, in answer to something she had whispered to him. "Don't send you away? Why, what an idea! Come, Dick, this is nonsense; what is it you want to say? Where is the use in alarming people in this senseless way? If some one has come aboard, tell us who it is."

"Well—it's the Police."

"The Police! Don't tremble, my love. It's nothing; it's some mistake. The police! Ask them to step this way."

Dick, only too glad of the opportunity, stepped out of the cabin, and a sergeant of police entered.

"Mr. Redmayne, I believe?" said the sergeant.

"Yes," said Redmayne, shortly. "Hush, my love," he whispered soothingly to Esther, who had said something to him below her breath, "it is only some foolish mistake; he will be gone directly. There is nothing to fear."

"I have come on a very unpleasant duty, Mr. Redmayne," said the sergeant.

"Let me hear what it is, please. Some mistake, I suppose."

"There is no mistake, I am sorry to say. I have a warrant to arrest your wife on a charge of wilful murder——"

A shrill scream from Esther, who sank forward a dead weight in Redmayne's arms. Redmayne tried to stagger to his feet, but fell back again. The sergeant had gained his promotion in a law-abiding community, and had never before had the privilege of arresting any one for murder. He had been in doubt when he entered the cabin whether to lay his hand upon Esther's shoulder and go through the formula of "arresting her in the Queen's name," or not. He was glad now, seeing how she had taken it, that he had not.

"Curse your infernal idiocy," cried Redmayne; "you see what you've done. If I was within arms'-length of you I'd pitch you overboard. There—a glass of brandy, quick—on the table there. Here, Dick," he shouted, "come here a moment."

The sergeant poured out a glass of brandy and gave it to Redmayne, who put it to Esther's lips.

"It's no use calling any one, or making any unnecessary disturbance," observed the sergeant. "You may be surprised," he went on, with a judicial air of making every allowance; "but the warrant's out, and I've got my duty to do."

"What!"

The sergeant beckoned, and a policeman who had been standing at the door came in.

"I have no wish to hurt your feelings, Mr. Redmayne; but I have already stated my object. I arrest Esther Redmayne on a charge of wilfully murdering Edgar Stadding, at Lowry Bay, on the 11th of June."

Redmayne started at the mention of the date.

“ When ? ” he said.

“ The 11th of June,” repeated the sergeant.

“ Let me see your warrant.”

The sergeant was oppressed with a feeling that the whole procedure had been wretchedly informal ; but the circumstances were peculiar, and he had been influenced by a certain feeling of delicacy and consideration.

“ Well, Mr. Redmayne,” he said, “ I let your friend come in, in the first place, to break it, and make things as easy and agreeable as I could all round, knowing the position you were in, and I’ve strained a point or two in your favour myself, and all the return I get is a threat to throw me overboard—an officer in the uniform of the Queen. I’m a known officer, and if the person arrested may demand to see my warrant, at least I’m not bound to show it to a third party ; but considering I *am* in a sense not within my precincts, and considering you *are* in a peculiar position why, there’s the warrant, and you’ll find it all fair, square, and above-board.”

Redmayne glanced through it, and handed it back.

“ Esther, dear girl, what is this ? ” he said. “ Speak, and clear up this horrible mistake.”

“ I warn you that whatever is said now may be used in evidence against you upon your trial,” said the sergeant to the shrinking girl, at the same time devoutly hoping that something *would* be said that might be used in evidence against her upon her trial.

“ Esther, Esther, look up ; don’t kneel like that. Speak, for heaven’s sake.”

At a sign from the sergeant the policeman had produced a pocket-book, and now stood slowly turning the tip of his pencil round and round between his lips, prepared to take notes of all that passed.

“ One thing more, sir,” said the sergeant, “ I must see the lady’s hands. Will you please remove the gloves.”

Her left hand was resting upon Redmayne’s knee. She

seemed too stunned and bewildered to speak, but she snatched her hand away, and held it behind her.

"Esther, this is folly," he cried, as she put out her right hand in dumb protest. "For your own sake—for mine—convince this man of his error, so far, at any rate."

"Better that you should do it than me, sir. Very necessary I should see the lady's hands," said the sergeant.

"I refuse to be treated in this way," cried Esther. "I refuse to be searched like this. Matthew, how can you see me——"

"Ettie, listen to me. You don't realize your position. You don't realize what you are charged with! I entreat you—I command you—let me see your left hand! Draw off your glove!"

She obeyed with one bursting sob, but still held her hand from her husband's view.

"There's no ring," exclaimed the sergeant, turning to the policeman. "Make a note of that."

"Esther, let me see your left hand!"

"*Both* hands, sir, if you please," said the remorseless sergeant, bending forward with a critical expression of face, and both his own hands clasped behind his back.

"Esther, let me see your left hand!" repeated Redmayne.

"Matthew, you do not believe Spare me——"

"Let me see your left hand!"

No tears came to her eyes, but a sob shook her whole frame as she placed her hand on her husband's knee, and then bowed her head over it.

"A-a-h! Esther, where is that ring where is the wedding ring I placed upon that hand four days ago? Answer me."

The sergeant's eyes twinkled, as much as to say he could have thrown some light upon the subject if he had liked. Esther let her head droop forward till her face rested on the hand that had betrayed her, and sobbed speechlessly.

Redmayne sat looking down upon her with an expression that baffles description; the sergeant felt that the supreme moment had come, and stood with his right arm crossed in front of him, the hand clasping his left elbow, his chin resting in the prong formed by his left forefinger and thumb; the policeman, with the note-book open in his hand, was turning the point of his pencil round and round again between his lips, ready to take more notes.

"Where is the ring, Esther?" demanded Redmayne again, his face growing hard and stern.

"I do not know," she sobbed, without lifting her head. "I cannot tell you."

"Those three days—where were you?"

"I cannot tell you."

"Did you—is it true that— There was a ring found beside the body, was there not?" said Redmayne, turning to the sergeant. "Speak out," he cried fiercely, as the sergeant hesitated.

"Well, there was," answered the sergeant, slowly; his eyes plainly adding. "Considering you *are* in a peculiar position."

"A woman's ring?"

"A woman's ring."

"A wedding ring?"

"A wedding ring."

"What else? Were there any marks on it?"

"The initials——"

The sergeant stopped abruptly. He had repeated what the numerous "extras" posted about had already made public, and his consideration for one's peculiar position could take him no further.

"I'm not at liberty to say," he replied, finally.

"Esther, Esther, for God's sake speak," cried Redmayne, carried away by his passionate excitement. "You will drive me mad. What am I to think? You own you knew this man, that he had deeply injured you——"

(The sergeant opened his mouth to repeat his warning

hesitated—could not find it in his heart to forego such telling points that might be used in evidence—considered the first warning sufficient—motioned to the policeman to go on taking notes - and relapsed again.)

——"You are away for three days for some unknown reason, and on one of them this man is killed; you refuse to say where you were, or why you went; you start and shudder when the murder is mentioned; your wedding ring is gone from your finger, and a wedding ring is found beside the body. Great Heaven, will you not speak one word to clear yourself?"

He paused and looked down at her, but she remained silent. Her convulsive sobbing had ceased. Her face was buried in her hands, and she was weeping silently.

"Esther," he cried again, shaking her as if to awake her; "speak! Where were you those three days? Only say one word, and I will believe you."

"I cannot tell you," she faltered.

"Cannot! You must! Look at me! At least say you are not—you are not——Heaven! I cannot even put it in words," he said, falling back.

"Best leave it unsaid, sir," said the considerate sergeant. "And if you've no more to say to one another, why——" and he placed his hand upon Esther's arm.

She started to her feet wildly, then seeing Redmayne did not move or speak, threw herself on her knees beside him again.

"Matthew, Matthew, at least say you do not believe me guilty!"

"Where is the ring? Where were you those three days? Tell me the truth, Esther, and I will believe you before the world." He took her hands in his, and their eyes met. For an instant she hesitated.

A prolonged whistle from the sergeant, and stooping down he stretched out a fold of her dress between his hands, his eyes riveted on what he saw there.

It was the print of a hand in blood, clearly outlined on the light material of the dress.

"Blood, as I'm a living sinner! Here, make a note of *that*, man!"

"Great Heaven! look at it!" cried Redmayne in horror. "Oh, Esther! Esther!"

PART IV.

THE REDMAYNE CASE.

XIX.

"THE Redmayne trial has now reached its third day" (wrote the Wellington correspondent of the *Evening Bell* on July 9th), "and the interest which it has attracted from its commencement is at this present moment of writing strained to its highest pitch. Indeed, I doubt if there has ever been tried before any court in New Zealand a case possessing such striking points of interest as rivet our attention in this one. It is the royal right of women to compel our interest, and it is impossible not to feel interested in the girl Esther Redmayne (for, indeed, she is little more than a girl) as she stands hour after hour, and day after day, in the prisoner's dock, while the most fatal chain of circumstantial evidence is slowly, inexorably, link by link, being fastened around her. Apart from any consideration of her guilt or innocence, her position is unspeakably sad, for she is a bride of but a few weeks' standing. Public opinion here runs strongly in the direction of a belief in her guilt. Her conduct, of course, as is usual in such cases, may be interpreted either way, just as prejudice may dictate. She is nervous and sensitive in the very last degree. It is pitiable sometimes to note the expression in her eyes as the course of the trial sets more and more strongly against her—as it is most unmistakably doing. Often she will start and press her hand to her side as if she had suffered a spasm of actual physical pain. This was especially the case when the witness Hetherwick was giving her evidence

—evidence, too, which was given with such an appearance of spitefulness, and with such uncalled-for insinuations, that she had to be checked more than once from the Bench. Words seem at times on the point of bursting from the prisoner's white, tremulous lips; but whatever they may be, they are never uttered; and she shrinks back into herself with a kind of shudder, and looks round the court with a helpless, hunted look, as if she had for the moment forgotten herself and her position. This silence, which she persists in maintaining, is the most extraordinary part of her conduct. She literally refuses to make an effort to defend herself, even when that effort, one would think, might be most advantageously made. It is only reasonable to suppose that she has sufficiently strong reasons for the course she pursues; but, as far as I can see, there is only one possible effect it can have, alike upon judge, jury, and public at large.

"The best legal advice has been secured for her by her husband; but the keenest intellect might well be staggered at the mass of condemnatory evidence to be grappled with. A glance at it will show its nature. The theory of the prosecution is that a quarrel had occurred between prisoner and Stadding, arising out of previous relations that had existed between them;—and that they were on more or less familiar terms will be found borne out by the evidence of the witness Hetherwick. A letter received by prisoner shortly before the murder was committed and concerning which she maintained the utmost reserve, even when questioned by her closest friend, a Miss Winterson, saying it conveyed 'bad news from a friend,' and that she was 'not free to speak' as to what it contained is supposed in reality to have contained obnoxious proposals from Stadding. Whatever relations may have existed between Stadding and prisoner previously, it is natural the latter would be exasperated at a reference to them immediately after she had contracted an advantageous match a match, too, it is pointed out, that had been kept secret till the

very last moment. A menace being thus held over her
head, she availed herself of her husband's absence to seek
out Stadding, with the result that she took the most
summary way of for ever ridding herself of him.

"How far this agrees with the facts will be seen. Stadding,
the murdered man, put up at the Truss o' Straw, at the
Hutt, at about six or half-past on the afternoon of the 11th
June, and he left the hotel again at about eleven o'clock at
night; so that the murder must have taken place between
that hour and five on the morning of the twelfth, when the
body was found. Now, Esther Redmayne received the
letter I have mentioned a day or two before the arrival of
Stadding in town. In consequence of this letter she absents
herself for three days and two nights (from the morning of
the tenth of June to the evening of the twelfth) from the
house where she was staying; and she refuses to say one
word as to where she was, or what she did during those
three days.

"On the evening of the eleventh—the night of the murder
—Esther Redmayne was seen by a girl named Sarah Bundle
to step out of one of the carriages of the 5 p.m. train on to
the platform of the Wellington Railway Station. It is
known that Stadding was also a passenger by this train
the obvious inference being, of course, that she was following him. It seems the girl Bundle was the bearer of a
letter from her mistress to her mistress's son, who lives at
Monk's Bridge. She had to call at the station on her way,
and while there she happened to see the gentleman to whom
she was to deliver the letter, and gave it to him at once.
It was dusk at the time, and a high wind was blowing;
and what with the buffeting of the wind, and the confusion
of the people moving about on the platform, she declares
she would never have been able to recognize Esther Redmayne at all—and so an important piece of evidence might
have been lost—had it not been for an ostrich feather
which the latter was in the habit of wearing in her hat,
and which had, indeed, been given to her by the brother of

this very girl Bundle. The crowd prevented her getting near enough to speak, but she is positive it was Esther Redmayne she saw. (The hat, with the ostrich feather, and the dress in which Esther Redmayne was arrested, were produced in Court, and the girl identified them at once as those worn by the prisoner on the occasion in question.) It was only by dint of searching cross-examination that what this witness knew could be obtained from her; her nervousness and confusion preventing her giving anything in the way of voluntary evidence. She had been a friend of prisoner's, and cried bitterly when she saw the effect her evidence had produced.

"When the prisoner left the house on the tenth she had a wedding ring on her finger. When she returned on the twelfth that ring was missing. Strange to say a wedding ring was found beside the body of the dead man, which not only fitted prisoner's finger to a nicety, but inside it was engraved a monogram containing the letters 'M.R., E.R.,' which correspond with the initials of 'Matthew Redmayne' and 'Esther Redmayne,' while Mr. Hugh Bittlejohn, the well-known jeweller of Lambton Quay, positively identified the ring as one he sold to Mr. Redmayne, by its unusual breadth, and the initials which he engraved upon it in accordance with Mr. Redmayne's orders.

"The crowning piece of evidence, however, was yet to come. It was that of the policeman who had arrested prisoner. He deposed that she refused even to tell her husband where she had been, and that he (the constable) had found outlined on her dress the distinct imprint of a man's hand in blood. The dress was again produced with the stain upon it, and caused an immense sensation. In addition to this, the evidence of a certain Mrs. Hetherwick went to show that an understanding of some kind had existed for some time between Stadding and Esther Redmayne, and that the latter had been turned away from her situation at The Peak because that understanding had become a little too plainly displayed.—What did she mean by that?—Well, she had once found them talking together in the garden very shortly after the prisoner's arrival at The Peak, and Stadding had been much put out at the conversation being interrupted. They were on much more friendly terms than is usual with persons who have only known one another twenty-four hours.—Was it because of such a trifling incident that prisoner was turned away?—Well, she was turned away at a moment's notice by her mistress—Mrs. Shaw—because her mistress had thought it best in the interests of all parties that prisoner should not remain any longer in the house. (At this point the Court adjourned for the day.)"

   *   *   *   *   *   *

"Surprise" (says the report on the following day) "is not the word to express the feeling of the public here when the verdict of the jury was announced to-day. As far as my experience goes, there was not a single person, who had paid any attention to the course of the trial at all, but expected a verdict of guilty; and yet the jury, after long and presumably careful consideration of all the points in the case, and after listening to a summing up on the part of the judge, which apparently left no loophole of escape for the prisoner, have seen fit to bring in a verdict of Not Guilty, and Esther Redmayne was permitted to step out of the dock a free woman once more.

"No further evidence beyond that telegraphed yesterday was taken, and the day's proceedings were comprised by the speech of the Crown Prosecutor, and the reply of the defending lawyer. The former contented himself with the mere enumeration of the most telling points in the evidence, apparently regarding the conclusion to which they pointed as being too plainly self-evident to need strengthening. He might point out one thing. He had already had occasion to show that the probabilities against the ring being any other than that of prisoner were simply incalculable. It was now attempted to show that great muscular strength would be required to deal the blow that resulted in Stadding's death. Now, they knew that the blow had been delivered on the side of the temple of deceased—the most vulnerable part of the head, and where a well-planted blow by a vigorous child would be quite sufficient to cause death, much more easily a blow by an enraged woman.

"The defending lawyer made the best of an unfortunate position. He was plainly hampered by the obstinate reserve of the prisoner. The fact of her whereabouts on the day of the murder, as far as it had been stated in that Court, he maintained, had literally no significance whatever. To regard her absence from Fernridge as evidence of her presence at Lowry Bay, where the murder had taken place, was absurd. The one obvious thing to do was to prove that she had been either at Lowry Bay, or at any rate in the vicinity, and this had not been attempted;—and for the best possible reason—she had never been there. Again, her happening to be in the same train as Stadding was no more to be looked upon as evidence that she was following him, than it was evidence that any one else in the train was following him. He admitted that the finding of the ring beside the body and the absence of the ring from prisoner's finger was a coincidence, but nothing more than a coincidence. Such freaks of circumstance occurred every day, and were familiar to everybody. Besides, one wedding ring was as like another wedding ring, as one pea was like another. Mr. Bittlejohn might easily be mistaken in such a thing as a wedding ring. The letters engraved on the ring might stand for ten thousand other names besides those of prisoner and her husband. He must impress upon the jury the necessity of putting from their minds at once and for ever all consideration of such an arbitrary construction, and be guided only by the facts vital to the case. The mark of the hand, too, must be held to prove nothing. It was the mark of a human hand, and no more. What man would have the audacity to declare it was Stadding's hand? There was absolutely nothing to distinguish it from any other hand. If Stadding's hand had had any peculiarity or deformity, and that peculiarity or deformity had been reproduced in the imprint of the hand, then, and then only, could it be regarded as incriminating evidence in the case. Besides, he maintained that the blow which had caused deceased's death could never have been struck by the weak hand of a woman, whatever his learned friend might say to the contrary. It was a blow requiring considerable muscular strength, and could only have been delivered, if not by a man, at any rate by some one of much more powerful physique than the prisoner. Briefly, this was the substance of his address. It was weak, and every one regarded it as weak. The strongest point in the whole address was the appeal on behalf of the prisoner's youth, her unblemished reputation, and the peculiar pathos of her position.

"The jury were absent from Court about two hours and a half, and on returning the foreman pronounced the verdict I have indicated. And so ends the great Redmayne case."

In its leading columns on the 11th July the same journal makes the following comments on the case :—

". . . . . . . This has been, from beginning to end, a most extraordinary case; and though we must accept the verdict the jury have brought in, after, we doubt not, the most conscientious consideration, and though we are prepared to give the suspected person the benefit of whatever doubt the twelve gentlemen may suppose to have existed, we make bold to say that there can be no moral doubt but that she who yesterday stood in the dock was guilty of the most heinous crime known to the law. We consider that the evidence brought forward during the trial, if we are to give circumstantial evidence any weight at all, justifies us in saying that the verdict declares nothing more than a mere technical innocence. It is the crying evil of our criminal jurisprudence that it is possible for the law to be thus nullified—that the judicial acceptance of the solution to which the evidence pointed with such absolute conclusiveness should be rendered impossible on what every thinking man and woman must be convinced were, from a moral point of view, utterly inadequate grounds. We have never, happily, had occasion to speak in such terms before; we trust it may never fall to our lot to be compelled to do so again; but we should consider ourselves unworthy of the position we hold in the eyes of the public if we spoke in less trenchant terms than we have. We feel that in this verdict of Not Guilty, we have thrust upon us that which our consciousness of right cannot endorse; that which is an indication of inefficiency in our law, and that which is inimical to the best interests of society. It is to say in so many words, that the laws are framed not to eradicate crime itself, but rather to punish unskilfulness in its committal."

PART V.

THE ENLIGHTENMENT OF MATTHEW REDMAYNE.

XX.

On the 24th of April, three years after the events recorded in the last chapter, Matthew Redmayne, the junior partner of the firm of Redmayne, Redmayne & Co., Levuka, Fiji, locked his door, and remained shut up in his own room from the hour at which the post had been delivered, early in the afternoon, till far past midnight. On that day Esther's diary and confession, which have been open to the reader from the commencement of this story, were for the first time placed in his hands and read by him. Since the day of their separation, he had not even known what had become of his wife. He had heard, indeed, that she had gone back to live with Miss Dorothy Ann, and then that they had gone away from Island Bay. But feeling that they who were the declared friends of the guilty woman he had called his wife, could no longer be his friends, he had never seen or heard from the old lady again. No communication had passed between him and Esther since the day of the trial, save one, which was handed to her on the very day of her acquittal—an offer to make provision for her on his side, and a gently-worded but unmistakable refusal to entertain the proposal on hers—and like all the rest of the world he had believed her guilty, and they had drifted out of one another's experience. How else could things have been? With the array of facts against her on the one hand, and her silence on the other, what could he think but that he had placed his affections upon the falsest and guiltiest of women—one whose memory he owed it to his manhood to thrust from his heart for ever. For three years he had schooled himself to forgetfulness. He had seized eagerly upon everything that promised change of scene and occupation. He had travelled, travelled, travelled. He would have scorned himself had he allowed the old love to assert itself even for a moment in his breast. His belief in her guilt had been too complete for that. The very recollection of her name had brought a sense of loathing and horror. He had thought how on the last night when they were together, while his heart swelled with a joy beyond words at their re-union, while he kissed her and caressed her, while he rested unquestioningly in the belief that she loved him with the single-hearted affection with which he loved her, she bore the guilt of murder in her heart, and on her very dress the hideous brand of her crime; her eyes had looked into his, he thought, with the reflection of the love that shone in his own, while the brain behind them was scheming to make him the dupe of a murderess.

And yet she was innocent.

The manuscript that had brought this revelation to him was lying scattered about on the table. He took up the accompanying letter, and began to read it again—

"MY DEAR HUSBAND,

"When you read this your wife of a day will be dead. . . . ."

He could go no further, and his hand shook as he put the letter on the table again. She was dead. He rose and paced up and down his room, as he had been doing mechanically for hours already. The first shock of the revelation of his wife's innocence, and the groundlessness of his own suspicions, had brought with it a confusion and paralysis of thought. That had worn off now, and he began to feel the firm earth beneath his feet again. He thought of the three

years' martyrdom he had suffered, and that his wife (he
loved to think of her as his wife again, now) had suffered
also.　He thought of the chain of evidence that had
deceived everybody, and that had made him too the dupe of
his own senses ; he thought of the wealth of womanly love
and purity that he had thrust out of his life, and which he
had only learned to prize now it was for ever removed from
him.　He cursed the bitterness of the fate that condemned
him to all this, and that tantalized him with the knowledge
of the truth only when the warm loving heart was cold and
still in death, which had been true to him while he had so
cruelly doubted it, and which, had he only known, might
have beaten against his once more, as it had done in the
short sweet dream of their early love.　He was too full of a
sad satisfaction at the knowledge that the woman he had
so often told himself he should learn to loathe and scorn
was after all worthy—more than worthy—of the best and
strongest love a man could bestow, to feel one thought of
reproach against her, now that she was dead, because she
had allowed her love for her sister to make her forget what
she owed her husband.　He blamed what he called his own
suspicious nature.　He should have known her character
well enough to be convinced it was impossible she could be
the guilty criminal he had taught himself to believe her.
He blamed the blind chance that had woven this fatal web
of circumstance around them.　He cursed the villainy of
Stadding, which, in rebounding upon his own head, and
bringing about his own retribution, had spread its effects
beyond his death, and blighted the lives of others, who had
scarcely even been aware of his existence.　.　.　.　.　.　.

The hands of the clock stole silently round the dial.　In
the east a faint opal light was shuddering among the mists
that hung above the horizon.　The chilly atmosphere of the
room roused him.　He shivered and looked up at the clock,
noticing the hour with a vague wonder at his abstraction.
The window was slightly open, and a cold breath of air stole
into the room and rustled the loose sheets of Esther's

manuscript, which still lay strewed about the table as he had tossed them from him in the excitement of reading, and he gathered them reverently together. His lips trembled as his glance rested on the words—"When this reaches your hand the grave will have hidden all the faults and follies of your loving wife, Esther." All the bitterness the thought that she was dead could bring, he had felt as he paced all night about his room ; but he sighed again as he read the words, and raised the paper to his lips and kissed it.

In his agitation he had not noticed it before, but it now occurred to him that there had been no address given in either letter or diary. He looked hurriedly through the leaves again, and not finding what he wanted, laid them by, and took up the wrapper in which the packet had been enclosed. It bore the New Plymouth post-mark. And, as he raised his eyes, he looked out to where, in the dim morning light he could see the masts of his yacht cutting the sky in two dark filmy lines.

"At least, I will see where they have laid her," he said to himself. And then he put the manuscript away in his drawer and locked it.

In former days he would simply have gone on board, and set sail ; but times were altered now. His father, who had been the founder of the firm and its moving spirit for many a long year, was no more. He had died three years ago, and his place had been taken by his brother. Matthew had succeeded to an interest in the business as junior partner, but it was only within the last few months that he had settled down to work, and really taken upon himself the responsibilities of the position ; and never did those responsibilities thrust themselves upon him as they did to-day. It was evening before he was free to make his preparations for sailing, and it was morning again before the *Meg Merrilies* finally stood out to sea, and left the Fijian coast dwindling in the distance astern.

XXI.

" Miss Winterson."

" Matthew!" Miss Dorothy Ann was about to enter at her gate, but she let it close again with a snap as she gave Redmayne her hand; and there was a glance of keen scrutiny in her eyes as she looked up in his face.

" You did not expect me?" he said, with an air of embarrassment.

"I did not know what to think," said Miss Dorothy Ann, with an appearance of even greater embarrassment on her side, and looking rather doubtfully in his face. " I was not even sure that you knew she was with me, or whether you knew where we were."

" I knew she was with you, and though she made no mention of her whereabouts in her letter, I found out by the post-mark where you were. I knew that though her husband had failed to do his duty, you had more than done yours," he added, his voice trembling under his sense of gratitude; "and that you had taken her under your protection in spite of all the world might say ——"

" Nonsense, Matthew! Don't come talking sentiment to an old woman like me," said the old lady, reassured by his tone. " As for suspecting her—why, it is nonsense blaming yourself at this time of day; not being inspired you couldn't do anything else, as things fell out, as far as I can see. *I* should have done the same if she hadn't told me herself they were wrong," she added, simply.

" Did you never wonder that she did not give me the same assurance as she did you, and that we never saw one another after?"

" A simple assurance of innocence," said Miss Dorothy Ann, shrewdly, and in a tone bordering on reproof, " you would not have believed, Matthew. I've known you from a boy, you know. You always *were* so self-willed. Why she did not send the packet before—or, indeed, what was in it when she did send it, I am not quite sure ; but I trust it has let you understand the truth——"

"It has cleared up everything—everything," he said, looking up quickly.

"Thank God for that," said Miss Dorothy Ann, earnestly, and taking Redmayne's hand again in both of hers. "Thank God that things have come right at last. Oh, the sad, sad time it must have been for you ; I know what it was for her."

"I know it comes with a bad grace from me to thank you for all you have done for her, Miss Winterson, seeing how ready I was to believe in her guilt and desert her at the first breath of suspicion ; but believe me I do thank you——"

"There, there," said Miss Dorothy Ann, waving off any more thanks with her hands, " you have nothing to thank me for, Matthew, nor has she. We had been the best of friends before that terrible trial, why should we not be afterwards, for, as I say, she told me she was innocent. She did not tell me all her story mind you till just before her last illness ; but she told me she was innocent, and that was enough. We just fell back into the old positions we held when we first came to know one another ; and though I knew she was never happy, she kept up a brave heart under it all, and we both did what we could. Ah! Mat, Mat, my poor fellow," said Miss Dorothy Ann, patting him on the shoulder maternally, "there is only one recompense I could wish for, and that is to see you happy once more."

"Me happy! There is not a more impossible thing under heaven than that, Miss Winterson," he said, sadly. " Ah, what a fool I've been ! If I had only known the story that diary contained before ; if I had only had a hint of the truth, how different both our lives might have been. And now ——"

"And now," said Miss Dorothy Ann, cheerfully, "there's all the future before you."

"There is all the Past before me, Miss Winterson, with all the reproach and torture it will bring ; but whatever it may be, I deserve it. Miss Winterson," he said, his voice faltering, and his eyes moist, "you have had her near you for years ; you've read her character from day to day, as I have had it laid open to me in the diary she sent me. I have read her love for *me* there in language in which a woman only speaks to her own heart, and which makes that love doubly precious to me, and my madness to doubt her the more insupportable to think of. I know now, in some degree, what she must have suffered through my unworthy suspicion of her these last three years. While I have been looking upon myself as a wronged and injured man, and trying to execrate her very name as the cause of it, all the wrong and injury have been hers. She would have given her life for my sake, and I—I made hers miserable by suspicion and neglect."

"Well, well, Matthew," said Miss Dorothy Ann, with practical philosophy that jarred upon him almost painfully, and patting him on the shoulder again, "it's all over now, and it's no use crying over spilt milk. Of course it looks foolish, now we know the truth, not to have seen it at once. But as for that, you know she would be the first to forgive you —if there was anything to forgive, and forget all about it."

"Yes, I know only too well how ready she was to forgive and to sacrifice herself ; and it is that that adds tenfold to the bitterness of what I feel when I know that the explanation she has given has come too late for her happiness and mine— too late to make amends for the past."

"How too late?" said the old lady, with a look of vague apprehension, and with what seemed to Redmayne an uncharacteristic want of feeling in her manner. "What has happened ?"

"What has happened! Can you ask ?" he said, reproachfully.

"Yes, I really do ; I don't understand you," she said, the look of apprehension deepening on her face.

"You must surely know what I have come for," he said, sadly.

"I supposed—I had hoped—to see Esther," faltered Miss Dorothy Ann.

"To see her grave, rather."

"Her grave!" cried Miss Dorothy Ann, starting, and looking at him in hopeless bewilderment.

"Do not think to spare me by hiding the truth, Miss Winterson. I know the worst. I know she is dead, and that I shall never see my darling again."

"Dead!" cried Miss Dorothy Ann again, grasping the top of the picket fence as if she were in danger of falling to the ground from sheer amazement. "Never see her again!"

"There is some terrible mistake, surely. Is she *not* dead?"

"Is who not dead?"

"Esther—my wife!"

There was a sound from the direction of the house of a door being opened and closed, and then of light footsteps approaching along the gravel walk.

"Esther dead! Whoever heard of such a thing! Why, bless the man, no! Use your eyes," said Miss Dorothy Ann.

A vision in white suddenly revealed itself from the other side of the garden hedge, and then stopped abruptly as if turned into stone.

Redmayne took a step towards the vision in white, and then stopped abruptly as if also turned into stone.

"Matthew!" cried the vision in white, thinking it was being imposed on by another vision.

"Esther!" cried Matthew, thinking it was indeed nothing but a vision.

But each was too completely overcome by amazement to move a step towards the other.

"Well, it isn't often one has to introduce husband and wife to one another," said Miss Dorothy Ann, in exceeding good spirits, but still lost in bewilderment at what was going on—or rather, perhaps, at what was *not* going on— "but here's a wife writes and explains everything to her husband's and everybody else's satisfaction, and then can't believe her eyes when he comes himself in answer to it; and here's a husband who makes a personal visit in answer to his wife's letter, expresses a wish to see her grave, and can't believe his own eyes when he finds she's not dead. Upon my word, I'll have to make you known to one another. Mr. Redmayne, your wife, Mrs. Esther Redmayne; Mrs. Redmayne, your husband, Mr. Matthew Redmayne. Ah, now you're acting more like sane people," for Esther, having found that Redmayne was not a vision, and Redmayne, having found that the vision in white was actually his wife in the flesh, an interesting and incoherent little scene was going on in the friendly shelter of the hedge, which made the presence of a third person unnecessary, and Miss Dorothy Ann went inside accordingly.

.   .   .   .   .   . Suddenly, Redmayne woke up to the fact that his wife hung like lead upon his arm, and that her eyes were filled with tears.

"What, crying, my darling! Why, what is it, Ettie? Tell me."

She struggled free from him, and, throwing herself on a garden seat, hid her face in her hands and wept bitterly —not tears of joy at their meeting, but bitter tears of shame and sorrow.

"Ettie, my darling, tell me what has happened. I cannot bear to see you weep like this," he said, seating himself beside her, and taking one of her hands in his.

"I have forgotten myself—we should not have seen one another—you should not have come," she sobbed.

"I have forgotten *myself*, Ettie," he said gravely, "and I have come to make what atonement I can for the past. Say at least that you forgive me."

"Forgive! You ask *me* to forgive *you!* Oh, Matthew, do not add to my grief and shame by saying that. Do not make me scorn myself more bitterly than I do now for the ruin I have worked in your life."

"But, my dear Ettie, I do say that. Up till a few days

ago no one believed that vile suspicion against you more fully than I did. Until I learnt the truth—until your packet came ——"

"My packet—what packet?"

"Your diary that you sent——"

"I sent no diary."

"You did, my dear; and it has brought me back to you with deeper love than ever I have felt before, and to try and give you the happiness in the future we have both been robbed of in the past."

"But I sent no diary. I have not the slightest remembrance of it," said Esther, rising from her seat and looking down at him in perplexity. "It- it is not—my diary is in my room now."

"It came to hand, I assure you; and now I think of it, Miss Winterson mentioned it only a few minutes ago," said Redmayne, feeling the mystery thickening around him.

She stood for a minute or two thinking, her brows drawn together, and one hand, which Redmayne noticed looked very thin and white, as if after a long illness, resting on the back of the seat, her face flushing and paling alternately.

"Let us go in, Matthew," she said presently, without looking at him, and Redmayne, wondering in masculine bewilderment at the change that had come over her since their first greeting, drew her arm within his and they went into the house together. Miss Winterson met them at the door of the drawing-room, and Esther left them to go to her room. In a few minutes she returned, and looking into the drawing-room saw that Redmayne was alone. He was looking at something on the mantelpiece, and had his back turned towards her. She went up to him with a certain feverish decision, and placing her hand upon his shoulder, said sadly :

"Matthew, dear Matthew, I am doomed to ruin your life."

He had a shell in his hand, and as he turned his head

and saw the expression on her face, the shell slipped from his fingers and shattered itself against the fender.

At the same moment Miss Dorothy Ann re-entered the room, and Esther turned to her and said—

"While I was ill, Miss Winterson, was there anything I did that was—that you thought unusual, or did not understand?—while I was delirious, I mean. I have been ill, you know, Matthew," she said to him, "but I am better again now."

"No, my dear, nothing that I can remember," said Miss Dorothy Ann, turning a housewifely eye upon the fractured pieces of her shell, as they lay upon the floor.

"The packet that Matthew received," said Esther, hesitatingly, as if confused by some vague recollection which she could not fix in her mind—"it is not in my drawer; could it have been sent away then?"

"Yes, my dear, you sent it away yourself."

"I?"

"Yes; one night you had been asleep, and suddenly woke up and asked me to bring you the packet I would find in one of the drawers in your room. I brought it and you addressed it, and I had it posted for you in the morning."

"And—and was I quite sensible at the time?"

"You had not been a few hours before, and you were not a few hours afterwards; but you seemed quite sensible then."

"Can you recollect what I said?"

"Not very clearly," said Miss Dorothy Ann slowly, removing her gaze from her ruined ornament to Esther's face, and putting on the tense look of one who is trying to recall a half-forgotten scene to memory. "There was one thing, though; I asked whether I should not write a note to go with it, explaining under what circumstances it was sent; but you would not hear of it, and begged me to send it just as it was, saying all that required explaining would be found explained in the packet. I did not think it was wise, but I saw that the subject distressed you, and did not refer to it again."

" And did I never refer to it afterwards myself ?"

"No, my dear; never! Nor did I for the reason I have already given."

" I can't recollect it at all," said Esther, in a troubled voice, looking down at the floor, and twisting her handkerchief about in her hands. " It is very strange."

"I hope it is nothing you regret, dear," said Miss Dorothy Ann, with a puzzled look from one to the other, and a return of the apprehension she had felt while talking to Redmayne by the gate.

" Oh no, nothing, Miss Winterson, only—only it was strange it should have happened." She looked appealingly at Redmayne, and Miss Dorothy Ann, noticing the look, and guessing there were mutual explanations to be made, left them together again.

"Forgive me for causing you this new distress, Matthew," said Esther, speaking in a dry, constrained, steady voice, and gazing straight before her in an effort to preserve her self-possession. " You see how it arose. I had not intended that it should reach your hand till I was dead; but fortune has ordered otherwise. I had been often thinking about what I had written just before I fell ill. There was something I had intended to add to it ; and in my delirium I must have done what I would never have permitted myself to do if I had been in my right mind. I have been away for the last day or two—since I got well again, at a friend of Miss Winterson's ; but even if I had been at home I should never have found out that I had sent the packet away, for it has been laid aside in a drawer by itself—a drawer I have not opened for months."

" And you are quite well again now? You don't look strong," he said, looking down at her pale face.

"Quite well again now," she said, as if she had scarcely heard him. " Oh, Matthew, I do so wish this had not happened."

"But what is there to regret, my love? Had your intention of keeping your narrative by you till you were dead been permitted to be carried out—and I thank God it was not—it would have meant a life of misery and wretchedness for both of us. As it is, your actions have been over-ruled by a wise Providence, and we have been brought together again."

"Yes," she said, tearfully, and still twisting her handkerchief about, "we have been brought together, but only to part again."

"My dear girl, what are you saying?" cried Redmayne, reproachfully, and looking at her as if she was not altogether free from delirium even yet. "After all we have gone through, can you find it in your heart to regret doing that which has cleared away the clouds that were between us, and shown us the truth about one another?"

"No, Matthew, Heaven knows I do not; but I do regret doing what must give us the pain of a second parting. Do not make my task harder, or ourselves more miserable by reproaches or arguments, Matthew," she went on, pushing her hair from her forehead and speaking very rapidly, as if she doubted her own resolution, and feared it would fail her. "It must be—we must part. Let us get it over as soon as we can. I am glad, Matthew—very, very glad—that you have had your suspicions removed; but I can only repeat now what you have already read in my confession. Let us—let us say good-bye, and go our different ways and—and forget one another," she said, with a sob.

Redmayne looked at her with the most intense surprise.

"Esther, my dear girl," he said, slowly, and with a return of his old stubbornness, "this is mere mid-summer madness. I haven't the slightest intention of going away till you go with me. I left you on shore the first time, and lost you; I took you with me in the yacht the second time, and lost you again; I find you for the third time, and you try to slip through my fingers once more. In

all seriousness, my love, what are you thinking of, and what
do you think I'm made of?"

She waited with nervous impatience, and broke in almost
before he had finished speaking

"Matthew, you have not thought in what position you
and I stand to one another;—I have. It is no use closing
our eyes to things, and telling ourselves they don't exist.
We can't live our lives over again; we can't recall the
past; we must just abide by it. Oh, my love, my love,"
she said, bursting into tears, and all the resolution that
had supported her thus far deserting her. "I wish—I wish
I were dead rather than I should give you one fresh
distress. I have caused you so much—*so much* sorrow. It
breaks my heart to know I must cause you still more."

"Cheer up, my love," he said, taking her in his arms
and kissing her tenderly. "Try and think of the past as
lightly as I do—though I know how much harder it must
have been for you than for me."

"No! no! Hear what I have to say," she said, removing
his arms gently and resuming her former tone. "I must
be true to myself, and true to you for your own sake. Let
us go back to the time of the trial. You remember all that
passed, and pardon me for saying it, Matthew: I must—
you believed me guilty."

"Forgive me, darling. I did."

"I know you loved me then, Matthew," she went on,
interrupting him, for she felt that her woman's fortitude
would fail her again if she let him say more, "and if you
who loved me and knew me so well were forced to suspect
me in spite of yourself, what must the world think?"

"That for the world," he said, snapping his fingers airily.

"Ah, yes; it's all very well to snap your fingers; but I
cannot for your sake and my own look at it in that way,
Matthew. I—I *burn* when I think what the papers said
about me. Beyond yourself and Miss Winterson there is
not a man or woman who has heard of the case who does
not believe me a guilty woman. I would sooner die than

let you bring the reproach upon yourself of having it said
that you were united to one everybody believes to be a—a
murderess."

" Esther," he said, knitting his brows heavily, " I will
not listen to you—I will not hear you speak like that.
You are my wife. *I* know the truth, and I swear the
world shall know the truth as I know it. I will have
justice done. I will make the facts known from one end
of the land to the other."

She held up her hand imploringly to stop him, and then
pressed it over her heart as if in pain.

" Neither of us has anything to prove the truth, Matthew.
You know what I have said is true; Miss Winterson knows
it is true; but who else is there but would look at it
as a plausible falsehood? Matthew, dear, dear Matthew,
let us face the truth at once. I—I had trusted that this
scene would never have happened. I thought our last
parting was over three years ago. I would never have
written what I did if I had thought—if I had thought——
Oh, Matthew!" she cried, wringing her hands, "think as
I do. Realize that it is impossible. We can never be man
and wife but in name. We must not see one another again.
Let it be as if you had never learned the truth and—and
leave me. I cannot bear it."

" Esther," he said, with suppressed passionateness, " for
three years I have looked upon you as you say the world
looks upon you now. My life was aimless, objectless,
miserable, for want of your love. I have been pressed—
forgive me saying this; but I am pleading for what is more
to me than my life itself—I have been pressed by those
who were as blind as I was to the truth about Stadding's
murder, to get—to—to free myself in the one way in which
I could obtain freedom——"

"I am prepared to hear all you have to say, dear
Matthew," she said humbly. " This is no time for affectation between us. You have been urged to get a divorce
from me. I know. Go on."

"I refused to do it. I said 'No; let it rest. There is only one woman in the world to me. If she can only be my wife in name, so be it. No other shall be my wife in reality.' At the end of those three years my eyes are opened to the truth. I find that my wife is the noblest and purest woman that ever breathed. I come and offer again the love you accepted before things happened to separate us, and you throw me off like this. It is unjust; it is cruel. I have not deserved it."

"But, Matthew," she pleaded, piteously, "try and see it from my side too. I know how hard it is on you—on us both. I know you may think it unjust and cruel."

"It is cruel. It's unreasonable."

"Matthew, do not—do not be so hard with me. I have not sought this interview. It is as painful to me as it can be to you. I am not very strong," she said, passing her thin, shaking hand across her eyes. "I am not able to argue. I have suffered much, and tried to suffer in silence. If my voice has reached you, it is not my fault. It is not for my own sake I am speaking. I have done much, I know, to ruin your life, and I will do no more. I have made up my mind to be truer to you than you would be to yourself. I feel I should ruin it altogether if I consented to your wishes."

"Forgive me, Ettie, if I have seemed hard. I did not mean to be. If I spoke strongly, it was because I love strongly—ah! you don't know how strongly. You do not know what you are asking me to give up when you ask me to give you up."

"But it must be, Matthew;—it must be."

"No, Esther, it must not be. I will not have it so. We have suffered enough—you and I—for faults that are not our own. We have our own rights to consider. You forget that you are my wife. And I refuse to let any one come between us. Who was this contemptible wretch, Stadding, that the results of what he has done should be allowed to part us like this?"

"It is not Stadding," she said, sadly, but still clinging to her point. "It is for my sister's sake, and for yours, and my own. I have been through the ordeal once. I could not face it again ; and to do what you require would set the country ringing with the story afresh."

"But am I not to be considered? Is my happiness a shuttlecock, to be bandied hither and thither at mere caprice like this? If the story is to be known, let it. Let guilty be guilty, and the innocent be innocent. Why should those who have not done the wrong bear the consequences?" He was thinking only of Stadding ; she thought only of Catherine.

"But consider—it would be to take the guilt from my shoulders to put it upon those of my poor sister, and make her sad story the gossip of the whole country."

He was about to answer, but checked himself and bit his lip in silence.

.   .   .   .   .   . "Is that your final answer, Esther?" he asked quietly at last.

"Yes, Matthew ; I cannot do otherwise. Let us part. Why prolong this interview? It can do no good, and is painful to us both. Believe me, dear, it pains me to the heart to act as I am doing ; but when you have grown happier and forgotten me you will acknowledge to yourself that the kindest act I ever did, and my truest love for you was shown when I refused to link my disgrace with your honest name."

"No, my dear, you are wrong. I will not permit you to ruin your own life and mine like this. You shall not bear a guilt that is not your own. There is only one way, and that is for me to find out the truth more fully, and to make that truth known. Do not think me hard upon you, my love. I am not. I am only preventing you committing an injustice upon yourself and upon others."

"No, no, Matthew ; give it up. Learn to forget me ; I am not worthy. Let me drop out of your life. Spare me —spare those I love from fresh distress——"

"Those you love? And what of me, Esther; am I not one of those you love?" he asked, reproachfully.

Her eyes filled with tears, and her face flushed crimson.

"I do not know what I am saying. Heaven knows I do love you, and desire nothing more keenly than your happiness, and it is that I am trying to bring about."

"Good-bye, Ettie," he said, holding out his hands as if he had formed his final resolution. "Happiness and you must come together."

She stood a moment struggling to control herself, and then threw herself into his arms, and laid her head on his breast.

"The last time, Matthew dear—the last time," she whispered.

"No, my love," he answered, as he bent over her, "not the last time. When I come to you again as I have to-day, you shall stand as pure in the eyes of the world as you do in mine. Till then, good-bye."

"Dear Matthew," she said, throwing her arms round his neck in a last appeal, "do not try to seek the truth any further; let it rest for poor Catherine's sake—for mine."

"For yours and mine, Ettie," he said, gently and firmly, gazing back into her eyes, "I cannot. I owe it to you. I owe it to myself. Till then, good-bye."

He lifted her up and placed her upon the sofa. His lips were pressed passionately to hers for a moment, and then he left the room.

She started up with a half-formed intention of recalling him, uttered his name, and then stood still irresolutely. The door was swinging to: it wavered a moment as she called to him, and then closed. Footsteps passed down the passage, and she was alone. She hesitated whether to try and overtake him before he left the house; took a step towards the door with that intention, and then paused again; and as she paused the door was re-opened, and Miss Dorothy Ann entered.

"My dear, you have excited yourself," she said, kindly,

putting her arm round her, and leading her to the sofa, from which she had just started up. "This has been too much for you so soon after your illness."

"Oh, Miss Winterson, has he gone?" she said, almost hysterically. "I have so much to tell him that I left unsaid, and perhaps I may never have another opportunity."

"Yes, Ettie, he has gone," said Miss Dorothy Ann, looking at her companion in a grave, motherly way. "He met me in the passage, and asked me to come to you. But do not distress yourself; you will see him again soon, and you can tell him then, when you are calmer, and more yourself than you are now, what he has not heard. Do you think, my dear," she went on, stroking Esther's hair back from her forehead, "that you have acted quite wisely in what you have done to-day?"

"Did he—did he tell you?" asked Esther, timidly.

"He only dropped a word; but I can tell from what I saw on his face, and what I see on yours, what the result of your interview has been. I am afraid that all this has come upon us so unexpectedly that none of us have acted as we should have done, if we had had time to form a second thought on the subject. And what a strange thing that he should come here with his mind quite made up that you were dead. How was that?"

"It was the letter I sent with the diary. I had not intended that it should reach him till after my death, and I had worded the letter accordingly. I always intended he should know the truth at last, and I had it all written out early last October. It had lain in my drawer, along with little Pure-in-Heart's book, ever since; but after Catherine became well enough to leave the asylum, and live with us, I had intended adding a few words, telling him of it. But I could never persuade myself to look at it again. I wanted to forget that part of my life; and I kept putting it off, and putting it off, till my illness came on and prevented me altogether. Was it not strange?"

"You speak as if you regretted it, my dear, which I

assure you I am very far from doing. And as for 'strange' —why, I'm only a superstitious old woman, of course, but it seems very much like a Providential interference in my eyes, and I think you did a wiser thing when you were out of your mind than you have just done in sending him away, now you are in it. Seriously, my dear, you must re-consider what you have done to-day. I can't see you wreck your own life, and Matthew's, from—from——"

"No, no, Miss Winterson," interposed Esther, quickly, divining what was coming, "not caprice—don't say caprice. It is not, indeed."

"Well," said the old lady, shaking her head severely, "caprice was the word I was going to use. I don't know where you draw the line. It looks dangerously like caprice to me, and I'm sure it must have looked dangerously like it to him, and I am not going to look on and see his life spoiled for want of a word. You must remember, Ettie, that you *are* his wife, and that he looks at things in a different way to you. You see he never even saw your sister, and it is rather hard on a man to ask him to give up everything for the sake of a woman he has never seen."

"But, Miss Winterson," she pleaded, "just think for a moment what it would mean. However quietly it might be brought about, our living together would be the talk of the country in a day or two, and all the horrible old story would be brought up again, and the truth, in our own defence, would *have* to be told. It would not matter so much if Catherine did not come to hear of it; but look at what it would mean for her. It is only lately that she has been well enough to leave the asylum and be with us, and you know her mind is still so weak and sensitive that even ordinary every-day excitements have to be guarded against. The very least reference to what she has gone through would be more than she could stand; if the bare, terrible truth were dragged up before the public again, it would either kill her outright or make her ten times worse than she was before.　No.　God has been very good to us, and I must learn to be content.　Now poor Kate is getting along so nicely, we must not run any risks."

"Well, I suppose we mustn't," said Miss Dorothy Ann, reluctantly, taking out her watch, "and that reminds me that Kate is not back from her walk yet.　Do you think it is quite wise to let her go out by herself so much？"

"I think it is—at least, for her.　It gives her a greater feeling of self-reliance and independence, and in this quiet hum-drum spot there is no danger of any kind to fear. Ah, Miss Winterson," she said, her eyes filling with tears, as she reverted to the former subject, "it is hard—you don't know how hard—to give Matthew up; but it is my duty—I am sure it is my duty—and I have broken myself into it these three years past.　But you don't know—no, forgive me, I believe you *do* know—the joy it is to see Kate getting better and stronger every day.　And, perhaps, who knows, when she is quite well · but no," she broke off sadly, "you see, however morally innocent she may be, she did do it, and the truth must never be known　at least by her.　It is all over now, and we must let it rest for ever."

"Well, well, my dear," sighed Miss Dorothy Ann, "I had been picturing a brighter prospect for all of you than that; but I think you are right, and we must just trust the future.　And is that the reason you did not give Matthew just now？"

"Yes, I told him everything but that—everything but that Kate was living with us."

"Don't look so heart-broken over it, child.　You haven't seen the last of him yet.　He will be here again before very long, and you can tell him then."

"I don't know," said Esther, doubtfully.　"That's just what I'm afraid of.　He said that when he came to me again I should stand as pure in the eyes of the world as I did in his.　Do you think he means by that　—"

"Oh, if that's what he says, it makes a difference.　And

as for what he means by it—he means, my dear, just
exactly what he says," said Miss Dorothy Ann, folding her
hands resignedly in her lap, with a general suggestion that
she was speaking of an earthquake. "I've known him, as
I've told you, from a boy, and you need *ne-e-ever* expect to
change his mind when he's once made it up. He *is* that
obstinate and self-willed——" Miss Dorothy Ann searched
in vain for a simile, and went on: "Before a couple of
hours are over, he will have decided, quite to his own satisfaction, and without consulting you or any one else, what
to do and where to go. But here is Kate back from her
walk at last," she said, as a tall, thin, pale woman, still
young, but with a face marked with trouble that had come
too early upon her, opened the gate and came slowly up the
garden path with a bouquet of wild flowers in each hand.
Esther rose from her seat, and went out to meet her, and
the two came on to the house together.

"Yours has been a strange story in the past," said Miss
Dorothy Ann to herself, as she watched them. "I wonder
what the future will have to show."

———

XXII.

"THE first thing I've got to do," said Redmayne to himself, as he paced about the deck of the *May Merrilies* next
morning, as she stood away seaward under every stitch of
canvas, "is to see those two women who kept that house on
the Happy Valley Road. *They* know the truth, and if I
can only get it out of them the battle is half over—though
it's ten chances to one if they are there now. Poor little
Ettie's diary—the truth is there, but I couldn't use *that*
after what passed yesterday, even if everything else failed
me; besides, as she said, it would never be credited, with
nothing but her own word to support it. Poor little Ettie,

I wonder what she is doing now? I wonder is she thinking
of me?" and he looked interrogatively into the blue sky
above him. "I wonder did I leave her like a brute yesterday? I was afraid to stay any longer for fear I should
make a fool of myself. If ever she does become my wife
in anything more than name I must keep my unlucky
temper more in hand. What a strange tale hers, and mine,
and her sister's is, to be sure. I wonder, now," he thought,
pausing to put a fair and square question at Space, with his
hands very deep in his pockets, and his legs very far apart,
for there was a swell on, and the *Meg* was rolling very
much. "I wonder if there ever was a man in such a
position as I am in at this moment? Here am I : for three
years I am convinced beyond a doubt that my wife is guilty
of the murder of this fellow Stadding. At the end of these
three years I find that I have been all at sea, and that so far
from being guilty of any wrong-doing she has performed
what seems to me a piece of quixotic self-sacrifice—and
which is deuced hard on me, too—and that she is dead. I
go to see her grave, and I find that I've been all at sea
again, and that she is alive after all ; and just as I am
building up my castles in the air, and promising myself all
the happiness I have been cheated of these three years
past, I find that I am all at sea for the third time, and that
what has kept us apart these three years is to keep us apart
still. Talk of a woman's will ; talk of a woman's caprici-
ousness ; talk of a woman's only being able to see a thing
from one point of view," he said, mutely inviting Space to
follow him to the climax, " but this beats everything. Now,
I sympathize with her sister a thorough rascal that fellow
Stadding, and deserved all he got, I say but I can't
simply for her sake, a woman I have never seen in my life,
sit quietly down and allow my wife to make a sacrifice of
herself and me too. I wonder if she'll ever forgive me if I
do find out the truth and make it known?" a new aspect of
the question presenting itself. "Well, well, what's right's
right : and now I've begun it I'll go through with it,

whether it brings good luck or bad luck ; and it can't bring worse luck than I've had, come what will."

Contrary winds were blowing heavily up from the ocean, and it was not till early on the morning of the second day that the yacht entered port. Without losing an hour, Redmayne drove out to Happy Valley. He was met with disappointment at the outset. The house he sought was no longer there. He knew he had come to the right spot, for there, on the slope about him, stood the three pine trees just as they had been described by Esther ; there was the cart track leading up to where the house had been ; but the house itself had disappeared. There was no place near where he could make any inquiry, for the one or two buildings he saw were mere decayed ruins. He was turning away again with the intention of returning to Wellington, when the thought occurred to him that Sarah Bundle was one who had given evidence at Esther's trial. It was unlikely that he would gain any further information beyond that which she had already given in Court. Still, in a search such as that he was engaged in, it would be unwise to throw away even that slender chance. Besides, there was his quaint little friend Pure-in-Heart, whom he had not seen since his last visit to the cottage with Esther before they were married. He sent the trap back to Wellington by the lad he had brought with him, and struck into the path along the coast by which Esther had come on that fatal day in June three years before, when the converging lines of her sister's course in life and her own had met and crossed.

It had taken Esther little more than an hour to complete the journey, but he walked so slowly, thinking of her and the events of that day, and what had arisen out of those events, that it took him more than two hours to reach Mrs. Bundle's. . . . Time had worked its changes at the cottage. Mrs. Bundle had aged greatly in the three years since Redmayne had last seen her, and though she recognized the name readily enough, her eyesight had become so impaired that she had great difficulty in recognizing Redmayne himself. Sarah, whom he had left a mere girl, had developed into a tall young woman, with some pretensions to good looks, and a still more marked appearance of being aware of the fact. But greatest change of all—little Pure-in-Heart's chair, on which he had so often seen the young invalid wheeling himself about—was standing disused in a corner.

"Ay, poor little fellow," said Mrs. Bundle, quietly, noticing the direction of his glance. "We'll not see him any more on *this* earth. He's bin dead now going on for three year."

"I am very sorry to hear that," said Redmayne, sincerely. "I can scarcely say it was the special object of my visit to you to-day; but I had looked forward to seeing him again."

"Yes; you were always a favourite of his. He spoke of you near the last; and his book—you remember his book, the dear little fellow—he sent that to Esth—to Mrs.—to your——"

"To my wife," said Redmayne, as Mrs. Bundle paused, awkwardly. "Little Pure-in-Heart was wiser than we were, Mrs. Bundle—judging by his present: he believed in her innocence."

"Ay, that he did to the last, and couldn't abear to hear so much as a word to the con*trairy*," said Mrs. Bundle, looking up, curiously, at his tone, and with an uneasy feeling that the conversation was approaching an awkward subject, and that Redmayne was the last person in the world she would care to discuss it with.

"And he was right," said Redmayne, with no appearance of a wish to avoid the delicate point. "Of course you know perfectly all that has happened, Mrs. Bundle, and no doubt you were deceived like everybody else, and believed just the same as they did. I am happy to say that at this minute there is not the shadow of a doubt in my mind as to my wife's innocence."

"You don't know how glad I am to hear you say that," began Mrs. Bundle, heartily, when Sarah broke in, eagerly—

"Has she ever spoken of me? Will she ever forgive me for the evidence I gave against her?"

"There's no question of forgiving, Sarah; you only did your duty, and you could not have said less than you did. It was for the purpose of gaining your assistance in establishing the truth, in fact, that I have come to see you to-day."

"Only tell me how I can help, and I'll do it. I'd do anything for Miss Esther—Mrs. Redmayne, I mean—to make up for what I've done."

"Very well, then, Sarah; to begin with, tell me all that happened on the night that Stadding was killed. Now I think of it, how did you come to be living at Lowry Bay at that time? You stayed first at Monk's Bridge, did you not? Was the house at the bay far from where the body was found?"

"Not very;—so near, I remember it frightened me dreadfully, and kept me awake nights afterwards thinking about it. Why we went to live there was because Mrs. Amelia Llewellyn—that was the young lady—and her husband used to quarrel so   "

"*What* was your mistress's name?" asked Redmayne.

"The old lady, I don't know what her name was—she was just Mrs. Llewellyn; but the young one was named Mrs. Amelia."

. . . . "'I can think of no one else day or night. My whole heart and affections are bound up in the two words, Amelia Ll   '"

These were the words contained in the letter which Catherine had shown to Esther during their interview in the old house on the Happy Valley Road. They were the words that flashed through Redmayne's mind the instant he heard the name Amelia Llewellyn mentioned. Could they refer to one and the same person?   . .

"Why did Mr. and Mrs. Llewellyn quarrel?" he asked. "Do you know?"

"For one thing, because she didn't like him, though he was her husband, and because I think——"

"He suspected her of keeping up a correspondence with some one else—was that it?" asked Redmayne, quickly.

"Yes, I think so. He was very violent sometimes, and both his wife and his mother were afraid of him, and they were quite glad to get out of the house."

"So," thought Redmayne, "this is surely more than a coincidence. Amelia Llewellyn must be the name of the woman to whom Stadding wrote the letter that night. This grows interesting." . . . . . "Have you any idea as to who the person was with whom young Mrs. Llewellyn was suspected of corresponding?"

"No."

"You did not know Stadding, did you?"

"No, I never saw him, to my knowledge."

"Did you see any signs of a correspondence being kept up by young Mrs. Llewellyn while you were at Lowry Bay?"

"Oh, yes; more then even than before. Letters came nearly every day, but they were always opened and read by old Mrs. Llewellyn before they reached Mrs. Amelia, and they were always in a lady's handwriting."

"Now, Sarah, I want you to be very careful in what you say. Try and remember everything that passed about the time of the murder as distinctly as you can. This may be the first step to a more important discovery than we think. We can't afford to overlook anything, even the smallest detail, with regard to Mrs. Amelia Llewellyn. You say that the old lady opened and read all her daughter-in-law's letters before giving them to her. Then things must have gone so far that Mrs. Amelia must have been almost a prisoner at Lowry Bay?"

"And so she was," said Sarah, her colour rising. "She was treated shamefully. She never went out but what

Mrs. Llewellyn or me went with her—if it was me I was
questioned and cross-questioned when I came back as if I
was a spy, till I felt quite ashamed of myself. And I'm
pretty sure Llewellyn himself used to watch her too, sometimes. He used often to ride over from Monk's Bridge,
where he stayed with his groom and his horse, Scythe-
bearer, when we took the cottage at Lowry Bay. I
remember one day when we were out, Mrs. Amelia pointed
to a pile of rocks in one of those little gullies off the
Lowry Bay Road, and said, 'Do you know who's in there,
Sarah?' 'No, ma'am,' I said. 'Who is?' She gave a
toss of her head, and an odd kind of laugh, and said, 'Who
is? Why, Llewellyn; that's who it is, Sarah. And do
you know what he's there for?' 'No, ma'am,' I said
again. 'I'll tell you,' she said. 'He's there for the same
purpose as you are sent out with me this morning—to
watch me!' She threw her hands before her face and burst
out crying. 'Don't give way like that, ma'am,' I said ;
'and I do hope you don't think——' 'No, no, Sarah,' she
said, still holding her hands before her face, and still
crying bitterly. 'I don't think you would do it. Don't
take any notice of me. Only I am so miserable. I haven't
a friend in all the world, Sarah—not a friend in all the
world.' I didn't like to speak, because her temper was so
changeable sometimes for want of some one else to speak
to, she would make a confidante of me ; at other times,
one daren't so much as open one's mouth. But I was
sorry for her, and I said, 'If there's anything I could do,
ma'am——' She stopped me again, and said, 'No, no,
Sarah ; you're a good girl, but there's nothing you can do.
Let us go back now.' We went towards the house again,
and presently she stopped and looked back over her
shoulder towards the pile of rocks. The tears dried up
out of her eyes as if they had been scorched ; her cheeks
flushed up, and she laid her hand on my shoulder. 'See
there, Sarah!' she said, pointing with her finger. 'What
did I tell you? Wasn't I right?' And sure enough there

was some one on horseback riding out from the gully on to the road, but whether it was Llewellyn or not, it was too far off for me to tell."

"Did you ever see Mrs. Amelia meet any one, and did she seem to have no other correspondence than that which passed through the old lady's hands?"

"No. I think old Mrs. Llewellyn distrusted me, for often at the last moment, just as we were setting out, she would call me back and say she was not very well, and that she thought a walk in the open air would do her good, and she would go herself, or some other excuse. I thought then, and I think now, that it was nothing more than an excuse. She thought we might have made some arrangement between ourselves, and that by taking us by surprise like that she would find out what it was. As for meeting or seeing any one while I was with her, I am quite positive she didn't. She never even seemed to care to go in any one direction more than another, and nearly always left it to me to say where our walk should take us."

"Strange," said Redmayne. "It seems to me that she must have had some way of corresponding, and her husband and her mother-in-law evidently had reasons for suspicion, too. Was there no one else about the place she might have employed?"

"No one. There was nobody but the three of us at the house from week's end to week's end."

"Well, then, did she seem to attach more than ordinary importance to the letters you know she did receive?"

"Considering they were only from another girl," said Sarah, with a somewhat conscious smile, "*I* thought she did; and if she didn't get one when she expected, there was more questions than enough about it. Was I quite sure the farm-boy had called at the post-office?—(there was no regular delivery of letters out there, you know)—and was I quite sure old Mrs. Llewellyn had not kept the letter from her?— and goodness *knows* she got enough letters as it was. But what struck me as the strangest thing about it was that

she scarcely looked at the letter when it was given to her.
She was all impatience till it was put in her hand, and
then all interest in it seemed to leave her, and she would
toss it aside with barely a glance through it."

"But how do you know they were all from some other
lady? And did old Mrs. Llewellyn *always* read her daughter-
in-law's letters?—it seems a strange arrangement."

"Every one," said Sarah, answering the last question
first, "from the day we went to Lowry Bay to the day
we left it, there wasn't a letter that reached Mrs. Amelia's
hands that the old lady hadn't read first. She wouldn't
even let me take them in at the door, but took them from
the farm-boy, or whoever brought them, herself, went to
her room close by, and opened them and read them. When
she had finished she would give them to me to take to
Mrs. Amelia; she never used to take them in herself.
The first time, I remember, she sent the letter without the
envelope, and Mrs. Amelia went back with it herself.
There was high words between them, and as Mrs. Amelia
came out of the room where the old lady was, I heard
her say—'I shall not submit to it. For the future, if
you do take advantage of your position to read my letters
yourself, you will at least have the decency to send them
to me in the envelope, so that the servant may not have
the same opportunity, too. It is disgraceful.' (Not that
I would ever have thought for a moment of doing such a
thing as read another person's letter," said Sarah in careful
parenthesis.) "I never saw Mrs. Amelia so much out of
temper before, for, generally, she was more than half afraid
of the old lady, who was a Frenchwoman, and had a good
deal of her son's temper at times, especially if she had only
another woman to deal with. I know the letters were
written by a lady, because, for all the fuss she made, Mrs.
Amelia seemed to care very little whether I saw her letters
or not, when once they were given to her in the way she
wanted them; and I nearly always saw enough of them,
as they lay on her table, to see they were in a lady's hand.

Besides, old Mrs. Llewellyn had poor eyesight, and was sometimes not able to make out what it was she was reading; and she would fold the letter with that part outwards, and ask me to make it out for her—which I know it was not right for her to do when it was not her own letter; but she did it all the same—partly, I do believe, to spite Mrs. Amelia for what she said that time. But that wasn't all. After Mrs. Amelia had read the letters she always handed them back to the old lady again, just as she got them, and the old lady used to put them away in her drawer."

"And what became of them after all?"

"They were burnt—I burnt them. There was almost a quarter of a drawer full of them. It was on the same day as the murder took place—in the morning. Old Mrs. Llewellyn took out what papers she wanted, and then told me to burn all the rest that was in the drawer before she came back from her walk. It was one of the days when she had taken it into her head to go out with Mrs. Amelia."

"That would have been a fine haul for Pure-in-Heart," said Redmayne, smiling, and the next instant regretting his thoughtlessness.

"Yes," said Sarah, sadly, "and he got them, too. He made me promise before I went to Mrs. Llewellyn's to send him all the stamps, and I cut them out before putting the letters in the fire, and send them to him."

"And the portions of the letters you read for Mrs. Llewellyn—do you remember what they contained?"

"Only just the ordinary news—what you would expect one lady to write to another."

"Not, at any rate, what a gentleman would write to one he was in love with?"

"No," said Sarah, with a decided shake of her head. "I'm quite sure it wasn't."

"But the letters Mrs. Amelia sent in reply—you would see some of them; can you not recollect to whom they were addressed?"

Sarah shook her head again. "No; I am quite sure it was a lady's name; but what the name was I can't remember."

"H'mph," said Redmayne, disappointedly. "But you haven't told me yet all that happened on the day of the murder. What effect did it have on Mrs. Amelia?"

"She fainted dead off as soon as she heard of it, and when she came to again she was wandering in her mind, and Mrs. Llewellyn wouldn't let me go near her, but attended to her herself, and sent me into the kitchen out of the way, and told me she would call me whenever she wanted me. She didn't want me to hear what Mrs. Amelia was saying, it's my opinion," said Sarah, nodding her head mysteriously.

<hr>

XXIII.

SARAH paused a moment or two, as if she were trying to call the circumstances more clearly to memory, and then went on—

"Old Mrs. Llewellyn must have been with Mrs. Amelia, for, I should say, not less than two hours altogether, and never called for me once—which I thought at the time was strange, for as a general thing she was not one to take more trouble than she could help; and besides that, up to now she had never seemed any too fond of her daughter-in-law. She was all in a fluster, and was in the room, and out of the room, and pattered about the place in her wrapper and slippers, now for hot water, now for cold, now for sal-volatile, now for this, that, and the other; and all the time, not but what she had her hands full and to spare, she wouldn't, as I say, let me do—no, not so much as a hand's turn to help her. Once when I was in the passage and the door of the room was ajar, I heard a faint groan, as if some one was in pain—it must have been Mrs. Amelia

--and then the voice of old Mrs. Llewellyn trying, in her short, ill-tempered way, to quiet her.

"At last Mrs. Llewellyn came a-tip-te-toe to the door of the kitchen, where I was waiting, and looked in, and told me to come to her in her own room. I followed her along the passage, wondering in my own mind whatever could have been going on in Mrs. Amelia's room while those two were together. It was not till she got to her own room and sat down in front of me that I caught a fair sight of the old lady's face. What *had* passed between her and her daughter-in-law, beyond what I had seen and heard, goodness only knows; but it seemed, in a manner o' speaking, as if she'd been struck down with old age in the hour or two she had been with her. She didn't say anything at first, but sat with her eyes towards me, staring in a dazed way, as if she was looking at me and not seeing me, as it were, and drawing her hand across and across her forehead so, and muttering something to herself.

"I began to think that what had happened that morning had been too much for her, and that she was not quite right in her head, and so I said—

"'What did you please to want with me, ma'am?'

"She thought a moment or two and then said—'I didn't see you last night after I sent you to Monk's Bridge with the letter I gave you. Did you deliver it to your master, as I told you?'

"'Yes, ma'am,' I said. 'But I didn't have so far to go as Monk's Bridge itself. I left the parcel you gave me at the luggage office at the railway station first; and when I stepped out on to the platform again, the five o'clock train was just coming in. I saw Mr. Llewellyn standing there with another gentleman, looking on, and I went up to him, and gave him the letter at once.'

"I had got this far and stopped. Mrs. Llewellyn was not listening to a single word I was saying. She was gazing straight over my shoulder at something going on behind me, her eyes so wide open and staring that it gave

one quite a turn to see her. She got up from her chair
with a half scream, and darted by me. 'That *miserable,
unfortunate* girl!' I heard her say to herself as she passed
me. I turned around, and saw the door swing open and
young Mrs. Llewellyn, in her night-dress and with her
face as white as death, and her hair loose and falling about
her shoulders, fall forward into the old lady's arms. She
seemed to be saying something to herself, but she was all
in a nervous fright, and jumbled her words one a-top the
other, so that any one standing a yard or two away, as I
was, couldn't tell what she was trying to say.

"'You foolish, wicked girl,' I heard the old lady say to
her, in a loud, rough whisper. 'Hold your tongue--do you
know where you are—do you know what you are saying?
Why did you leave your room? Go back again this
moment?'

"The old lady tried to lead her along the passage to her
room again, but Mrs. Amelia only shuddered and moaned,
and leaned against her so limp and heavy that the old lady
had to half-carry, half-drag her along the passage. Old
Mrs. Llewellyn, generally speaking, was a pretty strong
woman ; but what she had gone through since early morning seemed to have told on her. I could see that she was
trying herself beyond her strength, and I stepped forward
to help her.

"'Come near if you dare, you young eavesdropper, you!'
cried the old lady, turning on me in the tigerish way she
had with her when her blood was up. 'What did I tell you
half a dozen times already this morning about minding your
own business? And as for you,' she said to Mrs. Amelia, -
'you come to your room? Come to your room, I say!'

"'Oh, don't don't be so rough with me,' said the poor
creature, and she raised her head as if it was a heavy
weight on her shoulders, and tossed back her long hair.
'Don't leave me—don't let me be alone when he comes—I
know he *will* come—or he'll forget himself——'

"'Hold your *tongue*, I say!' the old lady almost

screamed, her hot French blood aflame in a moment; 'and come to your room, or you'll·make *me* forget myself,' and with that the poor young creature was taken away by main force to her room.   I think I can see her now—her head drooped forward so much that her face was hidden by her long hair, her white arms thrown around the angry old woman's neck, and her feet stumbling and dragging along the passage after her as they went.

"Sure enough, Mr. Llewellyn did come over that day—for, I suppose, that was who she meant when she spoke of some one coming. After old Mrs. Llewellyn had been with Mrs. Amelia the best part of an hour, she came out of the room and said I might go in and attend to her now, while she took a·little rest.   Amelia Llewellyn was fast asleep when I first went in, but presently she woke and asked me to tell her mother-in-law she wanted her.   I went down the passage to old Mrs. Llewellyn's room, and as I came near the door I heard voices.   One was the old lady's; the other was her son's—he must have come in without me hearing him while I was with his wife.

"'—— the girl I saw at the theatre, and if she spilts I'm done for,' I heard Mr. Llewellyn say in a low voice, but very distinct.   Mrs. Llewellyn burst out a-crying, and said something I couldn't make out, and as I knocked at the door Mr. Llewellyn was saying again—'As for old Scythe-bearer, he'll never put one foot before the other again, and every penny ——'

"Then he heard my knock and stopped.   Mrs. Llewellyn was sobbing when she came to the door, and she just held it ajar, and no more, while I gave her my message.

"' Very well,' she said, in a shaking voice, when I told her. ' Go away to the kitchen again, there's a good girl, and get on with the dinner, and I'll go to Mrs. Amelia directly.'

"I looked back when I got to the lower end of the passage before turning into the kitchen, and saw that old Mrs. Llewellyn's door was still ajar, and that she was watching me from behind it.

"I had been in the kitchen, I should suppose, about half an hour, when I heard the sound of voices, and a loud scream from young Mrs. Llewellyn's room. I looked along the passage from the kitchen door-way, and saw the door of her room banged open, and old Mrs. Llewellyn came out hanging to her son's arm, and trying to drag him after her. He put one foot over the door-step, then leaned back into the room, and I heard him say to his wife, very slow and threatening—

"'Thank—your—fate—my lady I found you out when I did——'

"His mother said 'Hush!' and whispered something to him. He turned and stepped out of the room at once, and as he gave one of his evil looks towards where I was, I saw his eyes were bloodshot, and his face as white as chalk. His mother whispered to him again, and they went into the sitting-room together. I went on with my cooking, and presently I heard a door open and close as if some one had gone away Mr. Llewellyn, I suppose it was.

"Old Mrs. Llewellyn had dinner by herself that day, Mrs. Amelia being far too ill to leave her room; —when I say dinner, she sat down at the table, but scarce bite or sup did she take, and her eyes were red and her voice shaky when she spoke, as if she'd been crying again -and I do believe she had too, after her son was gone. . . . . . . As soon as I had cleared all away and tidied up, she called me to her, and said with her head turned the other way, as if she was looking out of the window

"'I am afraid, Sarah, that I must part with you on very short notice. Mr. Llewellyn's groom has been very careless, and his horse, he tells me, has met with foul play of some kind, and my son intends taking steps about it that will compel him to be away for a time, and in view of that —and my daughter-in-law's illness I have thought it best to leave our quarters here, and go back to Monk's Bridge again. But our movements will be so uncertain for some time to come that, as I have just told you, I am

afraid we must come to an arrangement for dispensing with
the week's notice. You have been a good girl, Sarah, and
I am sorry to have to part with you, and if I can be of
any assistance to you in getting you another place, or anything of that kind, I shall be only too happy to help you.'

"The rest of the day was spent in packing up—for now
she had taken the notion Mrs. Llewellyn was anxious to
leave for Monk's Bridge the very next day, if she could ;
the murder happening so near by had upset her so, she
said. We mananged to get everything finished, and I
slept there over-night, and left for home next morning. As
for Mrs. Amelia, I never saw her again from that day to
this. Mrs. Llewellyn had attended to her as far as she
needed the day before, and when I came away in the
morning, she said her daughter-in-law had passed a very
poor night, but she was sleeping nicely just then, and she
wouldn't have her disturbed, not was it ever so."

    *   *   *   *   *

Redmayne did not speak for a while after Sarah Bundle
had finished her story, then he said—

"The letter you gave to Llewellyn on the station that
night—I suppose it had been read, as usual, by old Mrs.
Llewellyn ?"

"Yes ; both by old and young Mrs. Llewellyn."

"What effect did it appear to have on them—do you
remember ?"

"No very noticeable effect on the old lady, that I can
recollect," answered Sarah, slowly. "But it had on the
younger. She seemed more excited than ever I had
noticed before ; though, as far as that goes, I didn't see
very much of her after the letter came. She kept her
door locked most of the time, and if there was a knock she
would answer that she was busy and didn't want to be
disturbed. She answered Mrs. Llewellyn once or twice
that way, I remember, but the old lady wouldn't take no for
an answer, and *would* go in. The last time, they had high

words, and the old lady said she didn't like such behaviour, and she believed there was more going on than met the eye. 'There's not much goes on in this house but meets *your* eye, at all events,' says Mrs. Amelia, firing up for once, 'seeing you read every letter that comes into the place.' 'Yes, and need to, with such a two-faced hussy as you under one's roof,' snaps the old lady, firing up on her side. 'But I'll take care that sharper eyes than mine sees this last one. I'll send it to your husband, my lady, and see what he can make out of it.' It wasn't often Mrs. Amelia mustered the courage to answer the old lady back, but she did now, and gave her as good as she sent, into the bargain. 'A two-faced hussy, am I?' she said, looking her mother-in-law straight in the face, and speaking just as slow and spiteful as ever she could. 'If you find it so difficult to deal with two faces on one pair of shoulders, take care how you deal with two faces when they belong to different people—especially,' says she, bending forward, '*when — those — faces — are — female — faces*,' just like that. The old lady didn't say a word in answer, but turned as white as a sheet, and went out of the room, and in a quarter of an hour or so sent me off with the letter and the parcel."

"Those were strange words to use, Sarah. You have no idea what they meant?"

"Not the least; but they seemed quite to stagger the old lady, and Mrs. Amelia said them as if they meant something between themselves."

"And what was in the parcel you took to the station—do you know?"

"Only a parcel of books, I think, to be sent to some friend at Foxton or Feilding, or somewhere; but I couldn't be sure."

"One thing more. You said something about a groom staying at Monk's Bridge, while you and old and young Mrs. Llewellyn were at Lowry Bay. Do you know if he is there now?"

"No! He got blamed for what happened to Scythe-bearer, and Mr. Llewellyn turned him away at once. He keeps the Truss o' Straw now. Jerry Riddock was his name."

"There is nothing else you can remember?"

Sarah shook her head. "Nothing else that I can bring to mind; but if you'd like to ask any more questions ——"

"Thanks, Sarah," said Redmayne, rising. "I don't think I have any more to ask."

"And have I——do you see your way any clearer now, Mr. Redmayne?" asked the girl, also rising, and looking up in his face anxiously. "You know, I do so want to make up for what I had to say in Court that time—what I *had* to say," she added, with a sense of remorse at having told the truth still heavy upon her.

"Thanks to you, Sarah, I think I do see my way clearer now; but we must wait and see what the future has in store for us, and if it turns out as I hope it will, you will have won the gratitude of some one much better able to thank you than I am."

      *   *   *

Redmayne had taken up his quarters at the Occidental Hotel, and as he sat in his room that night and looked over the evening paper he turned to the shipping column from sheer force of habit, just as the better half of humanity turn to the notices of births, deaths, and marriages. He was not thinking of what he was reading, but was wondering how he could best turn to account the information he had obtained from Sarah Bundle a few hours before, when his eye happened to rest upon the following entry:—

ARRIVED—THIS DAY.

Helen Denny, barque, 728 tons, Cannell, from London, *viâ* Plymouth, Capetown, and Hobart. Passengers—Mr. and Mrs. Macfarlane, G. M'Kie, F. Leslie, Dr. Carmichael ——

"Carmichael!" he cried, joyfully, throwing down the paper. "The very man!"

XXIV.

Doctor Carmichael had prejudices on most subjects—hotels among the number. Redmayne knew at which one he would most probably put up; and after breakfast next morning he set out in search of him. He had to pass the post office on his way, and he called in to see if there were any letters for him. There was one in his uncle's round commercial hand, another from his sister Ellen, and a third from Esther; and he hurried out to find a quiet spot in which to read it.

"Dear Matthew," it began "When you left me the other day I was so agitated and confused that I left much unsaid which I am most anxious you should know. I am very much afraid you will think me an unreasonable, unfeeling, selfish thing in saying what I did, and I cannot contain myself till I have told you the whole truth, so that you may see what justification I had. Dear Matthew, I am sure you will understand my motives much more clearly when I tell you that my sister Kate has recovered, and is now living with us. Before ever the trial came on Miss Winterson had seen to her removal from that horrible place on the Happy Valley Road for me; and indeed if we had not found her out, I have no doubt she would have been turned adrift on the world, helpless as she was, for those two creatures who watched her were, of course, in the pay of Stadling, and it is easy to guess what would be the first thing they would have done when their payment was stopped. She was placed very comfortably in an asylum, and while there she regained her sanity to an extent that justified her being liberated from confinement altogether. Since then she has been with us; and although in other respects she is as well as I am, her health is still *very* delicate, and her mind is so morbidly sensitive on the score of her past treatment that to renew her remembrance of it, and to bring about a hopeless relapse into insanity, mean one and the same thing. She cannot bear the slightest reference to anything associated with her terrible experience; and the doctor can only give us hopes of a permanent cure on the condition of her mind enjoying perfect rest and quiet. It has cost a world of patient, tender nursing and protection from excitement, to bring about the hopeful condition she is in to-day. I feel as if a very mine were beneath my feet when I consider that a chance paragraph in a newspaper—nay, a chance word dropped in her hearing —might undo all our work, and condemn my poor Kate to a doom far, far worse than death itself. Oh, my dear Matthew, let me *beg* of you that yours may not be the hand that will ruin her future life—that you will not do anything that will cause this wretched case to be tried over again. But you will, you *must* if you carry out what you have set your mind upon doing. I know you have every *right* to make the truth known, so far as *right* goes; and were it only respect for my sister's memory—if she were dead—I could not, and would not for a moment seek to prevent you. But you see it is much—much more than that. I do not think any woman in the world was ever placed as I am. I do love you, Matthew—dearly, dearly; you know I do. For myself I do not say one word more than I mean when I tell you I would gladly give my life to make you happy. But there are some things more precious than life—some things which it is not ours to give up— and it is something more precious than life that is keeping me from your side to-day. I dare not seek my own happiness at the expense of my sister's life, or worse—her reason; and when you consider this I am *sure* you will not think of persisting in your purpose. I know it is like asking you, if you love me, to love me no longer. But, Matthew, you are a man, you have prospects, you have many interests in life: try and forget me; try and live for some high and noble purpose. And try and realize that not the least noble and unselfish action you can perform, will be to grant the request of the distracted girl who now appeals to your pity, your generosity, and your forgiveness.

     "Your loving and trusting

        "ESTHER."

"P.S.—Miss Winterson and *Catherine* send their best wishes."

The letter had been blistered by tears in several places when he opened it ; but it was blistered in several more by the time he had finished it.

"Poor girl," he said, slowly folding up the letter, and holding it in his hand. "Poor little Ettie. I didn't know her sister was with them. That makes all the difference. What a brute she must think I am. It's a lucky thing this didn't come a day earlier. If it had, it would have tied my hands once for all. I should have given up the whole thing, and gone and buried myself in Fiji again, and consequently would not have known what I do to-day. Dear little Ettie! I believe we've all been on the wrong tack, and that I've been all at sea for the fourth time; but I'll make you a happy woman yet, if I die for it," and forgetting that it is impossible to enjoy perfect privacy even in the most retired street, he raised the letter to his lips and kissed it.

Half an hour later he was smoking a cigar with Doctor Carmichael on the balcony of the Empire Hotel.

There had been a silence between them. Redmayne had just told the doctor what he himself had learned from Esther's confession ; and the doctor was leaning back in his chair, digesting what he had heard, one knee crossed over the other, his hands clasped behind his head, his hat tipped over his eyes, thin wreaths of smoke curling up from his lips at lazy intervals, his eyes watching the throng passing to and fro on the long stretch of gray sunlit street below him.

"What do I think of it?" said the doctor, slowly, at last.

“Why, it looks as if the whole thing was brought about
by a special Providence for the one express purpose of
proving the truth of my theory.”

The doctor had many theories, and Redmayne asked
which[*] of them he referred to.

“My theory that an actor’s character for good or evil is
affected by his profession; that he unconsciously takes upon
himself the features of the part he represents,” answered
the doctor, in the doggedly defiant tone of a man who is
accustomed to have his theory disputed, and who expected
to have it disputed now. “The last man I repeated this to
was this very Stadding. He was always a cad as well as a
villain, and he scoffed at the idea, and yet,” said the doctor,
solemnly, “and yet my words were a Prophecy: they told
him to the very letter the death he was to die—to the very
letter, sir. Let us look at the facts of the case. Here is a
girl, foolish and sensitive as all the rest of ’em, who night
after night, night after night, fills her mind with the
thoughts, and trains her hands to the acts of a deceived,
deserted, and jealous woman—goes through it all, likely,
in her very dreams. Her false character and her real
character become welded together in her red-hot excitement, more closely than she is herself aware of. Thanks
to Stadding’s treachery, she becomes in sober truth the
very character she has so long only trifled with behold
her in reality a Deserted Wife. The last check is removed:
her reason is destroyed. She meets her false lover under
circumstances most likely almost exactly similar to those
she has become used to behind the footlights. And now,
with the influence of her training strong upon her—that
training which we call acting, and which you and I pay our
shilling to gape at, and clap our hands at,” the doctor went
on, warming up, and describing tangled rings of fire in
front of Redmayne with his lighted cigar—“what does she
do? What do we expect her to do? What is it an absolute
certainty that she *will* do? Why simply put into execution
what she has so long practised. She stabs him to the heart

merely—As he deserved, you say? That is not for you nor me to judge, Mat," said the doctor, with a relapse into gravity. "But tell me now, what confirmation *do* you want beyond that? I am Amazed," said the doctor, looking around him with an expression of face that quite bore out his words. "I say to you I am A-*mazed* when I think how the terms I used to that man have come true to the word and letter—'Or mad,' says he to me, that night. 'Yes,' says I, 'especially if mad; I'm glad you follow me,' says I. I remember it as if it was yesterday."

Whether it was that Redmayne was particularly struck by the doctor's theory or not, he remained silent and thoughtful for some minutes.

"It is a strange coincidence, to say the least of it," he said, at last. "But I am ready in this instance to go a step further than even you do. It did not occur to me before, but what you have just said has suggested it to me. Let us go back to that night at the theatre. The deserted wife, otherwise Esther's sister, you will remember, only enters on the scene after the quarrel between the two men, and after one of them has made his escape. To bear out your theory she must actually stab the wounded man. Now, does she do that? Esther fainted just there, you know—another odd coincidence, by the bye—and doesn't say how the scene ends."

It was only a trifling question, but Redmayne was a sailor, and along with certain superstitions peculiar to the sea, he had a lurking belief in omens, and he waited for the answer much as a school-girl might have waited for a gipsy fortune-teller's decision as to what her future husband would be like.

"Well," said the prophet, drawing in a little, "only the downward sweep of the arm is wanting. As a matter of fact the wounded man clutches her dress, and before the knife can descend, he falls forward at her feet, dead. But the disposition of mind, the will to do the deed, look you, is there, just the same."

Redmayne drew a long breath of relief at the will to do the deed being there only, and not the deed itself; and accepted the omen.

"I think with you," he said, "that Esther's sister and Stadding must have met under circumstances startlingly like those represented on the stage. Talk of holding the mirror up to Nature! The mirror must have been held up to the Future that night—and caught an uncommonly truthful reflection, too, if what I think turns out to be actual fact. Look here, doctor," he said, lowering his voice, and leaning forward. "I have reason to believe that not only did Stadding and Catherine meet as you saw actor and actress meet on the stage, but that the Third Man was there too; that it was he who actually did the murder, and that he made his escape just as the play represented to you."

"And who was that third man?" asked the doctor, incredulously.

"Why, to make the whole picture complete, he was at the theatre too that night, though not on the stage. You pointed him out to Esther, and she, little thinking what Fate had in store for her, said she hoped his path in life and hers would never meet. It is Llewellyn."

"Llewellyn! I remember the name well. She shuddered when her eyes first rested on him that night, and I said, 'Miss Gower, you shuddered; I'll take my oath you shuddered.' I remember. But what makes you think he had a hand in it?"

"Listen, and I'll tell you." And Redmayne recounted to the wondering doctor what he had learned from Sarah on the day before.

*　　　　*　　　　*　　　　*　　　　*　　　　*

"Now, doctor," he said, as he concluded, "you know I'm better at sticking to an opinion once it's made up, than I am at making up new ones. Can you help my dull brains out of the difficulty?"

The doctor walked up and down the balcony, and between the puffs of cigar smoke said slowly—

"I say, Mat—this is the very—deuce of a complication—Let me—think."

He took another half-dozen turns, and then began—

"First of all let us grant that my theory is perfectly right in Principle, even though prevented by a mere moment of time from being fully confirmed by Fact—as it would have been. Putting that aside, my idea is this—it may be right, or it may be wrong: We can take it for granted that the Amelia Ll—— mentioned by Esther as the woman to whom Stadding was writing was no other than the Amelia Llewellyn spoken of by Sarah Bundle. It is evident that Llewellyn himself had pretty strong suspicions of what was going on, but in his presence she is too cautiously on her guard to give him an opportunity of arriving at the truth. Very well: he packs her off to Lowry Bay, where she is near enough to be still in his power, and just far enough away for her to make some incautious move that will reveal the truth ; and with the idea of bringing matters to a head all the quicker, by driving her to desperation, she is allowed to receive no letter from any one till it has first been read by her mother-in-law. Moreover, he rides out to Lowry Bay himself ; and in all probability his wife never left the house on a single occasion without being under his eye. Here is where the difficulty comes in : That these two people—Stadding and Amelia Llewellyn (while at Lowry Bay, at any rate, whatever may have been the case before) could have corresponded with one another in the ordinary way, one would imagine impossible, seeing the old lady read all the letters that came to the house. That they could have met was still more impossible, in view of the watch that was kept up by both Llewellyn himself and his mother. In fact, we only hear of Stadding being once at Lowry Bay, and that was on the night of his death. Now, it is at the least very improbable that, on what was very likely the one solitary occasion on which it was

possible for Stadding and Llewellyn to meet, that they
should do so. More unlikely still that they should stumble
across one another at midnight, when neither would be
abroad without a particular reason. Then again, young
Mrs. Llewellyn, according to the girl's story, after she
received that last letter, was more excited than ever she
had been before. In my mind all this points to two conclusions—first, that in spite of all the cunning of Llewellyn
and his mother, they had been out-manœuvred by one more
cunning still, and that Stadding, having broken the heart
of one woman, and then heartlessly deserted her, was for
the second time in his life about to carry out an elopement;
second, that the plan must have been found out by Llewellyn
at the last moment by means of the letter the old lady
sent him, and that instead of meeting the wife as he had
expected, Stadding met the husband, and paid the penalty
of his villainy with his life. That's my theory, and from
the behaviour of Amelia Llewellyn, I should say, that as
regards the murder, it was her theory too. There are only
two points that don't seem to agree. In the first place, it
seems, as I have said, impossible for Stadding and Amelia
Llewellyn to have corresponded through the post; and yet,
judging from the woman's conduct, that is evidently just
how she did receive this message—and that, too, in a letter
that had been already under the eye of a jealous mother-
in-law. Secondly, how was it possible for Llewellyn to
find out the appointment between his wife and Stadding by
means of this same innocent letter—as I suppose he did.
You see the position?" The doctor held up three fingers,
and checked off his periods on them one by one. "Mother-
in-law reads letter, and passes it on as innocent. Amelia
Llewellyn reads letter, and receives a message that excites
her unusually for the rest of the day. Llewellyn himself
reads the letter, sees the hidden message, keeps the appointment instead of his wife, and we know with what result.
Now, what is the explanation?"

Redmayne shook his head.

"Well, I believe it must lie in the fact that they corresponded in cypher. The simple commonplaces that old Mrs. Llewellyn saw would be read very differently by Stadding and Amelia Llewellyn, who had the key to the little mystery——"

"Right, doctor, right," cried Redmayne, joyfully, not waiting to hear more, and starting up from his chair. "Now, if we can only sheet this home——"

"Yes, yes, we know," said the doctor, waving him back to his seat again. "Esther, happiness, and all the rest of it. But even supposing that all this is correct—and bear in mind that, plausible as it seems to you and me, it is only supposition after all—the sheeting home is just where the difficulty comes in."

"Difficulty! Why, what is the law for if it can't give us justice?"

"As to justice, dear boy, remember that the scales are oftener on her eyes than in her hands. See here, Mat, let us take a common-sense view of your position. Don't trust so confidently to the law. Recollect this case has already been before the Courts, and with what result? Why, as things fell out, the connection between poor litle Esther and this crime was so clear that you yourself believed her guilty. No one, even for a moment, thought of associating any one else with the case. What evidence can you show to support this new theory of Llwellyn's guilt? What could have been his motive? Jealousy, you say. Of whom was he jealous? You can't prove that he even knew of Stadding's existence. You can't show that even a single letter passed between his wife and Stadding to make him jealous. On the contrary, on the surface everything points to their never having exchanged a note or a word. Even if we had all the letters that passed between them, they were evidently written so that none but themselves——"

"They are burnt," said Redmayne. "Sarah Bundle told me she burnt them herself, so that hope is gone."

“There it is, you see. No, Mat; feasible as our supposition is, we base absolutely everything on what? On the mere fact of having seen the two words ‘Amelia Ll——.’ If you yourself had not seen those words first, and been, above all, influenced by what you read in Esther’s diary, all that you have heard from Sarah Bundle would scarce have aroused a suspicion in your mind. Where do we find those two words, or rather this word and a half? Why, of all places in the world, where it is not worth the paper it is written on—in a narrative by the very woman whom everybody believes was guilty of the murder herself, and coming confessedly from the mouth of a mad woman even at that. Poor little Esther! I can imagine her feelings, after proving in that diary of hers to such a pitch of certainty that her sister was the guilty woman, and then finding out after all that she is innocent. Mat, Mat, Mat, what amazing fools of fortune you three have been, and what an heroic little woman she is.”

“Yes, isn’t she,” said Redmayne. “I think so now. But how to cope with this man Llewellyn,” he added—his mind dwelling on the one idea.

“Mat, my poor fellow,” said the doctor, putting his hand on Redmayne’s shoulder, “your object is to bring a wife back to your hearth, rather than to bring a criminal to justice; and after that letter from Esther you showed me an hour ago, we must give up at once and for ever all idea of ever taking this case into Court, or any publicity at all, and proceed by other means.”

“True, doctor, true; I had forgotten. But what are those other means? For now I have got the thread in my hand, I will unravel the whole skein if it takes a lifetime. I will never rest till I have found out the truth, and can place in my wife’s hand the proof of her sister’s innocence; the proof that shall sweep away her last shred of objection, and make her in reality my wife at last. If the law cannot drag the truth out of this man Llewellyn, I will.”

“Steady, Mat, steady. It is coming to a personal

struggle between you and Llewellyn now, and remember you haven't a single chance to throw away. One false move, and the game is lost."

"Never fear, doctor; I'm playing for my wife's reputation, and my own happiness—nay, my own life; and I have this advantage: three years have passed, and Llewellyn is living in fancied security, and is therefore off his guard. I shall open the game by making the first move this afternoon."

"And that is?"

"To see Llewellyn's groom—he's the landlord of the Truss o' Straw now, I believe—and see what he knows of Llewellyn's whereabouts on the night of the murder. He was the only servant kept at Monk's Bridge at the time, so Sarah Bundle says, and he is sure to know something of his master's movements."

"Two heads are better than one in this business, Mat. Stay and have lunch with me, and we'll walk out together."

Redmayne had been on the point of leaving. He halted, looked at his watch, and sat down again impatiently. The doctor had resumed his comfortable position again, and was quite at his ease.

"By the way, Mat," he said, "there is one thing we have both of us overlooked, and which it would be as well to keep in mind. What was it the girl Bundle told you about Amelia Llewellyn warning the old lady to beware of two female faces when those faces were on different shoulders? Tell me."

PART VI.

WHY SCYTHE-BEARER DID NOT RUN FOR THE CUP.

XXV.

*   *   *   *   *

Scene : THE parlour of the Truss o' Straw, a roaring fire, with three persons seated before it; the atmosphere somewhat heavy with smoke.

Time : The clock on the stroke of ten.

Characters : A young man, apparently a sailor; an elderly man, apparently a doctor; the landlord of the Truss o' Straw. The landlord in the act of drawing the back of his hand across his mouth, and about to speak.

"Yes, it's nearly three years ago since I was turned away by Mr. Llewellyn over that affair about Scythe-bearer—which, as you'll see as I go on, I don't think he acted altogether justly by me. However, I can't complain, for I lost nothing by changing from groom to publican. A party of the name of Beazely it was that had this place before I took it. They wanted to give it up just about the time I lost my situation at Monk's Bridge, and as I'd been of a saving turn, and had a pound or two put by, why, thinks I to myself, I can't do better than buy it, and buy it I did, and here I've been ever since.

"He was a strange man, was Llewellyn, ever since I knew him; but the strangest thing that happened while I was with him was that affair of Scythe-bearer and the Cup. People said, as they always do say, that it was a cut-and-dried affair, and that what he lost was only on paper; but, you see, I was on the ground, and I know different. I know to my own certain knowledge that what he lost ran into four figures—and pretty high up at that; and what's more, if it hadn't been for his wife's money he would have been a ruined man to-day; and if that don't go to show good faith I should like to know what does. Besides, it was through that very accident happening to the horse that I was turned away, because he thought I should have prevented it, and of course, in a manner of speaking, so I should; but you'll see how it was when I come to it.

"Mr. Llewellyn and his wife never seemed to get on together almost from the day of their marriage. They weren't cut out for one another. The puzzle always was to me how they ever came to marry, in the first place. They did say that he married her for her money, which is likely enough. However, I can't say as to that; but I've a pretty shrewd idea he had the use of the best part of it after they were married. He was always a great sporting man, was Llewellyn, and the luck was always against him; and what with one thing and what with another, he soon made ducks and drakes of every penny of his wife's money he could lay his hands on. The worst of it was, he not only had his wife's money, but he used to ill-treat the poor woman too, and though she never appeared to complain, or do anything to take her own part, even so far as a woman might, many's the time I've seen the traces of tears on her face not but what she had a spirit of her own, too, and tried to hide her trouble. As to quarrelling with her, you'd wonder how any one could do it, for she was kind-hearted to a fault, and that *fond* of children: she and my little Floss were friends from the first day she came into the house; and she used to make as much of her as if she had been her own. My little girl was deformed, I may tell you. She had caught the fever when she was quite a little thing, and had never properly got the better of it, careful as we all were—her mother was alive at that time ; and with the odd turns that diseases take in young children, ever since then her back began to grow out. As to old Mrs. Llewellyn, one would have thought she'd have taken her part, but not she. She took very little notice of her, in fact. Latterly, when Llewellyn became regular cruel to his wife, the old lady did sometimes interfere between them, it is true, for very peace sake ; but his temper was of a kind that even his mother daren't so much as say a word to him when he was roused. He wasn't quite so bad after the housemaid came to live at the house —along of her being a stranger, I suppose ; but I was glad above a bit when they made up their minds to live apart for a while, Mrs. Amelia, and the old lady, and the girl taking a cottage, and going to stay at Lowry Bay. There was some peace and quietness in the place then, for Llewellyn was never in better humour than when he had nothing but his horses to take up his attention.

"This was the time that he was training Scythe-bearer, and he seemed to grudge any hand but his own coming near him. The horse was a hot favourite for the Wellington Cup, and, as I say, I know Llewellyn himself stood to win or lose heavily by him—to lose as it turned out in the end, though little we any of us thought in what way it would come about.

"It was an odd thing that no sooner had his wife left him for a while, than Llewellyn fell into a way of constantly riding back'ards and for'ards to Lowry Bay, where she was staying. I thought at first he had found out the miss of her, and was going to make it up again. I found out afterwards I was mistaken ; but whatever his object was, he hardly missed a day but what he would ride over.

"Things went on in this way till the 11th of June came round—and good reason have I to recollect the date, as you'll see directly—which it is about the only date I do remember. That day Llewellyn had the dog-cart out early in the morning, and after giving me strict instructions as to Scythe-bearer, he handed me over the key of the stable and drove off. The day before was as rough a day as ever I see. But the next morning was quiet enough, only it was a cold wintry morning—the kind of weather when one would prefer to walk, and what little wind there was came keen and cold from off the hills, and I wondered at him taking the dog-cart out.

"That day had begun bad for me, but I little thought how it was to end. Little Floss had been feverish when she first woke, but she seemed to get better as the morning wore on, and she got up and followed me about at my work just as she used. If she had been a strong, healthy child, I shouldn't have thought anything of it; but at the time she came through her first illness the doctor had told me that he thought it only his duty to let me know, that unless I was very careful with her she'd never be reared. I thought of this, and I wanted her to keep inside out of the cold. But no, not she. Where I was, there she must be, and thinking that maybe the open air would after all do her more good than being in the house, I let her be with me.

"About three or half-past in the afternoon, Llewellyn drove into the yard again. He had some one with him in the cart—a short, German-looking man, with light hair and whiskers. He spoke to him by the name of Trupp, and called to him to come and see the finest piece of horse-flesh in all New Zealand. They went into the stables together, and after a while came out and went into the house. They hadn't been there more than a bare quarter of an hour, as near as I can recollect, before out they were again. They got into the dog-cart, and drove out of the yard once more. They went close past me, and from what I heard Llewellyn say I gathered that they were bound for the station to meet the five o'clock train. It seemed it was some appointment the man he spoke to as Trupp had to keep.

"Towards dusk little Floss began to grow so feverish

again that I got more uneasy than ever about her. She
complained that her head was hot and aching, and that she
felt sick. I tried to persuade her to go to bed ; but no—
she wanted to stay close to me, and there she was with her
arms around my neck, and her head resting on my shoulder.
Her face was close to mine, and I could feel how hot it was.
While we were sitting like this, she rolling and tossing her
head from side to side, and me trying to comfort her in my
rough way, and wishing that Llewellyn would come back,
so that I could set off into town for medicine, there was a
rattle of wheels, and the dog-cart came clattering into the
yard again. I laid little Floss down on her bed, and went
out ; and there was the German, Trupp, back again with
Llewellyn. They jumped out of the cart, and went into
the house. As I took the horse out of the shafts I see that
he had been driven at such a rate that he hadn't another
couple of hours' work left in him.

"'Oh, Jerry,' calls out Llewellyn's voice, as I led the
brute into the stable, 'I want you to run down and tell
Moffat'—(Moffat, that was the blacksmith)—'tell Moffat,'
says he, 'I want to see him first thing in the morning.
Nothing the matter with Scythe-bearer, I hope, since I
left ?'

"'Nothing the matter, sir,' says I. 'What about the
key of his stall, sir—will you take it now ?'

"He was half-way towards the house again by this
time, and he stopped for a moment, and then calls back—
'Never mind it to-night, now ; the morning will do. Don't
forget what I told you about seeing Moffat—I must speak
to him first thing to-morrow. You'd better go down at
once.'

"I stole round to my own quarters before I set out, just
to catch a glimpse of my little Floss, and there she was
lying asleep, just as I had laid her down. Her face was
still flushed, and she seemed a bit uneasy in her sleep ; but
sleep, anyway, I took to be a good sign, and I set off for
town in better heart.

" I called at Moffat's house on the way down, but he was not in. His wife told me he was working overtime, and I would see him at the forge. The smithy was about ten minutes further down the road, and as I came up to it I saw both half-doors were closed, but the firelight was shining bright and clear in the dark through the crack between them. I was just going to knock at the door, when a sudden gust of wind blew my hat off, and while I was groping for it in the dark I heard a voice from inside the smithy say with an oath—

" ' I tell you it's a straight affair. All my money's on it to the last red cent.'

" ' And Scythe-bearer ? ' says another voice.

" ' Scythe-bearer,' says the first voice, very slow, and in that tone that made me think the owner of it laid his finger alongside his nose as he spoke. ' Sythe-bearer won't go to the post. Or if he goes to the post, he won't see the finish.''

" I had got my hat by this time, but waited to hear more.

" ' He won't be stopped by fair means anyhow,' says the second voice, ' for I know Taffy's backing his own animal up to the hilt.'

" ' Ah,' says the first voice.

" ' Ah,' says the voice of Moffat himself.

" ' Ah,' says a third voice.

" ' Take my tip, dear boy,' says the first voice, ' help us scoop the blooming pool ; you'll never regret it.'

" ' It's a case of Welsher *versus* Welshman,' begins Moffat again, and then he breaks off. ' By —— there's some one at that door.'

" I had my eye at the crack, and I saw the blacksmith make a rush for the door with a bar of iron, white-hot, in his hand. I knew what Moffat was, when he was roused, too well to wait till he got near me, and I jumped back, but something caught my foot, and I fell. Luckily for me, in falling I managed to half roll, half scramble a few yards back into the darkness. Moffat swung back the upper half of the door and peered out, with three other men beside him.

"'There's no one there,' says one.

"'By heaven, there is though,' cries another, pointing direct to where I was. 'See, there, Moffat. Lend us your iron, and I'll burn out his lampas for him.'

"Moffat never said a word, but kicked open the lower half of the door, and darted out after me, the bar clenched in his hand. I saw he meant business, and sprang to my feet, and ran for dear life. I trusted he would miss me in the dark, but the other three joined in the chase and came after me like the wind. I hadn't run a hundred yards when I put my foot in a hole, and fell a second time. There was no time to get to my feet again, so I rolled as quietly as I could to one side and waited. The three men dashed past me ; the blacksmith had been out-paced, and came lumbering up and stood within half a dozen paces of me. It had all happened in such double-quick time that the bar of iron in his hand still had a dull red glow on it. He stood swearing and muttering to himself ; the glow on the iron died out ; the clatter of the men's footsteps, and the sound of their voices, grew fainter and fainter till one couldn't hear them ; then he turned and went back to the smithy, still swearing and muttering. I waited till I saw him enter the open door, and then, as there was no sign of the other three men coming back, I rose to my feet and went on again into town.

"I had hurt my ankle when I fell the second time, and through that I was a good hour and a half longer than I would have been in getting home. What I had over-heard in the smithy had made me uneasy. I suspected there was some plot forming to prevent Scythe-bearer from running.

XXVI.

"I had got about half-way towards home when I heard the sound of footsteps on the road behind me—soft, stealthy footsteps, that gave me the notion of some one quietly dogging me in the dark. I stopped and looked back. Just then the door of a house by the roadside opened, and the light streamed out over the man who was following me. The broad-brimmed felt hat he was wearing shaded his face so that I couldn't see what he was like; only that he was tall, and was dressed in what looked a shabby black; and then the door closed again. But short as was the glimpse I caught of him, I thought I recognized one of the men I had seen in the smithy. After what I had heard and seen that night, the mere suspicion was enough, and I turned and hurried on homewards again as quick as my injured foot would let me, for the long walk I had had was making it more and more painful every moment.

"Whether the man was really who I suspected him to be, and meant foul play of some kind but had given it up when he saw he was discovered, or whether he had only happened to be coming up the road after me by accident, I can't tell; but I saw no more of him nor any one else for the rest of the way home—though something else happened, as you'll hear.

"There was a low, thick gorse hedge skirting the road for about fifty yards or so from Llewellyn's gateway, and just as I was on the point of turning in at the gate I heard a rustle behind this hedge, and then I thought I heard some one say in a whisper

"'That's him now.'

"I called out 'Who's there?' and waited, but I heard nothing 'cept the rustle of the wind among the bushes.

"I might have been mistaken, certainly, but it had seemed too plain and distinct to be a mere womanish fancy,

and if it had not been that I was anxious about little Floss,
I'd have gone and looked whether there was any one there
or no; for, as I tell you, I had my own suspicions as to
what the talk could mean that I had overheard at the
blacksmith's.

"I wish now I had gone and looked, spite of all;—I
wish, by heaven, I'd been struck dead fighting with the
d—— thieves that were at the bottom of the villainy that
was afoot that night, I do—for when next morning came I
had little left in the world to live for, as you'll see when I
come to it; and maybe Llewellyn'd have believed I'd not
failed in my duty to him when I shed my heart's blood to
prove it.

"However, it was not to be. I closed and locked the
gate and tried to think no more about it, meaning to tell
Llewellyn what I had heard, first thing next morning. I
had to pass the stables on the way to my own quarters,
and though I knew Scythe-bearer couldn't have been
tampered with in the meantime—for I carried the key of
his stall in my pocket—I unlocked the door and looked in.
He was just as I had left him, and I closed and fastened
the door and came away again.

" I had lit the lamp in little Floss's room before setting
out—the little thing was afraid to be left in the dark—and
it was burning on the table beside her bed now with the
light turned low down. She had fallen asleep, and the
dim light shone over her face. It was flushed, and she
was restless, and kept tossing from side to side and muttering in her sleep. I could see that even in the short
time I had been away the poor little soul was a good deal
worse. . . . . I had opened the door very quietly for
fear of disturbing her, and walked just as quietly across
the room. But quiet an' all as I was she heard me, and
opened her eyes, and sat up, and stretched out her arms
for me to take her. She wouldn't rest until I held her in
my arms, so I took her up and walked about the room with
her till midnight. She took some of the medicine I brought

her, and sunk into what seemed a sound sleep, so I laid her softly down on the bed again. The hands of the clock, I remember, were pointing to ten minutes to twelve as I sat down beside her, quite tired out, what with the day's work and the anxiety.

"I must have dropped off to sleep almost at once, for I recollect nothing after that till I was woke up by a shrill scream of fright from little Floss. The last stroke of twelve was just sounding as I started up. In a half-dazed way my mind took in the sound of heavy footsteps running across the floor, and I caught a glimpse of the fingers of a hand resting for a moment on the edge of the door, and then the door was banged to.

"I felt in my pocket for the key of Scythe-bearer's stall. It was gone. I had been robbed of it while I slept— it was the thief who had just made off out of the room. All my fears for the horse's safety came back to my mind in an instant, and I was about to rush after the man, when little Floss gasped rather than called to me—

"'Father—father—come to me—I feel so ill—I think I am dying.'

"Her voice was so faint and husky I could scarce make out what she was saying. Weak and ill as she was, the fright had been too much for her; she seemed all of a sudden to have sunk indeed well nigh to the point of death. She fastened her eyes on my face—I fancy I can see them now—and then they seemed to grow fixed and filmy; she pressed her hands to her temples so and fell back'ard and moaned. . . . . There was a scurry of footsteps on the stones in the yard outside. Everything hung on that one moment. I knew that whatever the plot might be that I had heard hinted at in the smithy, it was on the very point of being carried out. . . . . I feared my little girl was at death's door. Nature was strong. I couldn't tear myself away from my dying child— and yet what was it that was going on outside only a few yards from me? I sprang to her side, caught her in my arms and kissed her, then laid her gently down again, and pausing, and stopping, and glancing back, I darted into the yard. . . . . Too late! The heavy stable door swung back; I made a mad dash for'ard and grappled with some one in the dark; there was a stunning shock, and I was sent back gasping and staggering; I heard a clatter of hoofs; a shower of sparks was struck up from the stones, and I knew that Scythe-bearer, the favourite for the Cup, was stolen.

   *   *   *   *   *   *

"I heard little Floss calling to me to go to her, and sick and miserable and desperate, I staggered rather than walked into her room again. . . . .

"I don't remember what it was she asked; I don't remember what it was I answered her. I only remember taking her up in my arms again and walking about with her through the night; of her rambling in her talk, which was always of the strange man she had seen bending over me when she woke up; and then of her growing quieter and quieter and weaker and weaker; and of her closing her eyes and lying so still and breathing so low I didn't know hardly whether it was sleep or death that had come to her. I've passed many a troubled night since then, but I pray God I may never pass such another night as that was.

"There was no doctor within miles, and I was afraid that if I went for one she would be dead before I could get back again. I don't know what I might have done at other times and with different surroundings, but I was more than half stupefied that night. I had some thoughts of going up to Llewellyn's room and asking him for God's sake to help me save the life of my child. What held me back was a fear—partly for myself, but more for the sake of little Floss—a fear that when he found out what had happened he would strike me dead where I stood. A-ah, I knew his temper, and I knew he would be capable of it. And so I walked for three weary hours about my room with my child dying—dying in my arms, my love driving me one way, and my stupid fear the other.

"About three o'clock I got into such a state that I could bear myself no longer. I felt that I must do something more to save her precious life than I was doing, or go mad. Poor Floss's breathing seemed, I thought, to grow a little more regular and stronger, and I thought there could be no danger if I left her for a minute or two. I crept up to Llewellyn's room and knocked. A strange voice—that of the German who had been with him all the afternoon—asked—

"'Who's there?'

"Think me a coward if you will, but I felt my knees shake and the sweat start on my forehead when I thought of the risk I was running and of what I was about to bring upon myself. I said—

"'I'm Riddock, the groom. I want to see my master.'

"'What for?' asks the voice. 'What's the matter?'

"'Something has happened,' I said. 'I want to see him at once.'

"'Your master has not been well,' answers the voice again. 'He's asleep just now. Can't you wait till the morning?'

"Once the words had left my mouth my courage had failed me again, and I seized on the excuse at once. I said—

"'Very well, I'll tell him in the morning,' and crept away down-stairs again, like the coward I was.

"I halted when I came to the threshold of Floss's room. . . . The feeling had come upon me as I turned away from Llewellyn's door. A voice from the air seemed to have spoken to me.

"'I feared that my little daughter was dead!'

"I could see her from where I stood, and her face, I thought, seemed very white and still. I called to her softly, but she didn't move. Then louder. She didn't hear. I told myself she was asleep, that she was just as

I had left her, and turned away and paced stupidly up and down the yard a minute or two in the dim moonlight, and tried to keep the fear that was taking possession of me at arm's length. I told myself over and over again she was asleep—only asleep. . . . . . . It was only for a moment or two. Then I stole to the door and looked in again. She hadn't moved. Her face lay upturned and white and still as before, in the lamplight. Ah me, so deathly white and still. I walked softly towards her bedside, and took up the lamp, and held it so that the light played over her face from every point. I tried, as a drowning man clutches at a straw, to make myself believe that her expression changed with the changing shadows the light threw over her face—but it wouldn't do. 'Oh, my God, my God!' I whispered to myself, the terrible truth forcing itself on me so that I couldn't even pretend to shut my eyes to it any longer. 'Can it be true? Can she have died in those few minutes?' And then the light fell from my shaking hand with a crash and went out.

"As sudden as a thunderbolt there came the clatter, *clatter*, CLATTER of a horse's hoofs on the pavement of tho yard, then the banging of a door, a sound between a sob and a gasp; then the room shook as something fell with a heavy shock against the wall outside.

"It was Scythe-bearer come back again.

"I sat still with never a thought of rushing out and grappling with the thief. What had happened had un-manned me. I trembled like a woman, and my hand grasped little Floss's in the dark. It was cold and heavy. I sat down holding those dead little fingers in one hand and stroked them with the other, and waited. . . . . A minute or two passed; doors opened and closed; I heard the sound of footsteps and voices; a beam of light shone in through the keyhole of the door; then some one cried—

"'Great Heaven! what is this? Look here!'

"In a moment more the door of my room was thrown

open with a crash, and Llewellyn came in. He held a lamp in his hand, and as its light fell over his face I saw he was white as death; his eyes were bloodshot, and he was trembling with passion.

"'Come here,' he said, as if his rage would not let him say more, and beckoning with his hand. I rose and followed him into the yard as a whipped dog might follow his master. 'Look at that!' he said, pointing downward to something lying upon the ground. 'D'ye see it! That's your work!'

"It was Scythe-bearer. He was lying in a heap against the wall of the house. One of his fore-legs was doubled under him; his flanks were heaving and covered with sweat and foam; his head, stretched out to the full length of his neck, lay over his other fore-leg, and he breathed in short, heavy gasps. He was bleeding at the nostrils, and there were splashes of blood on the stones around him.

"'That's your work,' he said, again. 'That's the favourite for the Cup. Look at it; curse you, look at it.'

"I did look at it. I scarcely knew what was being said to me, or what had happened, or what I was doing. I looked at the German, who was peering about through his spectacles. I looked up at the face of Llewellyn himself. It had been white before; it was red and swollen now.

"'How did this happen? Where is the key I gave you?' he said.

"'It was stolen from me.'

"'Stolen! When? How!'

"'To-night, at twelve. It was taken from me while I was asleep.'

"'While you were asleep! Did you not see the man who took it, then?'

"'No, I don't know who it was; but I know this—it was all the outcome of a plot to stop Scythe-bearer from running—to stop him from running even if he had gone to the post.'

"'A plot !—a plot,' he sneered. 'Is that all you have to say for yourself ? A plot !'

"'What,' said the German, 'a plot to make das horse a lef'-at-the-poster——'

"'If there was a plot, out with it, then, and let me hear it,' said Llewellyn, fiercely, and I told him what I had overheard at Moffat's smithy.

"'If I thought I could believe this, now,' he said, scowling blackly at me, as if he would look me through and through, and then letting his eyes rest on the quivering brute at his feet. 'And you neither saw the man when he took the key from you, nor when he rode out of the stable ?' he said, raising his eyes again. 'What do you think of this story, Trupp ?'

"'It might be true,' said the German, shaking his head. 'It might be true. God knows.'

"'Well ?' said Llewellyn, looking towards me for my answer, with the black scowl still on his face.

"'I saw the man at neither time. It was dark——'

"'Just then Scythe-bearer lifted up his head and staggered to his feet, pushed his nose into Llewellyn's hand, tottered forward a pace, and then, with a groan that was almost human, poor brute, he fell down again with a crash, shuddered, and was dead. I had never seen Llewellyn affected by anything before, but he was touched now by the death of his horse. He knelt down on one knee and patted the animal's neck as gentle as a mother might stroke the hair of her sick child.

"'Ach,' said the German, peering down through his spectacles, and shaking his head again, 'Ach.'

"'The best friend I ever had, Trupp,' said Llewellyn, looking up in the face of the German, and speaking with a catch in his voice—'the best friend I ever had ;' and then with a sudden change of humour he cried, 'And there go five thousand pounds with him, and through you, you d—— negligent scoundrel.'

"He sprang to his feet and seized me by the throat. If

ever there was murder in a man's eyes I saw it in Llewellyn's as he glared down at me that night. He shook me like a terrier would a rat, and when I clasped his wrists to try and make him loose his grip his muscles felt like bars of iron. I tried to cry for mercy as I was borne back'ard, but nothing but a husky gasp came from my throat. I saw the German leap forward and seize his arm ; I saw his lips move, but what he said was drowned by the roaring in my ears.

"The next thing I remember was waking up and feeling some one hauling me along by the shoulders, with my heels dragging over the stones of the yard. My things were open around my neck, and I was cold and wet, as if water had been thrown over me. A door was pushed open, and I was carried in. It was quite dark, but though I was confused by what had happened, and hardly realized what was passing around me, I knew it was the room where little Floss was lying dead. I didn't know whether it was the German or Llewellyn who had been carrying me. Whichever it might have been, I felt it was like sacrilege for him to be in that room, and I struggled to my feet and said, 'That will do. Leave me, please ; I am better now.' The man made no answer, and passed out of the room, and I was left alone with my poor dead little daughter."

*　　　*　　　*　　　*　　　*　　　*

XXVII.

"And that is absolutely all you know of what happened that night?" asked the doctor, as the landlord finished his story.

"Yes," said the landlord, "all ; and good reason I have to remember it."

"You said something about Llewellyn turning you away?" suggested the doctor, as delicately as he could.

"Ay, and so he did.　Llewellyn was a strange man. He sent for me next morning, and without so much as mentioning what had happened on the night before, or allowing me to say a word in my own defence, he told me I was turned away from my situation.　He never had no pity or consideration for other people, and he had none for me.　Neither the death nor the burial of my child, he said, concerned him.　I must make my own arrangements.　One thing he had made up his mind upon—I was to leave instantly.　I should not stay another day in a situation I had proved myself unfit to hold."

"Was there nothing in his behaviour that struck you as unusual?"

"Nothing, except that the heat of his passion seemed to have worn itself out; I had seen him on less provocation than he had had then keep his passion for days so that one scarce dare come anigh him."

"And did he take no steps to find out who it was that carried out this villainous plot against him?"

"No," said the landlord, "nothing was ever done.　There was a talk made about it, but it come to nothing in the end, and some thought one thing and some thought another, but the truth of the matter is just what I've told you."

"Did not Llewellyn's wife and mother come back to live at Monk's Bridge very soon after this?"

"I believe they did, but I was not there when they came. I knew Llewellyn's humour too well to stay an hour longer than I could help.　I made what arrangements I could, and left at once."

"Perhaps you may have heard on what terms he and his wife lived after her return?"

"Very unhappy," said the landlord, shaking his head, "very unhappy, if all be true that I've heard.　If he cared little for her before, he cared less for her after, and they lived mostly apart till her death."

"When did that happen?"

"As near as I can remember about ten or eleven months after I was turned away."

"When you tried to stop the man who was riding out of the yard, did you not see enough of him to give you an idea who he was, or to help you to recognize him afterwards if you had seen him?"

"I saw nothing of him either then or before; and as to who he was, unless it was the man who had been following me on my way back from town, I don't know who it could have been."

"You have no suspicion, at any rate, that it could have been Llewellyn himself?" broke in Redmayne, impatiently.

The landlord had been following a floating black speck round and round his glass with a spoon. He paused, and after an interval of speechless surprise, he said—

"Llewellyn himself! Llewellyn get up at midnight to steal his own horse! Llewellyn the man to throw five thousand pounds into the street! Llewellyn ruin one of the best bits of horseflesh ever foaled in New Zealand!" and, unable to carry the proposition any further, the landlord went back to the black speck again.

Redmayne felt annoyed at his own question as soon as it had left his lips, and his annoyance was increased when he caught the expression on the doctor's face.

"There is nothing more that we want, I think," he said, and they rose by common consent to go.

"Nothing, unless you can tell us where we are likely to find the man Trupp," said the doctor.

"I know nothing of him," said the landlord. "I have never heard of him since."

"Well, Mat," said Doctor Carmichael, as they walked along the road towards Wellington together, "you have Llewellyn's whereabouts on the night of the murder accounted for so far; and now, which is it—Are we a step nearer the solution of our problem, or a step the other way? On my life I don't know which to think."

"Tell me who rode Scythe-bearer that night, and I'll tell you who killed Edgar Stadding," said Redmayne, with dogged conviction. "And tell me whether the landlord of the Truss o' Straw is a conscienceless liar, or whether we have to deal with the cunningest villain in all New Zealand, and I'll solve the next step, and tell you who rode Scythe-bearer too."

"Oh, the man spoke the truth—it was impossible to listen to him and not believe he was speaking the truth. Let's hear what you think, Mat. You have made up your mind as to who rode Scythe-bearer, and as to why he was ridden?"

"I have."

"And it was?"

"Llewellyn himself!"

"H'm; you say that after taking into consideration all the points of the groom's story?"

"Yes, all of them."

"In spite of what the groom overheard in the smithy?"

"Yes, in spite of that."

"And of his being followed, and of the key being stolen from him?"

"Yes, in spite of that."

"And of the five thousand pounds in hard cash?"

"In spite of everything, I tell you. The plot to prevent the horse from running may have existed, the groom may have been followed home and watched from behind the hedge, and by the death of his horse Llewellyn may have lost all the money he is represented as having lost. But my belief is that Llewellyn deliberately set his gain against his loss, and sacrificed Scythe-bearer, with his possible winnings and everything else, for the sake of revenging himself on Stadding."

"Ay, Mat," said the doctor, nodding his head sagely, "and there speaks prejudice rather than reason, I am afraid. What you say is feasible enough in one sense, but I must admit this story of the groom's has to some extent unsettled my belief in Llewellyn's guilt. It seems to me we have been too hasty in jumping to conclusions. You are losing sight of the fact—we are both losing sight of the fact—that only a few hours before his death Stadding really was being closely followed by the woman who of all people in the world had the keenest desire to be revenged on him——"

"Yes, yes, the finding of the ring, the stain on the dress, and all the accursed rigmarole that came out in the Court. Are we to go over the whole ground again? Don't you and I know how false was the whole thing," said Redmayne, with a touch of bitterness at the doubtful tone of the doctor's words.

"False in one sense only, let us remember; for strong as the facts seemed against Esther, you and I know they are ten times stronger in the case of Catherine. It was morally impossible for Esther to have committed the crime of deliberate murder, but not so her sister; she was insane, had expressed the intention of killing Stadding, and had been put through the mechanical training of the part time and again on the sta——"

"Why, only an hour or two ago," burst in Redmayne, "you had proved quite to your own satisfaction——"

"Hear me out. I am *not* forgetting the conviction we arrived at this morning; at the same time I am just as far from forgetting it was not absolute Revelation. It is just possible we may both have been wrong after all. Here is quite a new complexion given to affairs, and as thinking men we must give it reasonable consideration. If what the German said in reply to the groom's inquiry for his master is true, it is plainly impossible that Llewellyn can have been in any way concerned in Stadding's death. Let us be rational, in spite of—or, rather, because of—the stake you yourself have at issue. Let us follow this thing out with reasonable hopes of success only. What I was going to say was this—we have already admitted to ourselves that it is hard to see how Llewellyn's suspicions could be roused by a letter which his mother considered a mere commonplace communication. Very well. Further than that we must now believe that those suspicions were strong enough to lead him to sacrifice one of the most valuable race-horses in the island, with all the possible thousands that were depending on that horse; that in the space of an hour or two he worked up an elaborate plot to avert suspicion from himself; and that he deceived his groom by a piece of consummate stage-acting after he returned from his midnight ride."

"Exactly what I do believe—it only requires a little low cunning. As to the stealing of the key—— You must have noticed in listening to what the landlord said how closely Llewellyn questioned him as to whether he saw or had any idea as to who the man was who took the key. As for the groom's little daughter saying something about a strange man, why, any child in such a situation might very easily be deceived by her imagination."

"Granted, granted, granted," said the doctor in a descending scale. "I simply want to look at both sides of the case, and put probabilities against other probabilities. Now that I have done so I am prepared to go more than half length with you; only don't let us lose sight of the difficulties in our way. Above all, don't let us forget that if our conclusion of this morning is in point of fact the correct one, and if what we have just heard is the truth, we have, in your own words, the cunningest villain in all New Zealand to deal with."

"Well, well, doctor, as I told you before, I am better at sticking to old opinions than at making up new ones, and I stick to the decision I have already come to. I don't see this new complexion you say affairs have taken on themselves at all. I've made up my mind that Llewellyn *is* the guilty man. It is my dearest interest in life to establish his guilt, and what is more—established his guilt shall be if it can be done by two strong hands and a brain of which perhaps the less said the better;—yes, cunning and all as he may be. He may fight with the halter round his neck; but I fight with my wife's arms round mine."

"Then you are under circumstances of the most perfect equality, Mat. But another thing—Lowry Bay is not a stone's-throw from here, remember. Scythe-bearer was stolen at twelve o'clock at night, and came back again at three in the morning. Now, it is hardly possible that the journey there and back could be performed in three hours."

"Hardly possible to ordinary horse-flesh, perhaps, but still possible; and Llewellyn knew that probably even better than we do, and, Turpin-like, tries to make the thing incredible by means of the speed of his horse. If suspicion had happened to rest upon him, what better plea could he set up than that you have just mentioned?"

"Yes, yes, like enough, like enough," assented the doctor. "But look you here, Mat, if Llewellyn does turn out to be the author of Stadling's death, be sure of one thing—it was not jealousy that furnished the motive."

"Not jealousy! If there is one thing clearer to me——"

"Not jealousy, Mat, I repeat," said the doctor, deliberately. "I thought so myself at first. I don't think so now. He was not fond enough of his wife to be jealous; or, if jealous, not jealous to the extent of five thousand pounds not jealous enough to go the length he did. If I have learned nothing else from the groom's story, I have learned that. Mark what I say: if you ever get to the truth of this affair you will find it turns upon something very different from what you expect."

"Don't speak in oracles, for Heaven's sake, doctor. If you know anything let us hear what it is."

"I know no more than you do, so far as knowing goes. But I have done what you haven't: I've put two and two together, and suspect a great deal more. One thing is evident enough to me: Llewellyn loved his horse, but he most certainly did not love his wife, and he would not have sacrificed the one thing he did love for the woman he was within measurable distance of hating. You will find the key to the whole complication, it's my belief, when you find out the meaning of Amelia Llewellyn's words to her mother-in-law—'Take care how you deal with two faces when they belong to different people, especially when those faces are female faces.' Those words, be sure, point to some hidden fact in Llewellyn's life; they have their significance, and when you have found out what that significance is, you will find the tangled skein unravel in your hands—possibly have Llewellyn in your power. The one thing wanting, Mat—the one—thing—wanting—is a glance into the correspondence that passed between Stadding and Amelia Llewellyn—the correspondence that Sarah Bundle burned on the day of the murder. One glance at that, and mystery as it may have been to the old lady, I would read you the riddle to some purpose."

"That being impossible, we must do the one remaining thing, that's all, and hunt up this man Trupp, who slept at Monk's Bridge that night, and get what information we can from him."

"I don't anticipate anything from it; still, I suppose that is the only thing to do, but we must expect to have a very different witness to deal with in him from Sarah Bundle or the landlord of the Truss o' Straw. We have some reason to believe he has told one lie already on the subject, and if he really is in Llewellyn's confidence, you may rely upon it he will either be prepared with more lies, or else refuse us information altogether."

"The prospects are not the most cheering, certainly, but, as I say, we must make the best we can out of them. Next to Llewellyn himself he is the man who knows most of what happened that night, and it will be strange if we can't extract enough from him to help us to arrive at some more or less definite conclusion. . . . . I tell you what, doctor," Redmayne went on, with fierce impatience, "I feel my blood beginning to rise. This stealthy mining and counter-mining, and cut and thrust in the

dark, is not to my taste. I wish I knew this Llewellyn
—I wish I might meet him in the street and take him by
the throat and wring the truth out of him."

They had entered Wellington by this time. A thin
drizzling rain had begun to fall, and the wet, slippery,
black-looking pavement reflected the light of the street
lamps in long shimmering lines of brightness. As he
spoke, Redmayne felt the doctor's hand close around his
arm, and heard the doctor's voice say, "Look!—as I live,
that is he now, in front of us!" A man's figure had
turned out of one of the side streets from the direction of
the Railway Station, and halting beneath a street lamp,
commenced fumbling with his cloak. He took out three or
four letters from one of his pockets, and as Redmayne and
Doctor Carmichael came up to him, he was holding them up
to the light to read the addresses, selected one and put it
by itself, placed the others in an inner pocket, buttoned
his cloak around him again, and passed on. Redmayne
and the doctor followed him. The doctor seemed to regard
the wish Redmayne had just uttered in a very literal sense,
for he kept his hand clasped tightly around his friend's
arm throughout their progress through the sleeping town.
The wind was rising, and was sweeping along the silent
length of the streets in heavy gusts, and the drizzle soon
became a thick, steady downpour. Llewellyn halted before
a house where alone of all the buildings in the street a
light was burning in the window. Redmayne and the
doctor paused only long enough to see him let himself in
by means of a latchkey, and then retraced their steps
towards their respective hotels.

"You might have noticed a two-storeyed building with
a balcony directly opposite the house that Llewellyn
entered?" observed the doctor, as they turned away.

"I did; I made a note of it as a landmark to guide
me in the future," said Redmayne, significantly.

"Well, particular friends of mine live in that house, and
it is just possible——"

"You may gain some information from them," said Redmayne, quickly. "Quite right, doctor, there is not a point in the game we can afford to lose. But first of all we must find out this man Trupp, and gain what we can from him. We must not let the grass grow under our feet now we have gone so far."

"We must not, indeed. But there is one thing that prevents me giving the assistance I would like to give, and which I believe I could give."

"And that is?" said Redmayne, as the doctor hesitated.

"That is an opportunity to look through the diary your wife sent you, if you will let me. I want to go to the fountain head—— There is more in this affair than I can grasp with information given at second-hand."

"And more than we can afford to sacrifice for the sake of a little false delicacy. You shall have the diary as soon as I can get it sent over, doctor. I will write home to Ellen for it to-night. And now here we are at your hotel. Good-night."

XXVIII.

EARLY the next morning the doctor called upon Redmayne at his rooms.

"Well," he said, "what of the whereabouts of Trupp?—have you looked up your Directory?"

"I have. The only Trupp mentioned there lives in Auckland, I find. It is an uncommon name, and I expect it's the same man."

"Yes. I'm inclined to think so. But let us have no more jumping to conclusions after last night. The question is now, what are we to do?"

Redmayne, nothing if not prompt, already had a portmanteau partly packed; he looked up in surprise at the doctor's question. *He* had settled what was to be done, as far as that went, the moment he saw the entry in the Directory.

"Do? Why, there's only one thing we can do," he said, with a dumb appeal to the gaping portmanteau. "We settled that last night."

"We didn't know then that we would have to look outside Wellington for our man though, and even if it be the right man, which remains to be proved, it would be some days before we could be back in town again, and Llewellyn should not be lost sight of in the meantime. It would be better if one of us went to Auckland in quest of Trupp, and one stayed here to watch Llewellyn."

"Yes, a good idea," assented Redmayne, nodding. "There is no telling where he may shape his course for twenty-four hours hence. I leave it with you, doctor; what do you think?"

"I think if you can trust yourself to keep your hands off Llewellyn meanwhile, it would be better if I went on to Auckland, and you remained here. Another thing, my friends the Hawkshaws—you remember that two-storeyed house that I pointed out to you last night—have a couple of rooms to let. Suppose you were to shift your quarters from here and take those rooms till we could settle what further we should do, when we have learned the result of my journey to Auckland? You could act the private detective to perfection while you smoked your cigar on the balcony of a day. You won't have packed your portmanteau for nothing after all."

"Agreed. Anything that throws Llewellyn across my path. To live over the way is so much nearer to coming within arm's length of him; and that will come sooner or later, doctor, mark my words. Ours is a chain of three links, and we've reached the last of them in this man Trupp."

"That's more than either of us can say, my dear fellow. It was Sarah Bundle's story that made you seek out the groom, and the groom's that has made us seek out Trupp.

Who shall say what the fourth step may be? In all probability when I come back, we'll only find we've climbed one hill to see another beyond it. By the way, did you write to Levuka last night for the diary, as you promised?"

"I did, the letter is in one of my pockets waiting for the post at this moment."

"Come with me, then, and let me introduce you to the Hawkshaws at once. You can post it on the way. I think you will like the Hawkshaws when you get used to them. There are five of them. The two old people, and Edith, Miriam, and Theodore—who, I may tell you for your guidance, is looked upon by the rest of the family as a genius, and whom the rest of the family expect other people to look upon as a genius too. But I will leave you to form your own opinion of them when you come to know them."

Mr. and Mrs. Hawkshaw and their son were the only members of the family at home when the doctor and Redmayne called. The rooms were very conveniently situated for Redmayne's purpose—one of them opening on to the balcony—and satisfactory arrangements were speedily made with Mr. Theodore, who represented the family in all business transactions. Mr. Theodore was an artist, and presented himself with a much-used painter's palette and brush in his hand, and a look of artistic abstraction on his face. He had all the appearance of a genius. His smoking-cap had lost its tassel, his dressing-gown was threadbare, the front of his waistcoat was smeared with paint stains, and his slippers were very much down at the heels.

"You come upon me, Mr. Redmayne," he said, "in a careless moment. I am an artist, you observe, and am at present engaged on a work which takes up so much of my time, that I know I am prone to neglect myself.

"Indeed," he went on, working the tip of his brush round and round in a dab of moist colour on his palette, "the time of every one of us is almost entirely taken up now. The fact is, doctor—you know my old leaning that way—the fact is, I have written a play, and a little company of friends are about to perform it."

"And you have the old difficulty about filling the parts," said the doctor.

"*And* we have the old difficulty about filling the parts," assented Mr. Theodore, with a wave of his palette, "Exactly."

"Male or female ?"

"Well, both, as a matter of fact. There are two small male parts vacant—we are rehearsing without them—and a female part at present filled by a young lady who is doubtful whether she will not be called away a day or two before the time if a certain contingency in the family happens. And of course it's a moral certainty that the contingency *will* happen and she *will* be called away."

"Miriam ?" suggested the doctor, tentatively.

Theodore shook his head.

"Miriam, doctor, is dead against anything of the kind. She has a quarrel with even the most harmless religious novel, inasmuch as it assumes actuality. Her rigid idea of what candour imposes would require a novelist to put 'on'y s'pose' before every chapter. And as for plays—— No, Miriam is hopeless, and Edith has doubled her part already."

"And what of the play itself ?"

"The play itself," said the genius, returning to the dab of paint again, "is, as I have said, an original play—my own. I've shown it to several friends, but, like most other people, you know——" and Theodore shrugged his shoulders and left his sentence unfinished.

The doctor shook his head sympathetically.

"Nothing so unsatisfactory as criticism, Theodore," he said—"nothing so unsatisfactory as criticism."

"That's what I find," said Theodore. "One falls foul of my method of arrangement, another is prepared to swear I have filched whole scenes from other dramatists."

"Other dramatists ? H'm, h'm."

"People are so apt to forget that in these times, when all the stories have been told, that however truly *original* a production may be so far as the writer is concerned, and as my play is, it is hardly possible for it to be *new:* it is quite impossible, I believe, to write anything of which a segment will not coincide with the segment of what somebody else has written before you."

"The moral of which is?"

"Why, I suppose," replied Theodore, with a laugh, "that what we call Original Production should cease, that a Trinity of Shakespeare, Bacon, and Milton should be set up, and that we should fall down and worship."

"But as for you, you'll publish right or wrong."

"I feel that that kind of treatment is unjust and absurd when it goes the length of condemning a man's play, as mine has been, for the simple reason that it happens to have a balcony scene in it. Surely the balcony is not to be tabooed and appropriated to Shakespeare to all eternity because he has used it prominently in a prominent play."

"Surely not," assented the doctor, "or what would become of the 'other dramatists'?"

"If the same principle were applied a little more widely, what *would* become of them? Now, my play naturally led up to a balcony; I conceived a balcony; I introduced a balcony; and, by heaven, doctor," cried the excited playwright, grasping his palette like a shield and his brush like a dagger, "I've as much right to use that balcony as I have to use the one we are standing on at the present moment."

"I agree with you, Theodore, I agree with you," said the doctor, with a keen appreciation of his own humour. "When a man's play naturally leads up to a balcony, and he conceives a balcony, and introduces a balcony, by heaven he *has* as much right to his balcony as all the William Shakespeares and puling Romeos and Juliets that ever breathed in England or Verona. You have a good view of your neighbour across the street from here, too, I notice."

"Yes, yes; but to return to my play. Perhaps you would like to see it?"

"I have promised myself that pleasure, Theodore. When do you intend to produce it?"

"I meant," said the author, with the mendicant air of people who keep plays about them in manuscript, and with a return for the third time to the modest refuge on his palette, "that perhaps you would like to see it in—in MS."

"I should like it of all things, Theodore; but I am starting almost immediately for Auckland, and it is doubtful how long I may be detained. But if, as I say, you could let me know when you think of producing it —"

"About three weeks from now, I hope, if all goes well. I want as many rehearsals as possible, for some of the little company are very slow in grasping the significance of their parts—very slow."

"Three weeks, very well," said the doctor, feeling that much might happen in three weeks, "if I can find an opportunity between then and now, I shall be very pleased to see the play; and meanwhile, Theodore, I shall consider myself commissioned to press into your service any eligible young lady I can prevail upon to take this vacant part; though I haven't an idea what the requirements of the part are, by the way."

"Whoever she may be, she won't have more than a dozen or twenty lines to say throughout, and I have made them very simple. Any one of ordinary intelligence will do. The title of the piece, I may tell you, is *The Lover, the Lock, and the Larder*."

"I understand: humorous—with a policeman in it."

"Well, if my title suggests that," said the playwright, with a restrained severity in eye and voice, "all I can say is that the title is unfortunate, and shall be changed. That the play should contain humour—a refined humour, I trust—was the end I placed before myself, certainly, but I found no necessity to introduce a policeman."

"But, bless my soul, Theodore, policemen are occasionally introduced——"

"Yes, I'm aware of it," said Theodore, showing an inclination to break off the conversation and return to his picture, "with a clown and a harlequin to keep them company. In my case I have endeavoured to write a Play, not a Christmas pantomime. But I shall take care that the title shall be changed."

"Theodore is not a bad fellow at bottom," said the doctor, when he and Redmayne had left the house, and speaking with an impartiality that plainly cost him an effort, "but he resembles the rest of the authors—as a tadpole resembles a frog. I never discussed picture, story, play, or poem with him yet—and he produces each with equal readiness, the young egotist—without having more or less of a quarrel with him over it. Him and his balcony scene ! However, the lodgings will do capitally ; that's one consideration."

"Capitally," said Redmayne, "though there's that play in manuscript—I know what it will be. He'll read it to me or make me read it, and I know no more about the merits of a play than I do about Sanskrit."

PART VII.

THE NIGHT OF THE ELEVENTH JUNE.

XXIX.

There had been a ring at Herr Trupp's door, and a card bearing the name of Doctor Carmichael had been put into the herr's hand. He was always known as the herr, though he had lived so long among English people, and had become so Anglicized in his ways of late years, that it almost amounted to eccentricity for him to retain it in his name now; but he did retain it, partly as a mark of his nationality, which he was loth to give up, and partly because this is an age of advertisements.

"Doctor Carmichael, Doctor Carmichael!" he said to himself vaguely, as he looked at the card. "I don't know the name. However, show him in."

An epoch had arrived in the herr's life. He was an enthusiastic palæontologist, and had only lately published a pamphlet with a theory on moa bones. It had not attracted any attention as yet, but ever since the time it had fallen dead-born from the Press, the herr had dwelt in daily expectation that every ring at his door was the ring of some intelligent reader who had been struck by his pamphlet and its theory, and had come to discuss it with him. He had been disappointed times out of number, but he entertained the same expectation just as strongly as ever again at that moment. . . .

He shook his head as he received the doctor, for the

latter's mission had had its effect upon the expression of his face—and it was not that of an enthusiastic palæontologist. "Alas," he said to himself for the fiftieth time, "another disappointment; this is not the man to discuss a work like my pamphlet."

"I dare say, sir," said the visitor, striking abruptly into the business that had brought him there, "that you will be surprised at this intrusion on the part of a stranger—all the more so when I say I have come all the way from Wellington with no other object in view than this visit."

"Wellington," thought the herr, whose inscrutable vanity contrived to put a favourable construction on this unusual introduction for no other reason than that it *was* unusual; "it must be my pamphlet after all. How little one knows how far one's name may spread," and he began to think he must have been mistaken in his estimate of his visitor, and to take his uncompromising stare for the kindly interest of a mind in touch with his own. . . . . "I am very pleased, I'm sure," he said, pressing his glasses back to a genial focus with his finger and thumb.

"I am engaged in an investigation in which I am sure you can be of the greatest assistance to me." . . . . And the visitor's eyes added as plain as eyes could add, "But in which I know it will be against your will to help me; but I am prepared to overcome that will;" and again the herr misunderstood the dumb language of his visitor's eyes, and hugged the belief that it really was his pamphlet.

"It is a question of palæontology, perhaps," said the herr.

"It is a question of murder," said the visitor.

The herr suddenly collapsed behind his spectacles, and threw himself back so violently that his chair creaked again.

"God bless my soul! A question of murder! And you come to me! What do I know of it?"

"It is a question of murder," repeated the uncompromising visitor, "and I have come to you because you know all about it. I refer to the murder of Edgar Stadding by your friend Llewellyn at Lowry Bay, on the 11th of June, 1886."

Doctor Carmichael leaned forward, the better to observe the effect of his carefully premeditated shot. There was no mistaking the expression that overspread the face of the herr. It was one of blank, hopeless bewilderment, and nothing more.

"I beg your pardon," said the visitor, before the herr could collect himself sufficiently to answer; his eyes taking upon themselves a new look, and his voice a new tone. "I have surprised you. I have been too abrupt. I should have explained myself."

"I certainly do not understand to what you refer," murmured the herr, helplessly.

"Think for a moment, please. It is three years now since the event took place. Do you not remember staying at Monk's Bridge one night, and what happened there?"

"You mean the night the horse Scythe-bearer died."

"That was the night. Do you not remember anything besides the death of Scythe-bearer?"

The herr's mind went through a process that was not thought, and which ended in a shake of the head. The old shade of suspicion came over the face of Doctor Carmichael again, and he put on a look of keen scrutiny that made puckers on each temple.

"May I ask if you are able to say whether Mr. Llewellyn left the house that night between the hours of twelve at night and three in the morning?"

"I have not the slightest conception of your motive, but I can say with absolute certainty that he did not leave the house between the hours you mention."

("You unconscionable liar!" said the visitor's eyes.)

"I am afraid the time that has elapsed has impaired your memory of the circumstance," translated the lips.

The usually bland spectacles of the herr flashed in the sunlight.

"No," he said; "now you mention it I recall the occasion perfectly. My friend Llewellyn did not leave the house that night—or rather that morning—till he led the way down to the stable-yard with me, and there we found my friend's horse lying at his last gasp upon the stones. The poor brute had been done to death by some miscreant during the night. But you spoke just now of an explanation," said the herr, recollecting himself, "and when you connect the name of my friend with a crime in the way you have done, you will pardon me if I say that this conversation can go no further till that explanation is forthcoming."

The doctor held his walking-stick clasped in both hands, bent into a half-circle across his knee, and his knee raised in front of him. The herr had pushed his spectacles on to his forehead with the motion of Ivanhoe closing his visor in the lists at Ashby. Dr. Carmichael had always given himself some credit for a degree of skill in reading faces, and he told himself that if ever he had seen a human face which was unconscious of hiding anything in the shape of a guilty secret, it was surely the one before him now. As for the herr, he only saw the reddish face of a very common-place, uninteresting gentleman, calling himself a doctor, who had not only insulted him through his friend, but who had never even so much as seen his pamphlet, and who would not have had enough intelligence to read it if he had seen it.

"I am aware my conduct must have seemed un-accountable in a stranger," said the doctor at last, relaxing his stick and his mental attitude at the same time, and my only excuse is the peculiar position in which I am placed. My, let us say, curiosity has been very powerfully aroused as to what actually took place at Monk's Bridge on the night I have mentioned, and it was because I had reason to believe you would be able to assist me in arriving at the truth that I called upon you to-day." (He would have stopped his meagre explanation at that point had he been permitted, but the herr still fronted him with close-shut lips and visor raised, and so plainly waiting for something further, that he had no alternative but to go on.) " You will remember that a murder was committed that night— a man named Edgar Stadding being the victim, and a girl being arrested and tried as the perpetrator. Events into which I am not at liberty to enter—but which you may be assured have given me every right to prosecute the inquiry you see me engaged in—have occurred, which cause me to entertain very serious doubts as to that girl's guilt——"

" And which, on the other hand, cause you to suspect that it was my friend Llewellyn who actually did the deed ?"

" Well, if you put it that plainly— yes."

" I am glad you have been so unreserved with me ; I shall try and be equally so with you. It would have been better if you had said this at first. I was with Llewellyn not only during the afternoon of that day, but during the whole of the night as well, and whatever information I have is entirely at your service ; for, if you once learn the truth, I am happy to say you will no longer entertain the shadow of a suspicion against my friend."

" You will pardon my questioning you somewhat closely?"

" Pray have no scruples on that score. I can appreciate your position perfectly, and have but the one desire to help you, and to remove from your mind your suspicions of my friend : the more closely you may question the more thoroughly will his character be cleared."

" My first question you have already answered when you tell me that Mr. Llewellyn did not leave Monk's Bridge on the night of the eleventh June. May I ask what is the evidence which makes you so certain on this point— for in proving that, you prove all ?"

" The evidence of my own senses. We slept in the same room ; his bed was not two yards from mine. I was awake the whole of the night, and could see him any time between the hours you mention."

"And did see him?"

"And did see him," said the herr, nodding his head with slow emphasis, and tapping his fingers on the table beside him. "I can say with absolute certainty that he did not once leave the room on the night of the eleventh June from the first moment of his entering it."

For the fourth time Doctor Carmichael's eyes scanned the herr's face; for the fourth time he formulated the doubt that had been floating through his mind during the whole interview, Is this man telling me the truth? and for the fourth time the frank and open face of the herr—all the more frank and open because his spectacles were on his forehead and not in front of his eyes—disarmed his suspicions. . . . "Yes," said the doctor to himself, "it is possible for a villain to have an honest man for his friend."

"From the first moment of his entering it," repeated the herr, deliberately, this time reading aright the hesitancy and questioning in the doctor's eyes. "Perhaps you will understand more clearly if I tell you all that happened that night. I went to my room some time before my friend. He had been reading a letter which I had seen put into his hand that afternoon by a girl as we stood on the platform of the Wellington Railway Station——"

"Did he say anything that would indicate the nature of the contents of that letter—did he appear impressed by it in any unusual way?"

"Not in any way by the letter itself, I should say. He merely glanced through it, and then tore it up and threw the pieces in the fire. But there was a note with the letter, which I thought seemed to affect him differently."

"In what way?"

The herr hesitated a moment, as if he thought his visitor was presuming on a too literal observance of his purpose to question somewhat closely, remembered the character of his friend was at stake, and went on—

"Before I answer that, I must say, in justice to my

friend, that I can only tell you what appeared to me to be the case, rather than what may have been the case in reality : I thought his face paled, and that his hand shook. He certainly seemed agitated, and commenced pacing about the room."

"He said nothing as to what the note contained?"

"No, he did not," said the herr, drily; "and, knowing his humour, I judged it best to leave him, and went up to my, or rather our, room accordingly. That would be about half past nine. It was between an hour and an hour and a half after that, when Llewellyn came into the room."

"Eleven o'clock."

"About eleven o'clock. The room was lighted by a night lamp, and he had turned the flame down and blown it out just before getting into bed, when he seemed to remember something. I heard him feeling about among the things on the table, and muttering to himself; and presently he asked—

"'Have you any matches, Trupp?—I've mislaid mine?'

"I gave him my box, and he lit the lamp again, and poured some colourless liquid from a phial into a wine-glass, and tossed it off, saying, 'Well, here's to Scythe-bearer's chance in the Cup.' His eyes, I thought, had grown unnaturally bright, and his face very worn and pale since I had left him; but I knew how much depended on his winning the Cup race, and I thought that the nervous strain was proving too much for him.

"'Nerves?' I said.

"'Yes, nerves,' he answered.

"'Not breaking down already, I hope?'

"He shook his head.

"'Something very like it, Trupp. I feel wretchedly weak and ill to-night.'

"He placed the phial and the wine-glass near the lamp, as if he intended to use them again during the night, turned down the flame so that it only cast a dim light over the room, and got into bed.   .   .

"I have been all my life a victim to asthma, but it was worse than usual that night, and the fumes from the lamp aggravated it afresh. In the course of an hour the irritation became unbearable, and I began to cough so loudly that I feared I should wake Llewellyn—which, ill as I feared he was, I should very much regret having done ; so I stepped out of bed and blew the light out. . . . .

"The night was as yet intensely dark, and silent almost as the grave—the only sound I detected was the deep, measured breathing of Llewellyn. Suddenly that silence was broken. I heard a noise I could not distinguish, save that it seemed to come from the direction of the stable-yard. Then—surely I could not be mistaken—the swift pounding of a horse's hoofs upon the ground, but deadened by the walls that intervened. Then stillness again. I lay motionless and listened, but nothing happened, and the sound was not repeated. Llewellyn did not seem to have been disturbed, for I could tell by his heavy respiration that he was still asleep.

"The minutes crept on into hours. The little clock in the room where I was sleeping struck 'one' and 'two,' and was echoed by another clock with deeper tone from an inner room somewhere in the house.

"A little before three there came a hesitating knock a the door. I asked 'Who's there?'

"A voice answered 'I'm the groom. I want to see Mr. Llewellyn.'

"I asked him what was the matter, and he answered that something had happened.

"'Your master is not well,' I said. 'He's asleep. Will the morning not do as well?'

"'Very well,' came the answer, after a pause, and in a tone so faint that I could barely make out the words, 'I'll tell him in the morning.'

"I was sorry afterwards I did not let the man deliver his message, for I learned next morning that his only child had died during the night ; but I attached no importance

to the poor fellow's words at the time. Had he insisted on
making himself heard—as one would naturally expect a
man situated as he was would have done—I should, of course,
have offered no further objection, but aroused Llewellyn
at once.

"He had not been gone long when I was once more
startled by the clatter of horse's hoofs in the yard. The
sound was fainter than before, but I was certain I could
not be mistaken. The thought crossed my mind for the
first time that perhaps something had happened to Scythe-
bearer. I sat up and listened intently. Llewellyn was still
asleep—I could see him in the faint moonlight lying with
his face turned away from me. I stole noiselessly to the
window, and looked out. The stables were round the
corner of the house, and I could not make out anything
from my point of view. I stood for a few minutes debating
with myself whether I should arouse Llewellyn or not.
Everything seemed to me the same as usual. Perhaps I
had been mistaken. If anything had really happened to
Scythe-bearer, surely the groom would let his master know
on the instant. But stay—could it have been that that
had brought him to the door a few minutes since? It was
possible——and yet, surely, in that case, he would not have
let me turn him from his purpose so easily. . . . I felt
for the matches to light the lamp again, but could not find
them. 'Llewellyn!' I called, 'Llewellyn!' He did not
hear me, and I stepped to his bedside and shook him by
the shoulder. 'Llewellyn! Get up. Something has happened in the stables.' He was broad awake in a moment,
and started up into a sitting posture. 'What do you
say? Is it Scythe-bearer?'—'I don't know. I have heard
the sound of horses galloping in the yard. The groom
knocked at the door a minute or two ago, and said something had happened.'—'My God! it must be Scythe-
bearer,' he said, as he threw on his things. 'It must be
Scythe-bearer. If it is I'm a ruined man!' He drew the
matches from under his pillow, and threw them on the

table as he dressed. I lit the lamp, and drew on my things almost as quickly as he did. 'Follow me, Trupp,' he said, catching up the lamp, and leading the way through the house, 'and let us see what has happened.' I followed him as he hurried along the passages, and the first thing we saw as we stepped into the stable-yard was the dying form of Scythe-bearer lying in a heap on the stones." [1]

.   .   .   .

.   .   .   .

XXX.

[FROM MATTHEW REDMAYNE TO DR. CARMICHAEL.]

"I CANNOT describe the shock your letter, describing your conversation with Herr Trupp, has given me. I don't doubt for a moment but that you are fully justified in your confidence that the herr told you neither more nor less than the truth, and I must admit that I am discouraged by it beyond words. If Llewellyn was not the author of Stadding's death, we know well enough who was; and you will understand all that that means for me. The dearest hope of my life is dashed to the ground for ever. I can look for nothing more conclusive than this last piece of evidence. I own myself convinced at last. When I think of the story told in Esther's diary—when I consider all the circumstances of her sister's life, I feel I have been a mere self-deluded fool ever to have formed the hopes I have lately indulged. A fool not to see that Sarah Bundle's story was far more easily explained away than was Esther's. A fool not to see that the landlord's story needed no explanation other than it bore upon the face of it. Well, it's all over now, and it only remains for me to bear my

[1] The herr then goes over the same ground as that already traversed by the landlord of the 'Truss o' Straw, with only the trifling variations that might affect the memory after lapse of time.

part as well as dear little Esther has borne hers. I cannot tell you how this heart-sickening see-saw between hope and despair has affected me now that I have arrived at the truth at last. . . . You are wrong in advising me to see Esther again. Another interview with her would be useless—worse than useless. It would be more, I believe, than she could bear. Better let things be as they are. Come back as soon as you can, for I have much to say to you."

XXXI.

[From Matthew Redmayne to Esther.]

(Ten days later.)

" Dear Esther,

"This will be delivered to you by Dr. Carmichael only upon a certain condition, which he has formed in his own private mind, but which he has not imparted to me. It is this same condition of his that has caused him to make the journey to New Plymouth alone, and that has caused him to think of bringing you back with him to Wellington on his return. I know that you will not approve of this step. After the decision you expressed at our last meeting, and situated as we two are, I fear it is very unwise—doubly so when I tell you that all our investigations have proved worse than fruitless. It is only on the doctor's assurance that his action will be justified by the event that I have permitted it at all. I can only say that if we do see one another again I will not seek by so much as a word or look to turn you from the determination you have formed; that I shall seek to do nothing that might make this second interview between us more trying for you than in the nature of things it may prove to be; and in earnest of that I refrain from writing so much as one of the many things I should have written only a few days ago.   You have decided that our paths in life must henceforth be apart from one another.   I will not play the hypocrite with myself by saying I believe that decision is a wise one ;—but so be it.   Only rest assured of this: that if in the future you should change your mind as to what you consider duty imposes upon you, you will not find me then with the restraints upon my affection which I place upon them under present circumstances.   You will find me then as to-day.

"Your true-hearted lover and husband,

"MATTHEW."

PART VIII.

"NO SUCH THING AS CHANCE."

XXXII.

*　　　*　　　*　　　*　　　*　　　*

" Now, Esther," began Dr. Carmichael, and then stopped
and bent over her with an old beau's gaiety, and whispered
something in her ear—only one word or two —which caused
her to start, draw her brows together swiftly in a momentary frown, and look almost fearfully up in his face, with
parted lips, as if she were about to speak, and then, reassured by his expression, to sink back in her chair again
with a new, almost pleased, and wholly mystified look in
her eyes and an incredulous smile on her lips, and —was it
or was it not—a sidelong timorous glance towards Redmayne ? Miss Dorothy Ann, too, who was sitting beside
her with a much more knowing look than the circumstances
seemed at all to warrant, took her hand in hers, and they
both sat with their eyes fixed upon the doctor's countenance—the only difference was that there was no mistaking
the satisfaction and expectancy on Miss Dorothy Ann's
face, while Esther's expression became gradually one of
settled perplexity and uneasiness.

" Now, Esther, and you, Redmayne," began the doctor
again (he did not include Miss Dorothy Ann, but Esther
thought she detected a swift glance pass between them),
" when I set out for New Plymouth three or four days ago,
I made it a condition that if a certain supposition I had

formed proved true, I should consider myself justified in bringing you two together again for at least one more interview before both your lives were ruined by your parting for ever, if you went so far as to turn the romantic tom-fool's game you are keeping up into earnest."

The doctor, whose always reddish face was redder than ever under the influence of some internal excitement, paused and looked at his audience. Redmayne, alive to nothing but the responsibility of following out the course he had pledged himself to in his letter to Esther, was sitting a little apart with an almost theatrical composure of face and manner. He nodded, and the doctor went on—

"Very well. That particular supposition did prove true, as it happened, and, consequently, I have brought your wife and Miss Winterson all the way from New Plymouth up here to your own sitting-room to-day. . . . . . And much good it appears to have done you, you ungrateful young dog," the doctor seemed to add mentally, as he contemplated his friend's unbending stolidity.

Redmayne nodded his head again, and then instantly subsided into his frigid shell of composure.

"But this interview over, and the explanation made that I think ought to be made, I wash my hands of the whole affair, and you must decide for yourselves whether for the future your paths in life are to be together or apart."

Esther started with an indefinite feeling of alarm under a meaning glance that escaped the doctor, and a meaning pressure of the hand from Miss Dorothy Ann. She could not free herself from the apprehension that some advantage was sought to be taken of her feelings; but a glance towards Redmayne reassured her, at least as far as he was concerned.

"Doctor Carmichael," she said, tremulously, "you have been the very best of good friends to me, and I know that your intentions towards me are always the kindest— but —but there can be no explanation. The only explanation possible between us was that which Matthew and I came

to days ago. This is becoming nothing less than perse-
cution, and I cannot bear it. I cannot—you know I *cannot*
do otherwise than I am doing. Why did you not tell me
what were your intentions before inducing me to come here
from New Plymouth ?"

"No, doctor, my wi—— Esther, came here," said Redmayne, with signs of a rapid thaw taking place in his own
composure, as he noticed the distress Esther's apprehension
was causing her, "under a distinct promise from me that
I should neither by word or look attempt to alter the
determination she has come to——"

"They have both thrown themselves on your good faith,
in fact, doctor," Miss Dorothy Ann interposed hastily.

"And I can't allow you, doctor, on any conditions whatever, to try and do for me what I am bound in honour not
to do for myself. All I can say is that I am—that we are
both prepared to await . . . the future."

A grateful look from Esther through the tears that
would come, and he withdrew into his shell more completely
than ever.

"H'mph," said the doctor, discontentedly, after a pause,
"and this is being in love, is it ? Human nature seems
to have changed considerably since my day. However,
Redmayne, you can keep your temper, and, Esther, you
can dry your tears. I said in the first place I should not
bring this meeting about unless the event fully justified
me in doing it; and I think you'll admit, before I've done,
that the event *has* justified me. . . . There is one
thing. I am afraid I shall have to refer to a subject that
may give you pain, Esther; but you know me too well to
think I would give you pain needlessly, or to imagine that
I have only brought you here to play with your feelings——"

It may have been something in the doctor's voice and
glance, or the recollection of the words he had whispered to
her at the beginning, or it may have been something in the
eloquent pressure of Miss Dorothy Ann's hand, but with a
woman's swift change of disposition and a woman's swift

intuition, Esther suddenly started up with her hands clasped before her, and her eyes sparkling with a light they had not known for many a day.

"Oh! dear Doctor Carmichael, you mean—you must mean my poor sister. Don't keep me in suspense. Tell me—tell me what it is at once!"

"Doctor," cried Redmayne, catching the infection, and throwing his carefully preserved composure to the winds, and springing to his feet, "you can't mean——you have found out no new fact?"

"You would ask, Esther, I know, if there is any hope that after all your sister is innocent—innocent, that is, in the sense you would wish her to be. Recollect what I have told you this last day or two as to our investigations and what their result has been, and do not let me rouse expectations that may be only doomed to disappointment."

"Speak plainly, doctor. Tell me at once *is* she innocent or not?"

"Let me answer you both at once, by saying if I cannot at present go so far as that, I have at least found out, however impossible it may have been for Llewellyn to have done the deed himself, he had so powerful a motive for wishing it done, that I have not the least doubt in the world at this moment but that the man who did commit this crime was no other than some one he had hired to do it——"

"Unless," faltered Esther, almost inaudibly, understanding only too well the meaning of the doctor's pause, and feeling her new-born hope turning cold and dead about her heart again.

"Yes, unless, indeed, he was forestalled," he added, gravely, understanding in his turn the breathless pause she too had made; "but judging by after events, that seems highly improbable—at least to me."

"I pray God her hand may be as innocent as her heart was," Esther breathed rather than spoke.

"But I do not understand," interrupted Redmayne,

impetuously, "what new facts—what new discovery can there be?"

"The discovery of all others that I have been longing for since you first broached this subject to me."

"You cannot mean the correspondence that passed between Amelia Llewellyn and Stadding?"

"That, and nothing else—those letters, at least, that passed from Stadding to Mrs. Amelia Llewellyn."

"But the girl told me distinctly she burnt every letter."

"Possibly."

"Did she not tell me the truth, then?"

"Possibly," said the doctor again, with vast enjoyment of the situation, "as nearly as a girl's giddy head would let her; but whether I had to extract the correspondence from the ashes of those letters, or from the air, I've got it, lad, every message—but one—that passed between those two people that is of any interest to us."

"Now—in this house?"

"Now, and in this house."

"Then, in the name of heaven, let me see them with my own eyes," were the first words that sprung from Redmayne's lips, and

"Oh, however *did* you come to find them out?" were the first words that left the lips of his wife.

"In the first place, by a very simple process of reasoning; and in the second place, in the careful keeping of those ten pretty little fingers of your own."

"In my keeping, doctor: whatever are you saying?"

"Neither more nor less than that you have been carrying about with you for months the one piece of evidence of all others that Mat and myself too would have almost given our right hands for—the one piece of evidence that more than anything else gives me hope that your prayer as to your poor Kate's innocence may yet be fulfilled."

"I?!! I did not so much as know the letters were in existence till you told me of them the other day."

"Doctor, you must be raving. If you really have the

letters with you, show them to us, and I'll believe you," cried Redmayne again.

"All in good time, Mat," said the doctor, waving his hand; "all in good time, Esther. Let me show you first how I ferreted the thing out. You know that when I came back from Auckland it was in the full belief (as I told you in my letter, Mat) that after all our cleverness and all our plausible putting together of this, that, and the other, Llewellyn was entirely innocent of even the knowledge of Stadding's death. Some days later, you remember, the diary you had written for was forwarded from Levuka—you needn't trouble yourself to blush, Esther; it was a very nicely written little diary, though apt in parts to make a young fellow vain——"

"Oh, for heaven's sake keep to your story, and let us get through, if we must hear it first," said Redmayne, impatiently, who now looked as if he had never known what composure meant.

"Well, well then, as I say, the diary came to hand, but I had little hope of gaining anything from it, for by that time all the airy castles we had been at so much pains to build had been all upset and gone off in thin air. I told myself that what I had all my life long believed to be the truth—that an actor's fictitious character may become by oft repetition his real character—had been borne out in this case." (Redmayne frowned at the speaker's forgetfulness, and looked quickly at Esther's face, but she did not seem to have appreciated the significance of what the doctor had said.) "This was what I told myself when I took up your diary; and it was in this belief that I read on till I came to your description of the scene in the theatre—the glade in the forest at midnight, the two men talking angrily, the struggle, the stage moon and the canvas clouds—where did you learn anything about stage moons and canvas clouds, I should like to know?—the escape of the guilty man and the entrance of the woman on the scene, and then of your waking up from your faint and seeing Llewellyn looking down at you from over the shoulder of Stadding. I read on till there, and then I stopped, and my opinion changed. I recalled the discussion Mat and I had had over it all, days before ; but it struck me with tenfold greater force now that I had seen it in your own handwriting and with added particulars. I put the book down, and said to myself, ' By the great god Pan, there's fatality and Providence in this, and I've been a blind fool not to see it.'

"There is nothing in the way of superstition about me— not an atom—but there are some things a man can't get away from, and this was one of 'em. I told myself this could be no mere coincidence : it must be neither more nor less than a direct providential forecast of what was to happen in the future, and I went afresh over the whole ground Mat and I had already gone over. I went back to the theory of Llewellyn's guilt, and, following that up, came to a consideration of Sarah Bundle's story and what I had heard from the landlord of the 'Truss o' Straw and Herr Trupp. We had concluded, Mat and I, that whatever Llewellyn's motive might have been, it was to a moral certainty furnished by the letter Sarah Bundle had given him on the railway station. Old Mrs. Llewellyn had said she intended showing the last letter Amelia Llewellyn had received to Llewellyn himself, and without doubt this was the letter Herr Trupp spoke of his friend reading, and then tearing in pieces and putting on the fire. What had the greatest effect on Llewellyn appeared to be the note his mother had sent along with Amelia's letter. Now, I asked myself, what could that note contain likely to disturb Llewellyn as it had apparently done. I remembered Redmayne had spoken of a quarrel which Sarah Bundle had witnessed between mother-in-law and daughter-in-law on the day the letter had been despatched. Amelia Llewellyn had said—' If you find it so difficult to deal with two faces on one pair of shoulders, take care how you deal with two faces when they belong to different people, especially when

those faces are female faces,' and the words had affected
the old lady in a rather remarkable way. I thought then
—and I know now—that these words referred to some
hidden fact in Llewellyn's past life, which fact, judging
from the look of things, had hitherto been kept from
Amelia Llewellyn's knowledge. If so, what would be more
probable than that the old lady would draw Llewellyn's
attention to these words in her note. They would show
him that whatever secret they pointed to was now known
to his wife.

"Thus far it had all been fairly plain sailing with the
assistance of the evidence I had ready to my hand. But
now the difficulty came in. Supposing all this was true,
and still going on the theory of Llewellyn's guilt, where
was the immediate occasion for his acting as he did? How
was it he, or his hireling rather, came to keep that fatal
midnight appointment with Stadding? The note would
show him, for one thing, that his wife had a method of
keeping up correspondence with some one outside, and, of
course, that whatever fresh information she had gained of
her husband's past history, must have been furnished her
by this person; but it could tell him nothing more. When
I had first considered this subject with Mat, the conclusion
that we had come to was that Stadding had planned an
elopement, which he purposed should be carried into execution that night, and that the message apprising Amelia
Llewellyn of this—or, more probably, of some final arrangement in connection with it; no doubt the plan itself was of
long standing—had been read by Llewellyn, and that at
the last moment when interference was possible, he had
ridden his racehorse Scythe-bearer out to Lowry Bay, had
met Stadding at the place appointed, and had then and
there killed him, probably in the course of a quarrel. That
conclusion I still thought the correct one, except that,
instead of Llewellyn himself, it must have been some one
he employed.

"Now then, I asked myself How was this fatal message

conveyed which Llewellyn had read? He had torn up the letter which Amelia herself had received, so it was not in that; and it could not have been in old Mrs. Llewellyn's note, for she was not aware that her daughter-in-law carried on any correspondence. That was the utmost point of my reasoning, and at that point I began to despair of going any further. Still, I felt sure the point that was puzzling me was the key to the mystery, and I went patiently over the ground again and again. If the secret was to be discovered at all, I knew it must be in that part of Sarah Bundle's story describing the habits of the women at the cottage at Lowry Bay. There was only one thing to do to settle the point, and I did it. Without consulting Redmayne I walked out to Newtown and saw the girl Bundle myself, and got her to repeat the whole of the story to me afresh.

"I questioned her very closely about the letters her young mistress received, and what she told me served for a time only to puzzle me the more. I had thought at first that they might have been written in cipher; but if that were so how was it that Llewellyn discovered the message *after* he had burnt his wife's letter? The only facts that I could make out were that Amelia Llewellyn did set great value on the letters she received; that they came very frequently; that she appeared to care nothing for them when placed in her hand; and that she had high words with her mother-in-law on one occasion when a letter had been brought to her without the envelope. The same watchfulness had been exercised when she sent letters away as when they were received; before being posted they were always given to the old lady by Amelia herself, and the girl had not the slightest idea as to whom they might be addressed. I questioned her as to whether her young mistress had appeared to greatly resent the old lady reading her letters before giving them up, and from what she told me, Amelia Llewellyn seemed amused rather than otherwise at the old lady's manœuvre, which, especially in the case of a woman, seemed incomprehensible to me.

"Here, then, I was once more fairly at fault, and with expectations lower than ever, I took up your diary again; and because it is always the unexpected that happens, the revelation came to me just at the moment when I had despaired of it. It lay concealed in a certain passage you had written long before any of these sad complications had arisen; and when I read it I dropped the book and felt for a moment as if I had been dazzled—the truth broke so suddenly upon me. It was like coming out of a dark room into broad noonday. Every link fell into its place by enchantment, everything was explained in one involuntary flash of intelligence. I knew now why old Mrs. Llewellyn failed to see what was passing under her eyes; I understood Amelia Llewellyn's anxiety to get her letters, and her apparent loss of interest in them when they were put into her hand, the frequency with which those letters arrived, why she had quarrelled with the old lady when she had sent her the letter and kept back the envelope, and lastly, how that mysterious message had fallen into Llewellyn's hands, and been read by him.

"With the influence of my discovery fresh in my mind, and without the loss of a single hour, I set off for New Plymouth; and this is what I found, and this is my sole justification for having brought about this meeting to-day."

The doctor lifted a book from where it had been lying unnoticed on a chair in a corner of the room, and placed it on the table. Esther recognized it with wonder: it was Pure-in-Heart's book of stamps. The group drew round the doctor without uttering a word. He fluttered the leaves for a moment or two, and then selecting a page, inserted the point of his penknife under one of the stamps and drew it neatly off—so neatly and unresistingly that it suggested the idea of prearrangement. Beneath it was a small square of paper which had originally formed part of an envelope, and this square was covered with writing in almost microscopic characters, and so crowded together that it could only be read with difficulty. As little of the minute space as possible was occupied by the address and signature, and here and there contractions had been resorted to. It read as follows :—

> *Dear A. Do not, I entreat, suppose I am seeking to mislead you in any one particular. Whatever other faults I may have I never yet deceived a woman. I tell you that before long you may defy his tyranny & cruelty & demand yr. freedom from him. Only a little longer and the facts I have referred to will be in my hands. He little knows with whom he has to deal when he deals with me and when yr. honour and happiness are the prize I defend.—Yr. own E.S.*

"How in the name of all that's marvellous came that there?" cried Redmayne, as the doctor ceased reading.

"The explanation is simple, even to absurdity. The passage I read in the diary was that containing the words of your little friend Pure-in-Heart—' Who knows but what the same Power that sets all these things going just to please a poor, weak little invalid, mayn't somehow make use of what he does in his turn.' The truth I had been blindly groping for for days dawned upon me in an instant. The mysterious correspondence had been carried on *under the postage stamp*. But, if so, what must follow? Why, clearly, that the missing correspondence—the correspondence we had so often lamented as lost to us for ever, with all it contained, was at that very moment in Esther's hands. Thus :—

"Amelia Llewellyn locks her room door to prevent possible interruption; the stamp on her letter is removed, and the message lurking beneath it read. The letter having to go back into old Mrs. Llewellyn's hands, the stamp must be replaced again. The old lady puts all the letters together in her drawer, right up to the morning of the 11th June. The girl Bundle is ordered to burn them, and does so, but first as she told Mat cutting out the piece of the envelope bearing the stamp, and sending them to her brother. We know his method is to paste into his book the stamp with the portion of the envelope it covers adhering to it (in this instance, as it happened, they were already prepared by his sister). Consequently every message would be preserved intact in his book of stamps. That book the little fellow had given to Esther, and so the irony of fate had completed itself by making the very person most interested in the disclosure of this evidence the unconscious means of its concealment. It was when I arrived at this point that I saw the opportunity of bringing you two together again for this last interview, but I made it a condition not only that my surmise as to the secret correspondence must be the correct one, but that the character of the communications themselves must justify me in my purpose. I went to New Plymouth, as I have just said, I examined Pure-in-Heart's book, and I found that the little fellow's desire to be useful had been fulfilled years after his death in a way he could have little suspected, and that the same Power that had set all these things going just to please a poor, weak little invalid, had indeed in this unthought-of way made some use of what he did in his turn."

Esther and Redmayne and Miss Dorothy Ann all turned upon the doctor to address him at once. He held up his hand.

"Wait and see what follows. Wait and see how thoroughly this bed-ridden little invalid fulfilled his unconscious task before he died—how his childish fad of collecting stamps has done for us what all our wise brains could not do for ourselves."

The doctor bent over the book again, and removed stamp after stamp, each revealing its little square of manuscript as had the first, till the whole page of little Pure-in-Heart's book presented the appearance of a closely-written folio. And with their hearts beating under a tumult of excitement, so powerful that it scarcely permitted them to understand what they read, Esther and Redmayne stood side by side, and saw gradually spread out before them the whole connected series of communications that had passed from Stadding to Amelia Llewellyn, thus strangely hidden hitherto, thus strangely brought to light at last.

"Here and there," said the doctor, "you will find the writing too indistinct to be made out, and it is full of all sorts of contractions, but you will find no difficulty in gathering the sense. Your little friend, of course, put the stamps in his book at random, just as they happened to come to hand, and in many cases the message was hidden beneath two stamps; but as near as I can make out, this is about the order they should be read in. Here's the first one—apparently in answer to a letter from Amelia Llewellyn describing the quarrel Sarah Bundle spoke of when the old lady sent her daughter-in-law the letter, and retained possession of the envelope herself."

I.

. . . You were wise in acting as you did, dearest Amelia. It might have become a horribly awkward situation. Had she persisted in keeping back the envelopes from you we shd. have been lost, for all our ingenuity wd. not have helped us then. You had the best possible excuse in objecting to the servant being allowed to read the letters she brought to you; but, for the future, we must carefully guard against such possibilities. .

"Now, between this one and the one I have placed next there is seemingly a letter missing—one in which something had occurred that offended Amelia Llewellyn—you can see that plain enough by the tone it is written in. Thenceforward he drops the 'dearest Amelia,' and is only the warm, earnest friend, full of plausibility and good wishes. I am inclined to think there must be another link in the chain missing between letters six and seven, too. You will notice when you come to it."

II.

. . . I am not aware of ever having presumed too much, & shd. not have forgotten that "all we can have in common" is the "finding out of the truth," even without yr. very pointed reminder. It is more yr. loss than mine that this correspondence shd. cease, when a few more days wd. bring the knowledge that wd. give you yr. freedom. I am surprised at & weary of this constant changing of your mind & tone, & of exerting myself for no return but ingratitude. If you wish it, I shall be quite content to let this communication be our last.

III.

. . . I *do* remember that you are friendless, & am not so despicable as to withdraw what little aid I am able to render. But can you so misunderstand me as to suppose that I, of all men, am seeking in any way to take advantage of yr. position? What aid I can give, I have given freely up till now for yr. sake alone, & will continue it just as freely in the future. Yes, I well know that you have bitterly learned to be suspicious, & sympathize sincerely with you; but do not, I beseech you, destroy all our plans by distrusting me. . . .

IV.

. . . Patience, yr. martyrdom shall not last much longer. I sympathize deeply in the distress of mind this must cause you; but are you not foolishly scrupulous? What I have told you is neither more nor less than the truth. Why will you not believe?—But it must be hard for such as you to credit that so much villainy goes on around you every day. . . .

V.

. . . You speak of duty. I should be the last to seek to win you from it, but what duty can you owe to a man who has so basely deceived you as he has? Yes, I can understand that his conduct is so black *you* can hardly believe it to be true, but in a little while I shall give you undeniable proof—proof that will enable you to gain absolute and entire freedom from him for ever.

VI.

. . . Do not be so easily discouraged. I cannot see in what sense our correspondence is even a deception much less degrading. It is yr. only means of information: therefore, justifiable. It is their interest to keep you in ignorance ; it is yours to know the truth ; to insist upon those rights of which you have been defrauded ; to free yourself from a position into which you have been deceived ; & that freedom can only be obtained in one way—by putting yr. unreserved trust in me. . .

VII.

. . . I know how unbearable this delay must seem to you, but I am in daily expectation of the prefect's reply to my letter, & as soon as the copy of Llewellyn's marriage certificate is in my hand I shall forward a duplicate to you, & then I trust you will see things in their true light, & yr. doubts & misgivings & mistaken ideas of duty will be at an end. . .

VIII.

. . . *It has come, & you are a free woman.* I received the prefect's letter to-day. It confirms all I have told you. Llewellyn was married years ago in France, & his first wife is still living there. You have been deceived as surely no woman has ever been deceived before. You are no more his wife than if the ceremony had never been pronounced. It only remains now to act, & I am prepared to use this information against him to the utmost. . . .

IX.

. . . Why did I not furnish you with the information I had gained ? First, because I am afraid of the influence of those around you. Second, because I doubt yr. courage to carry out yr. purpose against such a man as L. Third, because a single false step now means ruin. Listen to yr. truest & most sincere friend— make one bold stride for freedom ! Leave yr. prison without a day's delay ; & then, free from yr. tyrant, trust me to see you righted. . . .

X.

. . . You see I was right. You confess now that yr. courage leaves you at the very thought of thwarting L. in such a serious matter. But it must be done. It is impossible, knowing what you do, that you can, that you dare, acknowledge him any longer as yr. husband. I am aware that it is a terrible situation to be placed in. But yr. duty is clear. Trust wholly in me. After all we are masters of the position, & a little skill & caution will give us the victory. . .

XI.

. . . No, as yr. best friend I cannot tell you all the facts I have gained. You are, as yet, too distracted, too little mistress of yourself. The old beldame who watches you might betray you into revealing it, & as I have said, one false step now means ruin absolute and entire. Keep our secret, put yourself beyond his power, and then trust in me. I have friends and will see justice done you.

XII.

. . . You *must* overcome yr. terror at the thought of opposing L.—that is, you must liberate yourself from yr. prison at Lowry Bay. Knowing what you do, how can you remain an hour longer in the house ? Try, do try & come to a decision. Make my friends yr. friends, & not an hour shall be lost in winning for you those rights which are yr. most precious possession. . . .

XIII.

. . . Still hesitating, still fearful. What may be the end of this if you continue to delay ? No, in kindness—no. The very tone of yr. letters makes me more than ever doubtful of trusting you with the full truth, while you are in the power of these people. Only resolve to leave them, & all will be well. I will meet you at any time, & at any place, and the day that sees yr. escape will see you in possession of all that I am now forced to keep from you. Let yr. next letter tell me you have at last made up yr. mind. . . .

XIV.

. . . More gratified than I can tell you that you are at last realizing the position in which you are placed. Do not fear any incautiousness on my part. If you are so closely watched as to make escape impossible by day, some other time must be chosen. What matters it so long as you do escape ? Courage, only have courage, & the future will yet have all the happiness in store for you that you deserve. . .

XV.

. . . Make no preparations. Avoid anything that might arouse suspicion. To gain yr. own personal freedom is the one thing needful. Do not ask me even now to impart the information I have gained to you. Rather let the knowledge be a further inducement to you to hasten the day of yr. escape, for on that day you shall hear all I now withhold from you. I am waiting now every day for yr. final answer. Do not let yr. courage desert you now at the last minute.

XVI.

. . . Yes, so far as I know I & the person from whom I first obtained it are the only persons aware of this fact in L.'s past life. I care nothing for his violence & desperation. His power over you now will soon be gone for ever. Think of freedom from him & all it will bring. Think of the further brutality that awaits you if you give up. Wait no longer. Try & let me know how & when you think of making yr. escape.

XVII.

. . . Why do you tie my hands with such conditions ? But I can deny you nothing : they are granted. Let me urge upon you —delay not a single hour longer. In yr. place I should see nothing in him but my persecutor & deceiver, & would not hesitate for a moment in bringing down upon him the severest punishment his conduct deserves. I have not, & shall not, venture near Lowry B. till I have yr. permission ; but do, do hasten yr. decision. . . .

XVIII.

. . . Everything else you have
asked shall be granted; the
farthest I can go will be to send
you the name of his first wife,
with the time & place of his
marriage in the letter in which
you let me fix the time of yr.
escape & place of our meeting. I
shall have the prefect's copy of
the certificate with me. I pledge
myself that within an hour after,
you shall be safe in the hands of
friends who will protect you to
the uttermost. How can you still
doubt? . . .

(Here the communications end abruptly.)

XXXIII.

A silence followed the reading of the closing words of
the secret correspondence. For the first time that evening,
Redmayne and Esther looked into one another's eyes more
as husband and wife should look, and less like the constrained and embarrassed strangers they had hitherto
appeared. But though both were quick to discern the new-
found hope, both remembered it was still nothing more
than hope; both remembered the parts they had still to
play.

"And that," observed the doctor, marking the interchange of glances, and looking eminently satisfied with
himself, "is my justification for bringing this meeting
about; was I right or wrong?"

"Doctor," said Redmayne, with a long breath of relief,
and seizing the doctor's hand and wringing it, "after what
you have done for us and shown us to-night, do not speak
of imprudence or justifying yourself. Thanks to you, we
have come to the truth at last. You have given me—you

have given both of us—fresh hope for the future—stronger, more firmly grounded than ever we have had before."

"Indeed you have, doctor," said Esther, taking the doctor's other hand in both of hers. "You must be the most wonderful man that ever lived, I think. I cannot believe my own eyes. To think that I should have this by me all this time without knowing it; while you and Matthew have been searching high and low for the truth. It's wonderful."

"And how could any one who saw him ever imagine that the dear little fellow's wish to be of use in the world, would ever have been fulfilled in such an unheard-of way? And yet how simple, how—how inevitably to be so, as it were, it seems," joined in Miss Dorothy Ann, under a sense of responsibility of having to say something, and speaking with a suspicious want of spontaneity.

"Ah, Miss Winterson, it's only hypocrisy for you to say that now. You have been in the secret ever since the doctor came to us at New Plymouth; I am sure you have —it was you begged the book from me—you must have known it all from the beginning, and all this time you have never made any sign."

"You must blame me for that: as stage manager, with an eye to dramatic effect, I forbade it," said the doctor; "though one might as well expect heat from an iceberg as extract a spark of—of dramaticity from either of you."

"The dear little fellow! We liked one another from the very first moment. How this brings back the first day I passed at his mother's cottage. How I *wish* he was alive now!" And Esther kissed the open page of the book in a way that made Redmayne wonder to what extent he was still bound by the promise he had given in his letter. "God bless you, doctor," she said, looking up in the face of her old friend with the tears standing in her eyes; "you *have* given me a stronger hope than ever I have dared to indulge before, that my poor, dear Kate, may indeed be innocent after all—after all. Oh, what a weary, weary time it has been."

"It *is* odd how it should fall out that a little fellow, who never took a score of paces from a sick-bed in his life, should let daylight through the schemes of two of the deepest villains that ever formed plot and counterplot—for there's motive here, look you, motive, motive, motive," began the doctor, drawing Pure-in-Heart's book towards him, and tapping it with his forefinger. "Notice this last letter, how it ends. All we want to make the chain complete is the letter that fell into Llewellyn's hands on the night of the eleventh June; and this last letter shows it as plainly as if it were lying before us; it guarantees, as soon as Amelia Llewellyn gives a definite promise to run away from the cottage at Lowry Bay, that all the particulars of Llewellyn's first marriage shall be sent to her. And the letter containing that exposure, and at the same time fixing the time and place for the meeting, must have been the very letter that fell into Llewellyn's hands—the letter that, more than any other possible thing, would set the whole nature of such a man in a blaze, and work him up to any deed of violence. By some means the charm that had worked so well hitherto, failed with him; he must have at once stumbled upon the secret that we have just found out. And as if anything more were wanting after such a thunderbolt as that revelation must have been, here is Stadding's assurance, apparently in answer to Amelia Llewellyn's request, that when he meets her he will have with him the prefect's own letter. Is it possible to conceive a stronger motive?"

"Stadding was an adept at deception," said Esther, doubtfully. "May this not have been nothing more than a cunning plot to deceive young Mrs. Llewellyn? Perhaps there was no letter from France—perhaps there had been no previous marriage."

The doctor shook his head.

"No not but what I could easily credit it, for it would

have been quite in character with the fellow, so far as that goes. These letters bear the appearance of genuineness on their face. You notice how careful he is to keep the power in his own hands; how he hides the information from this unfortunate woman for fear lest she should be able to act in her own behalf; how he dangles this new-found revelation before her eyes, and seeks to goad her on to his purpose by appealing to the most sensitive part of a woman's character. All this points, in my opinion, to his being possessed of some secret in Llewellyn's past life; — and that there was some secret I have always believed ever since those words of Amelia Llewellyn to her mother-in-law on the day of the murder were repeated to me. I would give much to see with my own eyes what her letters to him contained, and not be forced to guess at it from Stadding's replies—not, that such knowledge would be of much assistance to us if we did have it. But the chief reason for my disbelief that it is mere invention on Stadding's part, is that in that case how should we account for Llewellyn's action. Remember, as I have said before, it was not jealousy that animated the man. You remember what I said on that score weeks ago, Mat. According to what we heard at the Truss o' Straw, it was only for her money that he married his wife in the first place; and Stadding, I suppose, on his part, wanted her for what was left of it. No; it was not because he loved, but because he feared, and had good reason to fear, that Llewellyn did this thing. Trust me, little Pure-in-heart has done what no one else could do, and has shown us the one only motive that moved the man."

"Yes, but there's another side to the question," objected Redmayne. "There are the words that Sarah Bundle overheard while he was talking with his mother on the morning after the death of Stadding. He speaks of the girl he saw that night at the theatre, and of the danger if she informed. If that means anything, it seems to me it must mean that he himself was the man who met Stadding.

and not that he employed some one else to rid his path of him. Besides, with a man of his disposition, the provocation he received by reading Stadding's letter to his wife would have the effect of at once urging him to wreak his vengeance with his own hand, not to adopt such a cold, deliberate course of deception as you suppose."

"You may add to that, if you like, Llewellyn's desire to get into his own possession the copy of the prefect's letter, which Stadding carried in his pocket. I own I have been puzzled by the same thought myself, but it is easily enough accounted for. Whoever it may have been that Llewellyn employed to do this work, there is little doubt but that he would at least have one interview with him afterwards. The man would describe the scene, and ——"

"And the sudden appearance of Kate," said Esther, slowly and resolutely, as she saw the doctor hesitate in his choice of words; and then, holding up her hand, she went on earnestly, "Doctor, and you too, Matthew, the time for that is past now. You must not consider me. I have been too long familiar with every aspect of this affair when when I feared for poor Kate's sake to shrink from discussing it, or hearing it discussed, now that for the first time for years I have ever had any sure ground of hope."

The doctor nodded appreciatively.

——"and Llewellyn having been present at the theatre that night the resemblance would strike him at once, and he would naturally enough refer to it when describing the scene himself afterwards. But however it may have been, there is this encouragement in it he appears to regard her only in the light of some one to be feared as a possible witness."

As the doctor paused the opening and closing of a door on the other side of the street could be plainly heard. Redmayne started from his chair, and throwing back the door of his room that led on to the balcony, stepped out. The others followed him. A light was shining dimly through the blinds of the house opposite. A tall muffled form crossed the window and went slowly down the street. It paused once to look up at the group on the balcony, and then passed on again, and presently emerged from the shadow of the houses in which it had been walking, into a bright patch of moonlight at the entrance of a side street, crossed the street, and then became lost in the shadows on the other side again.

Either Esther or Miss Dorothy Ann—the doctor did not know which—whispered, "Who was that?"

"The man we have been discussing this last hour," he answered, "Llewellyn. He has a knack of making dramatic entrances and exits at such moments as he is under discussion. Esther, you shuddered," he broke off to exclaim. "I'll take my oath you shuddered at sight of him. This is the second time. History repeats itself, by gad. This is the scene in the theatre over again."

"Matthew, doctor," said Esther, in an almost terrified whisper, and leaning over the balustrade of the balcony to peer into the darkness in the direction in which Llewellyn had disappeared, "if you have never trusted a woman's instinct before, trust mine to-night. I am sure your suspicion is the right one, Matthew. That and no other is the guilty man."

"What have I told you all along, doctor?" said Redmayne, as the group passed back into the room. "Account for it as you will, there has been deception worked somehow, and Llewellyn is the sole perpetrator of this crime. You must admit the motive."

"I admit the motive, I admit the suspicion of his conduct, I admit everything, but I will not admit that the man Trupp told me anything but the truth; for I am absolutely, and beyond all question, convinced that he did not. I haven't been in the world three-score years, and been a doctor for five and thirty, without learning something of human nature, and it is my deliberate conviction that that man spoke the truth ; and that being so, how *are*

you to believe your suspicions are correct? The thing is
a rank impossibility."

"Doctor, you see deepest; you discover most; and you
believe least. There is and must be a way of accounting
for it."

"Believe me, you are wrong," answered the doctor, with
a shake of his head. "The difference between you and me
is that I go on reason and evidence; you go on fancy and
prejudice. If the balance of evidence points to a conclusion
that is against my interest, I accept it, simply because the
balance of evidence does point to it."

"Well, if I am wrong there's one man who can clear up
the mystery. We have followed your method hitherto;
we have taken reason and evidence; and we have exhausted
every source of information. There is only one thing more
we can do. We have come to the fountain-head now, and,"
added Redmayne, slowly and significantly, "there's only
the breadth of a street between us and it. I will not be
baulked any longer. I have been informed and misin-
formed, guided and misguided, long enough. By this time
to-morrow night I will have heard the truth from the lips
of Llewellyn himself."

"Matthew, what would you do?" Esther exclaimed,
speaking under the influence of the stern, set expression
of his face, rather than his words.

"I mean to put it to the touch, Esther, whether we are
both to give up for ever the new hope we have gained
to-night, or whether I am to claim this little hand as my
own again," he said, lightly, with quick change of mood, as
he took fondly into his own the hand she laid upon his
arm.

"Mat, dear Mat, be careful for—for both our sakes. Do
not run into danger. Remember he is desperate."

"Not more so than I am. Till to-morrow night I am
bound by the promise I gave you in my letter; by then
we shall see, in the doctor's own words, whether our paths
in the future are to be together or apart."

The doctor moved the lamp so that its light fell full upon Redmayne's face.

"Go on, Matthew," said Esther. "Speak without any reservation. Tell me everything."

"I must confess I am curious to know how you are going to extract the desired information," said the doctor. "Reason and evidence fail *there*."

"There is only one way. I have not forgotten that even if we succeed never so completely, that whatever is done must be done in secret. I gave up all hope of ever bringing this man to public trial long ago —when I first read your letter from New Plymouth, Esther. To-morrow night I shall meet him face to face in his own house, tax him with the committal of this crime, bring forward all the evidence we have or can assume, and demand a full confession of his share in that night's work."

"My poor Catherine! Only show me the proof of her innocence!" cried Esther, breathlessly, interlacing her fingers, and clasping her hands closely together. "How I shall *pray* for your success."

"Beautifully simple, and eminently dramatic," said the doctor. "If that is all you trust to, Mat, I fear you must make up your mind for failure the most utter and entire. Consider for a moment what such a confession would mean for him ; and remember that however skilfully you may utilize what evidence we have gained to-night, Llewellyn has too strong a defence, even in Trupp's story alone, to fear anything in the shape of mere circumstantial evidence you can bring forward, short of that of an eye-witness— which is impossible."

"Let the event prove which is right. My mind is made up, and nothing shall induce me to alter it. To-morrow shall see me either finally successful, or finally defeated. I should be a miserable coward if I delayed a day longer."

The doctor shrugged his shoulders. "If you will you will, and there's an end of it. But at least, if you must venture on this course, let me go with you. Let us go together, Mat. I have been of some assistance up to this point, I may be of still more before it ends."

"Willingly, doctor. There is nothing I should like better."

"I know well I could not dissuade you if I tried, Matthew," said Esther, going up to him, and placing her hands on his shoulders, and looking in his eyes; "but if I could I would not. There is nothing I long for now as I do that this horrid mystery may be cleared up once and for ever. Since Doctor Carmichael has been with us he has told us all you have both done to unearth the truth, and now I think with you that there is only one way in which it can be cleared up. I do so long to have this terrible suspense ended, and to know whether Kate is really innocent or not. You have truth and right on your side. Go and meet this man, and—and God help us both. If I were not a weak, puny woman— I may not go with you, but I will pray for your success. Let me come here and watch when you have entered the house. It will seem as if I were nearer to you—as if the danger must be less."

"There is no danger, my love, do not think it. To-morrow night will see the end of all our doubts and misgivings, and make you a free woman, and me a free man, once more; trust me."

"I will try and believe it—for your sake and Catherine's. Poor Catherine. How strange it seems. How little she guessed it was for her sake we brought her with us from New Plymouth. How I shall long to tell her all I have seen and heard when I go back to her to-night. Yet she must not—perhaps may never know it. Oh, Matthew, if it were only possible to gain the knowledge that is locked up and forgotten in her past life, how easy your task would be."

"I have it already, Esther. You yourself have given it to me, though you little thought it at the time. I read it weeks ago in your diary. With that, and what we have gained since, I believe we know all we need to gain our end. When you say good-night to Catherine this evening, try and be happy with the thought that to-morrow will see the last shadow of suspicion removed from her for ever, and with it the last shadow from your life and mine. And now it is getting late. I am afraid I have forgotten myself, and said more than I should, and have excited you. Let the doctor and me see you and Miss Winterson to your hotel."

The doctor was a few moments later than the others in leaving, and as he walked along the passage to the front door he saw Theodore Hawkshaw, with an air as if he had been lying in wait for him, approaching with an open letter in his hand.

"Why, Theodore," he said, noticing the expression on his face, "something has happened surely. What is it? Nothing wrong with the play, I hope."

"Oh, nothing, nothing," answered the playwright, with the bitter irony of one who has been so long familiar with reverses of fortune as to calculate on them beforehand; "only what I have expected. Only that the girl I have been deceived into trusting up till the very last moment has failed me."

"No! The girl who feared a contingency requiring her at home?"

"The same. I have just received a note from her, telling me she can't come. I am in despair. This was the night of the last rehearsal. To-morrow night is *the* night, and now look at me," said Theodore, extending his arms before him in abandonment; "see the position I am in. I have exhausted all my acquaintance. I have appealed to every one. Can you help me?"

"I am sorry, Theodore," said the doctor, buttoning up his coat, and passing on with the air of a man refusing alms to an importunate beggar. "I'm afraid I can't on such short notice. Could you not postpone it for a day?"

"Great heaven, if I did I should have three places

vacant instead of one. It is impossible. I can see nothing but ruin," said Theodore, following the callous doctor along the passage with the open letter extended in his hand. "What am I to do? I must have somebody."

"It is an awkward fix certainly," answered the doctor, who had opened the door, and was looking along the darkened street to catch a glimpse of his companions. "But it is really no use appealing to me, Theodore. I should be most happy to help you in any way possible; but I am quite unable to suggest anything, except that the time has not come yet, and we none of us know what twenty-four hours may bring forth. And now I must be off—my friends are waiting for me."

XXXIV.

EVER since dusk a light had been burning in the window of Llewellyn's house, and on the balcony of the house opposite the motionless figure of a woman was standing. A door at the farther end of the balcony opened. A man paused for a moment on the threshold, looking keenly into the dimness, and then walked quickly towards the woman.

"What, Esther," he said, in surprise, "begun your vigil already? I have been looking for you everywhere. Let me ask Miss Winterson or Catherine to keep you company."

"No, no, Matthew. Do not disturb them. I would rather not have any one with me—I would rather be alone. . . . You—you have come to say good-bye."

"Good-bye? No, why should I say good-bye? I have come to ask you to wish me good luck."

She paused thoughtfully before answering.

"Since I have been up here, Matthew—all day long, indeed—I have been thinking of what passed between us last evening, and what you are about to do to-night. It is

the last moment, but it is not too late. Think again—is it
wise ? "

"Yes, Esther, under the circumstances it is the wisest
thing possible—and the only thing. But why this sudden
change of mind ? Last night——"

"I know—I know," she answered, regretfully. "Last
night I urged you to go. I was excited then ;—I am not
now. Since I have been watching that lighted window
opposite, I cannot keep my mind from running on the
thought of what the light behind it may see in the course
of another hour. Llewellyn is there, Matthew, and it
terrifies me. Let me unsay what I said last night. I am
afraid to think what I have urged you to do in meeting
such a man as he must be when he is driven to bay.
When that door closes upon you——" She shuddered,
and drew her shawl around her, and left the sentence
unfinished.

"Nonsense, dear. You have let your mind brood too
long over it, and have conjured a mole-hill into a mountain.
Look on the bright side. Think how near our best hopes
are to fulfilment—how much for you and me and Catherine
depends upon the next hour." He drew her arm within
his, and walked with her up and down the balcony.
" What a strange tale your life has been since that day—
how long ago it seems to me now—when I left you at the
church door before we had been ten minutes husband and
wife. We can afford to look back at that time now, for
the last chapter of that tale closes to-night, Esther, and
after all you have done and suffered, it must have—it can
only have—a happy ending for us all."

"I do not know," she said, sadly. "I have learnt not
to count so surely on the future. Don't think me foolish,
but I have been haunted all night long with horrid dreams
about you, and all day with a nameless dread of some
further sorrow awaiting us. I cannot shake off their
influence. Think again, Matthew, think again, and do
not go to-night."

"Do not try to dissuade me, Esther. I would rather have five years struck out of my life than fail to meet Llewellyn to-night. Courage, my love. This will never do. You are trembling like a leaf; you are letting your foolish fears run away with you."

"I cannot help it," she said, putting her hand over her heart. "Do not laugh at me. I—I cannot tell you all I feel, but I fear all is not to end well. Do not go," she pleaded, returning to the one thought that oppressed her. "Listen to me. I am your wife. Do not go. Do not tempt fortune any further. Do not face that terrible man to-night."

She had taken both his hands in hers in the earnestness of her pleading. In the dim light that struggled up from the street lamps, Redmayne looked down at her white, upturned face.

"Say, rather, you *will be* my wife when once this wretched mystery is cleared up, and set at rest for ever. It is that hope that is urging me forward to-night. My mind is made up, Esther. Do not seek to turn me from my purpose; I shall only pain you by refusal."

"What can I say?" she cried in nervous desperation. "Mat, dear Mat, you do not realize what you are about to do. He is desperate, he will do you a mischief—he may kill you."

"Even that would be better than to live as we are living now. But do not fear. It will not come to that. He will not be so desperate but that he will accept the terms that offer him his freedom. Come, Esther, let us forget the past and all the restrictions and conditions we have laid upon ourselves for a moment, and let us part like husband and wife."

"Ah, then you *do* fear——"

"I fear nothing, my love, but to miss this last opportunity that at least offers something more than a probability of bringing our two paths in life together again." He drew the white, frightened face close to his own, and kissed the trembling lips. " And now, good-bye for only two short hours."

Five minutes later she was standing in the darkness, holding her breath unconsciously, like one who knows she has arrived at a crisis in her life, all her other senses suspended and absorbed in the strained gaze she bent upon the lighted window opposite—so strained and so long continued that when she closed her eyes in mental prayer, spectral green and crimson windows still flashed before her.

. . . . She had seen the door of Llewellyn's house open and close upon the forms of Redmayne and the doctor.

XXXV.

REDMAYNE's knock was answered by a careworn, elderly-looking woman—Llewellyn's mother, they both concluded at once. She looked at them doubtfully when they said their business was with Llewellyn, her hands nervously clasping and unclasping her dress at her side. She left them at the door, and stepped into a room opening off from the passage. While she had been speaking, the sound of a heavy, muffled tramp—a sound as of some one pacing backwards and forwards in slippers—had been audible from the direction of this room. It ceased for a moment, and then, as the old lady re-appeared and invited them to enter, it commenced again. She spoke reluctantly, and the doubtful look on her face had deepened. She hesitated as she uttered the tardy invitation, hesitated as she closed the door behind them, and hesitated still longer for the third time as she laid her hand on the door of the room whence the muffled tramp, tramp was sounding. She glanced from face to face, raised her head as if to speak—and then opened the door in silence, and allowed them to pass through.

The tall, stooping, yet powerful-looking figure of a man, wrapped in a dark dressing-gown, with hands clasped behind his back, paused in his pacing to and fro, and looked up as they entered. There was the slight inequality in the height of the shoulders, all the more apparent from his stooping attitude, the same evil-looking face, with its close-cropt black beard and deep-sunk dark piercing eyes, that the doctor remembered seeing at the theatre more than three years before; and as he exchanged the preliminary civilities, there was the same quick, suspicious expression in his eyes as there had been a moment before in his mother's.

"I am curious to know," he began, and the suspicion in his eyes was reproduced in the tone of his voice, "what it is you want with me. I do not think we have ever had the pleasure of meeting before."

"You and I have certainly never met before," answered Redmayne, and Llewellyn observed, with a furtive apprehension, the appearance of concerted action with which the reply was given; "my friend and I, I may say at once, have called upon business concerning certain things which took place some three years ago things of which you alone can inform us."

The evil face seemed to contract, and grow darker and more secretive. The eyebrows lowered into a straight black line, the hands clenched rather than clasped one another behind him.

"What things?"

"We are alone here? There is no chance of what we may say being overheard?"

"We are quite alone. But I am aware of no reason why we should fear anything we may say being overheard. Pray, go on," said Llewellyn, in a constrained voice, his face becoming a dark, insensible mask.

"I refer to what took place at Monk's Bridge on the night of the 11th June."

There was a moment's pause before the answer came.

Llewellyn halted, and exchanged glances with his visitors, as if he were deliberating whether the moment had come when he should throw off the restraint he was putting upon himself.

"The 11th of June, 1886," he said slowly at last. "Yes, I remember the date perfectly, and with good reason. It was on that date I experienced the greatest loss I have known."

"The date is fixed in my mind by an event of a very different character. To me it is always associated with the death of a certain Edgar Stadding, at Lowry Bay. Do you not remember it?"

"I remember the trial—the murderess was a woman suspected of a *liaison* with the murdered man, was she not? —and acquitted, if I remember rightly, under circumstances of very strong suspicion."

"Whatever any one may have been deceived into believing at the time," said Redmayne, with an ominous precision of utterance, "it has since been ascertained that he who committed the crime, and he who rode Scythe-bearer that night, were one and the same person."

It came upon Llewellyn unexpectedly. Impassive as he had schooled his face to be, a swift spasm shot across it.

"You are perhaps not aware that the loss I refer to was no other than that of the horse you have just mentioned," he said, steadying his voice with a palpable effort.

"So far from that being the case, we are perfectly well aware of the fact," answered Redmayne, significantly.

"Then I am at a loss to understand the tone this interview is taking," said Llewellyn slowly, his eyes ablaze, a great vertical fold showing itself in the middle of his forehead. "I am not in the humour to be trifled with. Either state your purpose at once in intruding yourself here, or I shall be under the necessity of ridding myself of your company."

"Our ultimate purpose you have probably already more than guessed at—I will make it plainer later on. In the first place it is the fact "—his eyes fixed themselves intently upon Llewellyn's—" that your first wife was alive in France at the very time that you were living with your second at Monk's Bridge."

Redmayne had calculated upon the unexpectedness of his reply, and he was not disappointed. Had he accused Llewellyn point-blank with the murder of Stadding he knew the charge would have been met with an unmoved front; but as it was Llewellyn stood motionless in the attitude he had assumed a moment before--his face, the lip fast clenched between his teeth, was the face of a man concentrating all his powers in one sustained effort at self-control, but which, in spite of him, records the emotions of the soul behind it. The blood ebbed slowly away, and left it pale, leaden, and working.

Redmayne paused without removing his gaze, but Llewellyn made no effort to reply.

"In the second place, because you discovered on the night of the 11th June that this secret was no longer your own, but was the common possession of your wife and Stadding, and that the danger you had to dread was the immediate exposure of that secret."

Redmayne paused again, but beyond the wild, dumb language of his lowering countenance, Llewellyn answered not.

"And, in the third place, because, as I have said, the man who rode Scythe-bearer and the man who murdered Edgar Stadding are one and the same—and you well know who that man was."

"You lie!"

The voice was so tremulous with passion, the words so thick and guttural, that they were barely intelligible.

"I do not lie," said Redmayne deliberately, and as deliberately measuring the other with his eyes. "I have it in the very handwriting of the man whose death you plotted and carried out on the night when you first learned that he had discovered the secret of your life "

"It is a lie! The letters were burned."

"The letters possibly ; but not the stamps, and the messages beneath those stamps. They were preserved in a way I need not enter into now, and at this moment are in our hands with all the weight of evidence which they contain against you."

Llewellyn stood silent and motionless for some moments, and then, with a sudden, "We'll prove that," strode nervously towards the door. Redmayne divined his intention, and stepped in front of him.

"One moment ! Hear what I have to say, first ! If you have been outwitted—and you have been—it was neither from want of precaution on your part or your mother's— and you are not in a fit state to speak to her now. Believe me, before this interview is over you will have much need to keep at least one friend by you. I tell you it is useless —you cannot avoid fate—you have played your last card, and you have lost. Cunningly as your plot was laid, you have not succeeded in hiding what you did that night."

"Stand from that door !"

"Hear me out, and you will see how useless is any further attempt at concealment. On that night- the 11th of June—you had an envelope placed in your hands on the Wellington Railway Station. On opening it you found that envelope contained a letter your wife had that day received. You read it, tore it up, and tossed it on the fire, and then read the accompanying note. It was in your mother's hand. and it drew your special attention to these words which your wife had that day used : -' If you find it so difficult to deal with two faces on one pair of shoulders, take care how you deal with two faces when they belong to different people, especially when those faces are female faces.' These words, in themselves, might mean anything or nothing. When I first heard them they pointed to a certain suspicion, but nothing more. To you they had only one meaning, and that was —that your wife had dis- covered the very secret you had striven so studiously to

hide from her;—more, that it was also known to one who
had declared himself your enemy, and who was prepared to
use the knowledge he had gained to the very uttermost
against you. I know how you found out the message,—
the one message of many that passed between Stadding and
your wife, what that message contained, and what resolution
on your part followed it. It was hidden beneath the postage stamp. It gave the name of your first wife, the place
and date of the marriage; it named the hour of meeting
between Stadding and her whom you had hitherto called
your wife, and also"—Redmayne hesitated an instant
as if to read more surely the expression on the other's face,
and then added slowly—"that Stadding would have with
him the Prefect's letter the letter which would prove
beyond all doubt the truth of what he had said as to your
first marriage. It was between ten and eleven at night
when you read this. At once you realized the danger, and
made up your mind how to meet it. You saw the opportunity not only of ridding yourself of your enemy, but at the
same time of getting into your own possession whatever
evidence he might have against you. The hour was late,
and the distance far to go. There was but one way in
which your purpose could be accomplished, and you adopted
that one way. You threw behind you the consideration of
how much you had staked upon Scythe-bearer winning the
Cup. You stole down from your room " Redmayne
was speaking rapidly, yet cautiously, and here he brought
all his powers of observation to bear in the searching gaze
he bent upon Llewellyn's face; and insensible and impassive as Llewellyn strove to make his expression, there was
written upon it that which confirmed Redmayne in the
course he was taking. He went on " You stole the key
from your sleeping groom, took the Cup favourite out of
the stable, rode, at whatever sacrifice of your horse, out to
Lowry Bay, and there met Stadding."

"Go on," said Llewellyn, hoarsely, as Redmayne paused.

" Now I will tell you our object in coming here to-night.

In the face of all this, are you so mad as to invite public trial? I tell you at once it does not enter into my plans to seek to bring that trial upon you—one moment!—but only on the condition that you are sufficiently alive to your own interests to grant my object without it. Knowing who I am, you know in what relation I stand to the lady who stood her trial for this crime. Give me a clear, unequivocal account of your share in that night's work, and you are free to dispose of yourself as you will. I ask no more of you."

"You have provided yourself already with a witness," Llewellyn sneered, "but you have reckoned without your host."

"You refuse the terms I offer?"

"You speak of my share in that night's work. To what share in it have I pleaded guilty? I care not for your terms; they are nothing to me. Do your worst. You have seen this case tried once, and you know with what result. What sane man or woman is there who has heard of it but believes the woman who was tried was the murderess? If she were innocent why did she not speak, and even if she be innocent, what is that to me?—why do you come to me at all?"

"She who was tried for that murder," said Redmayne slowly, his voice quivering with rising passion, "was my wife. It is in her name I have come here to-night. It is consideration for her that has induced me to make the concession which I have just offered you; but, by heaven, if you persist in your refusal, no earthly consideration shall prevent me from taking you by the throat, and wringing the truth out of your miserable carcase. Let me tell you one more thing—you know as well as I, that it was not she, but another, who saw you commit the murder of Edgar Stadding."

Once more the dark face blanched, and Redmayne knew that the shot had gone home.

"Then if it were not she, why did she neither prove it nor even seek to prove it? She was silent then; she best

knew why—and you and she best know why she will keep
silent to the end."

Llewellyn had retreated to the centre of the room, and
he and Redmayne now stood confronting one another with
only the width of the table between them. There was a
long pause—each stood glaring into the other's eyes, one
flushed with uncontrollable indignation and contempt; the
other pale, almost ghastly, with sullen, obstinate desperation.

"Have I not yet convinced you? While you have been
dwelling in your fool's paradise in fancied safety your track
has been followed inch by inch. You have baffled me and
escaped me long enough, and caused misery enough. I
have longed for weeks to meet you as I never yet longed
for any earthly thing, and now we have met, do not think
I will ever leave this room till I have obtained to the very
uttermost all that I have proposed to myself to gain. You
think my wife will remain silent to the end? Do not count
too surely on that. Suppose she does not. Suppose she
were to describe before judge and jury, as she has described
to me, a certain glade in a forest at midnight, and two men
meeting and talking angrily together, and presently closing
in a death struggle; the moon bursting out upon them as
they struggle; one man plunging a knife into the other,
and the wounded man sinking upon the ground; the
murderer taking from the body of his victim a certain
Prefect's letter, and then making off; the woman who had
witnessed it all coming forward from among the bushes.
You recognize the scene? Suppose we call one man Stadding,
and the other *yourself*——"

In their intense pre-occupation and excitement neither
Redmayne nor Llewellyn were conscious of anything going
on around them; they had both forgotten the very presence
of the doctor in the room. Llewellyn could hardly be said
to breathe as he listened to Redmayne's repetition, almost
in Esther's own words, of what she had years before described in her diary. He started as if an electric shock
had passed through him when the doctor, for the first time

taking part in what was going forward, placed his hand upon his shoulder.

"Suppose, further, that we have with us that very woman. Look there! and own the evidence against you is at last complete!"

He pointed through the window. The blind had been drawn up to its full height. Llewellyn followed the direction of the doctor's extended arm, stood for a moment motionless, then reeled and gasped forth something—not an articulate cry, but a sound like that of a wild animal. Had it not been for the doctor's firm grasp upon his arm he would have fallen.

On the balcony of the house opposite, motionless, statuesque, in the centre of a flood of white light, stood the figure of a woman. It was Catherine. It was, moreover, Theodore's balcony scene.

*   *   *   *   *   *

Llewellyn flung his hands before his eyes with an abandoned gesture, and gasped out: "The very woman— the very woman!"

XXXVI.

HE remained sitting in the chair into which he had fallen, his hand shielding his face from the light. The last pretence of resistance was gone; the desperate obstinacy that had characterized his manner a few minutes before had given way to a broken, spiritless resignation. It was some time before his excitement subsided sufficiently to allow him to speak. He rose, and recommenced his slow pacing up and down the room.

"Perhaps you are more disposed to accept my offer now," said Redmayne, congratulating himself that the last obstacle was overcome, but still eyeing the other warily.

"It—it is no part of your intention——" began Llewellyn,

halting for a moment, and raising his head to glance at Redmayne, and then letting it droop dejectedly on his breast again.

"Whatever my desire may be, you may consider yourself free of any apprehension that you will be brought to public trial, if that is what you mean," said Redmayne shortly, with no effort to conceal the contempt he felt.

"It does not need - it does not need," said Llewellyn, mournfully. "My punishment is almost complete without that—almost, for the end is to come yet, and it is not far off. It is as well you came when you did. . . . . Yes, it was I who killed Stadding." He made the confession without any evidence of a feeling of compunction, without a moment's alteration in the dead, impassive manner that had descended upon him since he had seen Catherine's accusing figure, even without an appearance of understanding the full significance of the words he used. "It is not, I suppose, in the least your desire to hear what I may have to say in my defence and I say nothing; but you will see that I can at least plead the extremest provocation. As for the trial, it was incomprehensible to me from beginning to end. If it were possible to hide crime, mine would have been hidden. Mysteries and mysteries to no one more than to me—seemed to spin themselves from the very air between me and the law; the whole trial was a tissue of mysteries which I never tried to understand, further than that they meant for me concealment and safety the most complete, and the most unlooked-for so complete that had I found Scythe-bearer alive and uninjured after that night's work I should have received the story brought out in Court as every one else did, and believed that I had been duped by a mere dream, and that I had not even left my room, except in imagination. I fail to understand, indeed, what can be your reason for demanding this confession of me at all when you are able to describe the very scene of the murder; but since you wish it, so be it.

"As you have said, an envelope was put into my hand

on the platform of the Wellington Railway Station. I had
gone there with my friend Trupp. It was his appointment;
he was to meet a friend there, but his friend did not put
in an appearance, and I invited him to return with me to
Monk's Bridge. Stadding, as you know, was in the train
that arrived while I was at the station, and so also was—
was the other, whom the girl that gave me the letter, and
who afterwards gave evidence at the trial, swore she had
recognized. I saw neither of them.

"It was between nine and half-past when I opened the
packet. There was my mother's note, the letter my wife
had that day received, and the envelope in which that
letter had been originally delivered at the cottage at Lowry
Bay. I read my wife's letter first. I do not remember
what signature was attached. It was mere girlish gossip,
and before I had read to the end I tore it up and threw it
in the fire. I was sorry I had done so when I read the
accompanying note, for then I saw at once that, careful as
we had been to guard against anything of the kind, she
had a secret correspondent. —It would be useless for me to
affect anything in the way of reservation, and I do not.
My wife and I had been on the very worst of terms.—That
secret correspondent, I had good reason to believe, was
Stadding. He had been an acquaintance of my wife's
before her marriage; and after her marriage he presumed
sufficiently on that acquaintance for me to threaten him on
one occasion with the treatment he deserved if he ever
again made himself disagreeable by obtruding his company
where he was plainly told it was not desired.

" You were right as to the words to which my attention
was drawn; and also in your surmise that for me they
could have but one possible meaning. But what puzzled
me was the strange alteration in my wife's behaviour
after the receipt of the letter which I had only a minute
or two before thrown away as worthless. One would
suppose that it had been in that letter she received
the information which had brought about this sudden

change of behaviour, yet I could not conceive how that information could have been conveyed. I suppose it was fortunate, or unfortunate, which you will—that I had burned the letter, for it would only have misled me, and possibly I should have allowed myself to spend so much time in trying to extract a message it did not contain that my attention would either never have been directed to where the message really was, or I would have found out the truth only when it was too late.

"As it was, my first glance was towards the envelope to which the letter originally belonged. I took it up aimlessly, and turned it about and looked inside it, and then, unthinkingly, tore it into bits, and was about to throw it after the letter, when something happened to catch my eye. In tearing, a portion of the adhesive side of the stamp had become exposed. It was covered with marks which on the first glance bore the appearance of a faint reversed impression of a number of closely-written words. It was very broken and very indistinct, but it was enough to rouse my suspicions. I selected those parts of the envelope to which pieces of the torn stamp were adhering. I removed the portions of stamp carefully, and found that my suspicion had been the correct one. I had a connected message before me.

"It was necessarily a very short one, but it contained much in little space. It gave name, place, and date in connection with a marriage I had contracted early in life in France; mentioned half-past one in the morning as the safest time for the elopement to take place—my wife to make her escape when she heard the signal that he was waiting for her; spoke of friends who would see her vindicated, and promised that he would bring with him the all-important proof in the shape of the prefect's letter.

"For a moment this sudden, unthought-of revelation paralyzed me. I thought of the danger in which I stood.

"It is no part of my confession to tell you anything as to my first marriage. That is included in the affairs of my own private life, and shall remain so. Sufficient that it was

a fact. It may seem strange for a man guilty of such a
crime as mine to excuse himself for the lesser one of having
deserted one woman and deceived another. When I
married my first wife I was young; she was designing.
She developed into a drunkard and a termagant. She hated
me, and I hated her, and after a time I left her and came
out here, and married some one else. That was all. But
unfortunately for me my second wife had friends, and they
had insisted upon our marriage taking place at the French
Consulate. Mine was a common enough offence, but a
very serious one in the eyes of the law, and the penalty is
a heavy one.

"I did not fear what my wife might do alone. She was
a woman of very weak character, and any resistance
she could make might be easily disposed of.—Let me say
here that I am quite prepared to believe it was this weakness of character that had allowed Stadding to gain sufficient influence over her to induce her to keep up this secret
correspondence. I suppose she and I grew to detest each
other as much as had been the case with my first wife; but
whatever there may have been of evil design in what was
going forward was on Stadding's part; not on hers. I do
not know for certain where he obtained his knowledge of my
early life, but I have met at least one man in the street who
hailed from the same town as myself. News of that kind
travels fast, and the fact remained—he did know. It was
he I had reason to fear. I knew it would be his dearest
interest to set the law in motion against me.

"It was the supreme crisis of my life, and in five minutes
I had grasped the situation and decided on my course of
action. Possibly the unexpectedness of it—the excitement
may have carried me away. Had I had more time, perhaps
I might have acted differently. The scheme that suggested
itself to me may seem a desperate one—it *was* a desperate one; but I was in a desperate position, and
instant action was the first necessity. I looked at my
watch; it was now ten o'clock.

"This was the plan I had formed: I would myself keep the appointment which Stadling had made with my wife. Several considerations combined to form the motive for what I had made up my mind to do. Stadling was my declared enemy. He was about to do his best to involve me in proceedings which would certainly result in unbearable exposure—I did not know sufficient of the law to know the exact extent of my danger. My fears may have exaggerated it. I had the dread before me of, in all likelihood, getting a long term of imprisonment. Stadling was to carry on his person that night the very proof of the charge he intended should be brought against me—the proof I was prepared to risk anything to gain. Added to all this, he had outwitted me, and was about to elope with my wife, and use her as an instrument against me. Yes, I would meet him. But there were difficulties in the way. It would be fatal, in view of what the next morning would reveal, for it to be shown that I had been absent from my room during the night. Owing to Trupp being in the house I was placed in an exceedingly awkward situation; but a moment's reflection showed me a means by which I might make his presence one of the strongest possible circumstances in my favour if the worst came to the worst. At all hazards I must meet Stadling; it was equally important, as I say, that my absence from the house should not be detected. Very well. I would get a substitute to take my place in the room for the few hours I would need for my purpose. If it was skilfully managed there was very little danger of the deception being discovered.

"I had no difficulty in fixing upon the substitute. There was a man I had occasionally employed about the stable named Murdock.

"I need have no hesitation in naming him, for he is dead now. There was not a great difference in our height, and his hair was the same colour as mine—for my purpose a very powerful recommendation. He was a lazy, good-for-nothing rascal, who, I have little doubt, would not have required much inducement to take the whole task off my hands for me altogether. But he had one virtue—he knew how to hold his tongue. I was well enough acquainted with his habits to know where to find him at any moment, especially at night, and before eleven o'clock I had seen him at one of his haunts in town, and stated my proposal.

"He had gambled away his last shilling when I saw him, and had not as much left as would provide him with a lodging for the night. All he had to do was, instead of taking refuge in the first shelter, to sleep in a comfortable bed, to keep a still tongue, to forget anything that might happen between then and morning, and pocket a crisp ten-pound bank-note. It was very simple, and he accepted it willingly. We returned to Monk's Bridge together.

"The next step was to make what provision I could against the chance of discovery by Trupp, and as he was in a strange house the chances were all in my favour. Discovery was almost impossible so long as he did not happen to strike a light during my absence, and I made that impossible by getting possession of his matches, and placing any others out of his reach. I not only counterfeited illness, but when I got into bed I left the lamp burning, for the simple reason that it was the last thing in the world one would do who intended to leave his room by stealth, and so would furnish a strong piece of evidence in my favour should suspicion become directed towards me. I knew at the same time that the fumes would be intolerable to Trupp, who was greatly troubled with asthma, and that it would not be long before he would either put it out himself or ask me to do so.

"Everything happened as I had expected. In an hour or less, during which I had marked the herr's cough growing more and more irritable, he got up and put out the light. I seized the moment when his back was turned to give place to the man I had in waiting in the next room. No more disturbance was caused by my substitute in taking my place than would be made by a man turning restlessly in his bed—not so much as was made at the same moment by the herr himself. All my substitute had to do to avoid any reasonable chance of detection was to lie with his face turned away and the clothes drawn well round his shoulders, so that if it should happen that he were observed by Trupp at all, the back of his head only would be visible; and, as I have said, his hair was the same colour as my own.

"The first thing my hand touched in the next room was something lying upon one of the chairs, and which I knew must be Murdock's clothes. At once an idea occurred to me, which showed how I might still further disguise my identity. I would wear these clothes instead of my own. Knowing that the quickest possible change of clothing would be required on my return, I huddled on only the hat, coat, and trousers, and taking the boots in my hand I put them on when I was at a safe distance.

"And now the most dangerous piece of work of all remained to be done—to procure the key of the stable from the groom. He had offered it to me in the afternoon, and I bitterly cursed my folly now that I had not taken it. As I drew near Riddock's quarters I was surprised to see they were lighted up. This was very unusual. His light should have been out hours before. I approached the door of his room cautiously, and looked in.

"He himself was sitting in a chair asleep not far from the bedside, and on the bed itself lay his young daughter, apparently also asleep. Riddock, I could make out by the light of the lamp, was wearing the waistcoat into the pocket of which I had seen him put the key earlier in the day. There was no time to hesitate. The longer I waited the greater the danger of discovery. The key must be obtained at whatever risk, and pushing the door stealthily open I stole into the room. Never before in my life had I experienced the sensation I felt as I drew nearer and nearer to pick the pocket of my own servant, and knew that the whole safety both of myself and my scheme was depending upon the mere flutter of an eye-lid. If either father or daughter should wake I was lost. Had it been possible I should have drawn back then, but it was not possible. There was bare time, and I must go on. I took each pace so carefully, so cautiously, I dwelt so long upon each step that my footing seemed to become uncertain and the floor rise and fall and make me sway from side to side as if I were balancing myself on a narrow plank. The boards creaked now and then, and the sound made me halt and catch my breath, and look from one sleeper to the other with the dread of seeing one or both of them start up into sudden wakefulness, and find me standing there in my strange dress. It was the child I feared most. She seemed to sleep so lightly that she could scarcely be said to be unconscious at all. She was restless, and tossed about uneasily; but neither woke—and at last I stood beside the groom undiscovered. I slipped my finger and thumb gently into his pocket, all the while keeping my eyes fixed steadily on his face, as if I could mesmerize him into a deeper and more insensible sleep. I felt the hard outline of something with my finger-tip, and drew it out. It was the key. A sound from the bed made me turn. The child was sitting up and gazing at me with wide-open eyes, and looking as if she thought she were still asleep, and I was a dream.

"My presence of mind deserted me utterly. I forgot that to be seen was to be lost, that the first thing the groom would do, even if I were to escape an encounter with him, and secured the horse, would be to go to my room to rouse me, and that my scheme would be exposed and I ruined. I acted as if I were in reality a thief whose sole object it was to gain possession of the horse. I darted to the door, and as I reached it I heard the child cry out. Another instant, and I had reached the stables. Familiar as long acquaintance had made me with every square inch of their whole frontage, many precious moments passed— moments so long that detection seemed inevitable—before the door swung open. I seized the bridle from where it hung upon the wall, led Scythe-bearer into the yard, and sprang, unsaddled as he was, on to his back. At the same instant the groom rushed out of his room with a shout, and sprang at me with the bound of a tiger. My blood was boiling with mad excitement, and had it been Stadding himself, instead of my servant trying to do his duty, I could not have put more deadly force into the blow I dealt him. It did not take full effect, but he staggered back with a low cry, and I dashed furiously past him into the darkness."

Llewellyn paused in his story, and took two or three turns up and down the room in silence.

"Of that mad ride through the night at the imminent risk of life and limb both to myself and the animal I bestrode, I need say nothing. Enough, that I overtook Stadding on the way to his appointed place of meeting. As soon as I saw him I sprang from the horse, tethered him to one of the trees, and went forward on foot. We met in a narrow clearing. I taxed him at once with what he was about to do. Up till now, notwithstanding all the precautions I had taken, I had never clearly proposed to myself how I should act when we did meet; but now the purpose that had lain all the time in the background of my consciousness sprang up from its lair and overmastered me. . . . . .

"I need not describe to you what followed, for you have already described it to me.

* * * * * *

"I saw the woman suddenly reveal herself from among the bushes, and I fled. I paused when I reached the shelter of the trees, and looked back. I thought the woman might be my wife; but it was not. The moonlight shone white upon her face. I saw it clearly. I can never forget it. It was the face I saw half an hour ago. She came near. Stadding struggled to his knees, and held out his hands to her. At that moment something touched me on the shoulder. I started and turned as if it had been the hand of an arresting constable—only to see Scythe-bearer standing beside me. He had broken loose from his tether. When I looked again toward the woman her hand was raised in the air, and she held something in its grasp. What it really was I could not see owing to the position in which she stood; but whatever it may have been, I saw her arm sink by her side again. I saw the man clutch at her dress, and fall forward on his face. I saw her stand for a moment looking down at him as he lay, and then clasp her hands before her eyes as if weeping; and, unable to bear the sight any longer, I threw myself upon my horse, and urged him homeward at his topmost speed. . . . .

"In looking back, I believe it was only the tremendous excitement—the insanity—of that night, only my sheer inability to put two coherent thoughts together, that caused me to adhere to the plan I had formed a few hours before. Had I retained possession of my faculties I should have seen inevitable ruin threatening me on all sides. On the one hand it was a moral certainty that the groom and Trupp had already discovered the deception I had put upon them; and on the other, here was this unknown witness who had surprised me in the very committal of my crime. Had I been capable of thought at all, I should have looked upon it as rushing into certain exposure to return to Monk's Bridge at all. But I was not capable of thought; I was not capable of realizing my position or the full enormity of what I had done. I was not capable of forcing my mind to suggest a fresh course of action.

"Twice on the ride home Scythe-bearer stumbled and fell upon his knees, and when at last I rode into the yard again, I felt him reel and stagger beneath me. I threw myself from his back, and stole up the stairs to my room, divesting myself of my things as I went. I paused at the door and listened. Not a sound. I looked in stealthily, the blind was drawn aside, and I saw the black form of some one appear in the moonlight at the window. I guessed at once it must be Trupp, who had probably been aroused by hearing Scythe-bearer enter the yard. So far nothing appeared to have been discovered; but what if Trupp should turn to where he supposed I was sleeping to arouse me? What if Murdock, in the meantime, should have fallen asleep? I pushed the door open a little wider, and, to my unspeakable relief, the signal was understood. While Trupp was still standing with his back turned towards us, Murdock arose, and came silently towards me. We passed one another midway between the door and the bedside. I had only bare time to draw the clothes about me, and assume the attitude of a sleeper, when Trupp turned and called my name. I did not answer, and he came up to me and shook me by the shoulder, calling out that something had happened in the stables.

*   *   *   *   *   *

Note. —The remainder of Llewellyn's confession is omitted for reasons similar to that given in Herr Trupp's statement.

XXXVII.

It was late. The balcony scene, with its unrehearsed effects and unsuspected audience, was the finale of Theodore's play, and both actors and audience had gone home an hour ago—all except Catherine and Esther and Miss Dorothy Ann. The author himself, flushed with success, had gone to his own room, and was pacing up and down, putting the question to himself, " What *is* there in Shakespeare, after all ? "

Esther gave no thought to the time, but remained with her eyes fixed upon the door of that terrible house opposite. It was a long time now since Redmayne and the doctor had set out on their dangerous mission, and she placed a nervous woman's interpretation upon their delay. The light was still shining in the window, and there had been nothing from its direction to break the silence she had momentarily expected to hear some fearful outcry, the sound of deadly struggle. But nothing had happened.

She had not even seen the blind drawn up. She had stepped from the balcony into Redmayne's sitting-room, and had stayed there during the progress of the final scene of Theodore's play, and so was not conscious of anything that had taken place. Of all the interests that grouped themselves about the household lights of Wellington that night, those that grouped themselves around that light were surely the strangest!

. . . . . . At length she saw the door open, and two forms issue from it. They were the doctor and Redmayne. Then another door opened and closed beneath her—then the sound of voices. The reaction was intense. Now that she had grasped the fact that her husband was really safe, the one fixed idea in the eddying confusion of her mind was—what had he learned? Was Catherine innocent, after all, or was she not? She heard Redmayne's footsteps approaching, and her courage, well nigh worn out by the anxious watch, was not proof against the suspense. A glance at his face as he entered the room brought a cry of relief to her lips, and before he had taken three paces across the floor—rapid and eager as those paces were—she was by his side, his arms were clasped around her, and his lips were pressed passionately upon hers. . . .

"At last, Matthew!"

"At last, Esther!" and she noticed, notwithstanding his lover's-raptures and her own, there was an unmistakable gravity in his voice as he spoke, and in his eyes as they looked down into hers. "At last I can claim you as my own; all that has kept us apart has come to an end to-night, love. He has confessed everything."

"And—and Catherine——?"

"Is innocent, Esther, perfectly innocent."

She clasped her hands. "Oh, thank God for that," she said, earnestly, the weight of an intolerable suspense lifted from her heart; "thank God that whatever may have been the intent that formed itself in her poor, distracted brain, she was not permitted to carry it out."

you remember what you said when we saw one another at New Plymouth, about happiness and a certain person who shall be nameless coming together? There was a wrinkle in your forehead, and a look in your eyes a moment ago I could not understand. *Has* happiness come?"

Under the circumstances there was a method of answering more expressive than words, and her face being turned invitingly upward at the moment he adopted that method.

"Yes, my darling, happiness has come—the look and the wrinkle notwithstanding. Perhaps they were there because, in spite of all I said that day, I am disappointed at owing so little of my happiness to what I have done myself."

"Then they should be on your face still," she said, "for you shall depend still less upon yourself for your happiness in the future."

She turned her face up more invitingly than ever to smile, and the temptation was irresistible.

"But, Matthew," the smile died away from her face, and she spoke with a vague feeling of inconsistency with her last words, "we cannot stay in New Zealand, we must not make our home in any place where events may happen at any moment to revive Kate's remembrance of the past."

"I have thought of that too, Ettie. There is nothing to prevent our going abroad at once, for there is nothing more we can do." He opened the door leading on to the balcony as he spoke, and they saw that the light was still burning in Llewellyn's house. As they looked the bent shadow of some one passed darkly across the window. Esther shuddered, and Redmayne drew her closer to him.

"So, please heaven, passes the last shadow on your fortunes and mine, Ettie."

"And yet, how near he came to ruining both our lives," she whispered.

"Yes, but he has more completely ruined his own. I saw something in his face to-night as he finished his confession that took the last thought of vengeance out of my heart—it was the shadow of approaching madness. The memory of his crime haunts him."

"It was a terrible crime, and it is a terrible punishment. I shudder when I think of your meeting with him—to think what might have happened."

"Poor girl, yours has been the hardest trial of all, fighting alone with suspense and your own imagination," he said, falling into his old habit of stroking her hair caressingly. "But dreams and presentiments do not always come true, you see."

"When will you tell me all that passed between you to-night?" she asked, her eyes wandering with something of their former fascination to the lighted window before her, and the shadow that continually crossed and re-crossed it.

He closed the door, and led her back into the room before he answered—

"Best forget it, my love, as I shall seek to do. Let it go with the rest of our past. To-morrow we will take Catherine with us and look our last upon New Zealand."

She rested her hand upon his shoulder and her cheek upon her hand.

"Yes, Matthew, that will be best. Let us forget the past with its good and its evil. To-morrow we will enter upon our new life; and as for the old one, we will put it from our memory as completely as it has been removed from Catherine's." Then with a woman's longing to hear the declaration she can never hear too often, "And you will be content to make my life one with yours, content that the truth you have learned to-night should only be known among ourselves, content even with the prospect of it never being known to the world?"

"Content, Esther, to let the whole world go; content always and everywhere, as long as I have succeeded in convincing *you*, and having you for my reward."

THE END.